RETURN OF THE

STARFIGHTER

Reg. WGAw

ISBN-13: 978-0-9848820-3-8
ISBN-10: 0984882030
ISBN - E: 978-0-9848820-7-6

Printed in the United States of America
Timber Creek Press
Imprint of Timber Creek Productions, LLC
312 N. Commerce St.
Gainesville, Texas
timbercreekproductions@yahoo.com
214-533-4964

Cover art work by: Steve Daniels
Cover layout and back cover by: Warren Martin

ACKNOWLEDGMENT

The authors gratefully acknowledge the help from John Eastman Major USMC (ret.), Trent Davis, former USAF and commercial pilot, Kelly "Gunnz" Jackson USMC (ret.) and Doran Ingrham, USMC, in proofing and suggestions.

DEDICATED TO

Clarence Leonard "Kelly" Johnson, (February 27, 1919 - December 21, 1990.) Chief Design Engineer Lockheed's Skunk Works. Johnson's boss, Hall Hibbard once said, "That damn Swede can actually see air." Kelly Johnson designed the F-104 Starfighter in 1953. His design genius was seen in over forty aircraft designs. In 1955, at the request of the CIA, Johnson initiated the construction of the air base in Nevada now known as Dreamland or Area 51.

Chinese Ultra-Super Carrier
SUN TZU

BLACK EAGLE FORCE SERIES

Black Eagle Force novels are a fast-paced series of military techno-thrillers about a top secret Special Ops team created for missions that are not—and cannot—be officially approved. The BEF protects American interests and fights evil wherever it exists. Their motto is: *Semper Paro Bellum* (Always Ready for War).

BLACK EAGLE FORCE: Eye of the Storm
ASIN: B007ILFV30
ISBN - 9781617779640
ISBN-E: 9781620240243
The BEF has only minutes neutralize two suitcase nukes and rescue twenty sex slaves from an island in the Gulf of Mexico before Hurricane Ellen strikes.

BLACK EAGLE FORCE: Sacred Mountain
ASIN: B007RRUM02
ISBN-13: 978-0-9848820-0-7
E-Book - ISBN-10: 0-9848820-4-9
The President of the United States has been kidnapped by terrorists. The BEF has been tasked to go deep into Mexico for her rescue.

RETURN of the STARFIGHTER
ASIN: B009ECAX52
ISBN - E: 978-0-9848820-7-6
ISBN: 978-0-9848820-3-8
Rogue elements of the Chinese government have neutralized of the US latest high-tech fighters, bombers and missiles and are set to invade the west coast.

You never saw us. This never happened. We don't exist. We are the BLACK EAGLE FORCE.

HISTORICAL FICTION WESTERN

THE NATIONS

BK00008623
ISBN-13: 978-0-9848820-5-2
ISBN-E: 978-0-9848820-6-9
ASIN: B0090SIDOS

The Nations concerns the heroic deeds of the Deputy US Marshals that patrolled the Indian Territory for Judge Issac C. Parker in the late 1800s. It features Bass Reeves, the first black Deputy US Marshal west of the Mississippi.

ENDORSEMENTS
(ALL FIVE STAR REVIEWS)

A compelling plot with unusual events, suspense, and fascinating characters, October 7, 2012
By Israel Drazin (TOP 1000 REVIEWER) (VINE VOICE)

It is fashionable to think that our young will assure our safety by using modern equipment. However, in this easy to read and fast paced suspenseful novel the opposite is true.

The authors base their plot on generally overlooked facts. One is well-known, although its possible impact, which they explore, is not. The US owes China trillions of dollars for Chinese loans that the US is unable to repay. In this novel, China demands payment, refuses easy to print paper money, and insists on payment in gold that the US doesn't have.

Most people don't know the second fact. China claims that its people discovered America in 1422, seventy years before Columbus, in a ship far larger than Columbus' three ships. Admiral Zheng He's fleet anchored in an inlet off of what is now southern Oregon, on the west coast of North America. The admiral relied on maps drawn by Kublai Khan, founder of the Yuan Dynasty in the eleventh century. Thus, ignoring the rights of the Native American dwellers, as Europeans did, China insists it has a legitimate claim to the US west coast.

Unable to collect the huge debt, a maniacal rogue Chinese general decides to conquer the US western coast. Using a sophisticated cyber attack and a blackmailed mole in the US, he destroys the US fighter jets and the use of US missals. When the planes crash and the missiles are rendered ineffective, the US Armed Forces lose the air superiority it enjoyed since 1944 and the ability to defend itself. He then sails with a huge armada of ships larger and more sophisticated than anything left in the US armory to capture and hold California, Oregon, and Washington as payment for the American debt.

The general's tactic follows the advice of Sun Tzu: "Begin (war) by seizing something which your opponent holds dear; then he will be amenable to your will."

It is then that the US turns to its retirees who develop a plan to refurbish and use forty and fifty year old planes. Joining the old-timers is the famed post-modern deadly Back Eagle Force "composed of elite former military Special Operations experts and crack pilots from all branches of the United States armed forces: SEALs, Rangers, Green Berets, Delta Force, Air Force Combat Controllers and Marine Recon - by invitation only;" only the best.

Readers will enjoy this thriller in which the authors introduce them to a compelling plot, unusual events, fascinating characters, and the intricacies of war and planes.

****

Outstanding novel!! A blueprint for America's future..., October 8, 2012

By Doran aka Plata

The Return of the Starfighter is the third in the Black Eagle Force series hits a grand slam homerun! The returning kick-ass-take-no-names characters are joined by some new Patriots to fight off an invasion by China and the story roars to life like the supersonic interceptor F-104 aircraft it is named for, The Starfighter.

I have read many novels that weave technical data through the tale but none match the fluid flow that Buck Stienke and Ken Farmer have presented here. I felt the controls in my hands, the cold dry sensation of breathing oxygen, could see the gauges and dials on the consoles of the advanced and old iron birds as I flew. I remembered the adrenaline rush of closing with the enemy as the Raptor teams performed their infil and completed their covert missions.

Again, Buck and Ken present characters so vivid and complete I felt I knew them personally. As a Vietnam era US Marine and later my work in the Risk Management world, I know the bond that links warriors together, a bond that goes far beyond friendship. A brotherhood that only those who go in harm's way can fully know and understand. The men and women of the Black Eagle Force exemplify this special bond in spades. I mourned the loss of each one that paid the ultimate price and exalted in the success of those who survived to fight another day.

I would give The Return of the Starfighter a ten star rating if it were possible. A perfect blend of old iron and the men who fly them and the new high tech aircraft and warriors of today leap from the page.

I do not know of a military action adventure series that holds a candle to the Black Eagle Force. I highly recommend them all for those who enjoy this genre of fiction blended with facts of today's modern warfare.

Doran W Ingrham
Inactive US Marine
Retired Risk Management Specialist
Author ~ Actor ~ Director
****

"Those who cannot remember the past are condemned to repeat it"-George Santayana, October 10, 2012

By Mandomac

"Return of the Starfighter" by Buck Stienke and Ken Farmer is set in the current time, with a budget cutting government coming to grips with an opponent on a 100 year plan. The economics behind the plot are also current, and lend an authenticity to the story line. The twist in the story comes in the solution to the problem. Resurrecting 50's and 60's technology to avert an imbalance of power and confront the threat posed. I especially liked reading about the older aircraft. The authors have done their homework, and all the tactics for the individual aircraft are authentic. Current technology has been compromised in many areas. Cyberwarfare, stealing high tech drones, hacking networks. This is a story that addresses these issues as well as: How does an effective leader manage his team? How fast can your team react when your initial Plan A is no longer effective? Where, and how quickly, can you locate

and train the right people for the right job? How do you keep your enemy from discovering you are aware of his intentions, and that you might have a viable counterthreat? It's all good stuff. Read the book and find out!
****

Outstanding, November 4, 2012
By Donald Hammond Amazon Verified Purchase

I agree with the other reviewers. This was a great book. I am happy to see the authors have kept the same interest level in this one as they have in the others, many times that doesn't happen with sequals. Good show, looking for the next in the series.
****

Get in, Sit down, Buckle Up and Hang On!, October 5, 2012
By Larry L. Launders "lllvis"

The third offering in the Black Eagle Force Series shows no sign of losing any momentum! And "Starfighter" has a great combination of military/high tech/low tech detail, and top notch story telling, to keep all kinds of us geeks happy! For myself, I'm very much a fan of lower tech solutions to high tech problems, and I certainly wasn't disappointed here. You won't be either!

Another great ride from Steinke and Farmer that you don't want to miss!
****

Y'all ain't ready for this one! Best of the series, so far!, By KJ2066

This one is a nail-biter! A shorts-sucker-upper! An edge of your seat, holy-crap!, thrill-ride!

Dare and his BEF band of bad-asses are gonna team up with some of America's finest aviators and go head-to-head against an determined, organized, and downright ruthless enemy in a high-stakes game of global poker involving stealth, power, and some of the most intense dog-fight sequences ever put on paper. Y'all ain't ready for this one!! The writing team of Steinke and farmer just keeps getting better and better! In my opinion, this is the best of the Black Eagle Force series, so far!

TIMBER CREEK PRESS

CHAPTER ONE

HAWAII

"Raptor 1 flight, I see you entering the MOA. Airspace is active surface to FL500. Cleared to strangle squawk. Monitor 136.8."

"Raptor 1 copy. Good day."

Lt. Colonel James "Hollywood" Stewart, commander of the 199th Fighter Squadron at Hickam AFB, looked to his right at his wingman who simply nodded. Both set their UHF comms to the assigned frequency as *Raptor 2* slid out to a fighting wing.

Eight *F-15 Eagles* from the 44th Fighter Squadron out of Kadena AFB, Japan, were eagerly awaiting the training DACT mission. The *Eagle* drivers had embarrassed themselves on the last deployment to Hawaii. Zero to forty-two was a serious butt kicking. Everybody in the 18th Wing knew it and the fact that the *Eagle* had a stellar 100-0 record in actual combat was no solace whatsoever. The operations officer in the 44th had briefed the day's mission and set up four of the blue-gray birds as top cover in the mid-forties. Four would cruise at FL330 and make the initial engagement. That was the plan.

Sixty miles west of Oahu at FL330, a Pacific Air Force E-3 AWACS aircraft from the 961st AACS, also deployed from the 18th Wing at Kadena, provided radar and telemetry coverage for the training missions. The controller watched as the two *Raptor* identifying blips on his scope disappeared. Icons for the eight *Eagles* moved slightly with each rotation of the giant rotodome. The green icons indicated the fighter's speed and direction as detected by the transmitted Pulse Doppler Pulse Compression waveform.

Unfortunately, the same information was data linked via satellite to the incoming F-22s providing them with an instant display of forces unavailable to the *Eagles*. The *Raptor's* AN/AAR 56 Infra-Red and Ultra-Violet Missile Approach Warning System and the AN/APG-77 Active Alert Scanning Array radar allowed the mottled air superiority gray fighters to approach like unseen sharks in a pool full of swimmers. If the *Eagle* did not get a visual on the *Raptors* first, the outcome of the battle was almost a forgone conclusion.

"Cyclops, Devil 1," called the lead *Eagle* pilot.

"Devil 1, Cyclops, go ahead."

"Say last known Unknown Riders bearing, please."

"Devil 1, last bearing two o'clock, angels unknown, over."

"Devil 1, roger." The colonel felt like a sitting duck. "You heard the man. Head's up. Bogeys inbound."

Seven other heads joined his as they simultaneously swiveled and searched for the two *Raptors.*

Hollywood pushed forward on the side mounted control stick and began a shallow descent matched by his wingman. A weather briefing he had received just after noon indicated the contrail levels would be from FL280 through FL310. The two leveled off at FL220 and accelerated to .98 Mach without use of the afterburner.

Tally on the Eagles. Stewart did not bother with a radio transmission. Both he and his wingman had the eight *Eagles* on their AASA display as well as visual contact. The two passed two and one-half miles beneath the *Eagles* and four miles astern when Hollywood initiated his burner climb. His wingman counted to fifteen and began a similar pullup to engage the lower four *Eagles.* His G suit inflated to counteract the acceleration as the twin F119-PW-100 turbofans lit off to produce a combined 75,000 pounds of thrust. He watched the flat screen display altimeter roll up at over 50,000 feet per minute as he went vertical. Thirty seconds later he was inverted directly in trail of the four *Eagles* flying top cover. A thin vertical contrail roughly three thousand feet long was the only evidence that the *Raptors* were in range. Eight sets of Mark 1 eyeballs scanned the airspace for the illusive F-22s, but none caught sight of the tell-tail trace of frozen exhaust condensate six miles behind them.

Hollywood rolled smoothly back to an upright position six and one-half miles behind the further left fighter in the upper formation. His AASA passive radar system collected all the data needed to lock up the first two fighters without even transmitting a radar beam. Internally, one simulated AIM-9 Sidewinder and two AIM-120 AMRAAM simulated missiles were slaved to the MOA sensors back on Oahu and the E-3 AWACS. Lt. Colonel Stewart noted his speed had increased to Mach 1.8 and range was only three miles decreasing. He quickly crossed checked his wingman's position and confirmed his briefed engagement tactics were still good to go. He slipped his finger up and over the trigger on his stick and pulled it twice.

"Raptor 1, Fox Three, Fox Three."

"Raptor 2, Fox Three, Fox Three," came this wingman's call over the common frequency.

Inside the eight *Eagles*, the missiles away calls from the *Raptors* created a blur of activity. Heads were snapping right and left as each tried to locate the aggressors. Nothing showed up on any of their radars, and Colonel Dick Ramey leading the formation in *Devil 1* was not happy when he heard the transmission from the controller aboard Cyclops.

"Devil 1, kill. Devil 2, kill. Devil 5, kill. Devil 6, kill. Confirm with ident, please."

"Dammit to hell! Son of a green bitch," Dick yelled to no one in particular. He reluctantly pressed the ident button.

"Bandit! Six o'clock, one mile," yelled the captain in *Devil 3* as he slammed his throttles to the stop and broke vertical, watching his wingman roll inverted and break downward as briefed.

His *Eagle* pitched up rapidly through seventy degrees nose up as his G-suit inflated and encircled his legs and abdomen like an anaconda. He looked back to see the two diamond shape air intakes of the rapidly closing *Raptor* looming larger as it closed the distance.

"Raptor 1, guns."

Devil 3's pilot slammed the stick right and pulled back even harder trying to initiate a vertical scissors maneuver—anything to shake the aggressive *Raptor* high on his six. He snapped a quick look back inside at his airspeed on his HUD, and then strained to reacquire his adversary.

"Devil 3, kill."

Son of a bitch! That can't be right...Jesus. I can't believe that. He watched as the *Raptor* unloaded, rolled inverted and disappeared beneath his tail in less than two seconds. It looked as if the *Raptor* had literally swapped ends in a tiny section of his dark helmet visor.

"Confirm with ident, please."

The latest victim to fall prey to the *Raptor* grudgingly pressed the ident button and pulled his throttles out of burner. He maintained the back pressure on his *Eagle* until he was inverted and watched helplessly as *Devil 4* attempted a reversal to offer support once he had seen the *Raptor* climbing for his former flight leader.

Devil 4 looked back between the twin tails of his F-15 and saw the two contrails forming behind him as his blue/gray fighter streaked down though FL350. He tried to ignore the radio call as the lower *Raptor* took a simulated heat seeker missile shot on the closer of two lower *Eagles*.

"Raptor 2, Fox Two."

He reacquired the *Raptor* that had just scored a kill on his flight lead and just in time. His *Eagle* was accelerating through Mach 1.6 as he began his pullout to bring his nose up to engage the F-22.

"Devil 8, flare. Flare. Flare." The captain grunted as he fought the seven Gs, barrel rolled left and attempted to find a way to outthink the *Raptor* pilot.

Six silver white magnesium stars twinkled and tumbled across the cobalt Pacific skies behind the supersonic *Eagle* as *Devil 8* double clicked his flare button three times.

"Raptor 2, miss," announced the controller.

Raptor 2 noted the miss call as he pulled lead on the *Eagle* that was intermittently conning as he barrel rolled in and out of the contrail level. The *Eagle* made a hard pullup in front of him that *Raptor 2* more than matched with the vectored thrust from his twin Pratts in min burner. The HUD pipper floated just behind the *Eagle* for a second until the Major increased back pressure. The flight control computers effortlessly compared his inputs to existing airframe and flight parameters in milliseconds and gave him the additional pitch commanded with a mixture of vectored thrust and tail surface inputs. He grunted softly as his modified diamond shaped wing literally disappeared under a white vapor cloud of boundary layer air as it separated at the extremely high angle of attack. Unlike other stick and rudder aircraft, the *Raptor's* fly-by-wire maintained fully stabilized control of the 150 million dollar bird as the major centered the pipper and pulled the trigger.

"Raptor 2, guns."

He rolled off the target even before he got the confirmation. The last *Eagle* in the low fourship was turning back inbound from 260°, three thousand feet above him and eight miles west. The major broke right to engage head on.

"Devil 7, kill."

Devil 7 tried three times to lock up the *Raptor* with his radar missiles. *What the…they ground checked okay!* The return from the *Raptor* was said to be essentially the size of a steel marble. Layers of radar absorbing Teflon like material coated the airframe, and its angular surfaces were designed to *deflect* rather than *reflect* radar energy. *No go on the AIM-120. Let's try a heater.* The pilot could see the *Raptor* turning to face him. At least he could see his contrail before it dissipated. Switching to the AIM-9, he struggled to get tone. *Just out of range. A little…*

"Raptor 2, Fox Three."

Devil 7 broke for the deck and pulled back hard to the stick shaker.

"Devil 7, kill."

Hollywood slid the throttles smoothly out of burner and pulled aft to the stick limiter, his mechanical marvel responding as designed and brought the nose to bear on the *Eagle* attempting to climb. Even at eight Gs, the nimble *Eagle* sliced through a lot of airspace as it maneuvered. It was obvious *Devil 3* was setting up for a nose on gun pass. He was only forty-five degrees above the horizon in his transition when the dreaded call was heard.

"Raptor 1, Fox Three."

Devil 3 gave it all he had—positive G, negative G, rolling G. Telemetry from the F-22 sent to the E-3 AWACS confirmed his fate.

"Devil 3, kill."

In eighty-six seconds, the record of the 18th Wing *Eagles* had dropped to 0-50.

ARIZONA

Jack Stewart slowed his burgundy 1996 Harley-Davidson Softail Custom down from the 105 MPH he had been clocking southbound on I-10 just outside of Tucson. He checked his mirrors and signaled for a lane change and maneuvered to exit on East Valencia Road. The autumn sun lay low in the clear turquoise sky and reflected off the full face shield on his helmet. He turned left onto Claycroft Road past the lines of drab metal recycling buildings. Whenever Jack drove up to Tucson to bend a few with other ex-military fliers, he took the scenic trip around what was officially called the 309th Aerospace Maintenance and Regeneration Group. To Jack, and almost everyone else in Arizona, the place was called simply, the *boneyard.* A veritable cottage industry had grown over the years as surplus military and other Federal agency aircraft of all types had eventually become obsolete and sent to the dry desert patch on the south side of Davis-Monthan Air Force Base.

He could barely hear the rumble of his Harley over the strains of an old Eagle's tune played in the custom speakers in his helmet. Jack sang along as *Hotel California* rocked to its conclusion. He pulled over and booted the kickstand into position while he stood up and stretched the kinks out of his sixty-seven year old back. The ride up from his home in the mountains north of town was less than sixty miles, but he certainly felt the tightness the high speed journey often created. He unsnapped the comm cord running from his helmet to the iPhone in his jacket pocket and tugged the brain bucket off, revealing a tanned head with silver hair cut in a short military style. His gaze scanned the rows of parked aircraft, many completely cocooned in a protective coating of shrink wrapped white plastic.

"Dammit!" *There were twenty-six Starfighters in that row last time I was here.*

He counted again. The number didn't change. Only twenty-five of his favorite aircraft of all time remained in the inventory of mothballed fighters called *a missile with a man in it*, a term the press had created when the F-104 debuted back in 1956. A super sleek product of Kelly Johnson's legendary Skunk Works at the Lockheed Aircraft Corporation, the *Starfighter* had been the first operational fighter flown by the young 2nd Lieutenant Jack "Burner" Stewart after graduating from UPT at Reese Air Force Base, Texas.

He had graduated first in his class and ended up with an assignment at George AFB flying the *Zipper* as some of the guys called the *Starfighter*. He transitioned along with the rest of the 479th Tactical Fighter wing to the F-4 and then to the F-15 *Eagle*, but always in his heart was a love for the first one, the inimical *Starfighter*. The old saw about never forgetting your first love was certainly true in this case. Making a mental promise to call the guys over at the AMARG once he got to the club, Jack donned his helmet and fired up his Harley for the uneventful trip around lone runway to the D-M entrance.

The airman first class caught sight of the blue retired officer decal on the forward lip of the Harley's narrow front fender. The single gold star he spied told him the rider was a retired brigadier general. His salute was crisp and quickly returned by the rider.

"Must be the fourth Friday," he remarked to his shift mate. "Lots of retired brass hit the O club once a month."

"Yeah. You'd think they made enough money to party someplace with more action," came the disinterested reply.

Jack pulled into the lot next to the OC, euphemistically called *The Flame Out* by pilots. He parked his Softail next to a couple of other Harleys and noticed three riceburners lined up on the other side of the Hogs. *Must belong to some of the new kids*, he thought as he dismounted and removed his helmet and gloves.

Jack unzipped his black leather jacket as he walked up to the door.

He blinked his eyes several times as they adjusted to the dim light inside the bar and looked around trying to spot any old cronies.

"Well look what the cat dragged in."

Jack immediately recognized the voice of his old wingman, John "Boomer" Eastman.

"Thought you were dead, Boomer," he said toward the dark shapes at a table.

"Bite me, Burner. Luv ya, too," came the rapid reply. "Same ole Mexican horse piss?"

"You got it."

"Hey Crystal, bring this broken down MiG shooter a Corona. My tab."

The tanned blonde hardbody smiled as she reached to the bottle proffered by the equally buff redheaded barback—Fighter Sweep Fridays meant crazy tips. Young and old fighter pilots and WSOs gathered for a palpable camaraderie that Crystal could sense and admire.

Boomer rose and greeted Burner with a back slapping bear hug. Three captains and a lt. colonel at the bar caught the Boomer comment when he ordered the beer and turned to see to whom he was referring. Burner pulled out a chair, removed his jacket and hung it on the chair before he took a seat. Emblazoned on the back was a F-104 in silver silk with a gold wire afterburner plume. Inch tall block letters identified the *Starfighter*, but they were an unnecessary addition. Every pilot knew the iconic needle nose shape.

"Who's the geezer?" asked Harley "Hog" Hale, the youngest captain seated next to a lt. colonel.

Lieutenant Colonel John "Magic" Mann set down his beer and cocked his middle finger with his thumb. As Hog looked over his left shoulder, Magic flicked his right ear. Hard.

"Ow! What the…?"

"Boy, that *geezer* shot down four MiG 21s in 'Nam plus a 25 and a 29 in Desert Storm. I'm not sure you're qualified to shine his boots."

"No shit!" said the surprised captain as he rubbed his ear. "Damn! You didn't have to break the cartilage in my ear, Colonel."

"Tape an aspirin on it, boy…Tell you what. You buy Burner a beer and I'll introduce you. He's a friend of mine. Pay attention, you might even learn something."

"Here you go, General," Crystal said as she set the dew-blistered longneck with a wedge of lime stuck in the top on the coaster. "Another round?"

"Love a woman with ESP!" said retired Lt. Colonel Mabrey "Mabe" Goshen, the only WSO at the table.

The gorgeous waitress nodded and turned to retrieve three more drinks. Jack admired her long legs and suitably short shorts. *Dollar to a donut she can dance*.

"So, what's the status on your rocket ship, Burner? Last time I saw you, the fuel control was eatin' your lunch," said Goshen.

"Had the boys replace it with a NOS unit. Fires right up. I'm planning a test hop tomorrow afternoon."

"What time? You know we wouldn't miss the chance to see you spend $10,000 an hour!" replied C.J. "Heater" McElheney, another retired USAF Colonel.

"Got that right, Heater. The only thing more expensive than a boat is a plane!" Stewart chuckled.

"You have to find some way to spend all that Lockheed retirement money!" Eastman kicked in.

"The government helps me with that problem. Anyway, how does 14:30 at Sunbird Aviation sound?"

"Ejection seat still work?"

"Not sure, Mabe, you're welcome to try it out."

Crystal arrayed the three drinks on the table.

"Here we go. The pause that refreshes. Let's have a toast to the Return of the Starfighter!"

The four lifted their bottles and clinked in unison.

"Starfighters!"

HAWAII

Eight dispirited *Eagle* drivers climbed out of the two tan Ford rental cars parked outside the Pearl-Hickam Joint Base Officer's Club. A pair of red Corvette convertibles pulled in as if in formation and parked beside the two Fords. The drivers hopped out and Colonel Ramey instantly recognized the two as the F-22 pilots who had just completed the afternoon's debriefing session.

"Well, Colonel, you two coming by to watch us drown our sorrows?"

Hollywood smiled as he walked beside the TDY pilots.

"Actually, I was going to offer to buy you guys a round. I know it's hard for you guys to come here and fly against the Raptor. I flew the Eagle for fourteen years."

The mood lightened up slightly for the eight pilots from Kadena.

"We appreciate your offer. A gentleman and a scholar, you are."

"Well, one out of two ain't bad," Hollywood grinned, and then glanced at his watch and computed the time difference to Arizona. "Deacon, start a tab for me. I've got to make a call before it gets too late."

"Can do, Kimosabe," replied Major Bart Jones as the nine pilots crossed underneath the covered entrance to the club.

Hollywood walked up beside a pair of matched Royal Palm trees bracketing the walkway and pulled out a silver iPhone. He tapped it a couple times, and then rolled down through his contact list and selected a mobile number. Four seconds later, it rang.

ARIZONA

Four retired and four active duty fighter pilots were crowded around a small table covered with empty longnecks. Crystal slinked by and policed up the dead soldiers, and then solicited orders for another round. Burner was retelling the tale of the Iraqi MiG 29 trying to outrun a Sparrow missile as he made a dash toward to the Iranian Border when his cell phone rang. He held up one finger as he retrieved it and looked at the caller ID.

"Sorry, guys, it's my son. Got to see what the good Colonel has to say today." He stood up and began to walk to a quieter corner of *The Flame Out*. "Hey there, Hollywood! How's the *haole* boy doing today?"

"Great, pop! I just had to pass on the latest results of the air battle today with the Kadena birds."

"So, let me guess… Raptors won."

"Eight to nothin'. Deacon and I took on two fourships. We even limited out first engagement to two AMRAAMS each and the Eagles never got off a shot."

"Bad day at Black Rock, indeed. How long was the total engagement?"

"Eighty-six seconds. About like the others if we don't ripple off four missiles each. Those only last twelve seconds."

"Jesus…I'm proud of you, son. Just remember that someday, someone is gonna figure a way to defeat that stealth advantage."

"I know, General. That's why we gave a couple of them a chance to mix it up. We gotta stay sharp."

"Good hearing from you, son. Listen, have to run, got a few new kids back at the table wanting to learn some old tricks. Buy the Kadena boys a round on me. Don't wanna get their feeling's hurt."

"Way ahead of you, sir. Deacon is already in the club on my tab."

"Tell him hello for me. Hey, almost forgot! Taking the Silver Knight up for its first test hop tomorrow!"

"Cool! Man, wish I was there to see it! I know it means a lot to you."

"I'll have one of my buds post it on YouTube. Watch your six!"

**CENTRAL MILITARY COMMISSION
MINISTRY OF NATIONAL DEFENSE COMPOUND,
BEIJING, PEOPLE'S REPUBLIC OF CHINA**

"Admiral Huang, your report please," ordered Paramount Leader and President Hu Jintao from his seat in the austere Central Military Commission conference room.

"Comrade President, loyal ministers, generals and admirals, I am pleased to announce that our new Most-Secret nuclear catamaran ultra-super carrier, Sun Tzu, has returned from her initial sea trials. She has met or exceeded all of our expectations…her dual flight decks enabled us to launch a fighter every twenty-two seconds. As I am sure you all recall, she is over a third longer with almost twice the total beam of the United States Nimitz-Class carriers and can carry 160 fixed wing aircraft and helicopters…seventy more than USS Ronald Reagan. Flank speed checked out at an astounding sixty knots, twice as fast as any ship of the line the United States has. Of course, we can't launch at that speed, but it does enable us to move anywhere in the world virtually uncontested. The recently developed bow and stern jet thrusters give Sun Tzu unheard of maneuverability. Our new similar design escort frigates and destroyers were also able to keep pace."

Admiral Huang Meng was Fleet Admiral of the East China Sea Fleet, the Navy arm of PLAN, or People's Liberation Army-Navy. A forty-year veteran of the Chinese Navy, Huang still retained a youthful silhouette, his gray hair was cropped short and the only sign of his sixty-years-of-age were his wire rimmed reading glasses. He and his special staff had conceived the radical new carrier design concept for China's projected emergence as a blue-water sea power.

China's first carrier, *Shi Lang*, a refurbished former Soviet hulk originally called *Varyag*, was considered a joke by the world maritime powers, but China merely used the *Shi Lang* as a training, test and development bed. The twin-hulled, six-jet thruster, two nuclear-reactor powered *Sun Tzu* was the result of over twenty years of planning by the Central Military Commission of the PLAN and was far and away the largest, most versatile military war ship ever built—and she was just the first of three.

"Very impressive, Comrade Admiral. What about the ballistic missile firing tests?" asked High General Chen Bingde, Chief of the General Staff of the PLAN.

"Yes, Comrade Chen, the ballistic missile tubes mounted between the two flight decks at the stern performed without flaw. We will be able to carry twenty-four nuclear capable JL-3 ICBMs, each carrying four warheads with a range of eight thousand kilometers. All of our tests were conducted at night, between passes of the vaunted United States spy satellites. Our sea trial test area was also at the very fringe of their viewing window, as planned. Sun Tzu says in the *Art of War*, 'In making tactical dispositions, the highest pitch you can attain is to conceal them.'"

"I seriously hope it will not come to using the missiles against our future territory, Comrade Admiral. We have over six million Chinese who have immigrated to the west coast over the last forty-seven years since the passage of the Immigration and Nationality Act of 1965 that lifted national origin quotas by the US Congress," stated General Liang Guanglie, Minister of National Defense. "I should hate to think we would attack our own people."

"Sun Tzu also says, 'In the practical art of war, the best thing of all is to take the enemy's country whole and intact; to shatter and destroy it is not so good. So, too, it is better to recapture an army entire than to destroy it'," said Admiral Huang. "Now that Li Kashing's company, Lampoa-Hutchinson, controls both ends of the Panama Canal, we have unfettered access to Central America, the Gulf of Mexico and, of course the Atlantic," he added.

ARIZONA

Jack stepped down off the ladder into the pristine cockpit of the F-104. His personal crew chief and mechanic, Lars Hendricksen, had worked for the Luftwaffe in Phoenix when the Germans trained their pilots and crew chiefs on the then new fighter. He fell in love with the area and became a US citizen in 1986. His native German was still a faint singsong detectable in his speech.

"Take it easy with our baby, Burner. She's ready to go, but break the new engine in slow, okay?"

"I'll be gentle," Burner replied as he snapped the lap belt across his waist and reached back for the shoulder straps. "Just gonna take her through her paces this afternoon."

Lars handed him the two metal tips of the gray nylon harness straps. Jack grabbed both and inserted them into the top slots of the five way buckle on his ejection seat harness, and then tugged the adjusting tabs tight. Unzipping the green USAF issue helmet bag, he removed his white flight helmet, slipped a thumb inside the opposing sides of the helmet and spread it apart slightly as he pulled it down into position. Lars took the bag, stepped down the crew ladder and lifted it off the canopy rail. He set the ladder well clear of the long silver fuselage, walked briskly to the auxiliary power cart and fired it up. Once the power output was stabilized, he flipped the transfer switch and energized the *Starfighter*. Lars glanced at Burner and was relieved at the thumbs-up signal. *So far, so good.*

Jack flipped the electrical master switch from *Battery* to *External Power*. He ran his *Before Starting Engines Checklist* and called for his IFR clearance from Tuscon Clearance Delivery. The afternoon Arizona sun began to heat up the powder-blue Nomex flight suit he was wearing. The suit, a gift from his son, had a *Starfighter* matching the one on his leather jacket embroidered across the back. He had resisted any color but OD green, but finally relented.

"Even the astronauts wear powder blue," his son had said.

The checklist was soon completed. All flight gyros were up to speed and Jack looked right again to pass the start signal to Lars. The tall slender crew chief engaged the air function of the power unit and sent 90 PSI through the black flex hose attached to the port on the *Starfighter's* fuselage. A thin line of black exhaust rose from the yellow power cart as its diesel engine surged and spun the compressor over. Jack checked his gauges and initiated the starting sequence. He gave the *Disconnect Power* signal to Lars after the engine was up and running and he had transferred electrical power to ship's generator.

Boomer Eastman zoomed into the cockpit for a close-up of Jack and the wide smile he was giving Lars. Nine other friends had gathered for the launch, many who had never seen an F-104 that was still operational. Those that had forgotten to bring plugs stood by with their fingers in their ears as Lars moved to pull the chocks from under the right main tires. In the viewfinder, Eastman got a great shot of the retired General's crisp salute to his friend and crew chief. The time to get this sleek rocket airborne had come.

"Tucson ground, Starfighter Six Five X-ray taxi."

"Starfighter Six Five X-ray, roger, taxi runway 11 Left via taxiway Bravo, hold short of runway 3/21, altimeter three-zero-zero-six."

Jack read back the clearance and gave an enthusiastic thumbs-up to his small but equally excited crowd of admirers. Minutes later, members of the largest Air National Guard wing in the United States, the 162 Fighter Wing, dropped almost everything on the busy F-16 ramp to watch as the gleaming silver craft taxied across runway 3/21 to take its position for takeoff. With seventy of the Vipers operating out of Tucson, the sight of a pair of F-16s taking the active runway was commonplace. None of the young mechanics had ever witnessed a *Starfighter* depart.

"Starfighter Six Five X-ray, cleared for takeoff runway 11 Left."

With all the checklists complete and the flaps set for takeoff, Burner felt a surge of adrenaline as he closed and locked the canopy. *I'm doing it. Thirty years later and I'm gonna fly a Starfighter again.* He acknowledged the clearance and pushed the throttles up to taxi onto the painted centerline. His heart beat a little faster as he took one last glance at the Jeppesen departure snapped to the metal clipboard attached to his left thigh. The clear Arizona sky boasted unlimited visibility as he braked to a stop and eased the throttle up to full military power. Jack checked the engine parameters and smiled as he pushed the throttle around the gate into afterburner. Nozzles sprayed copious amount of JP-4 into the burner section of the J-79, creating a tremendous roar and smashing Jack back firmly into his seat. A cone of yellowish-blue flame extended aft of the nearly fifty-five foot fighter as it rapidly accelerated down the runway. He deftly kept the centerline directly under his nosewheel with minute applications of rudder and eased back on the stick as airspeed rapidly approached 170 KIAS. The Silver Knight lifted off at 185—Burner quickly raised the gear followed by the flaps as the airspeed needle rapidly swung past 240. He smoothly pulled the throttles out of burner as he approached 300 and heard the tower direct him to contact departure control.

Two miles behind him, Lars and the gang of well-wishers were exchanging high fives. A pair of AF Reservists taxied into position on runway 11 Left in their Viper two-ship formation. In the wingman position, the Captain instructor in the F-16/B rear seat commented to his Second Lieutenant student, "Now that's something you don't see every day."

"Guess not. Ancient iron."

"Maybe. But it still can scoot."

Burner Stewart leveled the F-104 at 12,500 feet and turned east toward a dry lake bed some eighty miles from Tucson. The cooler drier air flowing through the aircraft ventilation system had chilled the cockpit, but not his enthusiasm. The words of John Gillespie McGee's *High Flight* poem came to him effortlessly as when he had memorized them years before as a basic cadet in the 11th Squadron at the USAF Academy, Class of '66. The words still stirred him as he connected cosmically with the American pilot who died while flying a British Spitfire during World War II.

He reveled in the view as the sienna-colored earth passed by and felt as if he were the only one alive in the desolate corner of southeastern Arizona. But all things must end, even an absolutely perfect test flight. The smallish tip tanks on the *Starfighter* extended its range, but the low level shakeout flight burned much more fuel than a high altitude long range cruise. Jack snapped into a sixty degree left bank and made a two G turn back to Tucson. Ten minutes later, he entered a left break for an overhead landing pattern on runway 11 Left.

Lars signaled the chocks were in place and cleared Burner to shut down the silver bullet. A small crowd met Jack at the base of the pilot ladder with a bottle of chilled Dom Pérignon. After a round of handshakes mixed with more high fives, Burner tore the metal foil and wire wrap off and sent the champagne cork flying. He toasted his friends, his talented mechanic and the *Silver Knight*. Eastman caught all the action on his video camera, and then took a long drink of the bubbly once Jack passed the bottle to him. Expanding gasses in the pale amber liquid quickly exceeded the volume of space in Boomer's throat, sending streams of cold frothy spume out his nostrils.

Jack doubled over in gales of laughter, and then ribbed his old wingman, "Boy, if you can't hang with the big dogs, better stay on the porch!"

**ARLINGTON COUNTY, VIRGINIA
PENTAGON**

Deep inside the massive 6,500,000 square-foot, five-sided building in the analysis department of Naval Intelligence, Ensign Maureen O'Grady poured over sonar data from the western Pacific and the China coast.

"Commander, you need to look at this," the attractive red head said to Lieutenant Commander Jesse DeFelice.

"What do you have, Ensign?" he said as he walked over to O'Grady's station.

"I noticed multiple high-speed returns consistent with very large water-jet propulsion systems from our passive deep water sonar array along the Chinese coast. The sound signature doesn't match anything we have in our data base. All the returns were limited to the area of the Bo Hia Sea. There must be something wrong with the system."

"How's that?"

"The speed calculated by measuring the Doppler effect of the unknown vessel was just a little over sixty knots."

"Jesus H. Christ! You're right, there must be something out of synch. There's nothing I know of that could be that fast, except for a racer…those returns are much too big and are from open water," DeFelice said as he perused the print out.

"Aye-aye, sir. I've already recalibrated the data three times and done a systems parameter check. Everything's A-Ok…All the aberrant data occurred at night…sir."

"How about satellite imagery?"

"The anomalous returns all occurred between passes of our bird, sir."

"Well, that's a red flag in itself. We've got two choices, Ensign, retask one of the birds or analyze the data stream from our weather satellite...maybe both. Print out a report of what you've got so far along with your analysis, I'll take it up to the SecDef."

"Aye-aye, sir."

ARLINGTON COUNTY, VIRGINIA
PENTAGON
OFFICE OF THE SECRETARY OF DEFENSE

The Pentagon building spanned 28.7 acres—was the only building in the US with six separate postal codes—but a person could walk from any point to another in under seven minutes. Lt. Commander DeFelice only had to walk a little over one minute to reach Secretary of Defense Harold Baker's office.

Baker's Executive Assistant, Willamena Parker, "Bill" as everyone called her, had been Executive Assistant to every Secretary of Defense since she was hired in 1970 during the Nixon administration. She was now 63 years young, usually wore her hair in a bun and dressed in smart conservative business suits—she often reminded visitors of Katharine Hepburn, both in looks and demeanor—but with a touch of Thelma Ritter. Bill not only was Executive Assistant to the SecDef, but some people would say she actually *ran* the DoD.

"Bill, need to see the SecDef."

“You’re lucky Commander, he was just about to leave for an appointment. You have three minutes,” Bill said, glancing at the clock on her desk.

“Yes, ma’am, thank you,”

“Thanks not required, just don’t make me come get you.”

“No, ma’am,” DeFelice said as he entered the office.

The walls were decorated with numerous political and military photos, including a large hand painted rendition of the famous photo by Joe Rosenthal depicting five Marines and a Navy Corpsman raising the flag on Mount Suribachi during the Battle of Iwo Jima. Baker, a balding Vietnam veteran, had retired as a Brigadier General from the Marine Corps almost fifteen years earlier, been appointed to the post of Secretary of Defense by President Annette Henry Thompson and was extremely well liked by all the services. He still carried himself in a military manner, even though he had thickened up some around the waist.

“Sir, thought you might want to look this over. We’re running additional surveys to verify,” DeFelice said as he handed over the folder.

Baker took the folder, opened it and scanned the report.

“Are you sure this isn’t some sort of glich in the system, Commander?” Baker said as he glanced over his glasses.

“No, sir. Ensign O’Grady ran the data multiple times and double checked the systems. No chance of error. She’s pulling up sat photos to cross check as we speak.”

“Interesting. The CIA has indicated there was level four information of China developing some new high speed war ships…I'll shoot this data over to Langley. Maybe they can make some sense of it. Keep me informed."

"Yes, sir."

"Bill, would you come in please?"

Commander DeFelice passed Bill as she entered.

"You barely made it, Commander."

"No, ma'am, uh, yes, ma'am, thank you, ma'am," DeFelice stuttered as he left.

Bill grinned at Baker after the Commander had closed the door behind him.

"You gotta quit scaring the troops, Bill."

"Just breaking them in right, sir."

"Uh huh…Listen, need to get this folder over to Weber at Langley," he said as he handed the report to her.

"Problems?"

"China."

"Again?"

***

CHAPTER TWO

AIR FORCE SPACE COMMAND VANDENBURG, CALIFORNIA

Dr. Stacie Chen, opened the computer file on her newest program for MILSATCOM, or Military Satellite Communications, for the Air Force Space Command's Space and Missile Systems Center. She had been working on the update for over twelve months and would be ready to uplink in two weeks. The diminutive second generation Chinese held her Ph.D. in computer programing, specializing in military communications applications from Cal Tech. Only five feet-two, with the body of a gymnast, Stacie had been working for the Air force Space Command since her graduation two years earlier.

Dr. Chen's revolutionary program would enable the entire US joint-service military to activate a world wide link through the massive secure satellite communications constellation allowing for all operations to communicate in real time. All Carrier Strike Groups, aircraft and ground based units would be able to synchronize and download links simultaneously—Battle Command-On-The-Move capability for individual units would be a key.

"How's it coming, Stacie?" asked Dr. Goodhew, the head of the department, as he entered her lab.

"Oh, hi, Taylor. Only have two thousand lines to go in the proofing routine. So far, so good," replied Stacie without looking up from her screen.

"That's an amazing program you've created. Not sure I completely understand it, but then again, I don't have to, thank goodness… Chairman of the Joint Chiefs, Admiral Valenti is chomping at the bit to see it in operation."

"They're just like kids at Christmas, wanting to see their presents. Well, they'll just have to wait 'till I'm done. Not uploading until I'm one hundred percent sure everything will work like it's supposed to."

"Oh, say, got a group of F-16 pilots coming in from D-M next week to watch the launch of our comm satellite with your new program…thought we'd give them a tour while they're here. Would like for you to show 'em around, if you don't mind."

"Joy. I'll carve out a couple of hours, but that's all. I'll be up to my butt in checking the codes again during and after launch."

"Really appreciate it…How's your mom?"

Stacie paused for a moment, and then said, “Fine. She’s still in China, uh, visiting family…”

“She’s been there, what…several months?”

“…Uh, yeah. Seems longer.”

“I’ll email you the schedule for those jet jockeys,” Dr. Goodhew said as he walked toward the door.

Stacie got a far away look for a moment—then pulled her long black hair back into a pony tail, slipped a scrunchie on it and then turned back to her screen.

ARIZONA

Jack had spent much of Monday after the first flight of the Silver Knight responding to Facebook comments he had received after posting the YouTube links to the launch and landing. *Starfighter* aficionados worldwide had cheered the videos and he had been pleased to hear from many of the pilots he had served with during his time on active duty.

The age of social networking had certainly changed the way people with similar interests could share good times. The retired general was active in the Red River Rats, Phantoms Forever, Eagle Driver Symposium and, of course, the Starfighter Assembly. He belonged to several other Air Force and a couple of Naval Aviator organizations for the F-105 *Thunderchief*, F-8 *Crusader* and F-14 *Tomcat* enthusiasts. With the click of a mouse, he could locate the last known flyable models of each aircraft and have a contact list of the organization’s members and many of their backgrounds. His stint at Lockheed had also created a contact list of top managers within the huge conglomerate as well as within the Pentagon's procurement section.

A spirited debate had ensued, as usual, when one poster inquired about Jack's *Starfighter* avionics. He had described the stock flight instrumentation and original military installed radar system. Many were surprised the radar still worked after all the years in storage. The discussion had gravitated into a dissertation about the relative merits of the state-of-the-art 21st century systems versus the old iron. The obvious addition of the stealth technology created an avalanche of opinions, most of which Stewart had found amusing. *Grumbling about a deficiency never solved the problem.* One post however, did catch his eye and started the wheels turning: *Yugoslavian air defense commander Colonel Zoltán Dani claims to have detected F-117s over Bosnia by operating his radars on unusually long wavelengths. Several of their version of the Soviet Isayev S-125 NevaSA-3s were fired from about 8 miles. One missile detonated near the unlucky F-117A by proximity fuze.*

Another post by retired Lt. Colonel Dickey Williams: *General Wesley Clark confirmed this version of the shootdown. It my have been luck. The Yugoslavs thought that they picked it up when the bomb bay doors opened.*

Burner added: *I believe in making my own luck.*

Several posters hit the *like* button in response to his opinion before Jack logged off for the evening. He sat quietly contemplating the situation for a few minutes before he picked up the phone. Lars answered on the third ring.

“Hey, see you’re famous, General.”

“We both are. Want my autograph?”

“At the bottom of my paycheck! What’s up?”

“Got a question about the radar frequencies. Back in ‘68, we didn’t have high PRF, correct?”

“The best horns we had in fighters back then were not that shiny. The unit in the Silver Knight is adjustable between what is now considered low and mid range PRF. Why?”

“An idea I ran across in a post. Don’t want to discuss it on the phone. May have security implications.”

“Forty year old technology with security concerns? You been sippin’ the sauce?”

“Just a touch. Let you know what I find out.”

“I’ll hold you to that.”

Jack ended the call and scrolled down to find the home number for Lockheed-Martin Senior VP/Technical, Roland Perry. He wasted no time in tapping the number.

“Jack, you old showboat! Fifteen people emailed that link of you and the silver bullet. You callin’ to gloat?”

“Hey, Rollie, nothing like that. Got a minute?”

“Sure. How was it?”

“The flight? Kick ass! Wish you could have been there on my wing. Everything went perfect.”

“Looked great in the video, made me jealous. So, how you doing, Burner? I miss beating your ass on the golf course.”

“In your dreams. Hey, the reason I called is that I want to run some ideas past you about defeating the Raptor.”

"Now who's dreaming? Ain't happened yet. Don't you ever talk to your boy? We are almost 750-0 in air to air missions against Active Duty and Air Guard units fourth gen fighters. You *are* aware of that, right?"

"Yeah, I didn't go into hibernation after I retired from Lockheed. Listen, I have something I'd like to run past you in person. Can you find fifteen minutes on your schedule this week? Don't wish to discuss this idea on an unsecure line."

"Anything for you, buddy. Hang on a sec while I check my schedule…How's Wednesday at 11:45?"

"Sounds good. Can you arrange landing PPR for me at Carswell? I *hate* flying commercial."

"Isn't that the truth? Waitin' in line for some TSA moron to grope my crotch doesn't make my top ten list, either. What's type and N number?"

"Beech Starship, November Sierra Two Two X-ray."

"Sweet. You rebuilt two aircraft in the last eighteen months?"

"I know. Should have my head examined. But ever since Karen passed away, I've had time on my hands."

"She was a gem. What's it been? Three years?"

"A little over…seems like forever…and just yesterday sometimes."

"Yeah, heard that…Lookin' forward to seeing you, Burner. Call me when you get in range and I'll have transport meet you on the ramp."

"'Preciate it. See ya," he said as he disconnected.

It's a long shot but somebody needs to follow up on this. Jack poured himself three fingers of Crown Royal over ice and pulled his Dash One manuals for the F-104, F-4 and F-15 out of his personal library. He slipped a pair of small gold framed reading glasses out of their case and proceeded to review each manual's avionics section. When he met with Roland, he wanted to be absolutely sure about his technical specs and have a plan of action to test his theory. He closed the last of the manuals; the clock in his study read three minutes past one. Jack took a quick shower and slipped into bed. Sleep came quickly and, once again, Karen was with him.

HAWAII

A light onshore breeze blew over the Pearl Harbor Joint Base as Lt. Colonel Stewart pulled into the Officer's Club on his burgundy Harley Softail Custom—identical to his dad's. The two had purchased the bikes at the same time, getting a great deal in Tucson. What passed for a perfect fall day in paradise was coming to a close as the men of the 99th and 44th Fighter Squadrons met at the club after the debriefing. Minutes later, he was sitting with eight other jocks in green flight suits talking about the best beaches to surf in the fall. Winter time often brought monster waves to the north shore, but the early fall was similar to summer weather and in turn, wave patterns.

"Makapu'u Beach has killer waves for body surfing this time of year. The shore break can be a bitch! Don't recommend it for first timers. The signs they post about broken arms and head injuries aren't fiction. I had two newbie airmen in the squadron out for medicals just this spring," Stewart said.

"Come on, Hollywood! You guys are trying to hog the best spots!" Major Jimmy "Jo-Jo" Johnson protested.

"Negatory, Jo-Jo. If you never experienced getting tossed into eighteen inches of water by a fourteen foot wave, be my guest. Did I mention the rip tide? First, it busts your butt, and then it drags you right back down into the surf for a second round. Recommend you guys try Ala Moana Beach Park. They have board rentals and plenty of chicks in bikinis and thongs to keep you occupied."

Johnson frowned at the suggestion, and then brightened up as a drop-dead gorgeous redhead in a Air Force Doctor's dress uniform entered the club. Heads turned to follow the Rhonda Fleming look alike.

"Oh my God! Think I'm in love. Imagine that one in a thong," said Stewart.

"She doesn't like pilots," Jimmy offered.

"Always a first time."

The doctor worked her way through the crowded bar and headed for the table where the eight jocks sat.

"See, the Hollywood magic is working."

Out of his peripheral vision, Stewart saw Jimmy Johnson begin to rise. *Oh Shit! Does he know her?*

The captain broke into a dazzling smile as she brushed past Stewart. His head snapped around as heard them speak.

"Hi, sis, how was your leave?" Jimmy asked as they hugged.

"Great, the folks are fine. Was nice getting off the island for a couple weeks."

Stewart felt himself flush with a tinge of embarrassment. *Imagine that one in a thong? Way to go, Ace. Insert foot, bite off at the ankle.*

"Are you getting hungry, Kel? The food here is not bad," Jimmy asked.

"Actually, I have a sushi place over near the Hyatt Regency I wanted to take you to. I can run you past the VOQ to let you change to some civvies."

"Sounds like a plan. Oops, where are my manners? Guys, I'd like you to meet by baby sister, Dr. Kelli Ann Johnson."

Kelli nodded pleasantly as she was introduced to all the pilots. All the pilots stood. When it became Stewart's turn, he could only think of one interesting thing to say, as her beauty had him completely captivated.

"Kelly Johnson, just like the famous aircraft designer?"

She smiled and replied sweetly, "Not exactly. Mine is spelled with an 'i'. He was our great uncle, and the family is very proud of him."

"Nice to meet you, Kelli with an 'i'. What's your medical specialty?"

"Oncology."

"Interesting…We would invite you to join us, but I see you two have plans. Enjoy the Wasabi Hut, Jo-Jo. Their Ahi is to die for."

Kelli curiously noted Stewart's mention of the name of the sushi restaurant she adored. Her green eyes met his for a second, and then she glanced at his smile before she tore herself away. *I don't date pilots.* Jimmy laid a ten on the table to cover his two drinks and they headed to the door. She took one last look over her shoulder before she reached the door. Hollywood Stewart had his blue eyes locked on her. The smile was still on his lips.

AIR FORCE SPACE COMMAND
VANDENBURG, CALIFORNIA

Stacie leaned in close to her screen, studying the complicated lines of code when her email chimed.

"Damn," she said as she saved her work and switched windows to her email.

The message was from Dr. Goodhew containing the list of F-16 pilots from Davis-Monthan Air Force Base coming in for their tour. She scrolled down to the list.

"Well, let's see what these hot shots look like," she mumbled as she opened her profile page on Facebook, went up to the search bar and typed in the first name, Lieutenant Colonel John "Magic" Mann.

"Married and old enough to be my father." She typed in the next. "Married, but cute," she said of Captain Harley "Hog" Hale. Stacie continued down the list. Captain Cam "Shaft" Smathers had a nose like a hawk. Captain Norman "Nooch" Nitschke and Captain Richard "Gas" Garrett were also both married. But, First Lieutenant Jeff "Boom Boom" Babayan was single.

"Wow, a hottie," she said as she opened his page.

"Graduated Texas A&M, ROTC 2007, Republican, Christian, likes the Star Wars movies, Dale Brown, Jim DeFelice and Clive Cussler novels and rock climbing. Cool. This may not be such a waste of time after all," Stacie muttered.

Stacie Chen was a very attractive single woman, buried in her work. *I haven't had a date in over four months,* she mused. *Of course it does take two to Tango. But I really need a break. I have to stay sharp, Mom's counting on me.*

FORT WORTH, TEXAS

"November Sierra Two Two X-ray, cleared to land runway 18."

"Roger, Two Two X-ray, cleared to land on 18," Jack replied as he reached for the gear handle. The flight had been uneventful and he smiled to himself as he watched the brand new F-16 pull up to the hold short line as it awaited its turn for departure. The *Vipers* rolled off the Lockheed-Martin production line on the west side the NAS Carswell JRB. Reserve Air Force C-130s and F-16s shared the other side of the venerable facility with Marine F/A-18s and US Army RC-12s. Not every day would Carswell Tower see a civilian bird arrive, much less the rare Beech Craft Starship.

Jack touched down gently just 500 feet from the approach end of the runway and slowed for his planned turnoff at the midfield taxiway.

"Two-Two X-ray, turn right on taxiway 2, contact ramp control on 121.7, we will close your IFR."

"Thank you, Carswell, Two Two X-ray, good day."

A ground marshaller met the blue and white Starship and guided it to a parking spot next to three new F-16s awaiting delivery. The marshaller raised the two unlit yellow wands above his head and crossed them when Jack approached the stop point. With the aircraft chocked, he released the brakes and completed his shutdown checklist. A silver Lexus LS460 pulled up. A pretty 34 year old brunette stepped out and waited near the aircraft entrance door. Jack grabbed his briefcase and lowered the stairs. He smiled when he recognized the young woman.

"Kristi! Great to see you, girl. I didn't know Rollie would send his personal assistant to drive me to the head shed."

She returned his smile and stepped forward to give him a big hug. "Always a pleasure, General. How was your fight?"

"Not bad. I see Texas was a little dry this year."

"We are hoping for more rain this fall. We still miss you around here. Roland's looking forward to seeing you. Got a visitor's pass," she said as she looped the red lanyard over Jack's head.

He looked at the picture on the ID. She had used his last official employee photo for it.

"Didn't have the mustache back then."

"I like it. Makes you look dashing. Hop in. Have us there in three minutes."

As promised, the two of them were parked in Roland's assigned spot in short order.

Kristi slid her ID badge past a security scanner that unlocked the doorway to the headquarters. The two passed by a security guard seated inside a station next to the main foyer. He smiled and nodded at Kristi, and then recognized Jack.

"Morning, General Stewart. It's been a while."

"Yes it has, Bobby, yes it has."

Jack warmed at the recognition. Karen had really been the reason Jack had retired. She wanted to spend some time without sharing him with the Air Force or Lockheed. Her point was well taken. The two had been physically separated by the demands of his work off and on for many years. Deployments, combat tours and test programs all added up to years apart that she could never recoup. He had granted her wish only to have her develop an inoperable brain cancer fourteen months after his retirement. Jack had been devastated and only really recovered when he teamed up with Lars to work on the two restoration projects.

Kristi led him into the VP's outer office and touched the interphone button.

"Mr. Perry, Jack Stewart is here."

"Bring him in!"

Roland met Jack near the door. The two shared back slapping bear hugs as they greeted. Suddenly, Jack became aware another person was already in the room.

"I'm sorry. Am I interrupting?"

"Jack this is Roger Rutan, our chief designer for stealth systems. Not sure if you had a chance to meet him while you were here. Roger, General Jack Stewart."

The two men shook hands.

"Roger, nice to meet you. My friends call me Burner. Aren't you Burt's brother? I thought he would have you working over at Scaled Composites."

"We did work together for many years. I even helped refine the design on the Starship you flew here. But Lockheed needed some help with fabrication and they made me an offer I couldn't refuse. Plus, Bert retired recently."

"Coffee anyone?" Roland asked.

"Black," replied Jack.

"I'm good," said Roger.

Roland motioned for the three to have a seat. He nodded to Kristin.

"One black coming up," Kristin said on the way out.

"So, Burner, tell me how you are going to defeat our Raptors?"

Before Jack could start, Kristin was back with his coffee.

"Thanks, Kristin, that was quick."

"I don't mess around," she said over her shoulder as she closed the door.

Over the next ten minutes, Jack laid out his hypothesis. Almost invariably avionics engineers had been drawn to the pulse Doppler radar with higher pulse repetition frequency. With almost no moving parts on the phased scanner array, the latest radar systems were outstanding at rapidly gathering massive amounts of extremely accurate information about detected airborne targets. But the fact remained, that none of the modern radars were capable of detecting the F-22. *How did Lockheed explain the shootdown of the F-117 by the Yugoslav Army? Was the low frequency radar, similar to the airborne moving target indicator operating at, 450Hz instead of a high PRF at 100Khz capable of painting a Raptor?*

Roland looked over Roger for reassurance. He was not happy with the look Roger gave him back.

"Roger, you guys did test all available radar frequencies against the mockups on the F-22, right?"

"Not exactly."

"What does *not exactly* mean?"

"Due to the nature of the expected threats, we tested against former Soviet, current Russian, French and Chinese SAM or fighter radars designed since 1980. Basically, anything operating above 45Kz. Systems designed to use frequencies below that are unreliable, obsolete and simply not in use. Nobody has fighter radars that operate in those ranges."

"So there you go, Burner. Rest easy. Nobody has a system that operates so low as to be a threat to the Raptor."

Roland smiled broadly after he gave Jack the news. He expected his old friend to smile back, but the retired general did not. He, in fact, had a sadness about his demeanor that was uncharacteristic when he replied. "I do."

Roland tried hard not to show emotion as he processed what Jack said. He stood up, checked his watch, moved to his desk and keyed his intercom.

"Kristi, cancel my one o'clock with the budget committee. I want Mark Peterson, Bryan Rye and Ed White to join us in the conference room ASAP. Plan a working lunch and order for us."

"Can do," she replied through the speaker.

Forty-five minutes later, Jack had laid out the basis for an airborne test over Nellis' Test Range in Nevada. He would have his F-104 modified at Nellis for carrying dummy AIM-120 AMRAAM missiles as well as telemetry pods which would give the range monitors instantaneous download of his radar and missile systems. If his low frequency theory was proved correct, fate of the entire F-22 program was at risk. Roland agreed to have Lockheed-Martin/Boeing cover the tests costs on one condition—Jack must return to work for Lockheed during the interim. Jack agreed with the condition and added two of his own. His pay would be exactly the same as his current retired pay, and Lockheed would hire Lars as a maintenance technician to oversee the conversion. Both men shook hands on their agreement before Kristi was called in to escort Jack to Human Resources for the required inprocessing and security background check procedures.

WASHINGTON, DC
WHITE HOUSE CABINET ROOM

President Annette Henry Thomspon was livid even before her Treasury Secretary Homer Gibbons finished his briefing. She held up her hand to signal stop. "You're saying Bernanke decided to go ahead with his ill conceived QE4 even after I had personally advised him to discontinue any additional attempt to monetize the existing Federal Debt?"

"Yes, Madame President. That's the long and short of it."

"Where do we stand in total Federal Treasuries outstanding? I'm not talking unfunded liabilities, like Medicare, Medicade and such, just the T-bills…Today."

Secretary Gibbons leaned to one of his three aides who whispered into his ear.

"The current total is $18.4 trillion, Madame President. Spending authorization from the Congress prior to your taking office allows that number to be increased to $20.2 trillion without a additional vote being called for. The Federal Reserve is now taking steps to issue $2.4 trillion in 20 year notes during the next four months."

Her antique gold eyes flashed with anger. Secretary Gibbons swallowed visibly as he obviously did not want to be the bearer of such disappointing financial news. She sat quietly for a moment and processed her options. "You're going to tell me that unless our party gains a super majority in the Senate elections fourteen months from now, there is no way to rein in the Federal Reserve. Am I correct?"

"Yes, ma'am…May I speak freely?"

"Absolutely. This is not time to hold any ideas back."

"The reckless spending policies of the two previous administrations have essentially bankrupted this country. Our debt exceeds ninety percent of the GDP as it is, and any further expansion is inviting a true default as we saw in Greece, Italy and Spain."

"Mr. Secretary, you sound exactly like one of my many campaign speeches. I am well aware of the factors leading to the dissolution of the European Union. Do you actually have any ideas to stop the Federal Reserve from printing money? The value of the dollar hit another all time low today as gold topped $4,100 on the Comex this morning. The Chinese are raising bloody hell over the loss of buying power of their $5.76 trillion dollar investment in our bonds."

"Madame President, I can't say as I blame them, really. The money they spent on our bonds is now only worth $2.1 trillion in FY 1999 dollars."

"Which is why I am so adamantly opposed to papering over our debt. For decades, gutless politicians have pandered to their special interest groups and spent more than they took in. I intend to stop that practice and truly balance the budget. What can we do?"

The hapless Treasury Secretary looked down at his feet. He shrugged and slowly shook his head. "Executive order? Decree their bond issuance capacity is void?"

President Thompson glared at him in silence. Her icy hot glare drifted to Attorney General Alan Ames. The conservative former constitutional law professor from SMU looked over his half glasses and exhaled.

"Alan, do I have that authority?" she asked in a direct manner.

"From a purely constitutional authority, I would say no."

She sank back into the high backed leather hair that stood exactly two inches higher than the rest of the chairs in the cabinet room.

“However,” he continued, “the expansive use of the Executive Order since the events of 9/11 has not brought into focus exactly what are the limits of the EO as a tool. Many people have chaffed under the yoke of restrictions placed upon Americans in all facets of their lives by little known Executive Orders. It has become *law by regulation.* The Supreme Court has not agreed to hear arguments on a single one, to my knowledge.”

“What about Obama’s drilling moratorium in the Gulf following the BP disaster in 2010?”

“His order was overturned by a Federal District Court, and then basically the same restrictions on drilling were implemented through a very restrictive permit issuance process. He essentially shut down our offshore oil business driving up unemployment…that did not change until your administration.”

Her gaze fell back upon Secretary Gibbons.

“What effect will an Executive Order have on Wall Street? Give me a short term and long term scenario.”

“Madame President, no one has ever successfully challenged the Federal Reserve. It is not possible to gauge the impact.”

“Homer, I want your best guess and don’t play games. Your friends at Goldman Sachs are going to scream bloody murder. They get rich off of low interest money from the Fed.”

Gibbons had a brief deer-in-the-headlights look, and then spoke slowly, "Wall Street financials will take a huge hit. Down 20% in two days. Maybe down 40% in a week. The DOW will drop between 800 and 1,000 points before it stabilizes and recovers. Gold will shoot up to $5,000 before it drops back to $3,500 or less."

White House Chief of Staff Mark Carter spoke up, "Madame President, I would advise extreme caution in this matter. While you may enjoy a substantial party majority in the house, not all of our own party are as conservative as you. They would not sit still for a change in the relationship with the Federal Reserve system. The media would have a field day and your actions would be the topic of every talk show and network for weeks. Any impeachment attempt in the house would be precarious and I could almost guarantee a conviction with the opposition led Senate."

"Mark, I appreciate your candor. I'm not going to go into this unprepared in any event. It is a monumental task to try turn this nation from the collision course it has been on for decades. The riots in Europe were proof a bankrupt socialist economic policy can only go on so long. As Margaret Thatcher said, *The problem with Socialism is that sooner or later, you run out of other people's money.* I am afraid that day is fast upon us. I'll have a decision for you at the end of the week." She looked at the gold Omega watch on her left wrist. "I'd like to see Admiral Valenti and Secretary Harper in the Oval Office. Thank you."

The President nodded toward the doorway and White House CoS Carter exited quietly. The three glanced nervously at each other for a brief moment before she spoke.

"Charger, first I want to thank you for standing in for SecDef Baker while he's visiting our troops in Syria...Now what is your take on the Chinese military? Do you think their actions in retaking Taiwan will embolden them for further expansion?"

"My position has not changed, Madame President. As I told you when I gave you the limited options we possessed at the time of the takeover, we are severely and tactically weakened by the five concurrent conflicts in the Middle East. Budget cutbacks forced the elimination of two full infantry and one armored divisions. We have ceased production of the F-22 and F-35, and only one new carrier is scheduled to come on line next year to replace the two set for retirement. Total ships-of-the-line number only 203, down from over 800 during the Reagan administration. The only area we actually lead the Chinese militarily is in strategic nuclear missiles, both land based and on subs. When the Chinese fully realize how vulnerable we are, all bets are off."

"Admiral, you can't seriously believe the Chinese would attack US soil! We are their largest trading partner. I myself have renegotiated the extension of the Most Favored Nations trade agreement with them," Secretary Harper protested.

"Mr. Secretary, my comments are based on a lifetime of watching and countering Chinese expansionism. They changed tactics in the 1990's, but did not change their spots. The

Politburo still calls the shots, regardless of the contracts they have with our big box stores. All the US sales have done is to allow the Chinese to build a more modern Army, Navy and Air Force that they could never have created under the economic performance of Communism. The gross imbalance in our trade relationship has given them the cash to purchase over five trillion dollars in US Treasury securities and amass fifteen percent of the world's gold reserves in the last ten years. Those are the facts. Actions of the Federal Reserve to pay off our existing debt with devalued currency may be the trigger that prompts the Chinese to military action to recoup their losses."

"Come on, Valenti! I know the Chinese Ambassador extremely well. There is no malice in him. I spoke to him just yesterday over tea, and he was most cordial. If there was any indication they were actually…" the Secretary of State halted abruptly as the Chairman of the Joint Chiefs of Staff removed a black and white photograph from his valise and laid it on the President's desk.

"Just in from the Office of Naval Intelligence. Don't know the name yet. Twin-hulled catamaran designed ultra-super carrier. Caught a break in the clouds and had re-task a satellite to get this shot. Top speed is twice that of our Nimitz-Class carriers and our best guess is it can carry at least three naval air wings. We tracked her on sonar to the Dalian Port. What we don't know is if she's the only one built."

"How can they have built this without our knowledge? Didn't the CIA or NSA have an inkling about this?" President Thompson asked.

"I can't speak for them, Madame President. My people at ONI got suspicious over high speed jet screws operating at night and took action at the direction of the SecDef."

Valenti and Thompson looked at Harper who appeared to be a shade paler.

"Conrad, do you think you can ask your friend the Chinese Ambassador the name of their latest carrier? If it wouldn't be to much of an imposition."

"Yes, Madame President. I will see what I can do."

"Thank you, Conrad, that will be all."

The somewhat unsteady Secretary made his way to the door of the Oval Office.

"Charger, now that there are just two of us, can you give me any idea of what you think their next move would be?"

"Yes, ma'am. The old idea that the Chinese would never attack the United States may no longer be valid. We have permitted our manufacturing base to decline as theirs built up. They have a new stealth fighter, and a copy of the Russian top of the line Su-27. Our F-22 fighter is a world beater, but we only have 140 of them, spread out over the continental US, Alaska and Hawaii. Historically, the Chinese have been reticent to seize additional territory and are generally suspicious of other cultures, of course, they've always considered Taiwan to be theirs anyway. What we saw in both Korea and Vietnam was that the Chinese Communists were committed to aid the enemies of western style democracies. That geopolitical posture had been followed in Africa and the middle east with substantial sales of Chinese hardware to Iraq, Iran, Pakistan, Libya and Latin America."

"So, you are saying, Admiral, that while we have been busy trying to stamp out brush fires around the world, China has been preparing a non-nuclear first strike capability that could overwhelm us? Is one ultra-super carrier group that significant? Is it possible that you are exaggerating somewhat?"

Valenti chose his words carefully. He looked into the President's eyes for a full four seconds before he spoke.

"Conrad Harper is worst than an idiot if he thinks the Chinese are not a threat. They have consistently acted against American interests abroad while they undercut our domestic industrial production with their slave labor cost advantages. I cannot name a single area in which they have supported our actions in any fashion…peacekeeping, humanitarian, you name it. I see the current buildup by the Communists in historic terms. The parallels to Japanese empire building are not a matter of chance. The difference in this century is that our country has been truly weakened by outsourcing our manufacturing capability, constant foreign purchases by the big box stores and by the grossly negligent policies of our Federal Reserve. I am afraid we are at a point where we may not be able to recover fast enough to prevent a defeat. We are extraordinarily vulnerable."

President Thompson took the Admiral's assessment with a heavy heart. She knew he was not grandstanding and that he was a battle scarred veteran of the political infighting that led to the down sizing of the US Military. The hardest part for her personally was to admit that the Admiral was right.

NELLIS AFB, NEVADA

The late October sun had just cleared the horizon over Lake Mead when Jack Stewart and Lars Hendricksen pulled into the visitors parking space in front of the 757TH Aircraft Maintenance Squadron hangar. Both men exited the white rental Ford SUV and headed for the blue entrance door. A slight breeze from the northwest chilled them both as the dry air took on the characteristics of the high desert.

"Beats the 110 degrees they have in August," Lars noted.

"Got that right. I made many a preflight out there when I thought my flight boots were gonna melt."

Highly trained technicians from the host unit were installing the last of the four simulated AIM-120 AMRAAM missiles on the outboard under wing hard points of the *Silver Knight*. A week's worth of modification had adapted the modern missiles to the sixty year old airframe design. Two other technicians were testing the interface between the range communications telemetry module attached to the right inboard stanchions. A pair of captive AIM-9 Sidewinders graced the left inboard hardpoint.

"Gentlemen! You boys were busy beavers last night," Jack said.

A Tech Sergeant turned and looked up at the silver haired pilot as he knelt in front of the wing.

"Morning, General. The night shift got with the program. I think you'll be happy. It's still is a little odd to put 21st century armament on a 20th century fighter."

"I know. I used to fly the Eagle on active duty."

"They are actually going to allow you to test this old bird on the range! What are you hoping to find, if you don't mind my askin', sir?"

Jack just grinned. "Don't mind you askin', but I'm not at liberty to say."

"Any way you want it, General. We'll be through here in twenty minutes and will go over the system ground checks with Mr. Hendricksen."

"Thanks. I'll make sure to tell the Chief and Colonel White what a great job you guys did."

The Tech Sergeant smiled, nodded and returned to the captive AMRAAM mounting.

Two young F-15 jocks in flight suits walked across the huge hangar floor to check out the F-104. Jack noticed their squadron patches and recognized the logos of the 65th Aggressor Squadron. Jack stood up and addressed the pair.

"You two must be the ones Colonel Crockett sent over to set up the brief."

"Yes, sir. I'm Rick Hess, call sign Von, and this is Captain Harry "Buck" Rogers. Nice ride you have here, General."

"Thanks, I'm kinda partial to the Silver Knight. By the way, I'm retired. My friends call me Burner," Jack said as he extended his hand.

The Major and Captain both shook his hand and gladly accepted his offer to check out the sleek *Starfighter*.

"Not much of a wing there, Burner," the Captain noted as he checked out the razor thin leading edge.

"No, and it will do more than leave a mark of you're not careful on preflight."

"Don't imagine your turning performance is good by modern standards, sir."

Jack laughed. "No, Von, the Starfighter didn't turn well, even back in the day. It was designed as a point defense fighter. It's small, fast, hard to see and, as it turned out, does not have much of a radar cross section either. You Eagle drivers won't be impressed by the size of the cockpit. Kelly Johnson came up with the basic design in 1953."

The two Aggressor pilots looked at each other.

"1953? I wasn't even born until '81!" Captain Rogers exclaimed.

"Babe in the woods…After we finish the grand tour here, we need to get over to your ops area. The mission brief is going to be Top Secret."

Twenty minutes later, the three pilots entered the briefing room and met with the commander of the 65th AGRS and two F-22 *Raptor* pilots from the 433rd Weapons Squadron.

"Burner, your Blue Force opponents this afternoon will be Lt. Colonel Barney "Quaker" Berlinger and Major Archie "Smoke" Marker."

Jack extended his hand and warmly greeted the two seasoned pilots.

“Burner Stewart. My pleasure. Quaker? How’d you get that call sign?”

“I’m from Pennsylvania…Nice to meet you, sir. You’re Hollywood’s dad, right?” Berlinger asked.

“Guilty as charged. You guys fly together?”

“Classmates at the Academy. Went through UPT together, too. How’s he doing out in Hawaii?”

“Loving it. Proud to be a Raptor pilot. Hard to be humble and all that crap.”

“Yes, sir. We get their exercise results every week and it’s difficult to keep from believing your own press clippings, if you know what I mean. The Raptor hasn’t lost a single engagement and I don’t see that changing with your Starfighter. No offense, sir.”

Jack smiled and shook his head. “None taken. Son, if you didn’t think you were the best thing wearing wings, I wouldn’t want you on my team. Being a fighter pilot is all about competence and confidence. You gotta have both.”

“Roger that, sir. Now can you tell us what this shindig is really all about? You can’t really be serious your ancient iron is a match for the Raptor.”

The smile melted from Jack’s face. “Boys, I love the Starfighter. But, on its best day it can’t compare airframe to airframe with the Eagle or Raptor.”

The other five pilot's nodded. From the looks on their faces, it was obvious they didn't think the retired General had lost his mind. He had their rapt attention.

"What would you say if I told you I think I have a way to defeat your stealth capability?"

"Holy shit," whispered Colonel Crockett.

Berlinger and Marker glanced at each other in disbelief. A slightly sick look crossed over Marker's face.

"General, I mean, Burner, are you serious? That's not possible," he stammered.

"Guys, you don't know how much I hope this test proves me wrong."

"What are you going to do to defeat the stealth, sir?" Johnston asked.

"To make sure the test is a valid one, I'm not going to tell you what I'm going to do. I have coordinated a rectangular test block 80 by 120 miles. Neither of us will be afforded the use of a AWACS bird to find each other. The test will be using on-board systems only, one V two. We have the range from 1300 local to 1400 local surface to 60,000. I will enter the range five minutes after you two and the range monitor will notify you that the fight's on…" Burner paused, then continued. "One more thing. The results of the test will be Top Secret/Need to Know Only. You all understand the security ramifications if my hypothesis is correct?" The assembled pilots nodded. Jack waited a moment for his warning to sink in before he continued. "In a couple minutes, we're going to bring in the weather shop and range control folks for their standard briefs. You will notice

I took the precaution of changing your routine call signs for this test. If one or both of your Raptors is detected and or defeated, RTB as if nothing unusual happened. Do not discuss the test results with anyone…not even your crew chief. Is that understood?"

Lt. Col. Berlinger looked hard at Burner. *Jesus. He's serious.* He knew of Burner's reputation and his stellar record as a fighter pilot and commander. Jack had graduated from the Fighter Weapon School at the head of his class. Suddenly the, importance of the day's test flight took on a whole new meaning. Barney sat up a little straighter in his gray leather chair and prepared to take notes from the three mission briefed pilots who were admitted into the room.

CENTRAL MILITARY COMMISSION
MINISTRY OF NATIONAL DEFENSE COMPOUND
BEIJING, PEOPLE'S REPUBLIC OF CHINA

"All stand and pay respect to our illustrious President and Paramount Leader, Hu Jintao," said Vice President Xi Jinping.

The members of the Politburo Standing Committee of the Communist Party of China, State Council of the Central People's Government and the Central Committee of the People's Liberation Army/Navy all stood and bowed deeply as Hu Jintao entered the room. Hu Jintao nodded his head slightly at the assemblage and stood at attention until the Chinese national anthem, *Xiang Yang Hong* had finished playing—then took his seat. As soon as Hu Jintao had settled, the rest of the hierarchy of the Chinese government also seated themselves.

"Honorable Paramount Leader, members of the Politburo, State Council and PLAN, we are on the precipice of a momentous time in our long history," said the Chairman of the Standing Committee, Wu Bangguo. "We all know that the west coast of North America was actually discovered and claimed for China by Admiral Zheng He. Admiral He and his expeditionary fleet anchored in an inlet off of what is now southern Oregon in 1422. This was some seventy years prior to the Columbus voyage. It is believed by our scholars that Admiral Zheng had in his possession, maps drawn by Kublai Khan, founder of the Yuan Dynasty in the eleventh century, thereby giving China legitimate claim to the west coast of the United States."

"Why did we not claim it at the time?" asked Wen Jiabao, Premier of the State Council,

"After Zheng's last voyage in 1433, edicts were passed by the emperor prohibiting Chinese from traveling abroad due to the profligate waste of the expeditions. The feeling was that the money spent could be better used at home since China was already the all-perfect Center of the Universe."

"The time has come for China to reclaim its own," Vice President Xi Jinping offered.

"Do you really think that the United States will roll over like a dog wanting its belly scratched?" asked President Hu Jintao. "You live in a dream world, Xi."

"The United States has no stomach for war, illustrious leader. If they did, they would have done more than just file protests with our ambassador when we invaded and reclaimed Taiwan. They had assured the Taiwanese government they would protect and stand with them if they were invaded...So much for their promises. The previous administration apologized to the Taiwanese, just like they did to most of the Middle Eastern countries. They are cowards."

"Their military is also stretched far too thin, trying to fight five wars at once. The United States no longer knows how to fight...they've lost their heart," proffered High General Chen Bingde, Chief of the General Staff of the PLAN. "In addition, not only are they are tired of war, their military budget has been cut drastically due to their bankrupt economic practices. I agree with Vice President Xi, now is the time."

"I still seriously doubt that a claim from 700 years ago will carry any weight with either the United States or the world community. China will be ostracized and no doubt censured by the United Nations. It is a fool's journey, General," said President Hu.

"Paramount Leader, you must also know that our seat on the UN security council enables us to veto any move to censure. The UN is a paper tiger. We are the sole super power now," added Guo Boxiong, Vice Chairman of the Central Military Commission.

"Comrades, this is useless diatribe. I would point out that China owns thirty-six percent of all US debt, 5.76 trillion dollars. Repetitive actions by their Federal Reserve Chairman to inflate their currency through a trick they refer to as quantitative easing has essentially made our investment worth less than 2.1

trillion. I consider that theft! We are taking about a generation's worth of labor from all our people... gone!" shouted Premier of the State Council, Wen Jiabao.

"What can we do to protect our investment at this point? Can we demand the United States pay us in gold? Gold has been rising in value at a rate several times that of the interest paid on our treasury notes," noted Premier Hu.

"Excellency, the value of the gold itself has not changed. It is worth the same this year as it was a thousand years ago. The value of the fiat currency the American devils have placed as the world's reserve currency is what has changed. It is why oil is high and copper is high. I humbly apologize for my lack of ability to explain the harmful affect the tricksters in America have had upon our august nation. The American President Johnson halted the exchange of Silver Certificates for silver coins and bullion during their War of Aggression in Vietnam. President Nixon took the American dollar off the gold standard in 1971, two years before the war criminals were shamed and ran away from Saigon, like thieves in the night. The result of these two actions was to allow their treasury to print currency with absolutely no backing. It is almost like counterfeit money, except it is their corrupt state that is doing the printing," Wen Jiabao said before he paused and looked directly into Premier Hu's eyes. "Honorable Leader, your idea to demand our notes be paid back in gold is an excellent one. We can no longer afford to believe in the 'full faith and credit' of the liars in Washington."

"What if the United States refuses to recognize our demand to call our notes?" asked Premier Hu.

"With your permission, Paramount Leader, I would offer my plan to ensure success of our acquisition of the west coast of the United States," stated Admiral Huang Meng.

"Please, Admiral Huang."

"Thank you, sir. I propose to steam Sun Tzu and her newly completed sister ship, Yang Jian with their CBGs toward the American coast. Our Mau-Class carriers easily outclass the Nimitz-Class carriers of the US. In addition, behind the two Carrier Battle Groups, we will have a fleet of forty of our new Type 071 LPD troop carriers. Each of the 071s will carry one thousand troops, fifty combat vehicles, four Z-8K heavylift helicopters and four LCAC hovercraft. The flotilla will divide and anchor within easy striking distance of the cities of Los Angeles and San Francisco."

There were loud shouts of "Folly!" and "Fools errand!" throughout the room as many of the members of the various councils spoke at once.

"Silence!" spoke Paramount Leader Hu. "There will be order in this chamber. We will not be a rabble!"

"Comrades, I am not proposing to attack the United States of America. I am merely proposing a show of force, much the same as the US has done in the past. Now the shoe is on the other foot."

"But, even with our new carriers and destroyers, we cannot get into a confrontation with the US Naval forces and air power, especially so close to their mainland. We would, as the

Americans say, be sitting ducks," said another Vice Chairmen of the Central Military Commission Xu Caihou. "They outnumber us in submarines with fourteen ballistic missile, four guided missile and fifty-six attack subs...all nuclear. Compared to our sixty-six submarines, only ten of which are nuclear...and those very noisy. And needless to say, their air power is unmatched by any country in the world, Admiral, regardless if they are spread thin fighting five conflicts in the Middle East, they still have six Carrier Battle Groups in the Pacific."

"I have taken it upon myself, Comrade Xu, to devise a plan that will negate the vaunted American air power, the missile capability of their submarines and Aegis guided missile cruisers," said Admiral Huang Meng.

***

CHAPTER THREE

AIR FORCE SPACE COMMAND
VANDENBURG, CALIFORNIA
Monday, 7 October

Dr. Stacie Chen was sitting at her desk, her face buried in her computer. Her rimless glasses had slipped down to the tip of her nose—Dr. Taylor Goodhew entered with six Air Force pilots in tow.

"Stacie, these are the pilots I mentioned last week. Lieutenant Colonel Mann, Captain Hale, Captain Smathers, Captain, uh, Nitschke, Captain Garrett and ah, First Lieutenant Babayan. Gentlemen, meet our top communications programer, Dr. Stacie Chen," Dr. Goodhew said stumbling through the names.

Stacie got up from her chair, removed her computer glasses and walked around her desk toward the group of blue clad Air Force officers.

"Gentlemen, welcome to our facility," she said as she nodded and looked each man in the eye, and then their name tags, stopping at Lieutenant Babayan. "Babayan…Turkish isn't it?"

"Uh, yes, ma'am, uh, Doctor, uh I'm, ah, second generation. My first name is Jeff…friends call me Boom Boom," Babayan stammered, blushing and clearly smitten.

"It's *Miss*, Lieutenant, or *Boom Boom.* I'm also second generation…You can call me Stacie. You'll have to tell me how you got your call sign…sometime." Her eyes glinted like flakes of obsidian as she smiled and paused for a moment. She then continued, addressing the entire group. "We are pleased you came out here for the launch of our new satellite."

"Thank you, Dr. Chen, we've been looking forward to it. None of us has ever seen a live launch before," offered Lieutenant Colonel Mann.

"Well, you came to the right place, Colonel. We launch from one to three vehicles per week, including satellites and missile tests, that is except for the Pegasus XL. It's staged from here, but actually launched offshore from a modified L-1011 at 39,000 feet above the Pacific, southwest of Monterey. We have almost two hours until we launch the Transformational Satellite Communications System or TSAT into its polar orbit. It will be the final link to activate the Global Information Grid in the TSAT Network Integration Group, the TSAT Space Group and the TSAT Mission Operations Group. I won't go into detail of how it works except that your fly-by-wire aircraft and all of our missile based units will be operationally linked in real time. The system will control over 26 military communications satellites across four families, including DSCS, Milstar…WGS, and AEHF System."

"Holy cow," responded Colonel Mann in a barely audible whisper.

"There's not going to be a quiz, is there, uh, Stacie?" asked Babayan.

"I haven't given that much thought, Boom Boom, but it's an idea," she replied, grinning.

There were groans from the group and Captain Nitschke pitched in. "Way to go, Boom Boom, keep it up."

"Just kidding, guys…Anyone up for dinner before the tour? We launch at twilight…I'm buying," Stacie said as she winked at Babayan.

"Can't beat a deal like that," said Captain Garrett.

"The rest of you will have to tell me your call signs. I find the reasons behind them fascinating."

"Don't think you want to know how Captain Garrett got his, Stacie," proffered Babayan.

"Oh, what is his call sign?"

"Gas."

Inside the control center at Vandenberg, Stacie and her charges watched on the huge monitor as the long Taurus rocket carrying the TSAT system slowly lifted from its launch pad balanced on a fat finger of white hot fire. White to gray smoke billowed out from the base and for a moment, obscured almost half of the rocket until the solid fuel first stage, with its over 361,000 foot pounds of thrust, lifted it free of the gantry.

"Jesus, you can feel the vibration of the launch through your feet," exclaimed Babayan.

"With the kind of thrust required to escape Earth's gravitation, the launch of even the Taurus can be felt up to ten miles away. The Atlas V and the Delta IV Heavy can be felt much further, of course," said Stacie.

"Of course," offered Captain Cam "Shaft" Smathers, knowingly.

The other pilots just glanced at Smathers and shook their heads.

"That is an amazing sight," said Captain Harley "Hog" Hale.

"Hog, you get your jollys watching a bottle rocket go off," added Colonel John "Magic" Mann.

"Aw, Magic, do not."

Stacie and the other pilots chuckled at Captain Hale as they watched the rocket disappear into the deepening twilight.

"Well, there it goes, so far, so good," commented Stacie. "Now it will be several weeks until the satellite achieves a stable frozen polar orbit before we will have it synchronized into the GIG. I have to run a complete systems check on the new program first."

"This is all way above my pay grade," said Captain Norman "Nooch" Nitschke.

"Everybody has a job to do, Captain. I know *I* wouldn't be able to fly one of your F-16s."

"Point," replied Nitschke.

"Are you flying back to DM tonight, Colonel?" asked Stacie.

"No, Stacie, we'll wait 'till in the morning. Think we'll go over to the VOQ, clean up and head over to the Officer's Club."

"Oh, I'm going over to the base theater. It's western week. They're showing The Searchers with John Wayne. Anybody want to come along?"

"I'd love to go, Stacie. I watch anything the Duke does. The Searchers is one of my all time favorites," Babayan spoke up.

"Well, I guess we have a date. We'd better hurry," she said looking at her watch. "Starts in fifteen minutes...We can join the rest of your group at the O Club after the film...Is that all right?" Stacie said as she hooked her arm inside Babyan's arm.

"Oh, uh, sure. That'll be great," Babayan stammered. *Oh, my God, I've died and gone to heaven.*

NELLIS AFB, NEVADA
Thursday, 10 October

"Bravo 31 Flight, turn right heading 340, contact Nellis departure control."

"Tower, Bravo 31, right 340, going to departure."

On his wing, Major Marker simply transmitted his position in the flight.

"Two."

Lt. Col. Berlinger reached down and switched his tactical radio to the next preset without even looking at it. Flying out of the same base almost every day had its benefits. Barney checked in as usual and received clearance to climb to FL330. His wingman also acknowledged the altitude and both *Raptors* were soon tiny dots disappearing into the clear desert skies.

Jack locked his canopy down as he approached the arming area at the approach end of runway 21R following the airman's hand signals. He pulled up on the yellow lead in line and stopped at the hold point as directed. He held both hands up and rested them on the inside canopy rail as the two airmen removed all the *Do Not Fly* streamers from the test missiles and telemetry pods. The lead airman held up six fingers for the total number of streamers removed and snapped a crisp salute to the pilot seated in the *Starfighter*.

Jack returned the salute and transmitted his readiness to the control tower, "Nellis, Delta 22 number one for 21 right."

"Delta 22, tower, runway 21 right, taxi into position and hold."

"Position and hold 21 right, Delta 22." Jack felt his pulse start to pick up as he ran though the last of the *Before Takeoff* checklist. He advanced to military power 100%, noted the fuel flow, slowly pulled it back to 80% and quickly to idle as he released brakes and pulled into position. The General Electric J-79 engine idled smoothly as Jack taxied across the painted numbers and lined up on the runway centerline. A pair of F-15s and a desert camouflaged F-16 *Aggressor* taxied across the departure end of the runway after they had landed on 21L. The ever changing Las Vegas vista caught his attention. In the decades since he first flew out of Nellis, Sin City had grown far beyond anyone's expectations. The Eiffel Tower of Paris and the gigantic black pyramid of Luxor dominated the distant skyline. Tens of thousands of new hotel rooms and billion dollar casinos helped Vegas to be far more than a gambling destination. But the city had encroached upon the once distant air base, as certainly as it had surrounded the McCarren International Airport south of Nellis. The juxtaposition of old and new sites amused him. *At least some things never change,* he thought as he checked the nosewheel steering was still engaged. Jack slid his dark visor down into position and waited.

"Delta 22, cleared for takeoff, runway 21 right."

"Delta 22 rolling."

Jack smoothly pushed the throttle up to military and released the brakes. The acceleration pushed him back in the seat. He took the throttle to afterburner range and monitored the nozzle swing to 9.0. *Good light*, he noted as the engine thundered its mighty roar and the extra thrust planted him firmly against the metal seat back. He could not suppress the smile that came to his face. The very first time he had flown the *Starfighter*, he was really excited when the J-79 lit off and he could not help his enthusiastic, "Yee-hah!"

The only problem was his mic button on the throttle was depressed and everybody on the tower frequency heard it. The instructors in mobile control never let him live it down—so the call sign *Burner* was assigned. He disengaged the nose wheel steering at 120 knots and rotated the *Silver Knight* into the air as the speed raced past 170 to 190. Two minutes later and the last vestiges of Las Vegas passed under his nose as he prepared for hand-off from departure control to range control. Jack maintained 350 KIAS and climbed at full military power.

"Delta 22, Nellis radar services terminated. Contact Longshot Control on 238.8."

"Delta 22, good day," Jack replied as he switched to button six on his preset.

Creech Air Force Base passed under the left wing as the Silver Knight streaked though FL290. Ahead of him lay 12,000 square nautical miles of the world's most highly monitored airspace. Sensors, airborne cameras and electronic mapping provided for almost instantaneous playback of fighter combat operations with real aircraft. Jack had arranged for a test in a small section of the 5,000 square miles of airspace that is restricted to civilian overflight. Members of the 98th Range Wing at Nellis actually controlled the range and a limited number of personnel were cleared to participate in the brief test scheduled for the next hour.

"Longshot, Delta 22 with you at FL370."

"Delta 22, Longshot, radar contact. Cleared to enter restricted airspace after 2105 Zulu. Time now is 2102 Zulu. Confirm negative Darkstar."

"Copy time, that is charlie…Negative Darkstar, Delta 22."

Jack realized external factors such as an AWACS aircraft could possibly effect the outcome of the test. The test was not to see if the Raptors could find a *Starfighter* with an AWACS providing long range radar coverage. He also did not plan to enter the area using the same entry point as the *Raptors*. He turned slightly left, paralleled the western boundary of the target area, checked his watch and rechecked that his F-104 radar was in the *Standby* mode. Jack set the armament switches to his AIM-9 and AIM-120 missiles to *ARM* and rolled out heading east into the training airspace.

"Delta 22 entering the block, nose is hot."

"Delta 22, cleared to strangle squawk. Monitor Blackjack on 377.8"

"377.8, Delta 22. Good day."

A seriousness came over Jack as he selected the assigned frequency, one that only warriors can truly relate to—more than a game face, this mission was more than just a game, more than just a routine training hop. The whole survivability of the premier US fighter fleet was at risk. Jack tried to place himself in the mind of a *Raptor* pilot. Where would one set up in a relatively confined eighty by sixty mile airspace? Burner's intuition told him the *Raptor* lead would initiate a turn back toward his entry point at fifty-five to sixty miles from the entry. He eased the power up to full military, switched the radar frequency to low PRF range and tuned the unit to *ON*. He snap rolled to a right sixty degree turn and pulled hard in a three G turn to the east. With one eye on the radar, he switched the unit back to *Standby* and continued his turn until he was heading east.

Inside Bravo 31, Barney Berlinger started to react to a momentary alert on his AN/ALR-94 radar warning receiver. The *Raptor* had the most sophisticated passive radar system ever installed on an operational aircraft. With over thirty tiny antennas spread out and blended into the stealthy craft's surface, it can sense incoming radar signals from virtually any direction. The system can pick up signals from up to 250 miles away and process them through a pair of ultra high speed Raytheon Common Integrated Processors operating at a rate of 10.5 billion instructions per second. If a target approaches it can automatically turn on the AN/APG-77 radar to track the threat. All that capability came as a part of a huge cost of over 200 million dollars per aircraft. Barney noted the discrimination software had rejected the momentary hit as it fell outside the normal frequency parameters for fighter attack radar. The low PRF band was also shared by numerous hand held radar units used by highway patrol and county deputy sheriffs. Ground based weather radar and that used by aircraft out side the restricted airspace would occasionally trigger a flash alert, so Barney reacted by making a series of slow S turns at altitude to insure his unseen adversary could not be hidden under his wing. Marker matched his flight lead's maneuver as the two worked south in a spread formation at FL410.

Jack had seen a single momentary blip on his radar bearing 110 degrees and forty-five miles as he had performed his initial search sweep. Given the vast technological advantage of his *Raptor* adversaries, he knew he could not use his radar full time as designed. A stronger, steady low PRF frequency radar signal would be detected and trigger a hostile threat designation of his *Starfighter*. He made what he often referred to as a *SWAG,* or scientific wild ass guess, for the heading the *Raptors* were on and computed a intercept course. This time he limited the sweep to a twenty degree arc of the sky from his altitude of FL350. His speed was up to Mach .95 and his adrenaline began to pump just like back in the '60s. The *Raptors* were both in a gentle right hand turn when Burner's radar showed two small, but distinct targets at his twelve o'clock and thirty-one miles. He switched the radar back to *Standby* and slammed the throttle as far forward as it would go. Jack glanced back inside to confirm that the burner light at his backside was a good one. The mach indicator needle swung past Mach 1 and kept climbing as Jack riveted his attention to the deep blue expanse of sky before him. His pulse rate jumped and he could hear his breathing rate increase as the oxygen regulator cycled faster and faster. Already, the taste in his mouth had become slightly metallic as the bone dry air sucked away what little moisture he had remaining in his nose and throat.

"Smoke, any talley?" Barney asked his wingman over their discrete common frequency as he began a clearing turn back to his left.

"Nada, Quaker. You sure he's really out here?"

"According to Blackjack, he is. We'll start a turn back north in one minute. If we don't catch any sign of him on the next pass northbound, we'll just crank up the radar systems. He ain't stealthy."

"That's a 10-4."

Burner's eyes weren't like they were back at the Academy. Age had taken a toll. He no longer could see 20-10. They had deteriorated all the way back to 20-20 and he strained to see the distinctive gray shapes against the deep blue at 41,000 feet. He inched the throttle back as the F-104 passed through Mach 1.8 so as not to exceed the 1.9 Mach max maneuvering speed with tip tanks. Both tanks were dry, but there was no way he would jettison his baby's tanks on a training mission.

Suddenly, there they were. One o'clock. The lead element had climbed slightly and was starting his cross over his wingman as he initiated a turn back to the north. Neither could spot the much smaller silver craft as he pointed her needle nose directly at them. Burner slammed the throttle back to its stop and pulled up hard as he toggled the Sidewinder switch active and searched for a tone.

Bravo 32 was still heading south watching his flight lead cross overhead when Burner called, "Delta 22, Fox Two."

Rolling left to pull lead on the turning *Raptor*, Burner thumbed the *Guns* mode active, centered the HUD pipper on the cockpit and squeezed the trigger.

"Delta 22, Guns."

Inside Bravo 31, the activation of the *Starfighter's* gunsight AN/APG-30 radar triggered a major caution warning that brought Barney's head back inside the *Raptor* for just a second. He processed the information quickly and then attempted to turn into the threat, but as his head snapped back to search for the contact at his nine o'clock, a slender silver streak rocketed past his tail at almost Mach 2. It was all Barney could do to try to track the rapidly disappearing *Starfighter*. He pulled back on the stick, pulling up and breaking hard right just in time to catch Burner doing a slow victory roll through 50,000 feet. *What the hell just happened?*

"Bravo 31, kill. Bravo 32 kill," came a radio call from controller. "Delta 22, Blackjack, I see you are approaching the southern end of the exercise area. Say intentions."

"Blackjack, Delta 22 exiting the area. Test complete. Advise other elements to RTB."

"Blackjack copies, Delta 22 contact Longshot on 238.8, squawk 3125."

Jack slowly pulled the throttle out of burner as he continued his roll. The deep, almost cobalt, blue sky at that altitude was something few people ever got to witness personally. He could even detect the slight curvature of the earth. He stopped the roll wings level inverted. For a couple seconds, he hung there weightless, and took in the spectacular view. Burner could see the snow-capped Sierra Nevadas in California, the Pacific Ocean beyond and the full extent of the Colorado River basin from the Utah border to the Grand Canyon and all the way to Lake Meade. For a few seconds, he was twenty-five again.

Archie was livid. *What the hell does Blackjack mean, "Bravo 32 kill?"* He too, got a two second radar warning when Burner targeted Bravo 31. He had cleared to his right, and then back left and rolled to follow his flight lead that was then making a southern turn.

"Quaker, what's happening?"

"We're dead, Smoke. Didn't you hear Blackjack?"

"Yeah, I heard the man! Where the hell is Burner?"

"You didn't see him fly right between us?"

Archie was stunned. *That's not possible.* "Negative! When did that occur?"

"About twenty seconds ago…just after I crossed over you."

"No shit?"

"He blew through us like a dose of salts through a goose."

"How did that happen?"

"Don't know, but we're damned sure gonna find out. Rejoin on the left for recovery."

"You got it."

Jack taxied the Silver Knight into a parking spot just outside the 757TH AMS hangar and shut down. Lars was standing by as the young airmen set the yellow wooden chocks in place and brought the crew ladder to the right side of the *Starfighter*, setting it gently in the canopy rail so as not to mar the highly polished skin. Lars quickly climbed the steps and bagged the flight helmet as Jack proffered it.

"So, how did the old girl do?"

A smile told him everything he really needed to know, but Jack did have to answer the question.

"If we keep this up, I'm gonna need to get fitted for a pressure suit."

"You took it to fifty?"

"A little over on the post attack portion. I'll tell you at the debrief."

"Any write-ups, boss?"

"Not one. She's trimmed out and running great. Can't believe it. You did a great job, buddy."

"Labor of love, son, labor of love. We gonna pull off the test gear tonight?"

Jack shook his head. "No, I think we're probably due a couple other test flights to determine sensitivity and max detection parameters. We'll know more about what Lockheed and the DoD want after the debrief. But, I'm bettin' it's gonna hit the fan."

Lars looked concerned. Jack unstrapped his lap belt and shoulder harness, and then unbuckled his clipboard from his left thigh and handed it to the taciturn mechanic. He placed his hands up on the forward canopy bow and pulled himself up and out of the seat. Lars heard him groan slightly as he straightened up.

"Do we need to get you a crane there, old timer?"

"I'll *old timer* your German ass!"

Lars laughed aloud. "Ya, that's for sure. Neither one of us can be called spring chickens any more."

WASHINGTON, DC
WHITE HOUSE
Thursday, 10 October

President Thompson sat at her small antique roll-top desk in her private quarters. The first family's sanctuary, as it was sometimes called, occupied the second and third floors of the four story White House. Annette was under major stress and had several yellow pads lain out in front of her. Her computer, with its secure Internet links, sat on a small desk angled perpendicular to the roll-top. She rotated her chair toward the computer screen and typed in a command, opening a file on China. She pushed a loose strand of her auburn hair that was beginning to be flecked with gray, away from her face and massaged her temples. *I hope I'm not getting another migraine.* Suddenly, there was a light tap on the door. "Enter," she said as she smoothed her hair down, turned her chair around and stood.

Secret Service agent Jim Tatum opened the door slightly and stuck his head inside. "Got someone out here, Madame President. Claims he knows you," Tatum said grinning as he opened the door wider.

Gunter Hermann, Annette's husband of six months, walked in. Gunter was a still muscular, trim man in his early 60s, a little over six feet tall, with silver hair and sky blue eyes. After his two tours in Vietnam, he had rarely left his three thousand acre ranch in south Texas—Eagle Nest. He and Annette had been college sweethearts, but had drifted apart and each married someone else. Both had lost their spouses, Gunter's wife and mother of their children, Mike and Carla, had been killed in a car accident eight years earlier and Annette's husband had died of a massive heart attack during her campaign for the presidency.

She and Gunter had married after the Black Eagle Force rescued her from Javier Cojone's compound in the Sierra Madre Mountains in Mexico. They had a child from their love affair back in college, Mickey Williams, a former Secret Service agent, now a member of the BEF.

"Hi, Honey, what's up? I came quick as I could," Gunter said as Annette rushed over and embraced him.

"Thank you, Jim. That will be all."

"Yes, ma'am. Always a pleasure to see Gunter," he said as he closed the door.

She and Gunter continued hugging.

"I'm so sorry to pull you away from Eagle Nest, I know it's calving time," she said as she stepped back to look lovingly into his chiseled and sun weathered face.

"Sweetheart, you know as much as I hate this hellhole, I'll always be here when you need me. Your trips to the ranch are far too infrequent. I've missed you…Besides, Mike, Carla and Mickey are all at the BEF base on the ranch. Think they can handle anything that comes up…Looks like you need me a hellova lot more than the ranch does," he said, looking at the dark circles under her eyes. "Don't think I've seen you quite this stressed out. What's wrong?"

"Let's sit, this may take a while. I'll ring for some coffee," she said as they walked over to a settee by the window.

Almost an hour and several cups of coffee later, Annette leaned against Gunter's broad chest.

"So, there you have the entire situation, honey. I just needed someone to talk to that didn't have an ax to grind."

"Baby, you already know how I feel about the Chinese…we bail their asses out in WWII, and then they jump all over us in Korea. If Truman had left McArthur alone, wouldn't be havin' this problem. But, that was then and this is now." He rolled up his sleeve to a nasty scar on his biceps. "You've seen this one before and the one on my side. Both courtesy of the Chinese army in 'Nam. Had a cousin shot down over Hanoi and took prisoner. He's still MIA."

"I know, I've never trusted them either."

"Trust? Damn gooks are crooked as a barrel of snakes. Dealing with them financially is like being nibbled to death by ducks. You also know how I feel about swabbie brass pukes, but Charger does know what he's talkin' about…he's dead on. Shoulda been a Marine…You gotta go with your gut, honey. Far as I can see, the gate's off its hinges. I don't have to tell you the government's first responsibility…"

"I know. Protect its citizens and preserve order."

"There you go."

NELLIS AFB, NEVADA
Thursday, 10 October

Lars held the door open for Jack as they entered the 65th AGRS briefing room. Colonel Crockett, Captains Hess and Rodgers and the two mission debriefers were already in the room and stood when Jack entered. Colonel Crockett began to applaud and the other four men joined in. Jack smiled and shook his head.

"Guys, appreciate the gesture, but it's really not necessary."

"Burner, nobody has got a confirmed kill on a Raptor since it came on board. You got two in less than six seconds! Gotta be a little happy about that, right?"

"You know, Rocket, it's a mixed feeling. I love the way the old bird handled, but as a Lockheed man, I was kinda hoping the Raptor would handle the low PRF better. You'll see what I mean in the debrief. Where're Berlinger and Marker?"

"They called when they left the 433rd Ops. Should be here in just a couple minutes. Like a bottle of water before we got started?"

"That sounds good. Lars had one for me when I got down, but I'm still a little thirsty. Almost forgot how dehydrating flying is."

Col. Crockett pointed at Von Hess who immediately disappeared out the door. He looked back at Jack and Lars.
"See you didn't attempt a AMRAAM shot."

"After I acquired a fix on both the Raptors, I killed the radar. Besides, the AIM-120 couldn't meget a radar lock on them anyway."

"Never fight the enemy's fight. Right, sir?" Captain Rogers asked.

"Exactly. I see the Colonel taught you well."

"Not well enough to do what you did, Burner. I wish we had all the guys in here for the debrief," the Colonel added.

"I know what you're thinking. But we have to keep a lid on this exercise until we can do an in-depth analysis of the Raptor's passive radar system."

"I understand. We'll make sure nothing leaves this room."

Jack nodded agreement. Capt. Von Hess and the two *Raptor* pilots entered the room. After the captain handed the cold water bottle to Jack, the pilots approached him. Berlinger extended his hand.

"Congratulations, Burner. You've done what I considered to be impossible. Nice job."

Jack shook his hand. He could tell the younger pilot was still upset by the outcome of the exercise. Major Marker likewise offered his hand.

"Congratulations…I guess. Never even saw you."

"Smoke, try not to take it personally. You guys are the best. I really mean that. I'm here to identify potential sensor or software problems which can make the Raptor vulnerable. Gentlemen, don't forget, my son flies the Raptor, too."

"Yes, sir," Archie said before he took his seat in the small amphitheater.

After the small crowd was settled into their blue upholstered seats, Tech Sergeant Henry Thompson dimmed the lights and began the debriefing. A large twenty-foot wide screen displayed the projected computer images of the exercise area. Range telemetry had captured and stored vital heading, airspeed and altitude information of each aircraft as well as radio transmissions, on board radar imagery, aircraft systems operations, gun camera, infrared and radar missile seeker head data. When Jack had initially turned on his *Starfighter* radar, a computer copy of the return was displayed on the left side of the screen.

"And here we see a brief radar image from Delta 22."

"Can you replay and freeze frame that?" asked Jack.

"Absolutely, sir."

Thompson hit his remote and backed up the video and then began a slow forward.

"Stop. That's the first hit from one of the Raptors."

The other pilots looked at the display and saw nothing. Jack stood and approached the podium.

"May I borrow your laser pointer, Sergeant?"

"Oh, sure, yes sir," he said as he passed the small device.

Jack took it and placed the red arrow on top of a very small greenish gray dot on the scope. "Right there. Bravo 31 or 32. Bigger than Dallas."

The other pilots looked at each other in disbelief.

Captain Hess couldn't help but ask, "But, sir, how did you know it was a Raptor? There is no target ID or airspeed shown."

Jack grinned. "Son, this is 1968 technology. All it gives you is bearing and range. In this case, 110 degrees at forty-five miles. It can't tell you your opponent's social security number or birth date…Continue, Sergeant."

The group watched as the icons of the three planes diverged slightly. Then Delta 22 made a hard tight turn to the south and the F-104 radar was turned on again.

"Freeze that, please," Jack said as the *Starfighter* radar depicted tiny two returns.

“Burner, you said the radar didn’t give our heading and speed. How did you know we were heading south?” Berlinger asked.

“Didn’t know. Just a SWAG. Intuition, experience, whatever you call it. If I got a second hit where I thought you might be, I would have a rear attack on your six. If I didn’t get a hit there…I’d reverse and try north. I didn’t know where you were going, but I damn sure knew where you’d been.”

“And you got all that from one little green dot? Bloody genius,” mused Barney.

“Not my first rodeo…”

“But, sir, why did you keep turning off and on your radar? Wouldn’t it have been easier to track us with a steady sweep? You could estimate heading and speed with a constant sweep contact,” said Major Marker.

“True. Why didn’t your Raptors have your search radar on?”

“Because it gives our position awa…” Marker stopped in mid-sentence.

“Give the man gold star. Never fight the enemy’s fight. Right, Buck?”

“Yes, sir!” replied a beaming Captain Rogers.

Sergeant Thompson continued the briefing and froze the simulation when the AIM-9 got tone on Bravo 32.

“There was some disagreement in Blackjack Control if this was a valid kill. But, in the absence of an active search radar system on the part of the Raptors, the launch parameters and PK were greater than 95 percent. Range was only 2,200 feet and the overtake speed was…817 knots."

"Holy shit," Major Marker muttered under his breath.

Seconds later the gun camera film began to appear on the left side of the screen. The red dot within a circle floated quickly over the fuselage of the turning *Raptor* and settled on the canopy. Berlinger's helmet with his dark visor were clearly visible. The audio recording of Jack's "Delta 22 guns" call was heard just before Thompson froze the playback.

"Can I get a print of that?" Jack asked.

All Quaker could manage was an incredulous, "Fuck me runnin'."

Smoke asked for a real time playback of the last twenty-five seconds of the mission. Watching the *Starfighter* rocket through the *Raptor* formation was informative, as well as disquieting. "Jesus, Burner, you look like a great white coming up to feed on a couple of seals."

"I like that, Smoke. You don't mind if I use it in the written report, do you?"

Smoke just grinned and shook his head.

Sergeant Thompson turned the lights back up, causing Jack to wince and blink a couple times. Once they adjusted, he addressed the group. "Thank you gentlemen for the fine debriefing. I want to remind you all, this mission is Top Secret/Need To Know Only. I don't want to see that video on YouTube, Sergeant Thompson. We are going to discuss the lessons learned in private."

"No, sir," Thompson said before the two enlisted men departed.

"Well..." Jack continued, "...what have we learned?"

Lars jumped in before any of the pilots could. "Don't fuck with old men in blue flight suits!"

Jack threw the empty water bottle at Lar's head, just catching the top of it as he ducked.

"Ain't that the truth. Seriously, what do you guys think?"

"I don't know about the rest of the squadron, but I would have to admit complacency. The Raptor is so friggin' stellar in its capability, I'm afraid we've let our hunter-killer instincts get a little rusty. Didn't think you even had a chance. Damned sure didn't like the looks of the pipper on my head...Smoke?"

"I feel like a brown bar Lieutenant on my first solo. Never even saw you, General...duh!"

"People, in all fairness, if I had left my radar on, your software would probably have considered it a threat and burned it out with its jamming capability. I don't like the idea there is a radar frequency range that can ping off the Raptor. Something my friends over at Lockheed will have to work on. The good news is software upgrade to the AN/ALR-94 radar warning system can take care of low PRF now that we have identified a threat.

"Smoke, your AN/AAR-56 Infrared and Ultraviolet Missile Approach Warning System was working fine. However, in the absence of an actual missile motor inbound, there is no source of a hot IR signature to trigger the system. In that sense the range scenario is a little unrealistic. But they won't let me shoot real missiles at you."

"Damned good thing. What would the time-of-flight been on that Sidewinder shot? Under two seconds?" Smoke asked.

"'Bout that," Jack nodded.

"Then I probably would not have been able to react fast enough to stay alive. I see why you didn't use AMRAAMs."

"I was fighting my fight. The AIM-120 is a hell of a missile. It's what I used on my MiGs in Desert Storm…But the MiG is no Raptor."

"Can the Slammer be reprogrammed to use low PRF or Multiple frequencies?" Colonel Crockett asked.

Jack thought for a second as he pulled on his ear lobe. "You know, Rocket, not sure, but I'm sure as hell gonna find out. The biggest limitation with a low PRF is trying to calculate speed and distance. That is why most systems use high PRF because of the higher quantity data stream available. Computers crunch the numbers, so the more info, the better the accuracy and PK. If you had a visual on an unsuspecting target, you could use a lower quality data stream like the early SAM-2s did." Jack turned to Lars. "Write a note about checking with Raytheon about modifications on the AIM-120."

"What the hell? Do I look like a secretary? Where is the mechanics union when you need them?"

"Imagine ripple firing a half dozen Slammers at the Raptors when the missiles can actually see them," Hess added.

"Hey, Von…Whose side are you on anyway?" Berlinger asked.

"Don't get your panties in a wad, Colonel. You have no idea what it's like to have your ass handed to you day after day."

Barney smiled as he looked over at Jack, and then back to Captain Hess. "After today, I think I can relate."

Jack stood up and made his pronouncement, "Guys, I think we learned a lot today. I'm sure Lockheed will want to do some other controlled tests to measure range and reflectivity, and knowing them as I do, it will take a day or two to get the engineering types to agree on what they want. In the meantime… heard the bar's open and I'm buyin'."

"You heard the man. Head 'em up and move 'em out," Colonel Crockett said as he led the gaggle of sky warriors toward the door….

HAWAII
Saturday, 12 October

James pulled his silver Jeep Wrangler into a dirt parking spot worn into the east side of Diamondhead overlooking the warm waters of the central Pacific. A steady tropical breeze of ten to twelve knots blew in from the south southwest setting up perfect conditions for both surfers and windsurfers. He pulled the keys from the ignition and slipped them into a special hiding place under the dash. Once outside, he stripped off his white t-shirt with the blue Air Force logo, fitted his sunglass keepers onto his Oakley Photochromic shades and pulled the rubber semi-snug around his closely cropped blonde military haircut.

Quickly, he unstrapped the Starboard Windsurfers Flare Freestyle board off the overhead rack and set it down gently on the rough volcanic gravel at the base of Oahu's iconic picturesque peak. Hoisting the lightweight silver-gray carbon fiber board with the blue and green sail over his head, he crossed Diamondhead Road and worked his way two hundred yards down the well worn path to the rocky shore. Once there, he slipped out of the worn leather sandals and donned the rubber soled dive boots he had tucked into his floral print jams.

The clean scent of the pristine Pacific waters filled his lungs as he stood and gauged the three to five foot swells that gently rolled in and then broke on the shallows. James eased into the 78 degree water and waded out waist deep before he set the board down. He lay on his back with the wind behind him and the board pointed ever so slightly out to sea. Once he had slipped a foot into the rubber footstrap, he pushed up on the boom, lifting the sail out of the water a scant six inches. The quartering onshore breeze caught the sail and yanked the bronzed fighter pilot erect and sent him and the freestyle board skittering across the surface in the flash of an eye. Novice windsurfers and wannabe windsurfers looked on with envy. He made it look so stinking easy.

The statuesque redhead parked her yellow Nissan Extera with a surfboard racked on top next to the silver jeep. She was wearing a pair of Cruel Girl cutoff jeans and an emerald green tank top that coordinated nicely with her green eyes. She unstrapped the banana colored board and after checking traffic, headed across Diamondhead Road with the board under her left arm.

Once she reached the bottom of the beach trail, she propped her short surfboard up against a palm tree and stepped out of her well worn rubber Crocks clogs. Lastly, she tugged an elastic scrunchy out of her shorts and secured the flowing red mane back into a ponytail, and then shed both the tank top and cutoffs to reveal a very small Brazilian designed purple thong that left absolutely only the tiniest bit to the imagination. She gingerly made her way through the volcanic rocks on the shore, hopped onto the surfboard and stroked powerfully into the incoming wave set.

Hollywood wasted no time in tacking his way offshore into the wind. As he reached the half-mile point he made a slicing turn across one of the larger swells and turned quickly to set up a series of warm up jumps. The sight of the island of Oahu rising out of the waves, with a line of windswept palm trees swaying with the wind thrilled him almost as much as the sounds of the board carving the warm salt water. *Man, can't believe I'm being paid to work here.* He made a few minor jumps, leading into some major airtime that pleased the spectators scattered along the beach. As he drew in close to the line of surfers, he made a well executed Vulcan, a moderately difficult horizontal 360 degree spin off the top of a four foot crest. He nailed it and immediately headed back crosswind to clear the waiting line of surfers.

The redhead was watching the incoming set and caught his performance. *Nice body. Great technique. Kinda cute.* She picked the fifth swell inbound, turned paddled and was able to catch it for a two minute ride back to the shallows. She carved it like a pro and bailed out as a couple kids on boogie-boards frolicked innocently in her path. *Plenty of ocean to share. I'll take it back out where they won't go.*

For over two hours, Hollywood worked the winds and waves. The wind picked up as did the sized of the swells. He made a couple forward flips, always landing nicely on the tail and charged in hard for another swell a hundred yards out past the redhead. She had watched him causally at first, but he had definitely caught her interest with his smooth command of the board and sail. She marveled as he raced down wind attacking an eight footer, slid one hand forward on the boom and got the sail rotating. *That blonde college boy just caught some major air,* she thought as she tried to judge the height of the skegs over the wave top. He kept sheeting, continuing the rotation as he flew at least sixty feet laterally before landing well back on the skegs. A huge spray of white water fanned out from either side of his board, but the tanned stranger emerged unscathed and glided closer to her.

Hollywood couldn't wipe the smile from his face. He couldn't remember having a better day. As he approached within twenty yards of the redhead wearing the purple suit he caught a close look at her for the first time that day. *OMG. She's perfect. What a face. What a bod.* He was awestruck as she turned and paddled furiously to catch the wave he had just jumped. He eased off the boom to slow the craft and watch her grab the eight footer. As she stood up, he realized she was taller than he had previous thought. He cruised parallel to the shore for a few seconds and then tacked back inshore to watch her in action. *Nice. Really nice.* He saw she worked the big wave almost to shore before she kicked out and began to paddle back in. *Guess she's gonna call it a day. Not a bad thought.*

The crowds were thinning out as the afternoon progressed. Only serious surfers, mostly locals, were able to hang in with the eight footers. Rookie tourists learned the hard way how the rocky bottom treated failure off Diamondhead. Most had already headed back to the more protected waters off Wakiiki, Hanauma Bay or over on the northeast shore at Kaneohe. Teenage local Hawaiians, mostly boys, scrambled down the paths to revel in the big water. It would be months before the monster waves hit the north shore and most of these teens were not really expert enough to take on the deadly waves of Waimea Bay—but they talked like they could.

James set up for his last run of the day with a series of inspired jumps leading up to a really difficult back loop he had been wanting to try. He visually cleared an area between two groups of surfers waiting some 200 yards off shore to try and catch a personal wave to master. The wind propelled him to almost twenty-five knots as he strained to get the most out of his rig. Up the back side of the nearly ten foot crest he went and sailed for almost forty yards before he landed clean and then rapidly reversed crosswind back into the face of the wave just before it started to break.

The redhead leaned her board against the brush and started to blot the salt water from her face when she saw the muscular man execute what had to be the absolutely most perfect back loop she had ever witnessed. The man laid out with one hand on the boom as the board rocketed up at least three times the height of the wave and hung there for a full second. He was one with the world, a testament to skill and balance and all that was beautiful in her eyes. Her jaw actually dropped for brief moment as she witnessed the feat and heard a smattering of "Wows!" mixed with "Oh!" as he deftly worked the wing while he dropped below the level of the breaker. She didn't even breathe—at least, not until she again saw the blue and green sail moving beyond the white and green crest of the breakers. She draped the tank top over her arm and applauded with the rest of the crowd lining the rocky shore. The windsurfer caught the next wave and began to ride it like a normal surfer toward shore. She saw a local fifteen year old that had been riding the same wave for a hundred yards, carving and cutting back at will. He raced across the face of the wave right at the windsurfer and then cut back just before impact, spraying the taller man as if to say, "I'm not impressed, haole."

Hollywood seethed at the obvious affront. It wasn't the first time he had been subjected to Hawaiian racism. It still pissed him off, even if official US Military policy forbade retaliation.

Suddenly a pair of ten year old boys appeared in the water as they emerged from out of the next wave inshore. In a micro-second, James glanced back in the direction of his tormentor and computed a collision course between the teenager and the two kids. The teenager was looking at James with a self satisfied smirk on his face and didn't react quickly enough when Hollywood pointed at them and shouted a warning. One of the two kids saw the oncoming surfer and ducked. The other had opened his eyes late and had salt water pouring down from his shaggy brown hair when the board hit him a glancing blow on his forehead.

The redhead saw the collision, dropped her tank top and charged into the water. Before she leapt forward, she saw the windsurfer shed his safety line from his wrist and dive like an Olympic swimmer into the churning water.

Hollywood stripped his sunglasses down onto his neck and quickly adjusted his eyes to the stinging salt water. The listless body of the unconscious boy lay only thirty feet away in five feet of water. The next wave crashed over both of them and caused the boy to tumble toward the rocky shore. James kicked harder as he strained to reach the boy—a rip tide current stopped the youngster's shoreward motion and began to roll him back out to sea. His lungs began to ache for air as he saw another figure swiftly moving closer with an underwater dolphin kick. The two met simultaneously and grabbed the boy by the arms just as a nine foot wave crashed over them. They fought though the rolling surge and headed for the surface. Grasping for air, they saw they were still some fifty feet off shore.

In less than a minute, they had worked against the out flowing current from the latest wave and had the boy on the rocky beach. Without a word, Hollywood pressed on the boy's stomach to force out the salt water he had swallowed. *He's not breathing.* He began chest compressions while the redheaded woman opened his airway and took his pulse from his carotid artery. She leaned over him, breathed forcefully into his mouth while she held his nose closed, and then listened to the air being expelled from his lungs. She repeated the process three more times before the young man's chest heaved and his eyes fluttered. James stopped the compressions and gently palpated the boy's skull around a two inch contusion. *No soft spot. Good.*

"I don't think he's got a fracture, but we should get him to the ER for an x-ray."

"Good idea, surfer boy. I'm a doctor," she said as she took off her water spotted sunglasses and looked up at the heroic windsurfer for the first time since they left the water.

"Kelli Ann?" he asked with his mouth slightly ajar.

"Hollywood?"

***

CHAPTER FOUR

NELLIS AFB, NEVADA
Saturday, 12 October

As Jack had suspected, it took Lockheed-Martin two full days, including a copious amount of overtime for the corporation to construct the re-test parameters they needed to validate his low PRF ID on the *Raptor*. SecDef Baker had reacted with speed and had included the other involved aerospace contractors, Boeing, BAE Systems, and Northrop-Grumman as well as Raytheon at the Tuesday inbrief. He had run with the chance idea a low PRF mod to the Raytheon produced AIM-120 could actually help defend against the new Chinese and Russian stealth fighters. Jack sat in the small Lockheed corporate office they maintained on Nellis at a desk he had temporarily commandeered from a technician. He hung up the phone and looked back at the secured DoD computer screen to read the latest emails."Jesus, Lars! What a goat rope! They also want a night mission with the B-2 and a flight of F-18s."

"I'll...recheck the landing lights on the Silver Knight. Oh, what a tangled web we weave..."

"Hold on, you hard headed Kraut! I'm not trying to deceive anybody."

"Aber nein! What is it you always say...the law of unintended consequences?"

"Yeah, guess I sorta forgot how multi-billion dollar corporations get wrapped around the axle when their play things don't work as planned."

"I suppose it all depends on whose ox is being gored, and this week you're the bull."

"That I am, apparently. Say, about ready for a break? That chef salad I had for lunch is long gone."

"I'm supposed to meet my kids for dinner. They're in town for a few days doing the tourist thing. Why don't you join us?"

"I'd be like a fifth wheel. Thanks for the offer. Have fun, buddy. Give 'em my love."

"You got it, boss. What time tomorrow?"

"How 'bout I call you? I've got a preliminary schedule for Monday set. We'll need to talk to the training schedulers and try to work around existing hops so as to not draw any more attention to ourselves than absolutely necessary."

"I'll wait for your call, then."

Lars headed for the door as Jack reached for his iPhone. *A nice thick ribeye would do well right about now.* He tapped the

Safari icon and did a Google search for a Del Frisco's Double Eagle Steakhouse. *3925 Paradise Road, I know that area, just north of McCarren.* He saved the location in his map function and headed to his rental car parked outside. Jack made a quick swing by the hotel to shower and change, and grabbed a navy blue sports coat to coordinate with his silver silk shirt.

LAS VEGAS
Saturday, 12 October

It was 7:30 by the time Jack pulled into the crowded parking lot. *Saturday night. Damn, should've called for a reservation* he thought as he walked in the door and approached the maitre'd.

"Good evening, sir, welcome to Del Frisco's. May I help you?"

"Any chance of getting a good steak?"

"Of course, sir. Your name please," he asked as he opened his reservations folder.

"Jack Stewart, but I don't have a reservation."

"Oh…I'm very sorry, sir. Saturday evenings are reservations only. I'm sure you can understand."

"Any suggestions? I haven't been in Vegas for a few years."

"You might try the Golden Steer, sir. They're located on West Sahara. I don't believe they have a mandatory reservation requirement for weekends."

"Thank you. Didn't know they were still here. The Rat Pack used to hang out there. Eaten a many a steak there myself. I'll give them a shot, it's not far."

"No, sir."

In just a few minutes, Jack had driven the short distance to W. Sahara and straight to the Golden Steer. *Hell, think I'll just valet park* he mused as he pulled up under the portico. An attractive twenty something brunette quickly appeared at his door as he opened it and stepped out. "Welcome to The Golden Steer, sir," she said as she handed him a numbered yellow ticket. "I'll take care of this for you. My name's Cassandra. Are you having dinner?"

"Thanks, Cassandra. And, yes I am," Jack said, handing her his keys.

"Enjoy your meal, sir," she said as she entered his car and quickly drove toward the valet parking area.

He went through the ornate large double doors and approached the maitre'd.

"Good evening. My name is Jack Stewart and no, I don't have a reservation."

The maitre'd appraised Jack and asked, "Are you military, sir?"

"Retired Air Force."

"Officer?"

"Brigadier General."

"Not a problem, sir. The Golden Steer has a policy to always serve our country's fighting men, reservations or not. It will be about fifteen minutes. Might I suggest our bar while you wait?"

"Good idea, thanks."

"Would you like me to show you the way?"

"Not necessary, been there before," Jack said over his shoulder.

He entered the large main dining area, and then headed toward the full service bar on the side. Most of the tall chairs were taken, but he found one next to a very attractive blond with aquamarine eyes sipping on a martini. *Hmm, looks to be about forty-five, but a real knock out.*

"Is this seat taken?"

"No. Please," she said in a June Allyson raspy type voice. "My name's Penelope, Penelope Lough," she continued, extending her hand.

"Jack Stewart…Penelope? As in Homer's The Odyssey?" he said as he gently clasped her hand.

"Very good, Jack. Yes, my mother loved the classic authors…Plutarch, Cicero, Plato and, of course, Homer. I think my name was preordained. Just glad I wasn't a boy, she might have named me Odysseus or Ajax."

Jack chuckled. "That could have been a problem. Know of a retired Colonel from the Marine Corps, named Archimedes Phillips. Goes by Dare."

"Dare?"

"Yeah, no one dares to call him Archimedes."

It was Penelope's turn to laugh. "Once I had no shoes, then I met a man who had no feet…"

"Something like that."

The bartender walked up across from Jack.

"May I get you a drink, sir?"

"Silver Patrón, neat,"

"Of course, sir," the bartender said as he turned around and reached up to the top shelf for the short squat bottle.

"Um, love Patrón, so smooth," Penelope added.

"My thoughts, too. If you're going to drink, it should be the best."

Just then, the maitre'd walked up behind Jack. "Excuse me, General, your table is ready, sir."

"General? My, my," Penelope said as she looked at Jack with undisguised admiration.

"Retired," countered Jack. "Listen, Penelope, I, uh, don't mean to be forward, but would you care to join me? Hate to eat alone."

"An officer *and* a gentleman. Very kind of you, sir," she said as she nodded her head toward Jack. "I accept. I think my table must be further down the list."

The bartender set Jack's tequila neat on the bar with a coaster. "Your drink, sir."

"Thank you…" he said getting up from his stool. Jack turned to Penelope and offered her his hand. "Shall we?"

"Delighted," she replied as their eyes met. *Uh, oh, better watch yourself, girl. This one is special.* "You have gorgeous eyes."

"Isn't that supposed to be my line?" replied Jack, a bit taken aback.

"You snooze, you lose, General," Penelope said with a grin and a wink as the maitre'd led them toward their table.

Two hours later, Jack and Penelope were having after dinner coffee. Their waiter had removed what little remained of their Kobe ribeyes and side dishes.

"So, you're really an honest-to-goodness author, huh? What type of books do you write?" Jack asked as he looked across the candlelit table at her aquamarine eyes that seemed to catch each flicker of the candle.

"Well, I don't know if honest or goodness has any application in my work, but I write somewhat irreverent murder mysteries…with a touch of humor."

"Now that's interesting. Don't think I've run across that particular combination before."

"My novels have had some success, but I want to expand my horizons…so to speak."

"Oh, how so?"

"I want to write a military mystery, but I'm afraid my knowledge of the military is rather sparse. I know just enough to appreciate that it's an interesting culture, to say the least."

"I just happen to have over thirty years on active duty in the Air Force…not counting my time at the Academy. Maybe I could give you some insight, if you like."

"I wouldn't want to impose…"

"No imposition at all. Sounds kinda intriguing. What's your premise?"

Penelope paused for a moment. *Oh, wow! I must be living right.* "I just have a rough outline so far. But, I see a Chinese mole who has been inserted into the US military structure to sabotage our entire GPS satellite array with a computer virus…cyberterrorism, if you will."

"That's a good start, however, as far as the GPS system is concerned…everyone in the world uses it…Including the bad guys."

"Oops."

"How about the mole inserts a virus into our military satellite communications systems…"

"It would blind us!" Penelope exclaimed.

"No, but it would make us deaf, dumb and very vulnerable."

HAWAII
Saturday, 12 October

Kelli handed the cell phone back to James as the ambulance rolled east on Diamondhead Road, its emergency light flashing.

"Thanks for the use of the phone. Little Burt's mom really appreciated getting the call from me. I'm sure he's going to be okay…they'll check him out thoroughly over at Memorial."

"Sure, any time. Glad to be of service. Guess now is as good a time as any to go back down and get our boards."

"Yeah. I noticed one of the other windsurfers pulled your board in after we got Burt breathing again."

An orange sun hung low, casting long shadows from the rows of now dark green breakers approaching the rocky coast. The temperature had dropped into the mid- seventies and with the stiff onshore breeze, Kelli had begun to wish she had a more than just a tank top on over her shorts.

"What a great day! I can't believe I pulled off that back loop," James said looking at the last of the windsurfers coursing the darkening waters.

"You nailed it like a pro. Don't tell me it was your first one."

"Actually, it was. I had been wanting to try one for a while, and everything just seemed to fall in place today. I just decided to go for it."

Kelli just shook her head. *Jeez. This guy is pretty talented for a jet jockey.*

James looked at his watch. *No wonder I'm getting hungry . It's almost 1900.*

"Kelli, don't know about you, but I'm about a quarter past empty. I was kinda wondering if you'd like to have dinner at the Wasabi Hut tonight?"

"Thanks for the offer, but I already have plans."

Damn! Shot down right out of the gate.

"One of my friends at the hospital brought me some lobster tails. Perhaps you could join me for a cookout at home?"

Hollywood's spirit shot skyward as he tried to be somewhat casual. "That sounds great. Can I bring wine, dessert maybe?"

"Wine would be nice. I need a chance to shower off this salt water. Eight o'clock okay with you?"

They talked amicably as they headed back up the trail to their cars. Once each had secured their respective boards, Kelli gave James her address, which he promptly loaded on his iPhone.

After he got dressed in a pair of khaki colored silk pants and a black and gold floral print shirt, James grabbed a bottle of his favorite Chablis, picked up his Alvarez DYM90 guitar and headed downstairs the parking area. Ten minutes later, he was at an older four story apartment building with crimson colored bougainvillea cascading down the balconies facing the south and west. He nodded at two seventy year old women who got off the elevator, and then stepped inside and pressed the button for the top floor. In short order, he approached apartment 402 and rang the doorbell. A tall forty-something man opened the door. James smiled, nonplused, although his heart sank slightly. *Right. She didn't say I was the only guest.*

"Hi! I'm James Stewart."

"Hey, James. Trent Gibbs, Lori's fiancee."

James stuck the bottle of wine under his left arm and extended his hand. "Nice to meet you."

Trent took his hand and gripped it firmly. He stepped back, allowing James to enter as he pointed to the back of the apartment.

"Kelli is out on the balcony, trying to get the gas grill to light."

"I'll go give her a hand."

He stowed his guitar next to the couch and left the wine in the kitchen.

On the balcony, a frustrated redhead was bent over the propane bottle under the gas grill.

"Need any help, Doc?"

"I can't get the grill to light. I filled the tank last month, so I think there's plenty of gas."

He helped her up, bent over the grill and cycled the gas off and on with his ear cocked toward the burner. *Gas okay*. He pushed the cylindrical red button inward. The silence told him what the most likely source of the problem.

"The piezo igniter isn't firing. Do you have a new D cell battery?"

"Have one in the kitchen," she replied as she spun around to get it.

James knelt down and looked under the grill where the igniter was located. He pulled the battery from its stainless steel bracket. A slight ring of gray corrosion around the positive end confirmed his hypothesis.

"Here's your problem…" The sight of her standing there in her lavender Hawaiian Hibiscus Palms halter dress almost took his breath away. "Wow."

She blushed slightly, brushing her copper locks behind her ear, then handed him the battery. "I'm glad you approve. Do you think this will take care of it? Don't have any matches. I don't smoke."

"Me either," he said as he slipped the battery and tested for the audible clicking sound of the igniter firing.

Satisfied he turned on the gas and was rewarded with a slight *whoosh* as the flames lit. He stood up, place his hands on his hips and shot her his very best John Wayne imitation, "Well, little Missy, there ya go, good as…new."

"That was great. Pee Wee Herman, right? Come on, I'll introduce you to my roomie, that is, if she is out of the powder room. They have a big date tonight. Trent's folks are flying in."

James shrugged off the tiny put-down of his favorite actor. He followed the lovely lady back into the kitchen, where she reached for two crystal wine glasses. "Red or white?"

"Surprise me."

Kelli set the glasses on the counter, opened the fridge and retrieved a chilled bottle of the exact same vintage James had brought. "Would you do the honors?"

He grabbed the foil cap cutters and made a rapid half turn on the bottle. Picking up the chromed rabbit style opener, he quickly removed the cork, filled the two glasses and handed one to Kelli. "To another wonderful day in paradise."

"To my new friend, and knight in shining armor," she replied with a laughing lilt to her voice and a slight curtsey.

Hollywood couldn't help but laugh, too. Her captivating smile and enchanting emerald eyes had his full attention. They raised their glasses together until they touched gently, and then sipped the cool pale amber nectar. She grabbed his hand and led him to a seat in the small living area. They both took seats on the padded white wicker couch across from Trent.

"So, you met Trent already? He's a surgeon at the base hospital," Kelli said.

"Interesting line of work. Any particular specialty?" James asked.

"I trained originally as an ear, nose and throat specialist. But went to Harvard for my plastic surgery specialty. I do a lot of soldiers injured by IEDs these days."

"Their body armor protects their internal organs, but the extremities are still rather vulnerable, I understand," James observed.

"Right. How did you know? Are you in the military also?" Trent asked.

James shot Kelli a quick glance before he turned to Trent. "Air Force."

"Oh, that's cool. Kelli said you were, like, a professional wind surfer and life guard."

James smiled. "I had a couple nice offers to sponsor me in competition, but I managed to hold on to my amateur status. But I did get a merit badge in lifesaving when I was fifteen."

"You were great today. You saved that boy's life," Kelli responded.

"*We* saved his life. A local surfer ran over him and he was unconscious."

"'Here I come, ready or not!" Lori called from the hallway.

The tanned blonde in a light blue sun dress entered the room and spun around to show off her outfit. Her face beamed with delight when Trent held up both thumbs. "Perfect, doll baby."

"Drop dead gorgeous, roomie. Come here, I want you to meet my friend James," said Kelli.

Lori approached and stuck out her hand as Kelli made the introductions. "Lori, James. James, Lori."

Hollywood stood up and politely shook her hand. “Pleasure to meet you, Lori. You’re gonna make a beautiful bride.”

“Wow.” She blushed. “I guess I was all nervous over nothin’.”

“See, just as I told you. Now you two go out and impress Trent’s folks,” Kelli said.

Lori and Trent departed, leaving Kelli and James to prepare dinner by themselves.

The lights of Honolulu spread out far and wide beneath the hillside balcony. Distant boats danced on the inky black water beyond Pearl Harbor as the cool night breeze continued to blow. James noted Kelli crossing her arms as if she was getting a little cold. “We can move back inside if it’s too chilly for you.”

“Guess so. But I do hate to leave this view.”

“I know. It’s wonderful, just like your dinner. Thank you. I enjoyed it immensely.”

“You are so welcome, even if you had to fix my grill first.” she replied. “Did I see a guitar case in the living room?”

“Yes ma’am you did…Thought it might be relaxing for after dinner.”

“What kind of music do you play?”

“All kinds. What do you like?”

It was her turn to be congenial, but coy. “Surprise me.”

They moved onto the living room where James opened up the case and pulled out his Alvarez guitar with a mother of pearl rosette laid into the solid cedar top. He formed an A minor chord and slowly strummed to check that it remained in tune.

Then, for a warm up, James played a rendition of *Canon in D*. He transitioned into Mason William's *Classical Gas,* before attaching a capo and doing a cover of James Taylor's *Fire and Rain*.

"Oh, my God. You could play professionally. You're that good."

"Glad you approve. I sit in sometimes for a local band down on Waikiki at the Sea Gull Lounge. Do you like country music?"

"Depends. Some of it's great."

"Here's one of my Dad's favorites. He always sang it to my mom."

He started on a song by a group called Restless Heart. Although the title was *Bluest Eyes in Texas*, Hollywood changed the color to green for the song.

Kelli was touched by the tenderness of his song and tried to imagine what his parents looked like, how they talked, where they lived. His voice spoke deeper to her than the mere words as she listened and melted a little inside. *I don't date pilots. That's what I always say. But...what if I'm wrong?* She looked deep into his eyes as he performed a more up beat tune—a six string version of a Lady Gaga hit tune. *Lady Gaga? He knows Lady Gaga?* "I can't believe you know her stuff!"

"A bit of a stretch for a Neanderthal, I agree. But I do draw the line at Beiber. Okay?"

She didn't know what came over her, but she leaned over and gave James a passionate, if not somewhat sloppy, wet kiss.

He responded by deftly laying the guitar down on the coffee table and giving the passionate kiss the attention it deserved.

EASTERN CHINA AIRSPACE
Sunday, 13 October

The white and red Gulfstream G500 cruised its way through the clear sky over the Bo Hai Sea in a slow decent to its destination at Dalian. Admiral Huang Meng and several of his staff occupied the eight passenger jet that belonged to the PLAN, and were returning to Dalian Port from the meeting in Beijing.

"Commander Niu, when we arrive back at Dalian, I want you to initiate orders for Sun Tzu and Yang Jian with their CBGs to make ready for embarkation," the admiral said.

"Sir?" replied Admiral Huang's chief of staff, Commander Niu Tao.

"Is there something about that order you do not understand, Commander?"

"Sir, the Politburo did not authorize…"

"If we wait on that gaggle of old women to make a decision, it will cost our country dearly. Sometimes we have to take matters into our own hands, Commander. Our first responsibility is to protect the land of our ancestors. Sun Tzu says, 'Begin by seizing something which your opponent holds dear; then he will be amenable to your will. Rapidity is the essence of war: take advantage of the enemy's unreadiness, make your way by unexpected routes, and attack unguarded spots'."

“The world was different in the time of Sun Tzu…I have to respectfully disagree, sir. I must report this to the Politburo.”

“You do what you feel necessary, Commander…and so shall I,” Admiral Huang said as he looked hard at his assistant. Abruptly, he felt the landing gear touch down on the runway with a soft chirp and the twin Rolls-Royce BR710 C4-11 reversers deployed. “Follow your orders, Commander, and then take the plane back to Beijing. I’ll see that it is serviced while you are at the port. It will take Admiral Tengfei Wei several weeks to make ready.”

“Yes, sir,” Commander Niu said reluctantly.

Admiral Huang walked inside the maintenance hangar and motioned for the head mechanic to approach as Commander Niu and his three man staff drove away in a dark green Cheng Feng Liebao SUV. The mechanic and Huang huddled together for a few moments, and then the Admiral turned and entered a Cheng Feng Limo.

A few hours later, Commander Niu and his staff were back aboard the Gulfstream as it lifted off the runway in route back to Beijing. The sleek jet banked left after its gear retracted and was cleared direct to Beijing. In three minutes it was out of sight, climbing west over the Bo Hai Sea.

Later that afternoon, Junior Lieutenant Da Qiang rushed into Admiral Huang’s office with an urgent message.

“Admiral, Admiral, the G500 has crashed into the Bo Hai Sea! There were no survivors!”

Admiral Huang Meng looked up from his desk, removed his wire rimmed reading glasses and replied, "No survivors? Such a pity. Commander Niu and his staff were a credit to the People's Navy and the Party. They will be sorely missed. Prepare letters to their families for me to sign."

NELLIS AFB, NV
Tuesday, 15 October

Inside the 65th Aggressor Squadron briefing room, every seat was filled. Outside the room, two stern-faced Air Policemen had checked the names and identifications of each attendee, allowing no additional personnel to enter. Retired Brigadier General Jack Stewart addressed the group as the second hand on his wrist watch swept past the 0800 position.

"Good morning, ladies and gentlemen. I'm Jack Stewart, Senior Vice President for Special Operations at Lockheed Martin. Before I go any further, today's briefing is Top Secret Need to Know Only and should not be discussed outside this room without appropriate authorization. Are there any questions about that?" Jack looked over the assembled group as several persons glanced around nervously before he continued. "Getting right to the heart of the matter, a mission was flown Thursday of last week in which an airborne low PRF radar system was shown to be able to defeat the stealth capabilities of a pair of F-22 Raptors. Both Raptors were simulated kills in less than eight seconds on the engagement." Burner let that sink in for a second as a buzz of murmurs crisscrossed the room. "Here is a condensed clip of the mission highlights," Jack said as he pressed the remote. "Here you see a single radar return from either Bravo 31 or 32," he continued with a red laser pointer. "And here is a return from both fighters in the element...and finally, in real time, the Sidewinder and gun shots on the Raptors."

Jack stopped the clip as the *Starfighter* rocketed up to 50,000 feet.

"Holy shit!" said Lt. Colonel Bob Peterman, sitting in the first row.

Jack smiled at the F-15 pilot. They had served together when Peterman was just a first lieutenant. "Flash, I can tell you have a question."

"Burner, sir, what the hell kind of craft was that Delta 22? Some kind of new black technology?"

"I can't say a 1953 design would count as new...Newer than a P-51, maybe." He enjoyed toying with the guys just for a second. The confused looks on their faces were worth remembering. "Guys, Delta 22 was a F-104 Starfighter built back in 1963. By the way, the Silver Knight is highly polished aluminum...What we are here to discuss are parameters of today's test mission to find out exactly how far the older radar systems can detect and track each of your aircraft.

"SecDef Baker has given broad DoD support for the test as well as Lockheed-Martin, Northrop Grumman and Raytheon. Technical data we gather from this mission may very well have a major impact on mission planning, tactics, avionics and missile design. Not only does it affect our own stealth technology, but quite probably, that of the Russians, the

Chinese and any of their customers. So, you see, there is a lot riding on us getting this thing done and doing it right."

Fifty-five minutes later, the briefing concluded with most aircrews and contractors reps left to mingle for a few minutes. Crew members for the B-2 headed out to the flight line to board the transport helo for Area 51. They had arrived at the super secret Nevada site the night before and would depart the Groom lake facility for a night mission after crew resting during the day.

Lt. Colonel Peterman joined the small group around Jack Stewart. "So we get to fly together again, hey Burner?"

"Lockheed engineers wanted a control aircraft to chase the Zipper and provide a second set of telemetry to confirm bearing and distance on all contacts with the Raptor and Spirit. Raytheon wanted it too, if they are going to have to modify hardware and software on the Slammers."

"I don't suppose it's just luck of the draw I got this assignment, is it General?"

"No, Flash, I didn't want to just pull a name out of a hat. Besides, Hollywood keeps me informed of the whereabouts of a lot of his contemporaries. The fighter community is still pretty small."

"I'm honored you chose me, sir. Did you want to meet in the PE room before heading out?"

"Actually, my bird is not on the main ramp. It's over in the maintenance hangar. When you call for taxi, get clearance there and we'll join up for taxi out and departure."

“Sounds like a plan. I’ll be there at 1055 local.”

They shook hands and Peterman headed out. The senior design team engineers from Raytheon approached Jack. “Jason, good to see you. How’re Tricia and the kids?”

“Good, everybody’s all good. Now I see what you’ve been up to with that antique. No wonder you haven’t been hitting the links lately. You remember Eric Billings, my top sensor designer?”

“Sure, we met at the corporate shindig you guys put on at the Noah’s Ark Animal Shelter fundraiser. Good to see you again, Eric,” Jack said as they shook hands.

“You have a great memory, Mr. Stewart. That was almost three years ago.”

“Call me Burner. Always have warm feelings for the guys who make the missiles on my birds work. It’s a professional self-serving interest, you understand.”

“Burner, if you’re right about the low PRF, it changes everything. I understand LM’s happy to have the Raptors be undetectable and all that. We’ve been unable to get a decent lock on one with any of our radar missiles. The AIM-120 is dammed near useless against them, as you know,” Jason grumbled.

Jack nodded. “That’s why I didn’t even attempt a Slammer shot during the mission. I knew where the Raptors were, and they didn’t have a clue about me. No sense changing that dynamic. I understand from a technical aspect why the industry went to high PRF. The data stream provides much more accurate target movement information reference acceleration, lateral movement and so forth."

"Of course, PK is increased twenty-fold. That, in a nutshell is why we all use the highest refresh rate," Eric replied.

"And, interestingly enough, why you can't shoot an AMRAAM at a Raptor even if you can see it with your own eyes," Jack countered.

"That is undeniable, Burner. We're looking forward to the test results. Any thing we can do to make Raytheon products better, and aid in the defense of this country, we're all about that, big time," Jason said.

"I know you do. Hey, we're all in this together…Better get my butt in gear. I don't want half the world waitin' on me to get this dog and pony show up and runnin'."

Jack spun around and headed for the hallway. Jason noticed the embroidered *Starfighter* on the back of his powder blue flightsuit and grinned. "That's my boy! Low profile Burner."

"Sierra 55 flight, Blackjack, turn right three six zero. Maintain flight level three five zero for this pass. Primary search radar on, transponder squawk 5500, Sierra 56 strangle squawk."

"Blackjack, Sierra 55 right to three six zero, flight level three five zero, squawking 5500."

Jack adjusted his transponder for the last run at the *Raptors*.

"Sierra 56, roger, strangle squawk," Bob Peterman confirmed as he turned his transponder back to *Standby*.

Jack cleared back to the right as he rolled right and climbed slightly to clear the blue gray *Eagle* in tactical formation. He continued the roll to forty-five degrees and pulled back until he was in a two G turn as directed. Looking down at the F-15, he remembered when the first ones came on board at Luke Air Force Base, Arizona. The wing commander, Major General Fred Haeffner, at that time, was a free thinker. He took the liberty to change established tactics from the old *wing tip in the star* formation, where the wingman's responsibility was to back up and protect the flight lead, to a more fluid formation called the *spread.* Senior officers at headquarters 12th Air Force had resisted the concept because it went against the basics that they had learned a generation before. Eventually, the superiority and effectiveness of the *Fred Spread*, so called in honor of the Luke Wing Commander won out. Fred even experimented with painting a simulated canopy on the underside of the *Eagle* to further confuse other pilots in close aerial combat.

Flash Peterman watched Burner's *Starfighter* cross over and initiated a reversal maneuver well inside the turning radius of the F-104. But as he rolled out closer to a northerly heading, he realized he had lost sight of the much smaller fighter.

Dammit, that tiny ass fuselage gets small in a hurry. And the wings are invisible. He glanced inside at his radar and picked up the icon for the *Zipper* and closed the gap until he reacquired the elusive bird.

"Sierra 55, Blackjack, do you have contact with targets at your twelve o'clock?"

Jack check his radar picked up two definite targets at eleven thirty.

"Sierra 55 has two targets bearing 345 at 35. Targets moving eastbound. Estimate FL390, over."

Inside the lead *Raptor*, Major Hunnicutt, cursed to himself as he looked at the altimeter. *Son of a bitch! That's four for five passes that he has picked us up. And he even nailed our altitude.* He checked his onboard warning system which had locked on to the *Starfighter's* radar transmissions. Instead of identifying the source, the icon had the letters *UNK* beside it for *unknown.*

"Blackjack, Alpha Papa 21 has unknown contact bearing 170 at 31 and Eagle contact confirmed at 168 at 32, angels 350, over.

"Alpha Papa 21, copy contact there."

"Blackjack, Sierra 56, no joy on targets."

"Sierra 56, Blackjack copies negative contact with targets. Break, Sierra 55, Blackjack, this concludes the briefed portion of the tests. Any additional requirements?"

Jack pondered the situation of a second.

"Blackjack, standby, Sierra 56, say fuel in minutes."

"Sierra 56 has four zero minutes to bingo."

"Blackjack, Sierra 55, release Alpha Papa 21 flight to RTB. Sierra 55 flight will need one zero minutes for an additional test."

"Blackjack roger, Alpha Papa 21 flight, turn right heading 185 for exit point. Contact Longshot on 238.8, squawk 3225."

Hunnicutt set the departure transponder setting and acknowledged the radio frequency change. The transmission he heard before he flipped the radio tuner peaked his curiosity.

"Blackjack, Sierra 56 will be off freq for one, Sierra 55, go Winchester."

Bear set his secondary transmitter to 30.30 and checked in with Longshot on primary. He heard Burner check in with Flash.

"Flash, you up?"

"You bet, sir."

"Think you can handle one V one with a Starfighter?"

"You serious, sir?"

"Is a bullfrog's ass waterproof?"

"Set it up, General, I'm game!"

"Figured you would be. Turn south for two minutes. I'll continue north and call *fight's on*. I'll have Darkstar stand down to make it interesting."

Damn! I wouldn't want to miss that little engagement. Gonna see the old dude get a little lesson in humility. That deal with the Raptor was bogus big time. Bear pulled the power back on the *Raptor* as he slowed the two-ship down. His wingman figured out the plan as the two checked in with Longshot and performed a series of slow S turns toward the restricted area exit point…

Jack had pushed the throttle up to full afterburner as he made a easy climbing turn back south and leveled off at FL470. He made three sweeps of the area with his radar and located his wingman at FL410 still headed south. He turned the unit off and made a radio call. "Sierra 56, fights on."

Bob, in the *Eagle*, rapidly clicked his mic switch twice to acknowledge as he slammed both throttles to burner and broke into a hard left reversal to engage. The big bird responded instantly in a cloud of boundary layer separation as he took the F-15 right up to its maximum AOA. The lack of any target information on his HUD was disquieting. *Where the hell did he go? He has to be low. The Starfighter does not have a look-down shoot-down capability on that sorry ass radar.* Bob was partially correct. The *Starfighter* radar did not have sophisticated frequency domain signal processing. The first US fighter that did was the F-4 *Phantom*.

Bob's F-15C was equipped with a the latest AN/APG-82 radar upgraded in 2009 to combine the processor of the APG-79 used on the F/A-18E/F *Super Hornet* with the antenna of the APG-63(V)3 AESA originally installed on the *Eagle*. The new radar also boasted Radio Frequency Tunable Filters designed to enable both the radar and the electronic warfare countermeasures to operate simultaneously without degrading each other. It could track up to fourteen targets simultaneously. If it had picked up a significant radar return from the needle nose of the F-104 pointed directly at the *Eagle*, it would have tracked it and sent a target icon to the HUD, allowing Peterman to lock one of his AMRAAMs on it. But it didn't.

Jack pulled the throttle back to maintain a steady Mach 1.85 as he entered the shallow dive. Forty-three years of experience told him exactly where to look for the head-on pass at the *Eagle*. He knew the sun was not going to give him away as his adversary was lower and most probably looking lower. Jack had attacked the *Raptors* from below. His adversary expected him to be there again. A flash of movement caught his eye against the backdrop of red rocks in the dry Nevada desert far below. The supersonic *Eagle* had jinked to the east and was reversing when Jack made the move to light him up.

Flash reacted as quickly as any fighter pilot alive to the warning from his threat assessment software. He pulled the stick hard into his lap at Mach 2 until the stick-shaker shook and he eased up only fractionally. His vision was gray at the periphery as his heart struggled to overcome nine times the force of gravity and keep his brain oxygenated. The tunnel vision in his eyes was the first sign his aggressive maneuver strained the limits of human physiology. Even with his G suit inflated to the max, Bob grunted hard to help his body compensate. He heard the call, but didn't know where it was coming from.

"Sierra 55 guns."

Burner released the trigger on the stick as soon as the red pipper crossed behind the twin tails of the *Eagle*. He could not turn fast enough to pull additional lead at the high rate of speed, but the two second burst from the gun camera film and telemetry would be a sweet thing to show his *Zipper* aficionado buddies. *Nice reaction Flash. Almost quick enough.* The closure rate at Mach 4 works out to 4,465.74 feet per second. Crossing the last mile between the two fighters took a little less than 1.2 seconds. Flash had glanced down to search the area beneath the F-15 nose when his target was actually a thousand feet above and diving.

"Sierra 56 kill, acknowledge with ident."

Flash Peterman eased out of the breakout and rolled toward the area exit point. He reluctantly pressed the transponder button. *What the hell just happened? I never saw anything!*

Hunnicutt in Alpha Papa 21 glanced to his right at his wingman, who just shook his head. Neither had picked up a tracking signal of the sleek sided *Starfighter* as it approached the F-15. Suddenly, his own HUD showed an unknown radar target at his six o'clock and closing fast. He spun his head aft over his right shoulder and then snapped back to his left after he heard a transmission on the Longshot frequency.

"Rejoining on your left."

A slim silver bullet with almost invisible wings had extended its speed brake as Burner attempted to slow down to fly with the pair of F-22s.

Bear finally caught sight of it at six hundred yards in trail. The *Zipper* lived up to its name as it rapidly moved into fingertip position and the speed brake retracted. Bear had never seen a *Starfighter* up close, much less on his wing. He gave it a once over and shot Burner a thumbs-up signal then snapped a crisp salute. Jack quickly returned the salute. Sierra 56 checked on frequency three miles in trail of the three other fighters. Jack couldn't help feel a little proud of himself when he heard the transmission from Alpha Papa 21.

"Sierra 55, you have the lead. Take us home, Burner."

All the aircrews had a chance to shower and grab a quick lunch in the squadron break area before the 1300L debriefing. Several of the engineers from Raytheon were engrossed in their laptops reviewing the design specifications of the AIM-120 radar when Jack and the last three fighter jocks entered. Jack moved to the podium and addressed the group. "Guys, I want to thank all of you for the fantastic job you did today. Tech Sergeant Thompson will go over the detailed portion of the telemetry presentation so we can actually see in real time the various ranges the older radar actually got returns on the fourth and fifth gen fighters. Please remember that copies of the actual signal data will be made available for all contractors just as soon as we get the data files properly transferred to discs and classified. Henry…"

When he had finished the fifty minute briefing, Henry opened the topic for questions and discussion. One of the first questions asked by one of the F-18 jocks was why the older radar was more effective than the newer high PRF. Sgt. Thompson passed the question to Jack.

"Actually, Commander it isn't more effective. It only works in a different way that has been technologically surpassed as computer power grew. Given the world's bias for newer, better, faster, it was more or less overlooked in favor of what was thought to be more promising technology."

"But you actually found the Raptors on radar and defeated not one, but two, didn't you."

"Yes, but…Let me put it in perspective for you. Back in the Vietnam conflict, one of my buddies, Colonel Robin Olds shot down four MiGs. The reason he was not a Vietnam ace is that on several occasions, his missiles simply missed. The low PRF signals and processors at the time could not always compute where the target was going to be in order it compute and fly the correct intercept course. Does that make sense?"

"Sure, but there has to be something we can do to make sure we can find the Russian and Chinese versions of the Raptor. From what I've seen, they looked like they copied our bird pretty closely."

"You're right on both accounts. I don't believe they are as sophisticated as the Raptor in avionics, but they were able to duplicate the airframe design angles we developed at great expense at Lockheed Martin. How closely they did on copying the radar absorbing skin covering and other stealth characteristics remains to be seen."

Several questions fielded referenced maximum ranges Burner had ever identified targets with the *Zipper*. Finally, Peterman asked his question, "Burner, do you think we can roll that video of our last encounter?"

"I'm sure these folks are probably ready to get out of here," Jack said.

A chorus of *No's!* rang out from the assembled throng.

"Okay, okay, Henry, can you set up the engagement? Just the last ninety seconds, please."

Henry tapped a few stokes on the laptop. "Here you go, sir."

The left side of the screen depicted the radar from Burner's *Starfighter*, and the right was filled with the *Eagle* HUD and radar. The center field consisted of the restricted airspace with the four fighters.

"Sierra 56, fights on."

"Hey, Burner, that's cheating!" complained Peterman.

"Freeze program." Jack laughed. "How is that cheating, Flash?"

"You turned south before calling fight's on."

Jack smiled broadly. "Go back and listen to the setup recording, son. All I said was I would go north and call fight's on. I didn't say I still would be going north when I called it. Combat rules. Continue."

"And here, Sierra 55 gets a radar ID on 56," TSgt. Williams said as he froze the display.

"For those of you not familiar with the Model T radar, that green dot shows target bearing 185 at 24 miles, I estimated his altitude to be FL410."

"And General, your estimate was dead on as seen by the HUD altitude shown on Sierra 56," Williams commented as he touched the green dot, then the HUD. "After this sweep the Sierra 55 radar terminated. He departed FL470 and entered a shallow dive accelerating. Now consider the display Colonel Peterman had on his F-15. The AN/APG-82 was not picking up the F-104 frontal aspect. Interesting."

"Freeze frame," Jack requested. "Flash where did you think your adversary was and why?"

"I gotta be honest. I knew you were low because of your system limitations."

"Let me take a wild guess. You were thinking about look-down/shoot-down, right?"

"Jesus, Burner, you a mind reader, too?"

"I'll take that as a yes. I've been doing this since before some of you guys were born. And, this is hard for a Lockheed man to admit…sometimes it is not all about the equipment. The profession of arms requires a lot from a man, or woman, as the case requires. You have to know your equipment strengths and weakness, soup to nuts, as well as your adversary's. But you also have to develop a sense for how your adversary is going to try to kill you. Call it sixth sense, the force or whatever you want."

"So you used your Starfighter's friggin' needle nose to defeat the Eagle's radar. Poor man's stealth."

"Exactly, Flash. You broke the code. Now you know why I turned nose on before I called *fights on*."

"Never fight the enemy's fight."

"Bingo, roll the tape."

"And here we see Sierra 55's pipper on the nose of Sierra 56 who breaks when he reacts to the gunsight radar rangefinder."

"Sierra 55 guns."

"As we advance through the gun pass frame by frame, we see the pipper walk down the aircraft centerline. Unfortunately, the closure rate allowed a computed hit ratio of 82 percent and here Sierra 55 passes five hundred feet behind the target's six o'clock and exits the area," TSgt. Williams concluded.

"Kiss my rusty," Flash muttered under his breath.

Jack noted the *Eagle* driver's anguish. He'd been there before. "Nice reaction, Flash."

"I learned something…Actually, a couple of things."

"And would you be so kind as to share your lessons learned, Colonel?"

"One. Don't rely completely on technology. Two. Don't allow the enemy to fight his fight."

"Good. Anything else?" Jack questioned.

"Yeah. Watch out for old fighter pilots. They're some really sneaky bastards."

His response brought a gale of laughter from the crowd followed by a round of applause. Jack shook hands for a few minutes with well-wishers and had to beg off proffered rounds of beer from several of the pilots and engineers.

"Sorry guys. I have another brief for the B-2 test in six hours. Gotta get a little rest, if I can."

Jack and Lars both climbed into the same rental car and headed for the hotel.

"So, you think that software upgrade will help protect the Raptor?"

"Not sure. It should take care of the threat recognition problems. I don't think it will help the skin reflectivity. That's a problem for the physicists and chemical engineers."

"At least you gave them some data from which to start to find a solution."

"That we have, Lars. That we have."

***

CHAPTER FIVE

WASHINGTON, DC
WHITE HOUSE
Thursday, 24 October

President Thompson glanced at her watch as the Commerce Secretary took his seat in the White House Conference room. Aides began passing out sealed portfolios to all the National Security Council members who looked nervously at each other after seeing the large block letters TOP SECRET/DO NOT OPEN stamped across the red paper seals. Something big was in play and with the exception of the President, Secretary of State and Secretary of the Treasury, no one else in the administration had a clue. As the last of the aides exited the room, President Thompson began to speak, "Thank you all for coming on such short notice. Secretary of Defense Baker and

Chairman of the Joint Chiefs Admiral Valenti have notified me they will be running a few minutes late due to a critical intelligence briefing in progress. In front of you are copies of the demands presented by the People's Democratic Republic of China Friday morning. You may open the portfolios at this time."

Demands? The Chinese are making demands? My God, mused Attorney General Alan Ames as he tore through the thick red band. Many of the other cabinet members mimicked the same thoughts, bordering on fears, as they likewise opened the tan portfolios with more than a little trepidation.

"Secretary of Treasury Gibbons received the original paperwork with a summary of the original treasury bill purchase transactions dating back to 1991. Secretary Harper contacted the Chinese embassy in Washington to insure these demands were valid and not some form of a sick joke."

"Ambassador Chun was uncharacteristically cold and advised me that the demands were nonnegotiable," said Secretary of State Harper.

"Perhaps you should invite the Ambassador over for a dinner party, Conrad. Do you think they'll call it a even swap for $5.77 trillion dollars in gold?" snapped conservative Secretary of the Interior Rick Sullivan.

"That's enough! We don't need to get into a personality contest, people. This is serious," countered President Thompson.

"This is absurd. We don't have $5.77 trillion in gold! How many ounces is that?" asked NSA Director Austin Roberts.

“At the level we are discussing, we don’t refer to gold in ounces. The Chinese are demanding we deliver just a hair over 45,000 tons,” Homer Gibbons answered weakly.

“Out of the question! They knew the risks involved when they acquired the T-bills. There are no legal grounds whatsoever upon which to base such an outrageous demand. Tell them to go pound sand!” an obviously agitated Attorney General Alan Ames exclaimed.

“That’s pretty tough talk for a Harvard man, even if you have spent the last twenty years in Texas.”

The normally implacable Ames spun around in his chair to see whose voice had just impugned his manhood. The sight of a stone-faced Secretary of Defense flanked by an equally taciturn Chairman of the Joint Chiefs caused him to turn back forward, slightly red-faced and sputtering, “Why, I never! You…”

“We don’t have time for your grandstanding, Alan. With all due respect, stuff a sock in it.”

Few in the room had ever heard retired Marine General Harold Baker, now the Secretary of Defense, get short with another member of the NSC. The President jumped in to try to tone down the rhetoric.

“Secretary Baker, I’m…” Only to be cut off by Baker who raised his hand.

“Madame President, pardon the interruption, but we have a problem greater than whatever you are presently discussing.”

“Mr. Baker, we are faced with an unprecedented financial demand from the Chinese who presently own…”

"Two large ultra-super carrier battle groups are presently taking on supplies for a Pacific deployment as we speak," interrupted SecDef Baker.

President Thompson sank back into her chair as her eyes locked with his. She glanced to Admiral Valenti who had transferred a flash drive to the aide in charge of audio visual presentations. The look on his face told her his earlier misgivings about the Chinese naval expansion were more than a passing concern.

"Please take a seat, Harold. Samson, what have you got for us?"

The hard bitten Admiral moved to the center of the far wall as tall pleated curtains retracted sideways to expose a very large LCD monitor. He nodded his head to the aide who tapped a few keystrokes on a laptop and a big Department of the Navy logo filled the screen. Valenti thumbed the forward button on his remote, whereupon a FLASH TOP SECRET EYES ONLY PRESIDENT OF THE UNITED STATES screen appeared for a second before Valenti moved on. The third screen depicted a daylight satellite photo of a massive twin-hulled catamaran design aircraft carrier with parallel launch and recovery decks.

"Ladies and gentlemen, may I present the Mao-class ultra super carrier Yang Jian. Over fifteen hundred feet long…we've tracked her at over sixty knots. She's presently docked in the Dalian Port where she's taking on three air wings of the latest fifth generation fighters the Chinese have put together. Seventy-five miles off shore is her sister ship, Sun Tzu and her CBG, shown here."

A couple of muted gasps could be heard from members of the NSC.

"She, like Sun Tzu, is apparently fully operational…we have spy bird shots of her doing day traps for both the Jian-10 and the J-20 Stealth fighters," Valenti continued.

"But Admiral, there is no proof the J-20 was designed for carrier operations. My people…" argued CIA Director Clifton Ambrose.

"Your *people* failed miserably, Clifton. They missed the construction of the Mao-Class carriers, their twin-hulled destroyer escorts and the high speed troop transports, Type 071 LPDs, which, by the way, are presently boarding forty divisions of Chinese infantry."

"Admiral, are you certain of the numbers of troops involved? That is far in excess of any normal exercise we have seen from the Chinese Army," President Thompson said.

"You are correct about that, Madame President. It is almost impossible to move that many troops and their related support vehicles without us picking it up on satellite. We are talking over ten percent of the active Chinese combat troops here. Entire train loads of personnel as well as a steady stream of arriving buses and troop carrier aircraft. The process is running around the clock."

"Admiral, I think you are perhaps overreacting. Could this not be just an example of the Chinese saber rattling? I think that the Chinese are bluffing," said Secretary of State Conrad Harper.

"Mr. Secretary," Samson intoned as his eyes narrowed. "You don't play poker, do you?"

"No, I never was drawn to the game."

"Didn't think so. There is no need to bluff when you're holding four aces."

SecDef Baker had opened the portfolio and quickly scanned the cover letter summary and first page of the Chinese demands. *Jesus. Almost six trillion in gold.* "Madam President, if I may make a comment?"

"Please, Harold, I value your council."

"If it were not for this letter demanding gold for their paper investments, I would have said the red fleet preparations would have been a threat aimed at the Philippines. The Chinese have always been keen on the concept of projecting naval power throughout southeast Asia."

"Not to mention their historical records claiming exploration as far as the Americas and Africa from the twelfth through the fifteenth centuries. Had they decided to establish colonies back then, the west coast would not have been open and available for the concept of manifest destiny," Rick Sullivan added.

"Is there any independent proof of such claims? Where did you hear about this rumor? Sounds like Chinese Communist propaganda to me," NSC director Roberts said.

"Once the doors to China opened up significantly after Chairman Mao died, our universities had a major exchange program with their counterparts inside the country. My sister spent three years in Beijing helping the Chinese develop a modern on-line system of cataloging ancient texts and scrolls. As some of you know, their written history goes back over 4,500 years. Her colleagues from Stanford verified the dates of the Oregon coastal charts to be from around 1420…years before Christopher Columbus was born."

"Thanks for the history lesson, Rick, but I'm more concerned with the current Chinese ambitions and capabilities. Admiral, how quickly can the Mao-Class carrier battle groups be ready to sail?" asked President Thompson.

"Without knowing their full capability to transport men and materiel, I'm going to have to say a minimum of two weeks. It is a daunting task, which, up until earlier today, they have kept under wraps," he said as he shot a glance at the head of the CIA.

"Secretary Baker, can you summarize our defensive capabilities on the west coast?"

"Madam President, USS Carl Vinson and the Gipper are both deployed out of San Diego into the Indian Ocean at this time. USS Abraham Lincoln and George Washington are due to rotate back soon as the Nimitz can arrive off Somalia for support of the international anti-piracy campaign as we agreed with the EU. With USS John Stennis in Bremerton undergoing a long term refitting program, our actual naval capabilities on the west coast are minimal. Pressure from the locals opposed to jet noise and political pressures from the left have forced the closure of the Marine Air Stations at Miramar and El Toro as well as George Air Force base at Victorville. That leaves us with F-18s out of San Diego's Pendleton MCAS, North Island and at Lemoore NAS in Fresno California, with Air National

Guard F-16s nearby. Finally, we have an Air National Guard Wing flying F-15s at Portland."

"I should have agreed with Admiral Valenti's suggestion to attack the Somali pirate bases on land," the President sighed. "We do have significant other fighter capability in the mountain states though. Is that not correct?"

"Yes, Ma'am. Major bases in Idaho, Nevada and Arizona, but all would require a significant refueling effort to put them in place off the west coast. Moving them all to bases within a tactical operational range of the Chinese fleet would leave them dangerously concentrated against a first strike," Baker replied.

"Madame President, one other wild card we have not discussed is the Jian-20, the Chinese stealth fighter. It appears to be a copy of the F-22, although we have no known data of its actual effectiveness in combat," Admiral Valenti pointed out.

"Bottom line, Charger. What would the outcome of a battle between a wing of their J-20s against our F-15s and F-18s?" Thompson asked as she looked the seasoned sailor in the eye.

He shook his head as he tried to calculate the percentages. "Not good. If their bird is half as good as our Raptor, they would probably have an eight-to-one kill ratio in their favor. All of our west coast birds are fourth generation fighters. Not one has ever scored a kill on the F-22."

The members of the assembled National Security Council sat stunned by his assessment. The President closed her eyes and began to rub her temples as if to shake off an impending headache. "Harold, what are our F-22 numbers and disposition again?"

"We produced 187 aircraft, of which 182 are operational. Flyable today numbers...we can figure maybe 160. They are based at Langely, Tyndall, Holloman, Nellis, Hickam and Elmendorf," Baker rattled off using his almost computer-like memory. "Oh, Madame President, one small caveat to what Admiral Valenti said about the Raptor...we actually did have a couple Raptors shot down in a simulated test last week. The same aircraft was able to detect a B-2 at 30 miles. I'm meeting Monday morning with the heads of Lockheed-Martin, Northrup-Grumman and Raytheon to discuss engineering and software changes to the airframes, as well as sensors for both defensive and offensive systems."

"Harold, don't you think that a failure of the stealth technology to defeat a new radar system would be an important thing to brief the Commander in Chief? We spent billions to make those planes undetectable. Now you tell me someone has invented a system that could beat it! Just when did that occur?" Thompson snapped at her Secretary of Defense.

"1963, Madame President."

NAS FORT WORTH JRB, TEXAS
Friday, 25 October

Jack Stewart handled the dull gray plastic film in his gloved hands as several of the Lockheed-Martin technicians looked on. The film was less than 1.4 millimeters thick and had a translucent quality to it with something resembling fish scales floating inside the pliable polymer. "Ed, what makes this material so dangerous to handle? Everybody acts like it's poison."

"Well, the biggest problem is in the plasticizers used to make the material remain flexible under heat. A process called plasticizer migration. It can be absorbed in the skin and act as a synthetic hormone," Ed replied.

"Not like Viagra, I don't suppose."

"Nope, it mimics estrogen. Cause men to grow boobs…what I'm told." Ed laughed.

"Can't have that happin'. So, this will absorb all known frequencies of airborne as well as ground based radar? What makes it so effective against the low frequencies?"

"It's those tiny Aramid discs laid randomly into the matrix that cause the breakup of the low frequency radar waves. It can withstand up to 700 degrees which corresponds to Mach 2 air friction heat buildup. Now, on a stealth design like our Raptor, designed angularity as well as composite construction provides the basis for primary stealth radar attenuation. It just so happens that you came across a frequency spectrum that we did not design or test for when you resurrected that Starfighter," Ed White advised.

"Yeah, guess I stirred up a hornet's nest with that show up in Nevada."

"No doubt. I haven't seen so much scrambling around since we had that F-22 grounding for life support contamination. Major goat rope. Anyway, my counterparts up at NG called and wanted to license this coating technology from us. We got it done first and the SecDef wants some rapid response to this."

"Good for you, Ed. Besides it will help pay for the test cost we incurred at Nellis."

"Jack, your little show was nickel and dime compared to what some guys would have put together. The boss wasn't exactly happy you found the defect that you suspected, but he told me himself that you could have saved the integrity of both the F-22 and B-2 programs. Hate to think what would have happened if our enemies had discovered it first."

"My son flies the Raptor. That was more than enough motivation for me. Listen, I gotta make a couple calls before the end of the day. I want to see if Raytheon ran with the idea to multiplex their AMRAAM transmitter and seeker frequencies," Jack said as he set the sample back on the bench, removed his yellow rubber gloves and turned to head toward the door. He spun around just before he reached the doorway. "Ed, I just had another idea."

"Uh oh!" he replied in mock anguish.

"Could you run a computer simulation of the new coating on the Eagle, just testing for High PRF attenuation?"

"Sure, happy to."

"Thanks…wonder what the Silver Knight would look like with that coating on it?"

"Jack, you're pushin' it."

"See ya Monday," he said as he grinned and opened the laboratory door.

TUCSON INTERNATIONAL AIRPORT
Friday Evening, 25 October

First Lieutenant Jeff “Boom Boom” Babayan, dressed in tan slacks and a red polo shirt, waited in the Southwest Airlines baggage claim. He anxiously scanned the deplaning passengers from Flight 224 from LAX as they entered the baggage claim area. Then he saw her in the middle of the first group. She was wearing a bright yellow sun dress—her long black hair pulled back into a pony tail tied with a matching yellow ribbon. *Oh, wow!* Jeff thought as he waved and quickly walked over and gave Stacie Chen a quick hug.

“You musta been in the “A” group.”

“Got there early, hate sitting in the back,” Stacie replied. “I was really looking forward to this weekend. I think I’ve put in over sixty hours at the lab this week.”

“Do you have any other bags?” Jeff asked as he took the handle of her rollaboard.

“Nope, just that. Even though Southwest doesn’t charge for bags, don’t like waiting for them to be unloaded.”

“Let’s boogie then. Got dinner reservations at Miguel’s. Hope you like authentic Mexican.”

“Love it.”

They held hands as they walked toward the exit.

“That sun dress looks great on you,” he said.

“Thank you, sir. I have to dress a little more conservative at the base. This is more my style. You look great too…even though I like your uniform.”

"Thanks," he managed to get out while he tried to think of something interesting to say.

He was truly smitten, not only was she beautiful, but smart too.

"So, uh, how's your program coming?"

"It's coming," she said wearily as she glanced at his profile. "I'm only about a third of the way into the link system…That's one of the reasons I'm happy you invited me up for the weekend. I really needed the break."

"What's the other?" he replied, fishing.

"I think you know the other," she said with another demure glance.

Abruptly, Stacie's iPhone buzzed with a text message. She pulled it out of her purse and glanced at the screen.

Arriving L A Mon, 11am.

Stacie seemed to pale as she stared at the screen.

"Anything wrong?" Jeff asked.

"Uh, no…no. I, uh, have a…a relative coming in next week…that's all."

HICKAM AFB, HAWAII
Friday Evening, 25 October

Lt. Colonel James Stewart finished the last officer efficiency report and prepared it for transmittal to the Wing Commander for his endorsement. It was a necessary part of the job as Squadron Commander, but far from one of the most enjoyable. Three Majors with similar time-in-grade would be competing for two promotion slots. All three deserved promotions, but peacetime Air Force and budgetary cutbacks forced Stewart to make hard choices. He checked his watch. *Damn. It's 1715 hours already. Gotta get my tail in gear.*

Hollywood had another date with Kelli and a setting sun. He placed the personnel files in his file cabinet and quickly keyed the lock shut. Three minutes later, he fired the Jeep Wrangler up and rocketed out of the parking lot. A cool west-northwest weather system had passed over Oahu earlier in the day and left picture perfect conditions to watch the sun set over the western tip of the island in the Kuoakala Forest Reserve. He jogged from his parking spot to his condo elevator.

Inside the spacious three bedroom condo overlooking Waikiki, he took a seventy-five second combat shower and jumped into his hiking clothes. Almost as an afterthought, he remembered the chilled bottle of wine Kelli liked and stowed it, a lightweight blanket and two plastic wineglasses in his backpack.

Kelli looked stunning in a pair of khaki pants and a medium green pullover as the two headed westbound on H1 or, as it was commonly called, Queen Liliuokalani Freeway. Traffic dropped off once the two passed the cutoff to Makakilo City and headed northwest on the Farrington highway. The highway paralleled the magnificent coastline and skirted the last major populated area of Makaha and followed along the edge of the Makua Kea'au Forest reserve. The hilly tropical jungle bore little resemblance to the highly developed Honolulu metro area. Giant ferns dominated the hillside understory while the verdant green of a double canopy hardwood jungle defined the upper reaches. Rainfall topped 300 inches a year on the highest peaks that wrung moisture out of almost every passing cloud.

Entering the Kaena Point State Park, James checked his watch. *Forty-five minutes till sunset. Gonna make it.* He reached over and held Kelli's hand as they continued to the end of the paved road. A dirt road would take them within a half mile of the actual west end of the island. Late October was not really high tourist season in Hawaii, as snow birds often waited past Thanksgiving to migrate to the warmer climate and families with students were back in school after summer vacations. James waved at a single passing car driven by a retired couple as the deepening shadows in the foliage caused the Jeep's automatic headlight feature to kick in. The roadway itself was completely covered by luxuriant foliage and created a surrealistic tunnel effect.

"How did you know about this place?" Kelli asked.

"My folks brought me out here as a kid. My mom liked a break from the Arizona desert when we lived near Phoenix."

"I guess your dad was stationed at Luke."

"Several times, actually. That's where he met his mechanic friend Lars. Anyway, dad had seen this area from the air and wanted to share the view with mom."

"That's so sweet. I'd like to meet him."

"I think that can be arranged…Well, this should be the closest spot," James said as he looked as his map display on his iPhone.

He pulled off the dirt road into a small turnout and helped Kelli out of the Jeep. James slung the backpack onto his shoulders and led the way down the worn deserted path. The scent of musky jungle foliage mixed with sweet floral notes from flowers that bloomed naturally near the rocky shore. Ferns nearly nine feet tall lined the pathway.

"This is gorgeous, honey," she said as she marveled at the bright green parrots flitting from tree to tree.

"Yeah, I think it's kinda special, too."

As the path reached the shore just short of the actual promontory, all the vegetation gave way to a rocky, barren coast. The red-orange sun hung just above the cloudless flat horizon that stretched almost 270 degrees around the point. A gently rolling blue-green sea splashed almost noiselessly on the moss covered rocks a hundred feet below them.

Suddenly, a pod of humpback whales breached the surface less than 100 yards offshore. One of the males near the front exploded out of the water in an impressive display of aquatic aerobatics as it lifted almost three quarters of its body into the air, rolled over extending a massive pectoral fin jauntily skyward and landed in a thunderous white spray.

"Wow! Did you see that? They are so close you can almost touch them!" she exclaimed as a huge grin crossed his face. "Did you plan that?"

"Of course," he said looking at his watch. "But they are thirty seconds early," he replied.

"You lie, GI." She laughed as she riveted her attention to the water.

“Come on, girl, another hundred yards to the point. That was the whole idea of bringing you out here…I thought.”

“Okay, I’m right behind you…Look! There goes another one!” she exclaimed like an excited school girl when a smaller bull whale breached. “They’re so beautiful.”

James reached the tip of the jagged point sticking out into the ocean. He pulled off the backpack and spread the blanket down for the two to sit and watch the sun set.

“Have a seat Milady,” he said in his most chivalrous voice.

“Why, thank thee, kind sir,” she replied as she curtsied.

He sat down beside her as he dug into the pack and produced the bottle of wine and two glasses. Then he rummaged around for a couple seconds before the realization hit him. *I forget the wine opener.* He thought for a moment. *A shoe, a tree. Dammit. Where are the trees when you need them?*

“What’s wrong, babe?” she asked when she saw the look of disappointment flash over his face.

“Nothing, be ready in a jiffy,” he said as he untied his right hiking shoe.

“Got a blister?”

Kelli crossed her arms and watched curiously as he hopped on one foot over the rough volcanic pebbles to a large boulder just behind them. *What is he doing?* He took the bottle of wine and, after tearing the foil cork cover off, placed the bottom of the bottle inside the shoe. He proceeded to hold the neck of the bottle and smash the shoe firmly against the rock. He stopped after three strikes and removed the bottle from his shoe. James slipped his foot back into the tan colored shoe and walked back over to the blanket as if nothing had happened. It was only then she noted the cork was almost completely out of the bottle.

"They teach you that in fighter pilot school, do they?"

He laughed heartily. "Can't say that they do. Actually, a friend posted a link about it on Facebook. I thought it was pretty lame until I, uh, overlooked the wine opener this afternoon."

James twisted out the exposed cork and poured two glasses of their favorite. "To friends."

"To very good friends," she said as they touched glasses.

Savoring the amber nectar of the grapes, he pointed out the sights. "Just to the right of the setting sun, you can just make out the island of Kauai. It's that little green band, right there," he said, pointing. "A little farther west is the island of Niihau, but you can't see it from down here. You *could* see it from up there," he said as he spun around and pointed at a huge radio telescope atop the mountain.

"What's that?"

"Oh, it's a satellite tracking station. Does work for the DoD and NASA."

"I see," she said as she turned to watch the sun appear to touch the Pacific. "It's getting ready to go." She took another sip of her wine. He topped off both glasses. "What country is due west of here?" she asked.

"That would be China. Why do you ask?"

"Dunno, just curious, I guess. It's not sunset there is it?"

"No." He laughed. "It's Saturday morning over there."

"Not Friday morning?"

"Nope, they're on the other side of the International Date Line."

"If you say so...Guess I better stick to medicine."

They held hands and sat in silence for a couple minutes. As the sun sank lower, James leaned over and whispered, "Watch for the green flash."

Kelli looked at him slightly askance. "Is this some sort of trick?"

He simply smiled as the last of the sun's red rays disappeared beneath the horizon and a very brief green light flashed. She looked at him. "Make a wish," he said softly.

"I already have," she said she set down her empty glass and pulled his face to hers.

TUCSON ARIZONA
Sunday Morning, 27 October

The noise of a neighbor loudly closing their apartment door woke Jeff Babayan from a dream. He started to roll over when he realized something was pressing on his left shoulder. He blinked a couple time before he could focus on the soft features of Stacie's face nuzzled into his neck. *Oh, yeah. That part was not a dream.* He took a moment to watch her breathe in and out and reflected about the weekend to that point. The two were more than just attracted to each other, that was a given. They shared common interests in science and computers, dug the same music and were closet trekkies. Both loved *Next Generation* more than *Voyager* and neither liked *Universe* much as they both felt the whole concept of taking over some other person's body for a brief period of time was confusing and a gimmick instead of developing a great story line. She sighed a couple times and snuggled closer. *Man, oh man, I could totally get used to this.*

WASHINGTON, DC
THE PENTAGON
Monday, 28 October

Secretary of Defense Baker entered the room at precisely 0900 hours as was his custom. He hated waiting for people to start a meeting and extended that courtesy to others.

"Gentlemen, thank you for your quick response to this matter. At the outset, I would like to tell you that there are factors playing into this engineering discussion that I am not at liberty to discuss. When I say speed is of the essence in getting this done, I'm taking days, not months, not years." He took a moment for his words to sink in. Whatever the assembled contractors thought before the meeting, a new sense of urgency was etched into their faces. "General Stewart, as Senior VP for Lockheed-Martin, I'll start with you. By the way, I do want to thank you for your input and insight leading up to the discovery of this challenge facing us. Can you give us a rundown of your company's progress on the Raptor?"

"Certainly, Mr. Secretary. Our software engineers worked with our friends at BAE on AN/ALR-94 E & IS radar warning receiver. Essentially, a relatively small change in frequency discrimination software programming will allow immediate system response to the Low PRF ranges I transmitted on. Our friends at Northrop Grumman assure me the AN/APG-77 AESA radar will now transmit down there also. If the Russian or Chinese stealth fighters are observable in the low PRF spectrum, we'll be able to track them. That problem is essentially solved and only requires a file upgrade to be downloaded and a system reboot and we are done."

"Thank God for that," said an obviously relieved Harold Baker. "Now, what about the reflectivity problem? I don't think a software upgrade is going to help there."

Jack laughed as he shook his head, opened his briefcase and slipped on a pair of yellow rubber gloves. Taking out a 12 inch square of flexible gray material, he held it up for all the men seated around the conference table.

"Gentlemen, my apologies for the show-and-tell, but this is Lockheed-Martin's answer to the problem of stealth in *all* frequency ranges. It's lightweight, flexible, heat and cold tolerant. The *fish scales*, as I call them, are responsible for low PRF breakup and attenuation."

"May I?" Baker asked.

Jack handed him an extra pair of gloves from his briefcase.

"Please use these, Mr. Secretary. My chemical engineers call it plasticizer migration. Wouldn't want you singing soprano."

"Not on my bucket list." Baker laughed as he slipped the gloves on. "Interesting stuff. How fast can we get it on the Raptor and B-2 Spirit?"

"I took the liberty of contracting for 400,000 square yards of the material. It takes about six man hours per craft. Alex, what number did you guys at NG come up with for the B-2?"

"Burner, we estimate it's about sixteen hours with a four man crew. As you know it's not a difficult job, it just needs to be laid out smoothly," Alex Corden, the chief of the engineering section at Northrop-Grumman replied.

"Mr. Baker, I had my engineers crank out some figures for radar signature attenuation of the F-15, in their spare time. Frontal aspect reflectivity was reduced 96%, with full top or bottom platform view cut by 89%," Jack added.

"General, what does that mean in miles?" Baker asked.

"Well, sir, we still are not completely stealthy, but from a frontal attack scenario, it means we would not be detectable until we were within three to three and a half miles. That could be a game changer."

Jack noted that Harold Baker caught the import of what he just relayed. He could see the wheels turning inside the Secretary's head. *What is it he can't share with us? It has got to be big.*

"Alex, this new material could help the F-18 survivability also, would it not?" Baker asked.

"Of course, sir. Every mile you can get closer to your adversary without detection is a major increase in missile PK. We'll have to contact Lockheed for specifications on the energy absorption profile to give you numbers on our Super Hornet."

"Do that ASAP, please, Alex. Jack, Boeing is a major subcontractor on the F-22 aren't they?"

"That's correct."

"Now that they have taken over Rockwell and the B-1 program, I'd like some numbers on this film as applied to the B-1B. I'm thinking every one of our combat aircraft could benefit from it. Can you see to it Jack?"

"I'd be happy to, Mr. Secretary," Jack said. Almost as an afterthought, he continued, "The boys ran the numbers on my Silver Knight with this coating. With its streamlined nose, the Zipper was undetectable beyond four hundred yards…if I put that slimy stuff on my helmet."

Baker shook his head. "And tell me again why we spent 200 million a copy on the Raptor?"

"Well, sir, it is new and improved." Burner laughed.

AIR FORCE SPACE COMMAND
VANDENBURG AFB, CALIFORNIA
Monday, 28 October

Stacie sat at her desk watching the digital clock; it read 10:58, and the sick feeling in her stomach grew bigger with each passing second. She glanced over at the photo of her parents taken just before her father passed away two years earlier. *What am I doing? Will the Chinese really let my mother go? How will I ever face Boom Boom if he finds out I was responsible for sabotaging the Air Force Communications system?* The clock advanced one tick to 10:59. Tears formed in her eyes as she typed the activation code. When the display read eleven o'clock she pressed *Enter* and muffled a sob of deep despair.

Just before lunch time, Stacie accessed the system status information on the MILSATCOM and TSAT systems. To her surprise, the systems were up and running perfectly. *Maybe the virus does not work. Will they still release Mother if it doesn't? God, I wish I could talk to someone, but nobody can help me.* She dabbed the tears from her eyes, took in a deep breath and walked quietly to the cafeteria as if everything was fine.

SEYMORE JOHNSON AFB, NORTH CAROLINA
Thursday Evening, 7 November

A pair of F-15 *Eagles* from the 335th Fighter squadron departed in formation destined for a joint Air Force/Navy exercise off the Carolina coast.

"JC, what the hell we doing out here attacking the US Navy with Harpoon missiles? You know the Navy will never let us close enough to launch one at one of the big boys."

"Why do I always get WSOs who ask stupid questions? We are here because the SecDef wanted us to play with the swabbies on short notice. Who the hell knows?" Jason Carlisle Washington answered from the front seat of Racer 33.

Following the rejoin with Racer 31 and 32, the last of the four *Strike Eagles* in package two fell into position sixty miles in trail behind a flight of four F-22 *Raptors* headed inbound to a carrier group homeported in Norfolk, Virginia. The plan was for the *Raptors* to clear out the *Super Hornets* providing the air defense shield for *George H W Bush*, cruising three hundred miles off the Florida coast. The first contacts with the *Hornets* went as planned. Eleven F/A-18s from VFA 213 were simulated kills and sent to NAS JAX for recovery to keep the airspace clean. The sun began to set on the very busy CSG as it picked up eight *Strike Eagles* as hostile bogeys.

"Hey JC, there's a destroyer at 1130 for 90 miles and a probable cruiser at 1 o'clock for 105. Got 'em both locked up," WSO Six Pack O'Riley announced.

"Stand by to engage."

"Copy. Got the AGM-84 locked on. In range in eighty seconds."

Aboard *USS George H W Bush,* nicknamed *Avenger* because that was the type of craft President George H. W. Bush flew in WWII—part of her keel was made of steel from the Twin Towers. The air boss noted the loss of the primary ring of fighter coverage.

"Launch the reserves."

"Aye-aye, Captain. Uh, sir, Lacey 18 inbound with number one engine oil pressure low light."

"Roger, keep me advised."

The first of the reserve F/A-18s shot off the bow of the *Nimitz-Class* carrier with a pair of yellow and white cones of fire emanating from the afterburners. The aircraft rolled left and sucked up the gear as the pilot turned directly toward the incoming fighter bombers. Behind him, Lt. Commander Ron Hale followed the directions of the marshaller on the slightly pitching deck. As a trained team, the men and women of the *Bush* could launch a multi-million dollar fighter off the deck every 30 seconds. Commander Hale lined up directly over the catapult and set the brakes until the shuttlecock slid back into his massive nosewheel and was locked onto the stanchion by a Green Shirt. He released the brakes and waited for the run-up signal. When it came, he would advance the power to full afterburner and place his hands on the canopy rails, awaiting the launch.

"Lacey 18, cleared to land, call the ball."

"Lacey 18, ball, be advised I have secured number one engine."

Down in the ready room, members of VFA 31 viewed the TV screen with the sight of the *Hornet* with the white crosshairs of the automated approach tracking system seeming frozen over the aircraft as Commander Andy Anderson brought it in smoothly.

"Check that shit out. Anderson cool as a God damned iceberg with number one shut down. Boy's got some hands on him. He's a trappin' machine," said one of the ensigns.

"I'll get you Sonny's autograph, boy," said another *Hornet* pilot as he tossed a crumpled newspaper at the ensign.

On the cat, the blast fence rose behind Lt. Commander Hale's *Hornet*. He eased the throttles forward around the burner gate and quickly confirmed a good light on both engines. He started to raise his hands when the strangest thing happened. All his attitude, navigation display and HUD disappeared. A dozen

Master Caution lights illuminated simultaneously. Hale pulled his hands back down, yanked the throttle to idle and frantically shook his head. The Green Shirt crossed his arms and waved off the launch. Inside the launch cubbyhole, the cat officer, known as the *shooter*, gave the signal to the catapult operator who gingerly raised his hand off the spring loaded green release button and breathed a sigh of relief.

"Hot damn, that was close," the shooter muttered.

Andy Anderson reacted to the sudden loss of instrumentation with a decision to bolter. He slammed the one good throttle to full burner to execute the go-around. Unfortunately, the aircraft pitch did not respond as commanded. In fact, the nose dropped, and the aircraft rapidly rolled left. The aft deck of the carrier loomed above the stricken *Hornet*. Andy pulled the handles and ejected down into the deep green waters of the Atlantic a half second before the *Hornet* slammed into the fantail of the *Avenger*.

Inside the ready room, several pilots had yelled at the monitor in a vain attempt to tell the hapless jock to pull up. A second later, they were stunned by the sickening thud from the impact of the *Hornet*. The massive carrier shook from the resulting explosion as klaxons sounded throughout the ship.

Up in the CAC, crews sprang into full emergency actions as multiple *MAYDAY* calls echoed from the comm center speakers. The air boss' head snapped right, left, and back right as he witnessed the impossible. All the fighter aircraft transponders disappeared off the giant screen, including the inbound *Strike Eagles. That ain't right.* The sound of two dozen emergency locator transmitters filled the room.

"Kill that damned speaker! Tactics, talk to me! Where are my friggin' fighters?" the air boss bellowed.

"Sir, electronic tracking lost, primary radar indicated they are heading for the deck," answered the harried tactics commander.

Admiral Arthur Simms viewed the video feed from the aft hangar deck. Firefighters in full silver turnout gear fought fires engulfing a pair of F/A-18s with fan shaped spray from three hoses.

"Damage Control, report," he tersely demanded.

"Sir, four dead, eight injured. Five aircraft destroyed, but fires are under control," said Petty Office Third Class Wilson.

"Thank you, PO," he said as he reached for the handset hotline to the CAC. When the air boss answered, the Admiral gave a shaken Captain McBriety the ship status report. "Jeff, damage control reports the fires are contained. We lost five Super Hornets and four sailors. What the hell happened up there?"

"Art, I wish I knew. They just fell out of the God damned sky."

"What the hell are you talking about, McBriety? I meant the Hornet that slammed into the stern."

"Sir, I'm talking about the CSG defense package. Twenty-seven Super Hornet's."

"What about them?"

"They're gone, Admiral. Every damn one of 'em…They're gone."

DAVIS MONTHAN AIR FORCE BASE, ARIZONA
Thursday Afternoon, 7 November

Captain Garrett wished he had paid more attention to the parachuting instruction six years earlier in Undergraduate Pilot Training. He figured he would never ever have to use that little skill, because in his mind, there never was a good reason to intentionally jump out of a perfectly good aircraft. His flight of four F-16 *Falcons* had just taken off from DM on a mission over the weapons ranges south west of Luke AFB. He loved gunnery qualification and was very good at it. The four *Falcons* were south of Tucson at 2,500 feet climbing in tight finger tip formation when Garrett's HUD went blank. He glanced inside to see the entire flat screen displays blanked and heard a *Master Caution* alert as his aircraft rolled slightly left toward his wingman. Instinctively, he countered with ever increasing pressure on the side stick in his right hand. The quadruplex fly-by-wire system did not activate the flight control system. The *Falcon* continued to roll left.

"Lion Flight, break!" he shouted over the departure control frequency as he watched his close friend and wingman fly into his left wingtip.

The canopy impacted the wingtip and caused the lead aircraft to right itself for a second. Garrett slammed the throttle forward, causing his fighter to jump ahead of the other three before it entered an uncontrollable left roll and began a shallow descent. He reached between his legs, grabbed the yellow double D rings and pulled with all his might. A mighty roar assaulted his ears as the canopy departed and the wind blast of three hundred miles an hour swept around the cockpit. The zero-zero capable ACESII booted the pilot of the craft out into the dry Arizona air. A half second later, Garrett found himself being yanked out of the seat and listening to the wind fill the white canopy with a reassuring pop.

How the hell did that happen? he wondered as he watched three other pilots descending from different altitudes. He had actually ejected inverted and was just over fifteen hundred feet in the air. His wingman was over a thousand feet above him, with the two pilots from the other element spread between them. *Dammit. Friggin' cactus.* He remembered enough of the parachute training to steer clear of the towering Saguaro cactus and position himself for a PLF before he hit the sun baked desert floor. Garrett rapidly unbuckled the quick disconnects connecting him to his parachute. Two of the three pilots were landing near him. Garrett began to jog to their location when he noted one of them was not wearing a helmet. *Lost it in the ejection.* He closed to within twenty-five yards of the one with no helmet when the pilot landed without making an attempt to perform a parachute landing fall. *He must be unconscious, got to kill the chute.* Garrett grabbed a riser and held on to it as he flipped the quick disconnect on that side, effectively spilling the air from the chute. It was then he looked down at the young Lieutenant lying silent on the red dirt. His neck was bent at an unnatural angle and there was no light in his eyes. Garrett choked back the lump in his throat as he pressed two fingers on the young man's neck, checking for a pulse.

"Aw, Boom Boom...Dammit, son, no...," he said as he slumped down beside him and tears began to fill his eyes.

HICKAM AFB, HAWAII
Thursday Afternoon, 7 November

James Stewart turned well inside the pair of *Eagles* in a visual DACM exercise. He pulled up toward the streaking F-15s at FL410 and retarded the throttles slightly as he slid into a high angle off gun resolution. James placed the HUD pipper over the closer *Eagle* and prepared to pull the trigger when the pipper and, in fact, the entire HUD display vanished. *Come on, girl don't start that now.* He tried to sweet talk the *Raptor* HUD into re-activation, but once he glanced inside, he quickly absorbed the much bigger problem.

"Raptor 1 Flight, knock it off," he transmitted.

"Raptor 2, Mayday! Mayday!"

The call caught James off guard. *How can he be in an emergency, too? I'm in deep kimchee here.*

The nose of *Raptor 1* began to oscillate laterally as he moved the stick right. No result. Full aft stick met the same gut wrenching lack of response. The rudder pedals did nothing to slow the bigger swings in the nose.

"Anchor 11, Mayday."

"Anchor 12, I'm losing it! Primary flight controls are out!"

Holy shit. Eagles, too? We're all in the same friggin' boat.

"Rapter 2, Hawkeye, say nature of emergency."

James knew the AWACS controller was trying to help, but he could barely see his wingman as *Raptor 2* was fifteen thousand feet below him in an eighty degree dive. *Son of a bitch. Deacon's supersonic!*

"Raptor 2, say speed!" James yelled over the frequency. "Boards! Gear! Put your gear out! Eject, God dammit! Eject!"

The surreal sight of a pair of nearby *Eagles* departing from controlled flight captured his attention for a couple of scant seconds. He tried to calculate the time between the near one's nose pitching up and the other craft beginning a series of ever rapidly increasing rolls when he saw the two canopies jettison and both pilots eject into the minus fifty-five degree air. None of the *Raptor*'s Dash 1 procedures for recovery from uncontrolled flight had any affect whatsoever. His head slammed off the right side of the canopy and then even harder off the left side, a half second later. *Time to go*. He grabbed the yellow ACES II handle just as the *Raptor* pitched up almost vertical. The canopy blew with a definite bang—rapid decompression tore the air from his lungs as his heart beat wildly. It seemed like a long time before the rocket motor fired, sending Hollywood up the rails, but in actuality, was less than a second. The seat was equipped with a stabilizing drogue chute that deployed automatically from a storage container behind and above his head. It, the arm restraints and blast deflectors behind his legs prevented the five hundred knot ejection from breaking his extremities as he fell over thirty thousand feet before the man-seat separator engaged and released the lap belt securing him to the last remaining vestiges of his *Raptor*.

Four oil slicks and two fires were all that was left of the six heralded fighters that had dominated the skies minutes before. What saddened him beyond words, was the lack of parachutes beneath him. Major Bart Jones and two *Eagle* drivers never had a chance. As he hung from the canopy suspended over the deep blue waters of the trackless Pacific, he envisioned the task of looking Deacon's wife in the face to give her the news.

AIR FORCE SPACE COMMAND
VANDENBURG, CALIFORNIA
Thursday Afternoon, 7 November

Stacie glanced at the news feed from CNN and couldn't keep from crying. In her heart, she knew the Chinese who had blackmailed her into inserting their worm had lied. She didn't just compromise communication as they said. The diminutive communications specialist had personally been responsible for the destruction of forty-nine fighters, one B-2 and at least nine deaths. Seven pilots were still missing. Stacie picked up her cell phone and dialed a number in Tucson. On the fifth ring, some one picked up. *Thank God.* "Boom Boom! You're okay!"

"Hello, this is Captain Garrett. May I help you?"

"I need to speak to Boom Boom!"

"Who's calling, please?"

"This is Stacie, his girlfriend. Put him on, please."

Lief Garrett looked down at the pile of personal effects arrayed on the table in front of him in the briefing room. He opened the wallet and spied a snapshot of the two young lovers. *Christ. I met her.* Tears once again filled the pilot's eyes.

"Stacie, there has been an accident."

"Oh, God. Oh, God! No! Please dear God!"

"Boom Boom was…"

"Is he going to be okay?"

"I'm sorry, Stacie. He didn't make it…I'm so sorry…"

Lief swore he never heard a woman scream in anguish that loud. Ever. He never got the words *for your loss* out of his mouth. The line went dead.

Most of the other Space Command employees were in the break room watching the news coverage of the rash of unexplained military aircraft accidents. No one heard Stacie scream in her solitary office. After a half-hour, she regained partial control of her emotions. She picked up her office phone, and with a trembling hand, dialed the operator. After two rings a very pleasant sounding lady who lived in nearby Lompoc answered.

"Vandenberg operator, how may direct your call?"

"Can you connect me with the FBI?"

***

CHAPTER SIX

WASHINGTON, DC
WHITE HOUSE CONFERENCE ROOM
Thursday Night, 7 November

The mood was somber with a deep undertone of anger mixed with trepidation. As news filtered in of more pilots being rescued in both the Atlantic and Pacific, Secretary of Defense Baker addressed Admiral Valenti.

"Charger, bottom line, what are our capabilities with this electronic fiasco staring us in the face?"

The salt and pepper haired veteran exhaled and stared back into Baker's eyes. "Air power is gutted without a fighter force, and I don't have a Navy without carriers or ballistic missiles. Our Army is severely disadvantaged without the air superiority we have enjoyed since 1944. The Chinese have set themselves up for a virtually unchallenged invasion if we can't get to their troop carriers. Our helos are no damn match for fifth generation fighters, and don't have the range or firepower for offshore operations. That leaves us with the B-52s and B-1s with nearly no chance of survival alone against a well orchestrated modern fighter force. Our ECM gear is good, but never has been good enough since the Russians developed home-on-jam."

"We don't have a clue what caused the failures of so many disparate systems?" asked President Thompson.

"Not at this time, ma'am. All the facts point to a systemic virus or worm as they call them on the net. Something that sophisticated is not the work of a random hacker. The timing, coming just days before the Chinese Carrier Battle Groups are ready to depart, is more than a smoking gun. There is no such thing as coincidence," Baker replied.

"I agree with you Harold. Normally, this level of cyberterrorism would justify a declaration of a state of war. As you can imagine, the blow even managed to disable the targeting systems on both our land based and submarine ballistic nuclear missiles, as well as all the cruise missiles currently deployed. It could take weeks to get them back on line. We could declare war, but I'm not quite sure how we would wage one," Valenti continued.

"Why did they knock the systems out so early? If they wanted to attack us, could they not have waited until they were in position?" asked the President.

"You're asking the wrong people, Madame President. Ask the Chinese," grumbled Baker.

"I have an idea what they might be thinking," Valenti offered.

"Let's hear it," Thompson urged.

"The Chinese are obviously seeking payment or something for their multi-trillion dollar investment in the United States. It makes no sense to attack us and destroy our ability to create wealth. The value of our system is in the land, our people and the infrastructure," he replied.

"What's their plan, if not to defeat us?"

"The Chinese believe it's better to win via deception or intimidation, rather than to actually engage in combat and risk destroying what they covet. That's ancient Chinese philosophy," Valenti replied.

"You think they would rather have us surrender? That's not going to happen on my watch," the President said defiantly.

"Nor mine, Madame President. I'm just trying to speculate as to the Chinese thinking here. They caught us with our pants down, so to speak."

An aide entered and brought an envelope to the Director of the FBI, Marvin Huxley. He opened it and quickly scanned the contents.

"Jesus! Well here's some news I didn't expect. We know who planted the worm."

"Great work, Marvin! That was certainly quick," commented the President.

"Thank you, ma'am, but I can't take credit for the breakthrough," he glumly stated. "The perpetrator turned herself in. Turns out…it was one of our own."

HONOLULU, HAWAII
Thursday Night, 7 November

Kelli waited nervously near the doorway to the emergency room entrance to the Pearl-Hickam Joint Base Hospital. Finally, the distinctive sound of the approaching Coast Guard helicopter announced its arrival and she was able to discern which set of flashing red lights was associated with the rescue chopper. She never had paid much attention to how many flights came and went out of Honolulu before.

Kelli shielded her eyes from the dust and blast of the rotor downwash as the helo pilot gently touched down on the pad. Three sets of orderlies, each with a gurney, moved into position along side the orange and white Sikorsky HH-60J *Jayhawk* and had the first of the three pilots strapped down even before the rotors stopped turning. The orderlies wheeled an injured man quickly past her, but she determined it was not Hollywood. Neither was the next pilot that rolled past. From her vantage point, she could not see the face of the third man because one of the pararescue jumpers was walking in front of the gurney. Kelli didn't know whether to take that as a sign of a more injured man or not. She couldn't help it, but her heart almost pounded out of her chest—she simply had to know if Hollywood was one of the survivors.

"Excuse me," she said as she wedged herself between the PJ and the gurney.

"Sure, Doc," he said as he stepped aside.

The man's face was red with scattered bruising and a few shallow cuts above the eyes. The left eye was bandaged, but when the other eye saw her face, he broke into a smile.

"Hey, gorgeous! Know any good doctors around here?"

Later in the recovery room, where the Flight Surgeon insisted he remain for observation, James remembered something that he needed to do. "Hon, can you call Dad and let him know I'm okay? I left my phone in my locker."

She reached into her white lab coat and pulled out her phone. "What's the number?"

It was almost 10:45pm in Texas when the cell phone rang on the night stand inside the Fort Worth Marriott Residence Inn. Jack was seated in a chair at the desk working on his laptop. He reached for the phone with some trepidation.

"Jack Stewart."

"Mr. Stewart, Dr. Kelli Johnson in Honolulu. Your son…"

"Doctor, is he okay? Kelli Ann? Are you his…" Jack stumbled uncharacteristically at a doctor calling about his son's condition.

"I think he wants to talk to you," she said handing James the phone.

"Hey, Pop! Sorry to leave you hanging for so long. I thought the squadron would have called to let you know."

"Actually, the DoD put a news blackout on the whole cluster. They wouldn't give me the time of day an hour after the incident started. How are you doing?"

"Shaken, but not stirred. Well, got a couple cuts from the visor, and a neck bruise where my helmet tried to leave me at five hundred knots. Other than that, I feel like I carried the ball forty times against OU, or maybe the Cowboys."

"That good? Glad to hear you still have a sense of humor…takes a load off my mind, son."

"Dad…we lost Deacon, and two other guys from the 54th out of Elmendorf."

"Damn…I'm so sorry, James. Deacon was a good man."

"I don't know what the hell happened. All six of us lost complete control at exactly the same time. Fly-by-wire was completely compromised, all flight systems…and the backups."

"I know, son. I'm still in Fort Worth. Things here at Lockheed-Martin are pretty topsy-turvy, as you can imagine."

"I guess they are, seeing as how they made both aircraft types with problems."

"Son, it's bigger than that. The F-16s, F-18s and B-2s are affected also. It's not just a Lockheed problem."

"Jesus! Didn't know. This is way worse that I imagined."

"You had no way to know…We'll get it figured out, with time. Anyway, thank that pretty doctor friend of yours for calling. And if you need anything…Get yourself some rest, son. I'm so glad you're safe…I love you."

"Love you too, Dad. Love you, too."

FBI DIVISION OFFICE
LOS ANGELES, CALIFORNIA
Friday Morning, 8 November

Stacie Chen wasn't very attractive—she wore no makeup and her obsidian black eyes were red rimmed with dark circles underneath from almost fourteen hours of on and off crying. FBI Deputy Director Ben Corbin and Admiral Valenti actually didn't look much better after flying in from Washington to LAX on the all-nighter.

"I didn't know, oh my God, I didn't know…All those men…and it's all my fault…They lied to me…" Stacie began and then burst into tears.

"Why don't you just tell me how this happened, Stacie? From the beginning," asked Corbin after she was able to compose herself.

A stenographer sat at the end of the conference table with a Lightspeed keyboard connected to her lap top. A digital recorder with two microphones was positioned in the center of the table in front of Stacie. A camera mounted in the far corner at the ceiling recorded the interview.

She took a deep breath and began, "About four months ago, my mother took a trip to China to visit some of her aunts and uncles in the Zhejiang province…That's where my grandparents were originally from before they moved to Taiwan. After a month or so, I stopped getting regular messages from her and I became concerned. I tried contacting some of our relatives, but I couldn't get through. Telephone and Internet service is somewhat sparse in the province. Then I received an anonymous text message from China saying that my mother was being held as a spy and would be executed, but I could buy her freedom by performing some work for the PLAN…"

"Peoples Liberation Army and Navy," Corbin said for the benefit of the stenographer. "Please continue."

"They knew what I did and where I worked…they knew everything." She started to sob again.

Corbin handed a fresh box of tissues to Stacie. She pulled out one, dabbed her eyes and wiped her nose and then continued, "I was to insert some code into the new communications software I was developing, for MILSATCOM that would create the Global Information Grid…don't know how they knew about it, it was supposed to be Top Secret…Anyway, they said this code would just create what we call a *back door* into the entire communications system network. It would be a way for them to eavesdrop on our communications, even encrypted. The text message said that the US was already intercepting China's communications and this would just level the playing field. My choices were to either incorporate their code…or my mother would be hung. I didn't know what to do…My mother is the only direct family I have left…"

"Stacie, can the code be removed?" asked Valenti.

"Yes, but I'm the only one that knows where it's located. It's a massive program. I can remove it…Do you think it's possible to get my mother out of China?"

"Is that a condition, Stacie?" asked Corbin.

"No…no. I'm responsible for all those boy's deaths and my…" Her voice trailed off for a few seconds. She dabbed at her the tears streaming down her face. "I will remove the code…It could take up to a week, but I can scrub it out."

"There have been enough innocent lives lost already," stated Valenti. "Do you have any idea where your mother is?"

"Yes, actually I do. I said I wouldn't do it unless they let me talk to her. They must have forgotten that I'm an expert in communications. I back-traced the call by satellite. She's being held in the Liuhe Pagoda, Hangzhou, Zhejiang province. I also found out an Admiral Huang Meng has his central offices in the pagoda, he's Fleet Admiral of the East China Sea Fleet. I think he's the one behind this....Do you really think you can get her out?"

"No promises, Stacie, but we might…we just might," said the Admiral.

WASHINGTON, DC
PENTAGON
Friday Afternoon, 8 November

SecDef Baker's Executive Assistant, Willamena Parker, took the incoming call from Admiral Valenti.

"Bill, Charger. I need to speak to the man."

"Right away Admiral. I hope you have some good news."

"A little of both."

"Mr. Baker, line two. It's Charger," she said as she pressed the comm line between offices.

The bone weary Secretary picked up the handset.

"Speak to me, Charger."

"Harold, I sat in on the full debrief. Here's the bottom line. The worm was, in fact, a blended threat that included a virus, a worm, Trojan horse and malicious code. One nasty sum' bitch."

"Jesus! Any good news?"

"She says she can scrub the code from MILSATCOM in less than a week. They told her it was a back door to our entire communications system secured or not. She apparently didn't know about its affects on our aircraft."

"Uh huh…My tech guys say the worm permanently destroyed the hard drives on our fighters as well as the control centers of our ballistic missiles. I'd like to get my hands on the bastard who planned this attack!"

"Funny you should mention that. The Chinese hold hostage, under threat of execution, the mother of the young gal who did their dirty work. The girl, a Doctor Stacie Chen with Air Force Space Command, tracked the calls to a pagoda used as headquarters by Admiral Huang Meng."

"I've heard that name before. A real rogue hard-liner. He's the one pushing their super carrier program. Rumor has it he helped design it."

"Doctor Chen asked me if it was possible to help get her mother out of China."

"Would have been nice if she had come to us first, before she sabotaged the system…Charger, do you think there's any chance this girl is a double agent? We could be risking everything on her ability to clean that worm."

"I'm no spook, but if she is working for them, I would say she should get an Oscar for acting. Her tears were real enough. She was in love with an F-16 pilot that was killed at DM."

"Dammit to hell! So much hangs on this. I'm meeting early tomorrow with all our contractors for a recovery status briefing. Right now, it looks like there is no way in God's green earth to get our fighters, bombers and missiles up and running before the Chinese fleet sails. The Raptor has fourteen separate hard drives, the 15s and 16s have over ten each. Since we stopped F-22 production, a half dozen manufacturers of subsystems have gone out of business due the cutbacks. It's damned grim, in the short term, Charger. Damned grim."

"Harold, desperate times like this call for desperate measures. Can you imagine the advantage it would give us if we were to perform a rendition of their Fleet Admiral?"

"That Admiral Huang? There's only one group capable of a really short notice grab and go."

"And you and I both know who that is. Only you are cleared to make that call. If Dare Phillips and the Black Eagle Force can't do it, it can't be done."

WARBIRD RESTORATION, INC.
GRAYSON COUNTY AIRPORT, DENISON, TEXAS
Friday Afternoon, 8 November

Seventy-five feet below the three massive hangars on the east side of what was formerly Perrin AFB, was the home base of a top secret contract para-military organization—the Black Eagle Force. Under contract to the DoD, the BEF occupied an eight and one-half acre labyrinth of aircraft parking, gear storage, command and control center, office spaces and training facilities. The BEF was composed of elite former military Special Operations experts and crack pilots from all branches of the United States armed forces: SEALs, Rangers, Green Berets, Delta Force, Air Force Combat Controllers and Marine Force Recon—by invitation only. It was formed by direction of President Reagan in 1986 as a Black Ops quick strike organization outside the purview of the Posse Comitatus Act of 1878. Their motto is: *Semper Paro Bellum*, Latin for Always Ready for War.

In the Control Center, the CEO of the BEF, Archimedes "Dare" Phillips, Colonel USMC (ret.)—graduate of the United States Naval Academy in Annapolis ('81), was on a secure link to SecDef Baker.

"...and stay away from the new Global Information Grid, it's got a worm that knocks out our fly-by-wire systems..."

"That's why all those fighters and that B-2 crashed, isn't it?" asked Dare.

"You got it...It's the worst form of cyberterrorism...Dare, I'm tasking the BEF to take Admiral Huang Meng into custody and rescue Stacie Chen's mother in China. Designate Operation Dragon. Our information is that she's located in the Liuhe Pagoda, Hangzhou, Zhejiang province, China. It's at the foot of Yuelun Hill, facing the Qiantang River where it empties into Hangzhou Bay. I'll send you the coordinates. The pagoda is some thirteen stories. Both she and the Admiral are in there somewhere. You have to get them out before we neutralize the virus. We know where the virus is and who planted it, we just don't want the Chinese to know that we know and I'm sure I don't need to remind you of its full deniability status," Baker said.

"Understood…BEF accepts Operation Dragon, Standard Protocol, 1945 Zulu…Mark," Dare said, as he looked at his watch.

"DoD confirms…I'll arrange KC-10s out of Eielson and Japan for Mama Bird's refueling. You can link up over Seoul. You won't be able to communicate securely once you're feet wet. You'll be on your own."

"Roger that. Phillips out."

Dare turned to his second-in-command and Chief Operations Officer, former Army Ranger Major Kevin "Kit" Kitaen, who had been listening on an extension.

"Kit, contact Mike and the rest at Eagle Nest and get them here. We'll launch with four M600/As and Manta at 2000 local. Meet me in the planning room soon as you can. We got work to do."

"Be there in five."

Dare turned and headed toward the planning room. *Son of a bitch! Right into the mouth of the lion, or dragon.* He knew the BEF had done missions in China before, but that was before his time. The earlier missions came before the addition of the sleek and deadly M600/A *Black Eagle* VTOLs and *Mama Bird*, their huge C-5M *Super Galaxy* battle carrier. She could carry four *Black Eagles* in her monstrous cargo bay and the URF or Unmanned Reconnaissance Fighter craft dubbed *Manta* on an electromagnetic coupler under the left wing. The M600/As and *Manta* were launched and recovered in flight.

The M600/A Skycar—a four nacelle VTOL, or Vertical Take-Off and Landing craft, manufactured by Moller International, had been modified extensively starting with ultra-high-tech avionics and a stealth coating of multiple layers of a radar absorbing type of Teflon like the F-117 *Nighthawk*. The coating had a major difference—its final layer was a new clear photovoltaic, color spectrum frequency modulating adaptive coating containing chromatophores developed by BEF's resident electronic genius design gurus, Carla "Blaze" Hermann and Frank "Gears" Formby. The coating could, when electronically activated, adapt its color almost instantly to match its surroundings like a chameleon. When inert, the M600/A was a flat dark gray, but upon activation, would become a light sky blue when viewed in clear day sky, a dull gray in cloud cover, a dark blackish gray at night or even multicolored digital camo if under 500 feet AGL or on the ground. The sensors covering the entire skin area of the craft detected the ambient light spectrum and controlled the chromatophores on the opposite side of the craft. It gave the illusion that the aircraft was almost transparent. The BEF named this new technology, *LIZARD* in reference to the Chameleon lizard that inspired Blaze and Gears to mimic with their electronic wizardry.

Lightweight Dragonskin armor; composed of silicon carbide ceramic matrices, Graphene sheeting and titanium laminates, was installed inside the aircraft's skin under critical cockpit, avionics and engine nacelle areas.

The unique craft was twenty-six feet long, fourteen feet wide with the rear nacelles folded up and twenty-two feet wide with the rear nacelles extended. It had a gross weight of 3,800 pounds with eight 1500 cc rotary engines inside the four nacelles, developing 170 hp each. A Blaze G2 7.62mm six barrel, rapid fire, Laser-targeted, electromagnetic coil gun was mounted in the center of the aerodynamic nose. Six Griffin LRX 415 missiles on two triple pylons flanked by two PAASM or Hellfire missiles pylon mounted atop of the rear wing nacelle supports and four AIM 92 Stinger heat seeking air-to-air missiles were mounted under the front wing nacelle supports.

The *Eagle* had a top speed of over 400 mph with a ceiling of 36,000 feet and four passenger capability, plus weapons. The fuel cells were self-sealing inert foam-filled type bladders under the passenger compartment and gave the craft a range of over 700 miles. The M600/A could be in-flight refueled. *Mama Bird* was layered with the same stealth coating and *Lizard* adaptive technology making her virtually invisible optically as well as undetectable to radar.

Kit entered the planning room as Dare was orientating a large map of the US west coast, the Pacific and the east coast of China on a ten foot LCD on the far wall.

"Mike, Jill, Blaze, Mickey and Maria will be here with Eagles One and Two from Eagle Nest by 1800. That will give us the opportunity to prep and load them aboard Mama Bird with Three and Four in plenty of time for a 2000 local launch. I've notified flight crews and back-up pilots for Mama Bird and the Eagles along with Raptor Team Four. Already called in Tze Yen, since he's fluent in both Mandarin and Cantonese. Figured we might need someone who spoke the language."

"Damn, Kit, you read my mind," exclaimed Dare. "I've also put in a call for a Chinese female operative from the CIA. Thought we could use one other for our ground team."

From across the room, Communications Technician Sparky O'Neil—former Petty Officer Two, USN, a cute, petite, African American girl—signaled to Dare. "CIA Director Ambrose on line two, Dare."

"Thanks, Sparky…Dare here, Director," he said as he picked up the comm unit.

"Dare, got an operative for you, Special Agent Kim Wu, third generation Chinese. Grand parents from Tiapei, speaks Mandarin, Cantonese and Minnan as well. Kim is very experienced in field ops. You'll have to pick her up in Portland. She just finished an assignment in Malaysia and is taking a few days R & R at home. Let me know your ETA and I'll have Kim waiting at the Portland Air National Guard side of the airport."

"Get back to you in thirty, Director…need her sizes for a Chinese Navy uniform. Shoot me a hi-res jpeg photo of her for an ID…and thanks." Dare disconnected and turned to Kit. "Better get Bad in here. We're gonna have to do an infil."

In a few minutes Leroy "Bad" Poole, former Army Ranger Captain, wearing standard BEF black BDUs, strode into the

Command Center. Leroy was a two-hundred-forty pound muscular black man who left no doubt that his call sign "Bad" was well deserved.

"What's up, Boss?"

"Bad, we have a situation…"

Twenty minutes later, after a full briefing, Leroy's only comment was, "Well the shit has hit the fan, pardon the French, Boss."

"Couldn't have said it better myself, Bad," Dare said as he handed a folder to Leroy. "Here are all the pics and info we have on the Liuhe Pagoda. It's thirteen stories inside a five acre compound."

"Well, with four 600s, we'll be limited to eight Raptors, including Tze and the CIA agent, Kim Wu…Just hope she can cut it. Got a feeling it ain't gonna be no cake walk."

"According to her jacket, she has a stellar field record. Expert in all types of firearms and hand-to-hand combat…not to say anything about her linguistics," offered Kit.

"All right, we've got less than six hours till wheels up to get our basic plan together. Bad pick your primary team, get with Tze and see what you can come up with. You'll have another twelve hours to polish your insertion after we pick up Kim in Portland."

"Got it, Boss man, we'll be ready."

"I hope so, Bad, I hope so. It's going to be like bear huntin' with a switch," said Dare with deep concern showing in his eyes.

WASHINGTON, DC
PENTAGON
Friday, 8 November

SecDef Baker rubbed his eyes as the Boeing representative explained why there were no spares available for the flight management control system or the navigation modules that took inputs from the GPS system for navigation. Four hours of sleep in two days had drained his body, and although he didn't want to admit it, he was beginning to feel somewhat depressed. He made a command decision to reveal the exact nature of the Chinese financial demands, as there no longer appeared to be any national security reason to withhold vital threat analysis from the only persons who could actually make a difference in America's ability to defend itself. News of the Chinese carrier fleet buildup stunned the assembled engineers and managers.

For a long moment the thirty attendees sat mute. Finally an engineer from Raytheon spoke up, "Mr. Baker, sir, I know it's not our turn yet, but I did want to pass on some good news. We've taken the data provided by the recent tests at Nellis and reworked the AIM-120 to seek in low PRF multiplexed with high PRF and made significant detection improvements vis-à-vis the original stealth laminate used on the F-22."

"Ronny, can you project a effectiveness on the Chinese J-20?"

"Sir, we have confidence at over 80% detection at 30 miles."

"Nice work guys…now if I just had a couple wings of operational fighters to go with them," the SecDef sighed.

Jack processed the information he had just heard from the Raytheon rep. *Great. Now we can kick their ass if we get a chance. They won't be expecting us to be able to track the J-20.* He considered the game changing news and reflected about why he had not bothered to follow up on the Raytheon suggested actions. The mad scramble to fix the *Raptor* skin reflectivity issue was eclipsed by the cyber attack. *When you're up to your ass in alligators, it's hard to remember your job was to drain the swamp.* A crystal clear image of the vintage fighters lined up at Davis-Monthan popped into his mind. The thought of the *Silver Knight* equipped with new modified Slammers gave him surge of adrenaline. Everything suddenly fell into place for him.

"Mr. Secretary, I know where to get the fighters!" Jack blurted.

"Jack, don't make me guess. I'm almost running on empty here."

"Tucson. The boneyard! Why didn't we think of it earlier? We keep the third largest Air Force in the world mothballed out in the desert. What the hell are we waiting for?"

"I know they're out there. What kinds of aircraft are we talking about? They can't be flyable after all these years," Baker replied.

"F-104s, F-4s…105s, 111s, 14s, F-8s and even some early F-15s. The depot keeps 700 of 'em on a rotating schedule to run the engines and do systems checks."

"But Jack, those are obsolete models. Where can we find pilots and how do you expect to fight the newest fighters with the old iron?"

"I have connections to thousands of jet jocks, Air Force, Navy and Marines. Don't discount the fact that I surprised two Raptors and one Eagle with the Silver Knight. With Raytheon's upgraded missiles, and the new stealth coating Lockheed-Martin just developed, we can give the reds a fight they don't expect."

Baker gazed around the table at the experts brought in to bring him up to date. For the first time in days, he felt a surge of hope growing inside. He could sense the mood swing positive. *It's a harebrained idea. But what if it works?*

"Ronny, how many upgraded AMRAAMs can Raytheon get ready in one week. I need a hard number, not a guess."

"Fifteen hundred, using field modification to missiles currently deployed, sir. The mod is not hardware intensive. Rather, it's a USB software upgrade."

"Chip, can you mobilize the assets needed from Northrop Grumman to support the F-14?"

"Absolutely, sir."

Baker turned to the CEO from Boeing who began speaking even before he was asked. "Harold, you can count on Boeing. We have thousands of current and former employees who helped build the F-4 and the B-1 before they became part of the Boeing family. You tell us when and where they're needed and we'll be there."

"Thank you, Arlen. I knew we could count on you. Burner, you speak for Lockheed-Martin. I assume you have some sort of plan to support the legacy aircraft built by your predecessors as well as Lockheed?"

"We have one of the most capable aircraft ever built in the F-111 Aardvark that we picked up when we took over General Dynamics. After the F-15A model, it's also one of the newest, only being out of active service for less than fourteen years. The only orphans in the litter are the F-8 Crusaders and F-105 Thunderchiefs. I'll have to check with Colonel Budge Wilson at the 309th AMARG to see what is the actual status of those two." "Burner, for purposes of discussion, let's assume I drag you back to active duty and give you the responsibility to put together a composite wing consisting of as many stored fighters as you can cobble together. How would you go about the task of coordinating the effort? We don't have much time."

"First off, I would have your people cross reference active duty personnel files for any folks with experience on the available systems. The Eagles, Phantoms and Tomcats will not be a problem. I can use social networks to contact organizations with specific affiliations for the older birds. The biggest two problems are airframe reactivating and aircrew training. There is simply not enough hangar space at DM for what I have proposed. We would have to truck or ferry them to Luke, Nellis, Carswell, Holloman and MCAS Yuma. That way we could focus our efforts on a specific bird type at a single location or two. Simulator retraining would be at the UPT bases and at the RTUs for the F-15. We can spread out actual training flights in the advance UPT birds that are still flyable, like the T-38. We're talking about working with experienced fighter pilots, many of whom embarked upon a second career with an airline. They haven't forgotten everything they know."

"You make it sound doable, Jack. What's your best guess for a seven day and a ten day goal? How many birds can you get airborne?"

"Nothing like putting me on the spot, Mr. Secretary," Jack said with a chuckle.

"If I didn't think you could handle the job, I wouldn't be asking you for possible goal parameters on an almost impossible assignment. I've reviewed your Air Force record and I know what you did with Lockheed. Your test at Nellis shook up the stealth community, and I'm damned glad that there was somebody on our side who thought it up first. What numbers strike you as realistic?"

"I truly believe we can get 150 operational fighters in seven days and 225 within ten. I'd shoot for 500 trained aircrews. As far as mechanics and crew chiefs, I'd say we need a minimum of four experienced and two to four of our current mechanics per bird. One other thing. My experience on active duty tells me the Navy would never sit still for an Air Force puke running the show with Navy or Marine birds involved." He paused for a second and glanced at the faces watching him with rapt attention. "I would recommend that once the F-14s, F8s and the Marine Corps F-4s become operational, that they be deployed back to the fleet. Without fighters, the Navy is just an expensive sailing club. Of course, all of this depends on getting the President to sign off."

"Gentlemen, the President has authorized me to do whatever is necessary to provide for the defense of the nation. From what you have told me, there is no practical way to recover our fly-by-wire aircraft before the Chinese arrive to press their demands," Secretary Baker said solemnly. "Jack Stewart, under the powers invested in me as Secretary of Defense, I hereby direct you to return to active service in the United States Air Force. You will assume Command of the newly constituted 22nd Composite Air Wing headquartered at Davis-Monthan Air Force Base. I'll contact General Rodgers at Headquarters 12th Air Force to insure adequate office space and support."

Jack heard what the SecDef had said, but it still took him a second to process what had been laid upon his shoulders. The country's response to a modern day Pearl Harbor was now his responsibility, with the fate of the United States of America in his hands. Baker stood and whispered something to an aide. The aide departed the room. Baker asked the assembled men to rise, and then motioned to Jack to approach the head of the table.

Harold addressed the room in a confident, booming voice. "Gentlemen there are times when our great country has demanded much of its leaders. This is one of those times." The aide reentered and handed Baker a small white box. The Secretary continued, "We are all in this together and I am certain Jack will able to count on you support. It is my distinct pleasure to introduce to you our newest four-star flag officer, General Jack "Burner" Stewart!" Baker opened the box and handed it to Jack. Inside on a layer of cotton were two sets of four silver stars…

WASHINGTON, DC
Friday Night, 8 November

General Jack Stewart sat in the rear seat of the government limo for the ride back to the airport. He pulled out his iPhone and touched a contact. It rang four times before Penelope Lough picked up.

"There you are," she said.

"Still up?"

"Of course. I'm trying to finish up the outline…Let me guess. You're not coming in tomorrow, are you?"

"Not only smart and good looking, but psychic too."

"Doesn't take a rocket engineer to figure that out when you're three hours late calling."

"I apologize. Still in DC. Guess you heard about all the aircraft going down."

"That's so horrible. Can you talk about it?"

"'Fraid not. Except that they've pulled my butt back on active duty as a four-star, no less. Now I'm headed to Arizona."

"So, it's really serious, isn't it?"

"That's probably putting it mildly. Don't know when, don't know how, but I will make it up to you."

"I'll hold you to that…General."

"Look forward to it. Night."

"Night…You take care of yourself."

***

CHAPTER SEVEN

AIRSPACE OVER NORTHERN PACIFIC
Friday Night, 9 November

Mama Bird cruised at 34,600 feet in complete stealth mode one hundred sixty-eight miles north-northwest of Sandspit, a large sparsely inhabited island lying some four hundred fifteen nautical miles from Vancouver, British Columbia. All external lights were off, the *Lizard* chromatophore camouflage system was engaged, and it had been almost two hours since the flight canceled its IFR clearance and disappeared off radar. Mission Commander for the Black Eagle Force, Kit Kitaen, flew in the copilot's seat beside Aircraft Commander Gears Formby. The big bird flew a great circle route to the east Chinese target area and would overfly Anchorage, Alaska, crossing over the largest state before going feet wet again near Nome. The craft did not fly on airways, but as they did sometimes cross or parallel the routes used by airliners, the crew and their sensor operators monitored the skies for conflicting traffic.

"Looks like the FMS says we can climb to three-five-five for max fuel efficiency now," Kit said as he checked the flat panel display.

"Here we go," Gears replied as he spun up the altitude display and entered a flight level climb command to the autopilot.

"Roger, confirming flight level three-five-five, "Kit said as he pointed at the commanded altitude.

In the upper crew compartment, Leroy "Bad" Poole noticed the slight increase in engine RPM as the bird responded to the climb command. "Turn around, Kim, the front looks spot on."

Tall and willowy CIA Special Agent Kim Wu turned around and posed as if she were a runway model, looking over her left shoulder as her jet black hair flowed over the other. Bad closely scrutinized the Chinese Shao Xiao uniform, equivalent in rank of a US Navy Lieutenant Commander. He was pleased.

"How did the Dragonskin underarmour fit?"

"Like a glove. I can't believe it's so light. It's really effective, huh?"

"So far…Stops anything short of a .50 cal. Actually, it'll stop that, but your body will turn to jelly from the kinetic energy."

"Right…What's it made of?"

"Multiple layers of one molecule thick Graphene, the strongest substance known…bullets can't penetrate it, a knife can't stab through it and it has its own cooling system with nitrogen filled nano-tubes. Sandwiched between the layers are ceramic and titanium laminate disks that cover your vital organs, spine and the femoral artery area of your thighs. They're layered like scales on an alligator gar."

"Wow, wish we had this stuff at the Company."

"You will, the BEF serves as a test bed for a lot of new stuff…Well, looks great, Kim, or should I call you Liang Ping?" Bad said as he finished inspecting Kim's wardrobe and handing her the matching blue beret.

"Better start using Liang Ping," she said as she took a closer look at her Chinese Navy ID. "How the hell did you guys put all this together so quickly? It sometimes takes weeks for the Company to set up an op of this scale."

"They don't call us a quick reaction force for nothing. We have makeup, wardrobe and prop departments that can rival anything in Hollywood."

"How about me? Do I look like Tseng Jm Leor, Second Assistant to the Standing Committee?" Tze Yen asked as he walked up.

"Ooo, you look like what's his name from Manchurian Candidate," Kim exclaimed.

"You mean Denzel Washington?" Tze asked grinning.

"No, doofus, the original with Frank Sinatra."

"I look like Frank Sinatra?"

"Henry Silva."

"Oh, right. Bad dude," said Tze.

"Anyway here is the name of an actual Chinese Naval Captain we have identified as residing in the Pagoda. We monitored their communications with an ELINT ship off shore once the DoD identified the target. Kit figured you could go in as a high party official investigating the loyalty of one of the Admiral's Staff. The man is Shang Xiao Gwok Wei. He holds the rank as a Navy Ship's Captain, and it would be a reasonable cover story to have a party official, accompanied by a military escort to interrogate him."

"The BEF plays it high stakes, I see," noted Kim.

"We don't have time to set up an infiltration with low level cleaning staff or a cook. We will use the Chinese fear of the party apparatchiks. They look at their Central Security goons like the German Gestapo under Hitler," Bad confirmed.

Tze snapped to attention and clicked his heels together and smiled sardonically. Kim shivered at the sight.

"Scared me and I'm fearless…mostly."

"You'll do fine. I want the guards in the pagoda to be shaking in their boots when you two show up. If necessary, we can press the story that Shang Xiao Gwok Wei was supposed to transfer the spy to Beijing. We'll airdrop two Raptors on the roof to secure the thirteenth floor. That's where HVT one is most likely to be. Here are photos of both Admiral Huang Meng and Lan Chen. The rest of the team will be stationed just around the perimeter and able to provide support. If things turn really bad, the Eagles can level the place if needed. You'll be able to communicate with the rest of the teams with these," Bad said as he handed over two tiny cone shaped flesh colored devices.

"What are these for?" she asked.

"Two way transceivers, four mile range," Tze said turning his head and pointing to his ears.

She leaned in to study the almost invisible devices.

"I can barely see them! Ours at the Company are twice that big!"

"The BEF has its own R&D division."

"It still feels like I just found out that Santa Claus really exists."

"How's that?" asked Bad.

"You guys are supposed to be a myth, you know like Zorro? One of our agents claimed he was part of a big deal with the BEF in the Gulf a couple years ago. Everybody thought he was blowing smoke. Now, I not only find out that you're for real, but I'm actually going to be part of your strike team. I am totally blown away. How do you manage to stay so far under the radar?"

"Simple," said Tze. "We don't leave survivors. Anybody that finds out about us just ceases to exist."

"Ha, ha…Not funny, Tze."

"Which dialect are ya'll going to be using?" asked Bad.

"Mandarin," Tze and Kim said together, then looked at each other and grinned.

"They speak Mandarin in Zhejiang province," said Kim.

"Uh huh, better you than me," offered Bad while he set a leather briefcase on a table and opened it. "Here is your valise,

Ki…uh, Liang. You'll notice that inside, is a Magpul FNG 9 sub gun and your interrogation kit. And here are your hideaway hand guns," Bad said as he handed suppressed Sig 232 pistols to Tze and Kim. "You'll go down with Dare and Bull in Eagle 1. The rest of Raptor Team Four will follow in Eagles 2, 3 and 4. We have identified a nearby village where you should be able to commandeer a vehicle. If we can find a secluded spot to set down close by, we will, if not, we fast line. Done that before?"

"On occasion. Glad the women in the Chinese Navy are allowed to wear pants," replied Kim.

"Good point," said Bad. "Actually we have some black coveralls for you to wear over your wardrobe if you have to fast line. Just shed 'em when you get down and tie them to the line. We don't leave anything behind. We don't exist, remember?"

HONOLULU, HAWAII
Friday Night, 8 November

Dr. Kelli Johnson edged past the nurse's station in the Pearl-Hickam Base Hospital and smiled as she addressed the pair of third shift professionals, "How's he doing?"

"Fine, Doctor, the flight surgeon said he can return home tomorrow. He wanted to keep him one last night, even though the CAT scan came back negative."

"Thanks, I'm just gonna pop in and see if he needs anything."

"Yes, Ma'am, go ahead. I don't think he's asleep yet."

Kelli entered the room quietly, in case he had drifted off to sleep. The lights were dimmed, but she found James propped up looking out the window. “Hey, jet pilot, anything thing I can do before I call it a night?”

He rolled to toward her, and she was glad to see the patch had been removed from his left eye. The swelling was down considerably, although the bruising still made it look as if he had lost a ten rounder with a heavyweight contender. James tried to fake a smile and almost succeeded in fooling her. Tracks of a couple tears down his right cheek gave him away. “Hello, beautiful! We have to stop meeting like this.”

“Baby, are you in pain? What’s wrong?”

James took in a big breath then let it out. “I’m okay. Deacon’s wife and kids stopped by this afternoon to check on me. Can you believe that? I thought I was going to be the one to have to tell her the news about Bart…the wing king did it Thursday. And they were worried about me…”

“I know how close you and Deacon were, almost like brothers. I’m sorry her visit made you sad. Rhonda must be a very strong woman.”

“She is. I’d like for you to get to know her.”

“The nurse told me you get to go home tomorrow. It’s my day off…maybe we can spend it together.”

She noticed a fleeting look across Hollywood’s face. Something wasn’t quite right. “What’s wrong? Are you still thinking about Deacon and Rhonda?”

“I can’t tell you all the specifics, but I’ve been called to Arizona to command a squadron of F-15s. My transport leaves at 0930.”

"I thought all the F-15s were grounded! Why you? You aren't 100% yet. Don't they know…?"

"Sweetie…Sweetie, look, I, uh, don't know all the specifics, but my Dad was recalled to active duty as a four-star. He needs me to put together a squadron of combat veterans and Fighter Weapons School grads…I've got to go."

"This sort of thing doesn't happen very often, does it?"

"No…not in my career."

"Hollywood, do you think there is going to be a war?"

"As far as I'm concerned, the war started last yesterday. Whoever did this to us was not playing games. They sure as hell can't expect any mercy from me."

Kelli looked into his eyes and saw a change. No longer was he grieving the loss of his wingman and feeling the pain he empathized for his young wife and kids. James Stewart had reverted back into warrior mode. She pulled a chair beside the narrow hospital bed and laid her head upon his chest. He held her closer to him with one hand as he softly stoked her flaming red locks with the other. He stared at the light green ceiling as he tried to envision what the next few days would be like. Neither spoke a word.

AIRSPACE OVER NORTHERN PACIFIC
Saturday, 9 November

Relief pilots Julio Sosa and Bobby Mendez awoke to the gently shaking of their shoulders by Flight Engineer Mad Max Matthews.

"Hey, guys, it's time."

"Dammit, Max your timing stinks, dude!" Mendez grumbled from the top bunk.

"Who was she this time, lover boy?"

"Shakira! And we were on the beach at Puerto Vallarta. She had this totally hot gold thong thing and I…"

"Got the picture, Bobby. Almost makes me feel sorry for you." Max chuckled.

Julio popped out of the lower bunk and slipped into his fur lined house slippers with anti-skid rubber soles. He was still wearing the muted black Nomex flight suit worn by all Black Eagle Force pilots. As he folded the gray crew blanket for the pilots coming off duty, he ribbed Bobby, "Hey, cabrón, don't forget that dream. I want to hear every juicy detail, all the way to Korea."

Julio headed for one of the many lavatories to splash some water in his face and use the facilities before settling in the pilot's seat. Bobby stretched his arms over his head, yawned massively, and then eased his way to the galley coffee pot and poured himself a large cup. He worked his way into the expansive cockpit of the C-5M and stood behind Kit for a second.

"Where the hell are we, MC?" he asked.

Kit reached down and brought up a nav display menu, pressed an *AIRPORTS* icon and pointed at the nearest icon *ANC* at their twelve o'clock position.

"Magic box says Anchorage, Alaska. Sleep well?"

"You wouldn't believe. How's the bird?

"Great. No problemos. Just about ready for a step climb. Weather should be good until Nome. Forecast calls for light occasional moderate chop over the Bering Sea. Got us set up for a tanker out of Eielson at this point here just south of Galena," he said pointing at an icon on the route of flight.

"Cool. I have the duty, Kit, if you want to catch some Zs. Julio is leaking his lizard."

"Had that thought myself," Gears replied looking at his watch. It had been nine hours since *Mama Bird* lifted off the runway back at Grayson Regional Airport. "How's the temperature back there?"

"Must'a been perfect. Never missed a wink."

"We aim to please." Gears chuckled as Kit powered the seat back and right to facilitate his departure.

Kit stood partially up and stepped past the autopilot console between the two pilot's seats. Once fully clear of the overhead panel he straightened completely up.

"You've got it, Kemosabe," a tired and somewhat stiff mission commander said as he worked his way aft.

Bobby slipped himself into the gray lamb's wool covered copilot's seat, and then powered it up into position. He ran through a series of aircraft systems displays and cross-checked the navigation route of flight and refueling time schedule in the flight management computer. *Bueno. It's all good.* He turned to the flight engineer position and with a very creditable Cockney accent. "I say, old sport, might a man have a gander at the breakfast menu? I must declare, I am absolutely famished."

Five hours later, the second shift Loadmaster, Gunnz Garner, moved through the BEF pilot and Raptor rest area and woke the members of the planned assault teams.

"Briefing in 15," he said as he touched the arms of the persons closest to the outside aisle.

One by one, the members passed the word until all the appropriate team members were up and making their early morning preparations.

"So, Cowboy, did you finally get some sleep?" the statuesque blonde, Jill McElheney, asked her fiancé, Mike Hermann.

"Took me a while, Babe. Hard to shut off my mind sometimes. You know how that is?"

"Even hardheaded former Marines can use a little help some times. You should have listened to me about the Ambien. I told you Doc could hook you up. This half-way-around-the-world pre-positioning stuff is a bear."

"Tell me about it," he said sheepishly as he stood up to his full six foot three height and stretched. "I listened to you snore for two hours before I got Doc to give me one of those knock out pills."

"I don't snore!…Do I?" she asked.

"Like a grizzly bear in heat," he shot back at her as he smiled.

A tall woman with flaming red hair popped Mike on the back of the head as she passed him in the isle between the rows of recliners. "Ladies do not snore, brother dear. Besides, that's no way to talk to my future sister-in-law. 'Grizzly bear in heat'…my God."

"Come on, Sis, just havin' a little fun."

"Men…Anybody have an idea where we are?" Carla "Blaze" Hermann asked.

"About eighty-five miles west of Magadan over the Sea of Okhotsk. Two hours until we hook up with the KC-10 over Korea," Dare remarked as he returned from a short visit to the cockpit.

"Siberia? We're flying over Siberia?" Jill asked.

"A great circle route is shortest distance between two points on the globe. That's why we went so far north. We probably have been over Russian Federation airspace for a couple hours," Blaze added.

"I was going to say that was real nice of the Russians to allow us to overfly, but they don't know we're here, do they, boss?" Mike asked.

"Not likely. Lanie has been monitoring the Ruskies air defense network. Nobody down there seems to have a clue. We cross over a part of China and North Korea before we fall in behind our tanker."

"That's comforting to know. How's the coffee, Hon?" Blaze asked.

"Fresh pot. The usual, pretty lady?" Dare asked

"Please," she replied with her emerald green eyes sparkling.

"Coming up," he confirmed as he made his way to the galley.

The brainy Ph.D. from Rice University was almost twenty-one years younger than the silver-haired retired Marine colonel, but she still looked better two minutes after waking up than almost any other women he had ever known, even if they had been given an hour to prepare. She had been the design guru behind the BEF's array of futuristic electromagnetic coil guns and sonic weapons. Blaze had almost single-handedly saved the C-5M and its crew from destruction in an aerial engagement with a former Soviet MiG-29 pilot. Her rapid and effective actions had really impressed not only the *Mama Bird* crew, but also the CEO of the Black Eagle Force. She had not even been a member of the crew, but had read the operations manual of the complicated and capable aircraft, memorizing every system with her almost perfect "photographic" recall. The two had become colleagues, friends and eventually lovers. She served aboard *Mama Bird* as Defensive and Offensive Systems Operator.

BEF Raptor Snipers James "Ten Ring" Weber and William "Davy" Crockett crowded in behind Sean "Widowmaker" Baker" and Mickey Williams to get a cup of the fresh coffee to help shake away the cobwebs from the odd sleep pattern the all-night mission dictated. Rock Eddington jostled in line and rubbed sleep from his eyes. Dutch Offner, a multilingual member of the Raptor assault team had been picked to accompany Bad Poole on the paradrop on the roof. If they had trouble locating Admiral Huang Meng, his skill in Chinese would be vital in pumping information about his whereabouts in the headquarters.

"Come on guys, you move like old ladies. Ain't got all day. Gotta have my tea," Dutch grumbled to the warriors closer to the stainless steel galley.

"Man up, dude! Learn to drink Columbia's finest. You can't stand a spoon up in that weak ass shit you sip," Rock shot back at him as he filled his mug with the aromatic brew.

Dutch grabbed Rock by the collar and pressed his right thumb hard into a pressure point between Rock's ear lobe and jaw. The sharp pain almost caused Rock to spill his coffee.

"Say uncle!" Dutch commanded.

In a flash, Eddington snaked his free hand around behind him and grabbed Dutch by the crotch. His fingers were properly placed for a crushing blow, but stopped short of inflicted permanent harm.

A slightly high pitched squeak uttered from Dutch's lips, "Oooh."

"What was that word you wanted me to say, Dutchie boy?"

Dutch released his thumb pressure and was relieved that Rock likewise de-escalated.

Rock grinned and patted Dutch on the butt as he slipped by him. Blaze chuckled as she witnessed the interaction. She had grown to appreciate the camaraderie between warriors. Her brother Mike had served overseas in Iraq and Afghanistan for several years, earning two Silver Stars in the process when she was working on her doctorates.

"Boys will be boys," she said as she looked at Dare.

"Yeah, I can barely keep them house broken. Sometimes I think it's better that way."

In a few minutes, all the assault team and their alternates gathered around the planning table and Dare covered the details of the infil, execution and exfil portions of the plan. On a set of pull down wide screen video monitors, he showed detailed pictures of the pagoda grounds, the captive Lan Chen, and their high value target, Admiral Huang Meng.

WASHINGTON, DC
WHITE HOUSE
Saturday, 9 November

In the conference room next to the Oval Office, a harried President Thompson sat listening to the hawks and doves harangue each other. The entire National Security Council was present which included Secretary of Defense Baker, Secretary of State Harper, Admiral Valenti and Assistant to the President for National Security Affairs. Also invited were the Senate Majority leader, Speaker of the House, Head of the Armed Services, Committee, Director of the FBI and Director of the CIA.

"It's a God damned act of war, Madame President," shouted the Head of the Armed Services Committee, Senator Howard "Buck" Carter.

"We don't know who's behind it, Buck," replied Harper.

"The hell you say! Every one in the room knows it's the damned Chinese."

"They have unequivocally denied they had anything to do with that virus."

"Now that's a surprise," stated CIA Director Ambrose.

"When have they ever admitted to…"

"What about that fleet they're assembling?" interrupted Senate Majority leader Daniella Higgins.

"They claim it's just exercises, Madame Senator," offered Admiral Valenti. "But in my opinion, that's bull shit."

"I say let cooler heads prevail, no need jumping to conclusions," said Speaker Henry Harrison. "Let's negotiate."

"Negotiate my ass!" added Carter. "How many of our boys did they kill, Charger?"

"We've picked up two of the seven pilots that were missing, the other five are presumed lost, making a total of fourteen, and three were women…fourteen of our finest, not to count forty-nine fighters and one B-2."

"We only know that at least one Chinese, and that one possibly rogue, is somehow behind this. It is quite possible that the Central Committee truly has no knowledge. We hope to find out soon. The BEF should be on station in a few hours with orders to pick up Admiral Huang Meng and the American hostage. Plus General Stewart is putting together a fighter force as quickly as he can," said SecDef Baker. "However, I think we should make preparations to protect our nation…and that means do whatever it takes."

"Mr. Secretary, our last option is a nuclear strike on that Chinese fleet, should it approach our shores with hostile intent," said Admiral Valenti.

"With what, Admiral? Our planes won't fly," retorted Senator Higgins.

"Our B-52s will. Their electronics are still mostly analog. There are eighty-five active birds and nine reserve and we have sufficient warheads to arm them."

"Just how many do you think would actually get through to the fleet without fighter cover, Admiral?" asked Speaker Harrison, sarcastically.

"It would only take one, Mr. Speaker."

Upstairs in the living quarters of the White House, Gunter sat in his recliner reading a Dale Brown novel, *Fatal Terrain* when the President entered with a manila folder with the Department of Defense logo on the front.

"How's the book?" Annette asked as she walked over to her roll top desk.

"A lot better than what you're going to be reading, I suspect. Have to get away from the mad house down stairs?"

"You wouldn't believe the discussion going on down there with the NSC. I had to get out of there for a while, everybody pulling at me."

"Nature of the beast."

"Where do you think the BEF is by now?"

Gunter glanced at the antique clock on the mantel across the room.

"If they're not over Korea, they will be soon. It's Sunday night where they are."

"Sunday night?"

"They crossed the International Date Line."

"Oh, of course...All three of our children are going in harm's way, Hermie."

"I know, dear. This is something they chose to do. I'm very proud of 'em...They're just part of a lot of other of our best and bravest also going in harm's way for our country...There's something about a crises that seems to bring out true character."

"I hope mine holds up," she said with slight trepidation.

Gunter put down his book and replied, "You're doin' what you have to do, Annie. We've been attacked in a new way, but attacked we were."

"Charger thinks we should prepare a nuclear response with B-52s if the Chinese fleet lays off our west coast and all else fails."

"That is a viable option. But the SecDef has faith that General Stewart will be able to put that air wing together using the old iron and analog systems. The Reds won't be expecting that."

"You'd think the Chinese would have learned from the Japanese to not attack the United States of America."

"Apparently not."

AIRSPACE OVER EASTERN CHINA
Sunday, 10 November

Now on the other side of the International Dateline, the highly modified and deadly C-5M *Super Galaxy* passed over the lights of the bustling Chinese province of Jilin spread out below. In the foreground, just going under the nose of the only stealth transport/attack class aircraft in the world, was the city of Shenyang in the neighboring province of Liaoning to the south. From their vantage point at FL390, Gears and Kit could observe the night time panorama slipping almost silently beneath them. The Chinese cities sprawled out across the countryside with a spider-like web of lights and late night traffic headlights piercing the blackness. Beyond, an almost empty void of darkness defined the southeast Chinese border.

"Easy to tell where North Korea starts. Looks like a war zone down there. Almost no electrical power at all," Gears commented.

"Some folks just don't get it, do they? I pity the poor SOBs who have to put up with that moronic family keeping them at starvation levels. They spend whatever money they can squeeze out of their economy on modern weapons systems to terrorize their brothers to the south," Kit added.

"Once we are south of the DMZ, we'll begin a descent to pick up the tanker. I don't want our contrails to give us away."

"Good thinking. I'm allergic to visually guided SAMs…give me a rash."

"I heard that. Lemme give Blaze a call and see what's she's tracking," Gears said as he triggered the yoke mounted intercom rocker switch. "Weapons, AC, North Korea in seven mikes. Anything interesting?"

Blaze rolled her wireless mouse over the third flashing icon on her wide screen display. The drop-down box opened when she clicked it and described the nature of the threat.

"AC, Weapons, SAM search radars as expected along the border with China. No airborne radars detected."

"Copy. They're still in their standard paranoid state as if someone was going to invade and break their empty rice bowl. Let me know if anything changes."

"I'll do that, my friend. Weapons station clear."

Blaze glanced to her side at Tom Tallman seated at the *Manta* RPV station. Normally, Tom remained back at BEF headquarters in Grayson County, Texas. For this mission, Dare had decided to use his top people in every station. Tom had been an Army fixed wing and helo pilot, but had been recruited by the BEF for his computer skills. He had a Masters degree in Computer Science from Stanford that he picked up while on active duty in the Army. Like his name implied, Tom was, in fact, a tall man and, at six feet eight, too tall for US Air Force pilot training. The Air Force's loss was the Army's gain as he had been instrumental in the development of many of the Army's current small remotely piloted unmanned vehicles.

His confidence in Lanie, the usual *Manta* operator was unshakable, but the CEO had made the call and went with his absolute top remote pilot operator. Perhaps the cyberterrorism of the Chinese part led to the change, but Blaze had not bothered to ask her boyfriend why. She trusted his judgment with her life, as did all the other members of elite team.

The lights of Seoul, Korea just south of the DMZ demarked the visual change of the pro western democracy. The urban sprawl went on for miles, with the broad highways and boulevards snaking through the hilly South Korean terrain. The dark streak of black inside the capital city clearly showed the path of the broad, slowly moving Han River. Brightly lit glass high-rise buildings dotted the landscape, unlike the drab gray buildings in the darkened Communist country separated by the armed armistice line drawn across the Korea peninsula almost sixty years earlier at the 38th parallel. All the flight crew monitoring the position of the big bird breathed a tiny bit easier when the aircraft actually crossed the border to South Korea. The next hour and twenty minutes of the flight would be inside allied or international airspace.

Gears reached up and selected lower flight level in the flight management system and pointed to the digital readout for the altitude alert system.

"Descending to FL340," Gears announced.

Kit set the new altitude in the alert system and confirmed, "FL340, set and cross checked."

"Weapons, A/C, starting our descent for the refueler out of Kunsan. Let me know when you have a positive ID. Planned hookup is to begin over Lion intersection," Gears said over the interphone.

"Roger, A/C, Weapons currently tracking Texaco 59 climbing though FL210 at twelve o'clock and six-zero miles. Almost no additional air traffic noted. Not much moving within 200 nautical miles," Blaze noted.

"Just the all night freight haulers to the states. Let me know when Texaco hits FL340."

"Will do. Um…just out of curiosity, Gears, say the current winds at 350."

"Winds on the GPS show 275 at 190. Why?"

"Nothing, I thought I was getting a system glitch as the display just seemed off kilter. It took me a while to realize we had a monster right crosswind. Jet stream right?"

"You got it, girl. River of air makes it hard to fly into. Your ground speed just goes away heading westbound."

"What's the fastest ground speed you have ever seen with it as a tailwind?"

"727 knots over New York one night. By the way, Dare nearby?"

"I'm on the line Gears. Just finished breakfast and I'm looking over Blaze's shoulder at the display."

"Good. You wanted a call one hour out before the descent to launch the Eagles."

"'Preciate it, pal. Everybody has been rested, watered and fed. We'll have one last brief once we get the latest intel from the tanker crew, then head downstairs to saddle up."

Dare removed the interphone wireless ear bud and boom mic and laid it on the console. He placed his hand on the redhead's shoulder and gave her a gentle squeeze. "Be right back." Dare unbuckled the lap belt on the gray high back chair where the secondary weapons controller would be positioned if needed. He stood up and worked his way back to the BEF *Eagle* drivers. "Bull, how are all the primaries doing? Everybody good to go?"

"That's affirmative, Boss. They're lungin' in the traces. Haven't seen any action in a couple of months, you know."

"Yeah...One hour before descent to launch."

"Got it. I'll pass the word," Bull said as he checked his wrist watch.

Dare approached the BEF Raptor team leader and gave him the same information.

"Roger, Boss. Briefing update at 15 after?" Bad Poole asked.

"Sounds right, the tanker crew got the latest satellite photo intel and weather before dark. We'll get it when we hook up. It seems too bad we can't use the MILSATCOM to talk to anybody, but the DoD wants the Chinese to think we shut it down completely. Only line of sight encrypted radio and fiber optic is authorized...We'll find out soon enough."

DAVIS-MONTHAN AFB, ARIZONA
Saturday, 9 November

General Jack Stewart reviewed the inventory information provided by the 309th AMARG across the field. *At least the boneyard guys keep good records*. Even after a short night with a three hour nap aboard the C-37A provided by the 89th Airlift Wing, Jack was busy with his short term goals of identifying the best airframe assets with which to press forward. The top seven hundred candidates included those aircraft included in the highest level maintenance schedule, notably the B-1, F-14, F-15, F-111 and F-4s. Structural problems with the delamination of the air intake and wing root areas of the *Tomcat* had led to its early departure from the fleet. Only twenty-six of the mothballed veteran planes did not suffer from some sort of known structural defect. Sixty-one of the extremely capable F-111s were on the list, although some had their avionics cannibalized for other planes still on active duty when the early versions were sent to the desert. Forty-four would be left on his short list. The bulk of the remaining were Air Force, Navy and Marine F-4s with many of them being retired from active duty in 1996. Three hundred and eighty-nine sat wrapped in white plastic sheeting called *spraylat* after the company that produced the bug and dust proof stuff.

"General, a Colonel Bob Peterman is here to see you," Airman First Class Stevens called on the interphone.

"Thanks, Mindy, send him in."

"Good afternoon, sir! Colonel Peterman, reporting as ordered," the blond fighter pilot said as he snapped a salute.

Jack returned the salute and motioned for Bob to have a seat."Bob, as you are aware, a lot has happened since we flew together."

"I'd have to agree with you there, sir. My squadron lost six birds to whatever wiped out our FMCs. I see you've added some stars. They didn't waste time calling you back to active duty…What can I do for you, sir, considering all my Eagles are grounded?"

"Our mission here is to cobble together a fleet from the boneyard. We've got a week to ten days to get as many operational fighters as we can to interdict a presumed hostile

Chinese carrier task force. They'll be flying the latest J-10s and J-20s against whatever we have ready."

"A week? Not much time. Where are supposed to engage them?"

"If my gut is correct, off our west coast."

"You want me to command the Eagles we can make flyable?"

"You'll have one squadron. My son is inbound from Hickham to lead the other."

"I thought Hollywood was flying the Raptor?"

"He was. His experience in the F-22 will come in handy against the new J-20 Chinese stealth fighters. You two have the pick of any combat experienced Eagle drivers, world wide, past or present. Get them here, get them trained, and do it fast. Can you handle that?"

Peterman looked Stewart in the eye and never blinked.

"I'm your man, General."

"Thought you would be. See Airman Stevens outside for your lodging assignment. Personnel and Logistics are in the next two offices down the hall. Give them your requirements."

"I'll get right on it, sir."

With that, the able Colonel stood, snapped a salute and departed. Jack watched him walk toward the door when the interphone rang again.

"General, I have Colonel C. J. McElhenny and Admiral Sievers to see you."

"Send them in," he said as he rose to meet them at the door.

The colonel—at six foot three, was a trim athletic looking man with closely cropped blond hair turning to silver at the temples—held the door for a slightly shorter and heavier Admiral. Both men wore short sleeved polo shirts and looked as if they could have just walked off the base golf course. One of them had.

"Admiral, great to see you again. Thanks for coming on such short notice," Jack said extending his hand.

"Good to see you, too, Burner. Your message said urgent. Sounded important."

"Burner, just got your message when I got back to my car. Usually don't carry my cell on the course," McElhenny said. "Are those real?" he asked pointing at the four silver stars on the dark blue epaulets.

"Fraid so, Heater. Sit down guys. I have a proposition for each of you."

Minutes later, Jack had laid out his plan. McElhenny was offered the F-4 Group Commander slot and Admiral Snake Sievers the F-14 Squadron.

"General are you forgetting the fact that the Navy fired me after that Las Vegas Tailhook Convention?"

"Snake, we both know the administration was looking for a scapegoat to please that bitch Senator from Colorado. She got her fifteen minutes of fame and the best swabbie fighter commander I know of got his wings clipped. I'm not forgetting anything, Admiral. I have the authorization to reinstate you at full rank and pay. Dammit, Snake, I need the best people I can get with Tomcat experience. You can pick your crews and I'll transfer you to the Navy for deployment. I need an answer, yes or no."

Sievers ran through his reasons not to take the job in his mind. There were several. He wasn't forty years old and indestructible any more. The doctor had told him the previous week that the biopsy indicated Stage 3 pancreatic cancer. The Navy had burned him as the most senior officer in attendance at the Convention, even though he was fast asleep at the time of the most egregious acts taking place in the hallways. But the list of reasons to take the job was short. His country needed him and his talents. *I have one last chance to salvage my reputation.*

"I'll do it, Burner, by God, I'll do it."

AIRSPACE OVER YELLOW SEA
Sunday, 10 November

"Texaco 59, Galaxy 1 is one thousand in trail, how copy?"

Inside the KC-10, the copilot jumped at the call. He had been watching the radar system for sign of the scheduled refueling recipient without success. Major Montgomery shook his head at his younger copilot.

"Jesus, they could have told us it was a B-2!" the first lieutenant exclaimed.

"Galaxy 1, Texaco 59 roger, read you five by five. Say aircraft type and requested indicated airspeed," the aircraft commander responded on the designated secured comm frequency.

"We're a Charlie Five Mike requesting two-eight-five knots indicated," came the reply.

"Roger the airspeed. Boom will call you in sight. Fly the lights. I have message for you when you are ready to copy," the KC-10 pilot advised.

Aboard *Mama Bird*, Gears clicked off the autopilot in preparation for the hookup. He pulled the throttles back slightly to slow the speed overtake. Kit was handling the radios and fuel valves with Dare sitting in the cockpit jump seat to receive the message. Dare nodded to Kit that he was ready.

"Galaxy 1 ready to copy message."

"Message reads as follows. Quote: Hotel Victor Tango seen entering target area at 0200 Zulu. End quote, over," the major said slowly and clearly.

"Copy message. We'll turn our cockpit lighting up for your boom operator. We're a little hard to see."

"Texaco 59, roger." Montgomery switched to interphone. "Boom, you got anything?"

"Negative, sir. Not a...Holy shit! That C-5 was *right* beneath me! Never saw him coming."

"Just give the man some gas, like he asked for. You do remember how to do that, don't you?"

"Yes, sir. Hey, they just turned a set of small LEDs on near the receptacle. I don't know what they painted that bird with, but I can't see anything but two windows and a refueling box."

The staff sergeant skillfully guided the stainless steel fuel probe to the rectangular slot in the top of the C-5M and extended it until a contact light illuminated on his panel. “Galaxy 1, I show contact. Insure valves and crossfeeds set.”

“Texaco 59, Galaxy 1 confirms contact with fuel valves open and crossfeed set.”

The staff sergeant toggled three pumps aboard the KC-10 sending 1,200 gallons of fuel per minute down the probe.

“Galaxy 1, positive flow,” confirmed Kit.

Gears focused his attention on the delicate task of keeping nearly a half million pounds of aircraft positioned solidly beneath the tanker for the next thirty-five minutes. The C-5M would gain an additional 275,000 pounds of fuel before the tanks were full.

“You boys are busy and I have a briefing to give before we launch. Call me if anything changes,” Dare added as he unbuckled from the jump seat.

“Good luck, Boss,” Gears said without taking his eyes of the tanker.

“Thanks. Hope we don’t any, but we’ll take it,” Dare said as he placed his hand on Gears’s shoulder.

Kit shot a quick glance over his left shoulder at Dare. Their eyes met for a second before each nodded a brief warrior’s good-bye. Neither man said a word. They didn’t need to.

Thirty minutes later, with the briefing complete, Raptor teams and *Eagle* crews headed down the metal stairs to the cavernous cargo deck. Crew chiefs had the yellow DO NOT FLY pins and streamers removed from the gear and pitot static systems, but the armament safety pins would remain until just before departure. The first four people made their way single file down the crowded alleyway beside the line of parked M600/As. As they reached the last of the sleek dark gray craft, the sliver-haired man in a black flight suit spoke to the man following behind him. "Bull, you can start the interior check, I'll get the walkaround."

"Got it, Boss. Come on Tze, I'll let you show Kim the emergency oxygen system and the fastline setup."

A mechanic called to the pilot from just aft of the front nacelles. "No maintenance writeups, Dare. Eagle 1 is all ready except for the tiedowns. We'll get those just before we depressurize."

"Thanks, Marty."

Dare began his preflight inspection as Bull with Tze and the CIA agent Kim Wu, the team members selected to recover the American hostage, entered the crew door located on the left side of the fuselage just in front of the folded rear nacelle strut.

Upstairs, Kit noted the fuel gages were approaching full, and not taking any chances, called the tanker before the autofill shutoff had a chance to work. "Texaco 59, discontinue fueling and cleared to disconnect."

"Roger Galaxy 1, fueling terminated and probe coming clear."

Kit monitored the *Contact* light extinguish and reset the fuel cross feeds for normal operations. Gears watched the probe retract and rise up into the stowed position along the Extender's fuselage. He pushed forward on the Galaxy nose to descend slightly and reduced power to provide additional separation from the tanker. He felt the tension in his traps as he rolled his shoulders.

"Hey, you want me to fly a while?" Kit asked.

"You have the aircraft," Gears replied.

"Roger, I have the aircraft."

Gears reached up and turned off the refueling receptacle light, dimmed the cockpit switches then toggled the transmit switch on his yoke. "Texaco 59, Galaxy 1, thanks for the fuel. Ya'll don't give green stamps any more?"

"Sorry, friend, we're fresh out. But you guys pull over and park, we'll be happy to clean the windshield, check the tires for ya."

"Maybe next time. Ya'll have a good evening, now."

Gears looked up to see the tanker probe operator wave before he turned off his refueling lights. The position lights of the tanker began to move slowly away.

DAVIS-MONTHAN AFB, ARIZONA
Saturday, 9 November

"So you think we really have a chance at competing with the Chinese Navy fleet fighters with a handful of Phantoms, Tomcats and Eagles?" a somewhat incredulous Heater McElhenny asked. "Nothing personal, Burner, but the Phantom had its hands full with the MiG 21s and from what I gather, the Jian-10 is equivalent with the F-16. Nobody knows what the

J-20 is really capable of, but it looks like they copied the airframe of the F-22."

"I know all that, Heater, in fact it's part of my plan. I'm betting they did copy the F-22 to the best of their technology. Their ability to copy the Russian fighters is what got them the contract for the Pakistani Air Force. What the Chinese do not have is a bunch of battle tested fighter pilots who can think for themselves. We saw that in Korea and again in Vietnam. Most of them are taught doctrinaire Soviet style air tactics, massive numerical advantage and win the war of attrition. The new Raytheon mods with a low PRF capability will be able to detect their J-20, denying them the stealth advantage the Chinese believe they possess. When we add the Lockheed radar coating to our fleet, the difference will be tactically astounding. You are gonna have to trust me on that, but I've seen the numbers, and your Phantoms will be radar invisible until they are almost in gun range."

"That would make a difference. I got bounced by more Raptors that I care to remember. It made me feel almost like a sitting duck, not seeing the bastards until after they called Fox Three!"

"Now you see the method to my madness."

"Hell, this could work! What else do you have up your sleeves, you sly old devil?" McElhenny asked.

"What we have in abundance are airframes and weapons. I'm pulling out all the stops to get multiple readiness lines working round the clock. I've got eight hotshot maintenance DCMs with hand select crews. Three are already here with the rest on the way. As many wrench turners as we can get on the field will be focused on the task of airframe regeneration. The guys at AMARG have printed out copies of the tech manuals needed for the older birds like the F-4. I've even got groups working on the Aardvark, Thud, and Starfighter."

"And all this came about because you thought the low PRF could be a threat to the F-22. Freakin' amazing."

"Yeah, but actually, the catalyst was I didn't let myself get boxed into thinking newer is always better. It can be, but in the hands of a skilled fighter pilot, the old iron may just the ticket to kicking that Chinese fleet all the way back to Shanghai."

"I'll drink to that! When do you want me to start?"

"Heater, what the hell are you doing in my office? I believe you have work to do."

McElhenny stood, faced Jack and snapped a salute. "I'll get you two hundred crews, General."

"Countin' on you," Jack said as he returned the salute.

***

CHAPTER EIGHT

AIRSPACE OVER EAST CHINA SEA
Sunday, 10 November

The lights of the KC-10 grew smaller as Gears entered a shallow descent and turned slightly east of the airway. Traffic was almost nonexistent near midnight.

"Recon, AC," Gears called on intercom.

"Go ahead AC, Recon's up," replied the lanky Tom Tallman.

"Let's get Manta airborne. We'll be launching the Eagles as soon as we get down to 12,000."

"Can do, will call before release."

Tom turned to Lanie Hayes, former Sergeant USAF missile specialist. The petite woman with shoulder length light brown hair sat beside the former Stanford basketball star.

"Pre-launch checklist, please. About to start earning our pay."

The pair ran though the lengthy list of systems checks covering everything from battery voltage, gyro stabilization and satellite position feed. Tom toggled starter switch. "Starter engaged, we have rotation," he confirmed as the engine RPM was rising on the monitor's feed from *Manta*.

"RPM above 17%, fuel selector *On*."

"Roger, fuel selector is *On*."

"If no light within fifteen seconds of fuel valve open, discontinue engine start attempt."

"Roger."

Tom counted the seconds after the fuel valve cycled by watching the digital clock readout on the bottom of the screen.

"Fourteen, fifteen, aborting start," Tom said as he clicked the *Abort Start* icon. "Shit!"

"Confirm starter disengaged by RPM decrease."

"Roger, RPM is dropping below 5%."

"Do not reengage starter until RPM is zero."

"Roger, RPM coming to zero."

"Clear to attempt restart. Oh, by the way, the last mission over here it took three attempts. I think the engine was really cold soaked," added Lanie.

"Eighteen hours at minus sixty-five? Guess so. We'll try one more attempt at altitude, then wait until we get down in the denser air."

Blaze watched the exchange between the two seated at the next station. *I bet an electric heat blanket wrapped around the engine would alleviate that problem. Have to talk to Gears about it when we get back.*

The second attempt was a no-go also. As the *Galaxy* approached fifteen thousand, the third attempt was good.

"EGT stabile at 430°. RPM in the green band."

"Starter disengaged. Hydraulic pumps on," Lanie continued with the checklist.

"Hydraulic pumps on."

"Flight interface, engage."

"Flight interface engage is green."

"Standby to release."

"Roger, standing by."

Tom switched from stations only interphone to all aircraft interphone position.

"Manta ready for launch."

"Mike Charlie is go," replied Kit.

"Alpha Charlie is go," confirmed Gears.

"Power setting…match," Lanie said.

"Power setting is matched."

"Trim setting, point five degrees nose down."

"Trim setting confirmed."

"Cleared to release uplocks."

Tom moved his right hand to the joystick and clicked the red *DISENGAGE* icon with the wireless mouse. Strong electromagnetic locks opened, freeing the deadly ray-shaped URF—the weight of it leaving the port wing caused the giant *Galaxy* to roll slightly to the right. Gears stopped the roll at four degrees and held it until the URF cleared.

Tom pressed forward on the *Manta* joystick until his altimeter read fully 100 feet below that of the *Galaxy*. "Manta is clear. Climbing to FL220," he called to Gears.

"Copy that, Recon. All personnel stand by for depressurization."

Gears retrimmed the *Galaxy* until it was stable in a slight descent with both wings level. He removed his hands from the yoke. It remained stationary level and the attitude indicator didn't budge. He re-engaged the autopilot.

"Passing one-three for one-two thousand," Kit advised.

"Roger, one to go," Gears confirmed. "Time to launch the Eagles."

Gears reached over and changed the airspeed in the Flight management system to 250 KIAS.

DAVIS-MONTHAN AFB, ARIZONA
Saturday, 9 November

"General, the commander of the Arizona National Guard wing on line two."

"Thanks, Mindy." He picked up the hand-piece and pressed the lit button.

"Afternoon, Ted. Figured I would be hearing from you."

"Yes, sir, Burner. Look, I'll get straight to it. I don't know what you guys are up to, but I hear things are going crazy over at the AMARG. With my Viper fleet grounded until we get a boatload of black boxes, we are kinda twiddling our thumbs over here. I have close to two-hundred-fifty qualified mechanics in for the weekend drill. If you have something going on that can use skilled knuckle-busters, my guys are yours."

"I can't discuss the specifics for security reasons, but I need all the able bodies I can get. Have them bring their tools, also. Can you arrange for some bus transport? I'm told parking is getting tight on that side of the field."

"I got it covered. Hell, even some of my young jocks want to get in on the action. A couple of them saw your maiden flight in the Starfighter. Guess the old birds never lose their pull on us."

"I suppose they never do. Appreciate your assistance, Ted. I mean it."

"Any time, General. Mind if I swing by in a couple hours? I've got something else I'd like to run by you."

"I'll make time. Gonna be here until late, I'm sure."

"See you then."

There were two quick knocks on the door as Jack sat the phone down. The door swung open and Hollywood stepped inside.

"Colonel Stewart reporting as ordered, General."

Jack took one look at James' bruised face.

"Son, you're a mess! Gotta learn how to lead with your left or duck," he said as he walked around the perimeter of the walnut desk and gave his son a bear hug.

"Yeah, but you oughta see the other three guys…How's it going?"

"Better than I have a right to ask. We have a ton of folks ripping off spraylat and aircraft being towed in all directions. I got some really sharp logistics and maintenance types working for us and they are breaking down each fighter system and assigning teams to get the work flow done as quickly as they can. I brought in Flash Peterman to command the other Eagle Squadron. Heater McElheney is my number two and group commander."

"Good men. How about the F-4 squadrons? Who were your picks?"

"Got three enroute. Marty Ellington in from San Antonio…he was with the 479th at George. Even flew as Robin Olds' wingman in the Triple Nickel. Also, Alex Fuller, formerly with the Sundowners. And a crusty old Marine called Wardog Reynolds. Three time MiG shooter off the Oriskany."

"Now, there's the experience you wanted. I guess some of the Phantoms are Navy."

Right, and I know the CNO will want as many as we can generate. As I told the SecDef, a Navy without planes…"

"Is an expensive sailing club," Hollywood finished the sentence for his father.

Jack chuckled. "Had lunch?"

James shook his head.

"Come on, I hear they have a cafeteria open on the first floor."

"Can't fight a war on an empty stomach."

AIRSPACE OVER EAST CHINA SEA
Sunday, 10 November

"Max, depressurised at this time, clear to launch the Eagles," Kit transmitted over the intercom.

"Copy, clear to launch," replied the burly loadmaster.

Like most BEF members, he was cross-trained to handle multiple jobs. Max checked the safety strap attached to his harness one last time before he turned on the low-level red lighting and killed the bright halogen lights that lit the cargo bay like day. He grasped the aft ramp lever and pulled it down the center position. Outside, the clamshell doors of the C-5M empennage opened and the massive ramp began to lower. The noise inside the long cargo bay was deafening—as if a thousand angry hornets were circling. Each BEF *Eagle* had all eight Rotopower engines idling and even at low power, the spinning blades and exhausts created a mini-maelstrom inside.

Max eyeballed Dare in the left seat of *Eagle 1*. Dare gave him a thumbs-up and Max responded by engaging the track system mounted in the cargo bay floor. All four *Eagles* moved in unison until Dare's lead aircraft was positioned on the ramp, which extended out into the darkness. Max formed a signal resembling football goal posts with his arms, then lowered his forearms until they were in a level position.

"Here we go. Bull give me rear struts down and locked," Dare said in response to Max's hand signals.

"You got it," he replied as he shifted the mechanical lever down and pushed it in.

The M600/A struts responded to the hydraulic pressure on the internal bellcranks, and in seconds, the rear struts were completely horizontal. Titanium locking pins slid into place to assure strut rigidity. Bull observed the amber *In Transit* lights were replaced by green *Locked* indications that extinguished after five seconds.

"Down and green."

"Down and green confirmed," Dare said as he gave Max another thumbs-up signal.

Max spun his upraised index finger in small circles near his head. Dare grasped the side mounted single control stick with his right hand as his left hand eased the throttles forward. With slight back pressure on the stick, the four nacelles at the end of the wing-like struts tilted upward until they reached the maximum forty-five-degree point. A set of parallel louvers at the rectangular back end of the nacelles were computer commanded to a full down position to allow the craft to lift off vertically. Dare adjusted power until the green *Weight on Wheels* light faded.

"We're flying, Boss," Bull said matter-of-factly.

"Roger," Dare said as he focused on the extremely hazardous portion of the launch.

Max snapped a salute that was returned by Bull Gaspar in the WSO seat. Dare increased the stick back pressure, allowing the louvers to creep ever so slightly forward and inching the *Eagle* rearward. Three seconds later both men could see the aft edge of the ramp.

"Gear up," commanded Dare.

"Gear coming up," replied Bull as he grasped the small clear acrylic tire on a lever and pulled it out then up to the retract position.

Dare eased back on the throttles, causing the *Eagle* to sink and separate from *Mama Bird.* The tiny dark gray craft rocked hard a couple times when it hit the turbulent air beneath the *Galaxy*, and then smoothed out as it leveled off one hundred feet from the huge ship.

"Gear up and locked, after take off check list complete."

"Roger, checklist complete," replied Dare as he banked left and headed out to a pre-briefed position some five hundred feet from *Mama Bird.*

"Can I breathe now?" a very nervous Kim Wu asked.

"Sure. You can also quit crushing my hand," replied Tze Yen seated beside her in one of the two rear seats.

Kim sheepishly released his hand, not realizing she had grabbed it instinctively during the launch. "You guys do this every mission?"

"Yep. Sometimes twice," he said smiling. "Gets easier…Just wait 'till we dock."

"Joy…Looking forward to it."

Aboard the *Galaxy*, Max supervised the launch of the other three *Eagles* who formed a loose echelon formation below and south of *Mama Bird.* He raised the ramp to its upppermost position and watched for the green light signaling the outer clamshell doors had closed.

"AC, Load, we're buttoned up downstairs. Cleared to repressurize and turn as necessary."

"AC copies, pressure coming up."

Kit reached overhead and returned the pressurization to automatic. Everyone on board felt the change of pressure in their ears.

"All personnel, cleared off supplemental oxygen," Gears broadcast over the C-5M PA system. He removed his own quick-donning mask and stowed it in the receptacle on the left side of the fuselage. Pulling his boom microphone back down near his mouth, he called to Blaze on the interphone. "Weapons, AC, how we doing on the Chinese radar? Any change in search patterns or intensity?"

"Negative, AC. Cleared to turn back out to sea for your planned holding orbit."

"Copy that, sixty miles off shore is as close as I want to be."

Gears selected a cruising altitude of FL280 to minimize fuel burn and reduce ground noise from the sound of the four huge turbo fans powering the gargantuan aircraft. Intelligence from the DoD had pinpointed likely sources of Chinese defense radar along the coast, and mission planning had allowed the *Galaxy* to remain pointed at the closest and strongest source of search radar. Opening the clamshell doors and ramp was a problem only for sites astern where the aircraft interior could reflect radar beams.

Tom Tallman leveled *Manta* at FL230 where the noise of the stealthy URF would not be detected on the ground. A high overcast layer at twenty thousand feet above the Chinese coast obscured the terrain, but the lights of the cities could be seen as bright glows down in the gray mass. He set the cruise speed at 450 knots to stay ahead of the *Eagles* who relied on the slightly faster miniature B-2 look-alike to provide radar and battlefield situational awareness. Sophisticated telemetry and friend-or-foe software derived from the US Army Future Warrior program was adapted to the BEF's needs.

Even as the five craft neared the target area, the four *Eagles* maintained position by using the inputs from *Manta.* The advantage of the BEF *Lizard* adaptive chromatic camouflage made it almost impossible for one crew to see another *Eagle* when it was engaged. Formation flying, like that which thrilled crowds in air shows, was virtually impossible; therefore, each pilot attempted to maintain a thousand foot separation horizontally.

"Boss, I see Manta beginning its descent," Bull noted.

"Right, Tom has to get under this layer to find a set of wheels for our friends in back. We can't just have them walk up in the middle of the night."

"Yeah, a bluff will only work so far. A Cheng Feng Limo would do nicely if we had a driver," Tze added.

"Get me one of 'em and I'll drive it," Kim shot back. "The Company bought a couple for training purposes."

"A limo's a possibility, but how are you at hot wiring the ignition?" Dare asked.

"Don't want to talk out of school, but I could have starred in the movie Gone in Sixty Seconds without props or doubles." She laughed.

In *Eagle 2*, Jill "Lucky" McElhenny monitored the flight instrument display as Glenn "Bug" Haug crosschecked the battlefield threat assessment on the large LED display in front of him.

"Anything interesting, Bug?" Bad Poole asked from one of the back seats.

"Not much happening, thank God. These folks are not nearly as paranoid as the North Koreans."

"Guess not. They already knocked out our Air Force and Navy fighters. What the hell do they have to worry about?" Jill snapped back.

"Easy there, Lucky. Didn't mean to step on your toes. But really, we're gonna have their top Admiral in our custody in less than an hour," Bad added.

"Sorry guys, I'm more than a little ready for some major payback. I lost two good friends last Thursday in F-22s."

"They never recovered the guy off the east coast, did they?" Bug asked.

"No, and I dated him at the Academy. He was in a class ahead of me."

"Sorry for your loss, girl…Hey, here's a visual coming in from Manta."

Bad and Dutch leaned forward and tried to make out the greenish-gray infrared image.

"Where's the pagoda?" Dutch asked.

Bug slid his gloved finger over the screen to a point at the end and on the south side of the long bay leading to the East China Sea. "It should be about…"

"There," Bad said as a yellow circle appeared on the screen. "Looks like Tom beat you to it."

"Yeah, well, I hope so, his screen is seventy-two inches wide and he can split it to use two types of sensors at once," Bug admitted.

"Man, that's a long bridge across the bay. How far is that from the pagoda?"

"Roughly twenty miles, or twenty-six clicks as the crow flies. You aren't planning to hitch-hike are you?"

"Not me." Dutch laughed. "I prefer air mobile to infantry."

"Just wondering. Winds are just a light onshore breeze tonight. Should make your jump easier," Bug noted.

"Yeah. We gonna need some good conditions for a roof jump. That sucka's not even flat. It'll look like a bar of soap from 500 feet."

"Aw hell, Bad, if this job was easy, anybody could do it."

"Keep thinking that, Dutch. Just keep thinking that."

A thousand feet to the south, Mike Hermann and Maria "Double D" Sanchez in *Eagle 3* kept Ten Ring and Rock Eddington updated as to their current location.

"Double D, can you zoom in on the northeast section of the perimeter wall?" Ten Ring asked.

"Sure, the feed is high def digital and we can break it down to a four-inch res from Manta's present altitude. What're you looking for?"

"We need an elevated sniper hide and I want to check out the tree two hundred yards off the riverbank. Rock will pick a spot a couple hundred yards up hill."

"Bet I can find ya good one. How about this?" she said opening up the display by spreading her fingers on the screen.

"That's cool, can you make it bigger?"

"I'll put you inside the stinkin' tree, if that's what you need…There, close enough for you?"

"Whoa, I can see the branches fine. Don't suppose you can rotate that view ninety degrees and let me see a side view, can you?"

"Damn! You Marines are gettin' soft in your old age. What ever happened to crawlin' in on your belly like a reptile?" She laughed as she tapped the image twice. A white square appeared around the tree. She entered a series of commands in the Control Data Unit, called a CDU for short. The image rotated as she commanded, and after she touched both opposite corners of the image, expanded it to full screen. "How's that for you, Mr. Sniper?"

"Sweet! Didn't think you could really do it!"

"The software is like Photoshop, so it's really useful for some applications."

"Don't forget to tie your ass in, partner. A fall from up there is hard on the equipment."

"Bite me, Rock, I haven't fallen since that mission outside Fallujah."

"Told you that friggin' tree was unlucky."

"That you did, brother, that you did."

The two Raptors assigned to cover the waterfront of the pagoda grounds were Sean "Widowmaker" Baker and former Secret Service Agent Mickey Williams. Mickey had been the lead agent assigned to the primary team protecting President Thompson. When she and her fiancé Gunter Hermann disclosed the fact that they were his biological parents, he was forced to leave the Presidential detail. Mickey had been offered a chance to join the Black Eagle Force and readily signed on as an elite Raptor.

"Hey Rat, can you give us a IR scan of the riverbank a click either side of the pagoda?"

"Looking for hot bodies on sentry detail?" WSO Rat Hampshire asked.

"Precisely. You ever do any wet work?"

"I deny everything and demand proof…Air Force special ops, combat controller."

"Thought you were a pilot?"

"I was, but did both because of my shooting and marshal arts skills. They needed some snake eaters to get into Afghanistan right quick and work with the Navy fighters providing close air support. Some of my buds still work with Dev Group."

"SEAL Team Six?" Sean asked.

"The same…Here we go, girls. I see two on foot patrol and, uh, oh yeah, there the little buggers are…A hidden little gun position. Let's see what we got when we zoom in…Flash suppressor resembles the MG-42. I see three heat signatures inside. It's probably not visible from the pagoda."

"Wouldn't want to screw up the view. Jesus, Rat, you oughta be a Raptor."

"Yeah, yeah, I'm a freakin' renaissance man. I'll stick with this WSO gig unless you guys get into trouble. Don't make me have to come get you."

The two former Marines exchanged glances.

"No sir, Rat, we won't do that," Widowmaker said.

Rat looked over at former USAF F-15 jock, Richard O. Webb, AKA "Captain Midnight". Both smiled under their O2 masks. Richard was no relation to his famous actor namesake—his father named him Richard after his boyhood Saturday morning TV hero back in the '50s. Ovaltine and all—thus he got the call sign, "Captain Midnight". The BEF was comprised of the most highly qualified warriors ever assembled. Each was skilled in more than one discipline and served as the needs of the organization required. Like the two young former Marines in the back seat, all members came to the shadow corporation by invitation only. They were the best of the best and virtually no one outside of a handful of people in the President's cabinet even knew they existed.

DAVIS-MONTHAN AFB, ARIZONA
Saturday, 9 November

Colonel Marty Ellington scanned the stack of fan folded computer paper in front of him. On the reams of paper was a list of pilots with the qualifications he had given the personnel support staff just thirty minutes earlier. Department of Defense records were cross referenced with IRS tax records as well as land line and cellular phone company data bases to create a quick call list. *Ain't computers grand*, he mused. *But, who in the hell still uses fan-fold paper?* He ran down the list until he saw a familiar name. *Gotta start somewhere.* He picked up his cell phone and dialed the number.

In Colorado Springs, a retired Lt. Colonel and his wife were walking across the parking lot of Falcon Stadium, where the two had witnessed the USAF Academy football team win its annual homecoming game against Colorado State. Boomer Bamhauer reached into his jacket and retrieved his phone. He glanced at the caller ID for a second, and then a smile crept across his face.

"Duke! You old fart! How the hell are you and why weren't you at the reunion?"

"Hey, Boomer, nice to hear from you, too. Sorry, but Sally was a bit under the weather, so we canceled this year."

"You missed a good game, 24-10, we kicked CSU's butt!"

"Great, uh, this isn't a social call. I don't have much time."

"Okay, get to it, brother."

"Boomer, if I needed you to fly a combat mission in an F-4, could you do it?"

"You been drinking? Hell, I haven't touched a Phantom in almost seven years, not since the Idaho guard unit phased 'em out. I'm retired."

"I know your status. I'm asking if you're healthy enough to do it. We need experienced pilots."

"Are you talking about the F-15s, 16s and 22s? Is that what this is about?"

"I'm not at liberty to discuss that."

"Holy shit! That's it, isn't it?" Boomer exclaimed as he shot a glance at his wife.

She looked at him and became alarmed.

"What is it Hon? What's wrong?"

Marty heard her questions over the open line. *Shit! This is gonna be tougher than I thought.* "Boomer, I can't be more specific over an unsecured line. Can I count you in?"

A thousand questions raced through Bamhauer's mind. He had known Marty "Duke" Ellington for over thirty-five years. If Colonel Ellington needed him badly, the reason must be serious. He glanced one more time into his wife's eyes as he replied, "When and where do you need me to be?"

AIRSPACE OVER HANGZHOU CHINA
Sunday, 10 November

"Tze, how does that parking lot look to you? There are dozens of cars and I think the warehouse would provide a cover for our approach and landing," Dare said.

From his rear seat in the Skycar, the display was not really readily visible. Tze sat up and looked between the two pilots.

"Bull, can you expand that?"

"Here you go," he said as he spread his fingers over the touch screen.

"There! Hey, pard, you like that one?" Tze asked Kim.

"I like it. It's far enough from the apartments and there are no heat signatures of guards. Works for me," the tall dark haired agent agreed.

Bull rolled a red arrow over the planned landing site with his trackball and doubled clicked the input pad, putting a small green circle on the map display in all four *Eagles*.

"Looks like we have about ten yards clearance between the back of the building and the rice paddy. Should be enough to keep you guys dry after we set down."

"Thanks, Bull. We'll be able to shed these coveralls and leave them with you," Tze said.

"Eagle Flight, Eagle 1 initiating a decent for insertion. Eagles 2, 3, and 4, cleared to maneuver as briefed at this time," Dare relayed over the comm frequency.

All but *Eagle 2* began to descend to their deployment locations. Jill and Glenn maintained 8,000 feet and proceeded directly to the pagoda.

"Guys, standby for jump in three minutes," she said.

Bad Poole and Dutch Offner unbuckled their lap belts and began a quick check of each other's jump gear. Dutch strapped an H&K MP-5 9mm subgun carrying 147 grain subsonic ammunition to his front D rings. Bad attached his Blaze G3 Carbine in a similar manner. A portable semi-automatic coil gun electromagnetically firing 7mm, ferromagnetic projectiles—the Blaze G3 Carbine was the third hypersonic coil gun designed by Blaze Hermann. It bore a rough resemblance to the Steyr AUG, but fired a solid metal projectile sharply pointed on one end with an extended boattail on the other. It had a ranging and aiming device that looked similar to a Trijicon four power tactical sight, plus a crosshair reticle that was tied to an infrared laser range finder. It engaged whenever pressure was applied to the trigger and automatically computed range to the target within 2.5 mils of the center of the crosshairs. Elevation compensation was automatic and almost instantaneous. The G3 fired the solid tungsten steel projectile, which had been designed to penetrate up to four inches of rolled armor plate and seventy inches of stone or steel reinforced concrete. Velocity of the carbine was user selectable between 11,000 and 4,000 FPS. Being electromagnetic, there was no empty brass to contend with—once a two pound force was applied to the trigger, seven sequenced capacitors discharged their stored electricity through the field generation liquid mercury-filled carbon-fiber nanotubes. The ferromagnetic projectiles were levitated with a magnetic field and made no contact with the bore. There was no recoil and almost no sound from the rifle being fired. The projectile generated a supersonic shock wave that tended to confuse an enemy who heard the passing projectile as it flowed away from the shooter.

As time to jump neared, both Bad and Dutch donned their sophisticated Raptor helmets with comm gear and vision enhancing cameras. Resembling a full face motorcycle helmet, they enabled the wearer over 300 degrees of small arms armor protection in addition to wind and chemical agents. Each man wore a small ruck under his parachute with a camelback water system and additional ammo for his weapons. Dutch carried a small interrogation kit and nylon restraints. Both had a rappelling rope to facilitate access to the top floor from the roof.

Dare approached the warehouse from over the rice paddy at a steep angle. He pulled back pressure with his left hand as he ran the power up slightly on the eight engines controlled by the central computer with inputs from the centrally located throttle quadrant. All four nacelles rotated upward to their limit as he skillfully and smoothly slowed the descent rate.

"Gear down," he called as he observed the grass at the edge of the rice paddy begin to show signs of the down blast from the *Eagle* vectored thrust.

Bull responded by placing the handle down and quickly confirmed safe indication as the three gears extended, "Down, three green."

Seconds later, without the use of any external landing light, Dare eased the small craft down gently on the pavement. He pulled the throttle to idle and maintained a sharp lookout outside the craft with his NVGs. "Clear outside, let's get this party started," he said.

"Crew door coming open," Bull responded.

As the gull-wing crew door opened on the left side of the fuselage, Dare turned and shouted over his right shoulder, "Good luck!"

The two clandestine passengers stepped out of the aircraft onto the pavement and quickly worked their way outside the noise and wind blast of the eight idling engines. In seconds, they were several yards away as the door closed hydraulically and they heard the engines begin to wind up. Both shielded their eyes from potential dirt and debris as the M600/A lifted off behind them. The turbulent air dissipated as quickly as it built up. Kim, or Shao Xiao Liang Ping as she would be known for the next hour or so, turned and looked for the departing *Eagle*. She saw absolutely nothing. Even though her partner was standing next to her, a strange pang of abandonment swept over her for a brief moment.

DAVIS-MONTHAN AFB, ARIZONA
Saturday, 9 November

Burner checked his watch. *Almost 1800 hours. At least we're making some progress here.* The interphone buzzed again.

"General Stewart, General Solomon from the Arizona National Guard is here to see you."

"Thanks, Mindy. Please bring him in."

Burner rose to meet his one-star guest from across the field. The two friends shook hands energetically, even though the fast pace of the crash effort to reactivate the long term storage fighters had begun to take a toll on the formerly retired Jack Stewart.

"Jack, you look good with four stars," Ed joked as Jack offered him a seat.

"To tell you the truth, I haven't spent much time looking in the mirror to check it out. You said you had an idea you wanted to run by me. I'm open for suggestions."

"It's obvious from the activity over at the AMARG that there's a big push to get the old birds up and ready in short order. I saw the phone banks you set up down the hall to call in personnel to fly and maintain those birds."

"Yeah, it's not really possible to do this without being seen. I've got a short string to work with…seven to ten days."

"I don't know what the threat is, but scuttlebutt has tagged the Chinese with the cyber attack. Anyway, if I'm any good at trying to second guess the SecDef, you guys are planning to regenerate four wings worth of mixed airframes, some of which haven't seen the sky in decades."

"Ed, I'm sure you know I can't release our specific logistic and tactical information for security reasons. I appreciate your offer of mechanics earlier today. My guys tell me they were a major help."

"Burner, here's my idea. I know you'll be bringing in some qualified, but non-current pilots and WSOs for the fleet. One major problem I see is that the simulators for all the old iron are gone, probably sold off years ago."

"That's what we found out. What's your point?"

"My Vipers are down, but the sims work fine. Another major consideration is your guys that haven't logged fighter hours in a long while could use some stick time in a fast mover.

Today's sims are fully day or night VFR capable and would help knock out the cobwebs, so to speak. The AIM-9 and AMRAAM launches look so damned realistic you think you actually fired one off the rails. I'm offering you the boxes and instructors 24-7 for as long as you need them."

Jack sat back in his chair. "Ed, you're a lifesaver. I screwed up and discounted the Viper and Eagle sims. Of course we can use the help…Tell you what, I'm going to put you in charge of aircrew training. Our mission is to prepare for a Chinese naval assault with six air wings off the west coast. I'll have Mindy get you an alpha roster of the pilots as we get them and you can work with the group and squadron commanders to hash out the specifics."

"Jesus H.! Chinese Navy? I suspected as much but had no idea about the timeline. We got a lot of work to do, boss."

HANGZHOU CHINA
Sunday, 10 November

Kim Wu lifted up on the flat metal slim-jim specially designed to enter the driver's side door panel between the glass and weather stripping. Tze Yen stood by, scanning the deserted parking lot for movement. The slight click told Kim she was successful.

"Hop in the back, Tseng Jm Leor," she said as she unlocked the other three doors.

"Yes, Shao Xiao," he replied in pitch perfect Mandarin.

Kim quickly screwed a small slide hammer into the ignition set and, with a rapid outward motion of the hammer head extracted the original control column mounted lock. She inserted the replacement set and placed the extracted one and her slide hammer back into her briefcase. By the time Tze had walked around the back of the car and opened the rear passenger door, Kim had the charcoal gray Cheng Feng sedan running. He settled in as she slipped the car into gear. Almost silently, the pair exited the parking lot and turned on to the deserted two lane road.

"Mike Charlie. Element One inbound."

Aboard the *Super Galaxy* sixty miles from shore, Kit monitored the pair's progress on the 72 inch flat screen. Real time IR feed from *Manta* followed the lone vehicle toward an intersection a mile from the Liuhe Pagoda. Tom Tallman had assigned a blue dot to the vehicle allowing all the *Eagle* and Raptors to follow their movements.

"Mike Charlie, tracking," was all he said as he watched the wide angle view of the pagoda.

Two blue dots assigned to the Raptors aboard *Eagle 3* appeared as Mike and Maria dropped them off behind the small wooded hill south of the pagoda. Hovering above the stunted evergreens, Mike had employed the fastline for Rock and Ten Ring's insertion. Rock was first out and quickly moved fifty yards away through the dark woods. Ten Ring followed seconds later.

"Eagle 3, Raptor Six, clear."

Aboard the *Eagle*, Maria pulled the short rope attached to the much larger fastline and rapidly pulled it back into the craft. Once the end was clear of the crew door, she closed the door hydraulically. “Buttoned up, Cowboy.”

“And we’re off like a prom dress, D,” Mike replied as the nimble craft picked up speed in a pre-selected departure path designed to reduce the noise signature across the ground.

Rock Eddington lead the way toward a crossing point on the roadway leading directly to the imposing pagoda. He crosschecked the *Manta* feed to confirm no Chinese ground personnel were outside the pagoda complex on the south side.

“Six, Five, cleared to cross,” he radioed to Ten Ring as he covered the roadway from the pagoda with his G1 coil rifle. The highly modified Remington 700 Varmint rifle was mated with a Leupold 4.5x14x50mm Mark IV scope with an illuminated reticule. The upgraded version of Blaze Hermann’s original coyote rifle could shoot a tungsten steel projectile at over 12,000 feet per second, obliterating human targets at ranges farther than the unaided eye could see. Carbon-fiber nanotubes filled with liquid mercury acted as superconducting magnets when energized by the vanadium pentoxide batteries. The capacitors recharged in .62 seconds and the batteries could fire 120 rounds before depletion. The rifle was very quiet when fired, although the hypersonic projectile did emit a distinctive crack at Mach 10, much like the sound of a bull whip. It also left a very faint blue ionized trail as it sped to the target, although in practical use, no one ever targeted by the G1 was ever able to evade its lethal round.

Ten Ring looked both ways as he stepped into the clearing beside the roadway. There was no reason to run across, as his *Lizard* cloaking device made him virtually invisible, even to his partner. Once across the narrow two-lane road, he eased into the edge of the vegetation. Rock maintained a vigil over the empty roadway for a minute, and then moved to a high point where he could monitor traffic inside the wall on the south side of the pagoda. Rock removed a pair of camouflaged shooting sticks from his ruck and made ready to engage any targets as necessary.

AIRSPACE NEAR LIUHE PAGODA
Sunday, 10 November

Captain Midnight settled *Eagle 4* to a beach some one thousand yards up the Qiantang River from the ten foot wall surrounding the Liuhe Pagoda. As soon as the landing gear touched down, Rat Hampshire activated the crew door on the port side allowing Mickey and Widowmaker to make a quick exit. They sprinted toward the tree line as *Eagle 4* lifted off back into the darkness before the crew door was even closed.

"Lizard on, activate HUD," said Mickey.

"Lizard on, activating HUD," confirmed Sean.

All Raptor team members wore a Graphene coated Kevlar helmet resembling a full face motorcycle helmet crossed with a *Stargate SG-1* Kull Warrior headgear containing their secure communications gear, multiple front and rear cameras plus sound amplification mics. The HMD was projected on the inside of the polycarbonate bullet resistant face shield and gave the Raptors infrared and visual feed from *Manta* as well as the location of all the other Raptors in the target area plus the tangos. Raptors were designated by blue dots, the tangos by red triangles. Since the development of the *Lizard* chromatic adaptive camouflage system that made the Raptors virtually invisible, they relied on the feed from *Manta* to keep them apprised of the location of all team members. NVG cameras built in to their futuristic helmets gave them a ground level perspective of their objective. Each Raptor had a miniaturized wrist mounted computer to control all the aspects of their comm and *Lizard* gear.

They started moving just inside the edge of the trees toward the distant wall.

"You take the east side near the wall, I'll take the west. We'll have the gun emplacement bracketed plus coverage of the two man foot patrol," Mickey said into the tiny mic embedded in the chin protector of his helmet.

"Roger that. With Ten Ring and Rock, that'll give us a 360 degree field of fire," replied Widowmaker.

"Copy," Mickey said as he tapped the control pad on his left wrist—Rock and Ten Ring's icons inside his HMD indicated they were moving into position near the gate at the back of the river facing Liuhe Pagoda.

AIRSPACE OVER LIUHE PAGODA
Sunday, 10 November

"Winds up here are 085 at 30, Lucky," Bug said in his usual droll manner.

"Thanks, 500 meters up wind should be sufficient for this altitude," Jill replied. "You two ready?"

"Ready as we'll ever be," replied Bad.

"Let's do it to it," Dutch added.

"Coming to a hover, kids. Five thousand feet as requested."

The small dark craft slowed to a crawl, the eight Rotopower engines inside the upward pivoted nacelles provided the thrust to the pivoting vanes that allowed the *Eagle* to become motionless as Bug hit the door open switch. Even with special sound baffling hush kits installed on the four nacelles, the close proximity of the port rear engine generated a significant buzz like a hornet's nest inside the craft as the door hinged upward.

"Lizard up!" Bad commanded as he unbuckled.

Dutch touched the small green reptile shaped icon on his wrist control pad, activating the electronic cloak. Bug turned in his seat and extended his left fist toward the two Raptors.

"Good luck, boys. Grab that SOB and let's get it done right," he said.

Both Raptors fist bumped the retired Marine Lt. Colonel. A highly decorated graduate of the US Naval Academy, class of '78, Bug had flown Super Cobras in the middle-east.

"See you at the pickup point, Lady Luck," Bad said as he patted Jill's shoulder.

"Watch your step, Bad. I heard the first one's a bitch."

"That's what they say," he said just before he dove head first under the open gull wing crew door.

Dutch gave Bad a two count and followed suit. Each man counted a-thousand-one, a-thousand-two, then pulled the ripcord on their parawing. A gentle tug pulled them erect as the opening shock jumping from a stationary craft was not nearly as violent as either a HALO free fall or static line jump at 130 knots. Bad checked his chute with his Infrared helmet camera. He pulled the right riser to clear the canopy overhead and confirmed his partner overhead likewise had gotten a good opening—he did. Bad settled in to maneuvering the rectangular chute for a landing on top of the 12th century edifice.

Small areas of patchy fog began to rise off the Qiantang River and drift upstream. He crosschecked the disposition of forces screen supplied by *Manta* and noted the other four Raptors were now in position to provide fire support. The vehicle carrying Tze and Kim had come to a halt before turning down the road leading directly to the pagoda's rear entrance. The relatively slow 20 FPS descent took slightly over four minutes. Poole liked jumping at night. No one had every shot at him at night, which suited him fine. He made small turning circles to increase his rate of descent then set up for the last approach into the waning breeze. His IR camera depicted the sloped roof perfectly.

Each one of eight ribs in the massive octagonal building roof met at the central point then ran outward some fifty feet and curled upward as it extended past the roof line. The seven story structure stood 196 feet high, but featured thirteen balconies on its exterior. Bad timed his approach perfectly and pulled down firmly on both risers the slow the descent. He took two quick steps up toward the center spire and rapidly spilled his chute.

Dutch was slightly off on his judgment of his descent and strained to touch the roof. His toes missed the rising joists by mere inches but his forward momentum took him over the pinnacle and toward the far side of the roof. Seeing his mistake, he released the downward pull on the risers and touched down firmly on the far side of the slanted roof. He fought to get traction as his forward momentum took him closer to the edge of the roof. The rubber composition of his combat boot soles skidded across the painted metal coating, until he caught an edge on the gutter tiles. The weight of his rifle and ruck pushed him over the edge of the classic Chinese structure. He wind milled his arms to try to regain balance as he looked down almost 200 feet to the ground.

A scream began to form in his throat as the certainty if his demise rocked his composure. He felt himself beginning to topple over when a violent jerk pulled him back and to the right.

"Come on, Dutch! Quit screwing around." the deep bass voice of Poole ordered over the BEF comm frequency.

Dutch stumbled backwards and caught himself on his right hand and knee. He looked up and across the rooftop to see Bad with his canopy riser pulled tightly into his massive hands.

HANGZHOU CHINA
Monday, 11 **November**

“Raptors One and Two in Position,” came the awaited call over the tiny earpieces inside the ear canals of the two agents in the parked sedan.

It was now just past midnight when Kim looked in the rearview mirror at Tze. He showed no emotion at all—his icy stare sent shivers down her spine. He simply nodded, so she put the car in drive and made the turn toward the pagoda. *Game face on.* She became the Shao Xiao Liang Ping shown on her counterfeit ID badge. In less than two minutes the sedan approached the guard house at the south end of the pagoda complex. Kim waited until she was within fifty feet of the guard house to kill her lights as was the requirement to access the pagoda grounds. She knew the guard’s night vision would be impaired and neither would be able to notice the license plates were not military issue.

A tired, but stern faced guard approached the driver’s window. “Papers and identification. I do not show any arrivals scheduled for this time,” he grumbled.

Kim handed him her identification. “Tseng Jm Leor, Central Security Office for prisoner pickup,” Kim stated in perfect Mandarin.

Mention of the Central Security Office startled the naval security guard. He shined a flashlight into Tze’s eyes. The light evoked a rapid reaction the guard had not anticipated.

“Get that cursed light out of my eyes, you imbecile! What is your name, sailor? Who is your commanding officer? Have you never been taught how to treat a member of the Central Office?"

Kim looked at the shaken guard with derision. "I would not cross him again, if you know what is good for you," she said coldly.

The guard stepped back and saluted. "I will notify the front desk you are coming."

"No, you will not. Hand me my identification. We will notify the desk personally. I wish to speak to your superior without further interference from you. Do I make myself clear?" Kim said.

"Yes, Madame Shang Xiao, as you wish!" the shaken sailor said as he handed her the ID. "Open the gate! Be quick about it!" he called to the other guard in the post.

The sedan sped toward the parking area before the lights came back on. The guard manning the barricade gate tried to put a lighter spin on the situation.

"Perhaps the Gobi Desert air will agree with you, Li Pan."

"It is not funny, comrade. Not funny, at all."

***

CHAPTER NINE

LIUHE PAGODA
Monday, 11 November

Kim pulled into the parking lot, turned off the ignition and turned to face Tze.

"Comrade Jm Leor, may I carry your briefcase?"

"I prefer to carry it myself, Shao Xiao Liang Ping."

She exited the sedan and walked briskly to the rear passenger door. Kim opened it carefully and stood at attention as Tze exited. He glared disapprovingly in character as he led them to the rear entrance to the pagoda. He stopped before the massive double doors and waited for the Lt. Commander to open the door for him. Along the narrow hallway leading to the central security desk were drab framed photographs of Communist Party Leaders with a life size portrait of Chairman Mao Zedong prominently featured in the center. Even in death, his visage held sway over party faithful. Both Tze and Kim bowed almost imperceptibly as they passed, as was the custom. The opposite wall carried pictures of the Peoples Liberation Army Navy Chain of Command down to the East China Sea Fleet. Just before entering the circular foyer, the two passed a eight foot tall painting of Admiral Huang Meng in a heroic pose, standing aboard the bridge of his new flagship *Sun Tzu* with a cruiser and several other support ships in the background. The relative size of the portrait and the three halogen lights illuminating it left no doubt about his personal concept of his self importance. In years past, such an obvious affront to the memory of the departed Chairman of the Party would not have been tolerated. However, many years had passed and several Premiers had come and gone since Mao died in 1976.

The sight of a pair of unknown faces entering the foyer after midnight confused and alerted the low level guard. Shang Deng Bing Chong held a rank equivalent to a seaman in the US Navy. He was certainly not expecting visitors during the graveyard shift. He sat up slightly straighter as he addressed the female officer, "May I help you, Commander?" he asked before his gaze was drawn to the imposing man in the gray suit.

"You can assist me," Tze interrupted. "I am Tseng Jm Leor, Second Assistant to the Standing Committee."

Tze noted the color drain from the young man's face. *Good. He has heard of the Standing Committee in the Central Office.* Tze's countenance never wavered. His eyes possessed a soulless quality that made the young man question why he ever joined the Navy. No one in his south China village had ever spoken directly to a member of the Standing Committee. Tze swore he could smell the fear begin to emanate from the sailor's pores.

"We are here at the behest of Vice President Xi Jinping. It is his wish that the American spy you hold prisoner here be transferred to Beijing for further interrogation. Take us to her immediately."

Shang Deng Bing Chong felt his heart pounding in his chest. He swallowed as he realized he was not the object of interest by the Standing Committee. He closed his eyes for only a moment and said a brief prayer thanking the spirits of his ancestors for watching over him. A curt question broke him from his flash reverie.

"Are you sleeping, sailor? The Second Assistant is not to be interfered with. We traveled most of the day and half the night to get here." Kim bore into him.

"No, Madame, I am not asleep. I am trying to remember what room she is in," he protested.

"I suggest you remember faster, Shan Deng Bing," Tze said with an unmistakable edge of malevolence to his voice.

Chong could not bring himself to look directly at him as he fumbled for the master keys in the desk drawer. He found himself panicking again as the prospect of displeasing the interior security forces of China. Stories of mock trials and summary executions of those taken by the party apparatchiks were not fairy tales.

"Fourth floor! She is on the fourth floor," he exclaimed hurriedly.

"What are you waiting for? Take us there...now," Tze ordered.

"This way, please," the nervous security guard stammered as he left the semicircular duty desk and moved toward the elevator.

Bad and Dutch had stowed their parawing chutes in black nylon stuff bags, and then donned their rappelling gear. Dutch ran both green ropes around the massive wooden spire at the center of the roof, a load bearing part of the ancient structure. Both men wove the rope through their figure-eight descenders and snapped into their harness D-ring carabineers. They could hear the entire communication between the first element and the security guard downstairs, but only Dutch could understand Mandarin.

"They are headed up to the fourth floor. Kim just asked about the age of the elevator."

"That's the signal. Let's move," ordered Bad Poole.

Their weapons were strapped at the ready across their chests. Each took a deep breath, and then the Raptors pushed back off the rooftop into the darkness. With practiced precision, they fed out just enough rope to swing back under the overhanging roof and clear the wooden railing surrounding the balcony. They released a few feet of additional rope and settled onto the painted wood deck of the balcony. Silently, they fingered the carabineers, releasing the figure eights and then let their black rappelling harnesses slide to the painted floor. Without a word, they raised their weapons and moved like wraiths through the zigzag corridors. The blackness of the interior rooms was no match for the night vision technology incorporated into the Raptor helmets. In the greenish-gray world of the infrared light intensifiers, the trappings of an Admiral were still easy to identify. Priceless works of Chinese art adorned the walls and jade figurines from the Ming Dynasty sat under acrylic display boxes. A pair of elaborate carved satinwood doors led to what Bad determined to most likely be the master bedroom suite. He whispered to Dutch, "Cover the right side…on three."

Bad silently rotated the polished brass lever unlocking the two doors. He cracked one open a fraction of an inch to insure that they were in fact unlocked. At the count of three, both men pushed the doors wide open to reveal a massive bed covered in a fine silk spread. The emblem of the Chinese Army/Navy was embroidered in gold wire in a splashy display almost three feet tall. Four extra large down pillows cased in blue silk rested against the rosewood headboard. Bad lowered his rifle, as did Dutch. The bed was empty.

"This way please," Shang Deng Bing Chong said as they left the elevator. Each floor had similar zigzag corridors as part of a twelfth century Feng Shui sense of balance with nature. A guard was seated outside a featureless wooden door. He rose as the three approached. Kim and Tze glared at the hallway guard and allowed Chong to do all the talking.

"These people are here on direct orders of Vice President Xi Jinping. They are to take the prisoner back to Beijing tonight."

"No one told me. I'll have to talk to my Hai Jun Si Ji Shi Gua," the guard said as he reached for a phone on the wall next to his chair.

The thought of waking a PLAN naval non-commissioned officer first class, equivalent to a chief petty officer in the US Navy, did not sit well with Seaman Chong. Having both a Second Secretary and a senior non-com on his ass in the middle of the night was not an experience he wanted on his record.

"No! You do not understand. He is a Second Secretary with the Standing Committee. Do not interfere," Chong pleaded.

The mention of Tze's supposed Communist Party status froze the Shui Bing or ordinary seaman. If a superior enlisted man wanted him to release the prisoner to a lt. commander and a scary looking Committee member, the young apprentice seaman did not want any part of disturbing his sleeping section chief. *Besides, the old woman did not look smart enough to be a spy. All she did was cry about being held prisoner. It would be good to get rid of her.* He turned and slipped the key into the locked door.

"You made the right choice, seaman. I will notify your superior of your cooperation," Tze said.

Chong glanced at the Party enforcer and swore he saw a tiny hint of a smile, but he couldn't bear looking his way for more than a second. The four entered the small windowless room and the guard flipped on the overhead light.

"Get up Mrs. Chen. You are being moved," he shouted at the frightened woman.

"What…what time is it?" the gray haired petite woman asked.

"The time does not matter. Get dressed. Do it now," snapped Kim.

Tze opened a small closet with only two changes of clothes on wooden hangers. He quickly grabbed a dress and tossed it to Kim. "Have her put this on. She will not need any other."

Seaman Chong furtively glanced at the other guard, whose eyes widened at the exchange. Both men were certain that the fate awaiting the American spy was a chemically enhanced interrogation followed by a shot to the back of the head and a quick trip to an incinerator. He felt sorry for the old woman, but dared not telegraph his feelings to these party insiders.

Dutch and Bad felt a sense of failure for a second. *Maybe this is not his room*, Dutch considered for a second. His sweep of the room picked up a second doorway, smaller than the entrance. A third door lay on the far side of the room. Dutch whispered to Bad, "Take the doorway on your side. Could be a closet or bath."

"Got it," Bad replied.

Both men toe-heeled across the silk throw rugs. Bad opened his doorway to find an elegantly appointed modern bath with gilded fixtures on a marble freestanding sink. "Bathroom," Bad announced softly.

Dutch slowly turned the lever and pulled the door open, revealing a smaller bedroom with plain furnishings. He spied a shock of straight black hair on a simple flat pillow. "Bingo. We have a player."

"On my way."

Poole crossed the bedroom and joined Dutch. Together, they eased on either side of the bed. Dutch raised his visor as Bad screwed a suppressor onto the H&K model 23. When Bad was in position, Dutch placed his hand firmly over the young man's mouth and spoke to him in Mandarin, "Do not resist. Do not scream. We only want information."

The man's dark eyes snapped open and wildly searched for something, anything in the blackened room. Someone was holding him down, but he could not see anything. Suddenly, he felt a tiny prick on the side of his neck followed by a warm feeling that seemed to spread from the point of the pain. His heart pounded as he tried to wake from the nightmare, then he noticed he was not nervous anymore. *I must be asleep. But why can I not move?*

Dutch withdrew the needle from the man's carotid artery and slipped the protective tip back on the hypodermic before dropping it back into his thigh pouch. "Where is Admiral Huang?"

"He left four hours ago, to join his flagship," he said with slurred speech.

Son of a bitch. We missed him. "Why did you not go with him?"

"I am headquarters house boy. I am not sailor."

“That explains the hair,” Bad noted.

“When will he return?” Dutch asked.

“Not soon. He have me pack many uniforms.”

“How many staff officers are left here?”

“Very few. Many go two days ago, rest go with Admiral Huang tonight.”

Dutch retrieved a second hypodermic and injected half of it into the already sedated house boy. “Sleep tight…He’ll never remember we were here.”

“I’ll check the closet to confirm the kid’s story,” Bad said as he removed the suppressor from the .45 caliber pistol. He holstered the handgun and stashed the bulky can in his ruck. The disappointed Raptor opened the louvered doors to the closets in the house boy’s room. Two sections of open space between several sets of summer Navy uniforms validated the boy’s answers, although both men had high confidence in the sodium pentothal and scopolamine’s ability to break down the mind’s defenses and induce amnesia. “Looks like he was straight up, Dutch.”

“Never doubted it. Time to go, big guy. Tze and Kim have the woman in the elevator.”

“Right. Make sure you close the bedroom door behind us.”

In less than a minute they were back on the balcony, and Dutch was pulling the rappelling ropes off the roof in preparation for a second descent to the ground. They had planned to take the HVT hostage down the elevator and stun the guards with sonic weapons, but that was a higher risk exfil plan.

No contact at all reduced the risk of exposure. Each slipped back into their rappelling harness.

"Mike Charlie, Raptor One."

"Talk to me, Bad."

"HVT is aboard his flagship. Slipped out after dark, over."

Aboard *Mama Bird*, the sense of disappointment was palpable. Kit reviewed the disposition of forces display and noted the members of Element One had exited the building and were in the presence of a third person to whom *Manta* had assigned a red triangle. One solitary red triangle had just initiated another security patrol around the ancient building. Two other foot patrols covered a portion of the grounds behind the machine gun position overlooking the river from the center of the pagoda complex.

"Copy, no joy on the HVT. Element One clearing with subject south side of building. You have foot patrol on opposite side of building. You got one minute to clear north exterior."

"Raptors One and Two coming down."

Bad cleared the descent path for any IR signatures and tossed the line over the side, where it dropped silently and hung at the level of the sixth balcony. There was no practical way to carry two four hundred foot lengths of rope needed to make the descent with a single rappel and pull the rope down afterwards to leave no trace of their presence. Dutch also dropped his rope around a major balcony support beam and reconnected the figure eight to his harness. Bad led off and once again, pushed away from the pagoda into the inky blackness. Except for the slight hissing sound of the rope passing though the large loop of the rescue eight, he made no noise as he leapfrogged from balcony to balcony. Dutch was set up on the other side of the beam and descended along side Bad, separated by the upturned and pointed beams characteristic of traditional Chinese architecture. The Chinese believe the points discouraged witches from resting on them. Too bad the idea didn't work for Raptors.

At the sixth floor, Bad swung out onto the eighteen inch wide upturned beam and reeled in one side of his rope. He whipped it around the vertical balcony support and quickly looped it back to his descender rig and pushed away. At the fifth floor, he passed Dutch who was likewise reattaching his rope. Moments later, Raptor Two pushed off the fifth floor.

Ten Ring observed the two bouncing down a floor at a time. Suddenly a figure appeared exiting a side door on the pagoda. Ten Ring swung the crosshairs of his fourteen power scope at the figure.

"Raptors One and Two halt!" he ordered over the comm.

Instinctively, Bad and Dutch braked to a halt at twenty and thirty feet above the shrubbery, their ropes snaking across the shrubs.

"Raptors, have sentry forty feet west lighting a cigarette. I have him covered with sonic rifle. Mickey, do you have visual on the guard coming around the west side?"

"Negative. Moving in to cover."

Mickey began a tactical jog up the sprawling lawn. Baker closed up the east side with his rifle at a low assault position.

"Raptor Three coming in fast," Widowmaker called.

Bad reached out with his toe and slowly spun himself around. He brought his rifle to his shoulder and lined up his sights with the sentry's head. *Come on, dude. Get the hell outta here*. The unsuspecting sentry almost directly beneath him took a big drag on his cigarette. The red flare of the burning tobacco showed bright white in the IR cameras mounted on every Raptor helmet.

"Wan Li how are things going tonight?"

The sentry coming around the pagoda shook his head. "Nothing ever happens here, donkey breath. Didn't you get the email? The whole damn Navy is gone off on some big ass adventure and we are stuck here waiting for termites to attack the building."

"Yeah, I bet you would rather be fighting hand to hand with Bruce Lee or Chuck Norris."

"I would whip out some monster Kung fu on those two. They never dreamed of a battle to the death with Wan Li, Master of Doom."

"You are so full of Yak dung, Wan Li. Come on, we can go down to the gun port. Sometimes they have a deck of cards or dice."

"And mosquitoes."

"Quickly as you can, snatch the mosquito from my hand, grasshopper. Whatever happened to the Master of Doom, you weasel?"

"Kiss it, mental midget. At least I am not sucking on a cancer stick. Who is dealing?"

"I do not know. We shall see."

The two sentries turned to walk down the manicured lawn. Neither had a clue how close they had come to becoming casualties of an undetermined nature. Ten Ring could have killed each with a two second burst of sonic waves from the deadly and silent weapon. The theory of quantum entanglement had been put to good use, combining low frequency sonic energy at 140 decibels, but well below the threshold of human hearing, with an infrared laser beam. It was selectable to extremely low frequencies, such as 18 Hertz for a head shot or 20 Hz for the heart. It could match the resonant frequency of a critical human organ, creating massive internal bleeding and death in seconds. A sliding power selector located above the trigger mechanism allowed the operator to choose from moderate discomfort, incapacitation or death.

"Raptors One and Two, you're clear," Ten Ring radioed as the Chinese sentries moved down the hill toward the river.

Dutch and Bad resumed their descent and pushed off hard to avoid the shrubbery on the last portion of their rappel. They quickly snaked the ropes down off the exposed beams, coiled and stuffed them and harnesses into their rucks. Both worked their way to the west end of the wall surrounding the pagoda complex where they joined Widowmaker and Mickey. In slow, overlapping movements the four men silently departed the complex where the wall met the river bank. They began a slow jog to the west along the deserted riverbank.

Ten Ring carefully worked his way down from his tree sniper position and back south of the pagoda where he met up with Rock. The two moved south to the pre-selected pickup site along the roadway between the nearest town and Liuhe Pagoda.

Tze glanced at the middle-aged woman that they had whisked out of the prison cell inside the pagoda. She appeared to be terrified of her situation and for a good reason. Neither Tze nor Kim had broken character. As far as she was concerned, she was still being held prisoner. Kim turned off the main road back toward the village from which the two had stolen the sedan. Lan Chen had no idea where she was being taken.

"I already told your people, I am not a spy. I was visiting my aunt who is quite old and not in good health. You have to believe me."

Her Mandarin was slightly rusty, after living in the United States for over twenty-five years. She and her husband had worked hard at assimilation and rarely spoke Chinese at home.

"Relax. We are just going on a little trip," Tze said matter-of-factly.

She did not believe him. No one comes for a political prisoner in the middle of the night to take them on a little trip.

Kim pulled behind the warehouse and parked beside the large rice paddy. She shut the engine off and got out. When she opened the rear passenger side door, Lan began to panic.

"Move over. Give me your hands," Kim said.

Reluctantly, Lan complied. Kim smiled as she took both of Lan's hands in hers. The old woman tried to find some sort of sense in the lt. commander's actions. Her grip was firm but her eyes were not threatening like those of her other captors and interrogators. *What is going on? What do they want from me?* The female officer merely smiled. Lan felt a tiny prick on the right side of her neck. She started to scream, but a strange sensation rushed over her before the sound could emerge from her throat. Lan Chen slumped back into the seat as darkness overcame her.

"Let's get her out," said Tze before he opened the right rear passenger door.

He placed his arms under Lan's arm pits, lifted her up and pulled her to over the outside edge of the seat. Kim slid across the cloth bench seat and took hold of the old woman's left arm. Together, they carried her to the rear of the warehouse wall.

"Eagle 1, Element One ready for extraction," Tze said.

"Eagle 1 enroute."

Kim retrieved his briefcase from the back seat and set it beside him. She returned to the driver's side, entered and started the car and drove back to the same spot she had left from forty minutes earlier. She popped open her briefcase, removed the original ignition lockset and switched back to the original. Taking a handkerchief out of her uniform coat, Kim wiped down the steering wheel and inner door handles. Finally, she cleaned the rear seat exterior and interior door handles. The seasoned CIA agent looked around the parking lot and checked the apartment building for any room lights which may have been turned on since she returned to the lot. She picked up her briefcase and began walking back to the warehouse. As she approached Tze's position, she could hear the faint distant whine of the approaching Skycar.

Eagle 1 streaked across the placid rice paddy, ten feet above the soggy vegetation. Dare pulled back on the throttle and eased the nose up slightly as he prepared for a quick pickup.

"Gear down."

"Gear coming down," Bull replied. He never took his eyes off the disposition-of-forces screen *Manta* was generating. The other *Eagle* crews had already picked up the three Raptor teams and were providing air support from an elevation of six thousand feet. No additional targets appeared on Bull's display. "Gear down, three green, pickup area is a go, Boss."

"Copy that," Dare replied as he used a combination of aero braking and parasitic drag to help slow the craft. He could see Kim, Tze and a figure he assumed to be Lan Chen. Without using the bright halogen lights, the approach and landing required the use of NVGs, something Dare had done hundreds of times in his Marine Corps Super Cobra. Tze and Kim shielded their eyes from the down-blast of the nacelles as he touched down approximately eighty feet away and chopped the power back to idle.

The two operatives lifted the unconscious Lan to her feet, and then Tze ducked under her arm and hoisted the small woman's frame up onto his shoulder in a fireman's carry. He followed Kim to the opened crew door and laid the woman down on the carpeted floor of the *Eagle*. Kim pulled her inside as Tze stepped in to help place Chen into the fold-down jump seat behind Bull's WSO position.

"Door is clear," Kim yelled up to Bull, who immediately began to hydraulically close the wide gull-wing crew door.

Dare advanced the power as soon as the *Door Open* light extinguished and the small craft was airborne over the rice paddy even before Kim and Tze were strapped in the two rear Raptor seats. He called for gear retraction, and then glanced over his shoulder to see Tze pulling on a intercom headset.

"Any problems, Tze?"

"Not that we know of, Boss. By the time they try to find out what the Central Committee did with the prisoner, we should be halfway home."

"That's the idea. How's the prisoner?"

"She was scared half to death. We stayed in character. Don't think she'll remember much. Figured we didn't need to expose her to the Eagles. We'll let Doc decide if we're going to keep her out until we hit the west coast."

Dare nodded then switched to the BEF comm frequency. "Eagle Flight, Eagle 1, initiate recovery as briefed. Eagle 2, you have the lead."

"Eagle 2 copies. I have the lead, form up on the right," Jill replied.

She began a climbing turn back to the east and plotted an intercept with *Mama Bird*. The other two maneuvered to a loose echelon formation on the nearly invisible craft before it climbed into the gray overcast night sky. The three were four miles ahead of *Eagle 1* by the time he reached their recovery altitude of 12,000 feet MSL. *Mama Bird* was some seventy miles off shore and heading outbound on her orbit.

AIRSPACE OVER EAST CHINA SEA
Monday, 11 November

At 400 KIAS, the M600/A attack fighters were considerably faster than the orbiting C-5M. Gears calculated the rejoin time and began a descent to the recovery altitude. One hundred miles off shore, he made a right hand turn and notified the crew to prepare for de-pressurization. Blaze relayed the heading to the nearest air defense radar installation that was sending a slow steady sweep across the coastal air defense zone. Gears turned the nose of *Mama Bird* orienting it almost directly at the radar emitter—the chances of being detected were markedly reduced.

"Eagle 2, cleared to initiate docking sequence," Gears radioed to Jill and Glenn.

"Copy, Mama Bird, Two is three hundred yards in trail."

Toggling the yoke mounted switch, Gears selected the interphone side. "Load, pressurization is off. Cleared to drop the ramp. Eagle 2 inbound."

"Roger that, AC. Set for recovery," replied Max.

Inside the empty cargo bay, several other crew members awaited the recovering Skycars. Each had an assigned task. Some would safe the weapons and pin the gear. Others would tie down the deadly craft for the long tip home. Max was again connected to the airframe with a long safety strap and a harness. He could move out to the extended ramp and was wearing NVGs just like Jill and Glenn to see what was happening as the tiny craft made the tricky and delicate recovery. The red lights of the cargo bay gave it an overall ominous glow, but did not give the position of the aircraft away when the ramp was lowered. Max engaged the ramp control handle and lowered it to a level position.

"AC, Load, ramp down and locked."

"Copy, Load," Gears said as he turned to Kit. "Flaps 15, give me 200 knots."

"Flaps to 15, and 200," Kit confirmed.

Mac could feel the change in deck angle as the massive C-5M responded to the flap position and the nose dropped three degrees.

"Gear down, before landing checklist," called Jill as her *Eagle* closed to fifty feet behind and twenty feet below the almost invisible mother ship. A tiny row of red LEDs in the centerline of the cargo bay roof of the cloud-gray bird were really all she could see clearly from her position. She could feel the muscles in her neck begin to tighten in anticipation. Her lips became dry as the physiological aspects of the nerve-racking recovery began to manifest themselves.

"Down, three green. Before landing checklist is complete."

"Thank you, Bug," she said without taking her eyes off the monster craft looming larger above them.

The moniker *aluminum overcast* ran across her mind for some reason. Perhaps it was the gigantic size differential between the two craft. Perhaps it was the fact that she was over hostile territory on a clandestine mission. More likely it was the fact that she had to bring the sleek little craft to a hover, like a hummingbird, exactly matching the C-5M's 200 knots while being sandwiched between the extended ramp, the empennage and the clamshell doors.

It was dark, the turbulence of the massive transport began to cause small pitch and roll oscillations as she brought her M600/A within ten feet of the bottom of the ramp. Unlike the really vicious wingtip vortices, each a horizontal tornado capable of inverting the Skycar in a half-second, the laminar flow around the fuselage was merely unstable. It consisted of invisible eddies and burbles, not unlike a small rock protruding above the surface of a fast moving stream. The closer to *Mama Bird* Jill flew, the smoother it would become. But first she had to penetrate the outer portions of unstable boundary layer air.

"Easy there, Lucky," Glenn cautioned. "Relax, you got it made."

She could not see his right hand sliding up behind the side stick on his side. Her vision was concentrated on the greenish-gray view as the Eagle's nose edged above the end of the cargo ramp. Jill made tiny, almost imperceptible inputs to the side mounted stick—the Skycar computers made corresponding inputs to the vanes at the back of the four nacelles. Compared to precision formation flying in smooth air, this recovery would be rated twice as difficult as in daylight.

The blackness of the Chinese night sky between layers of clouds made it even tougher. She concentrated on the small red LED inset into the aft end of the ramp. They glowed as tiny white dots in her NVGs. Her heart pounded like a trip-hammer. *Settle down, girl.*

Max monitored her approach and began to motion her forward as the M600/A settled into the pocket of relatively smooth air behind the C-5M ramp. He stood inside on the centerline of the dimly lit red cavern of the cargo bay. Once he could see the main gear securely over the ramp, he turned his hands palm-side down and made short downward movements. Jill responded with a slight hint of forward pressure on the stick and retarded the power slightly. The craft touched down first on the main gear, followed almost instantaneously by the nose.

"Weight on wheels," Glenn announced with the illumination of the cockpit amber light.

Jill tried to swallow, but her cotton-mouth made that an impossibility. She did pull the throttles to idle as directed by Max. One of the other loadmasters slipped behind the nose wheel to lift the tractor chain assembly paddle into position.

"Fold 'em up," she finally was able to utter.

"Rear nacelles coming up, little lady."

"Lucy, I'm hooome!" Dutch Offner said with his best Ricky Ricardo imitation.

In seconds, the rear nacelle struts had folded up vertically. Jill shot Max a thumbs-up signal when the transformation was complete. He, in turn, opened his fingers from his closed fists, signaling *Brakes Release*. Jill complied and returned the signal, whereupon Max started the tractor chain that pulled the tiny fighter forward into the cargo bay. Total time since Gears had cleared *Eagle 2* to land was less than ninety seconds. One down, three to go.

EAST CHINA SEA
Monday, 11 November

Three hundred nautical miles south east of the port of Dalian, the one hundred and thirty ship combined Chinese task force steamed across the East China Sea at a modest rate of thirty knots. The task force was comprised of two CBGs or Carrier Battle Groups; *Sun Tzu,* serving as the flag ship, and her sister ship *Yang Jian* were at the center. Each ultra-super carrier had a total of twenty-two escort vessels: cruisers, destroyers and frigates, four perimeter nuclear powered subs and forty Type 071 LPDs troop carriers in trail.

Sun Tzu had peeled off from the main force. A Chinese manufactured Shaanxi Y-8G transport, similar to a US made C-130, made its approach to the carrier's stern—lining up with the blue runway lights in the center of the chosen flight deck. Two other strips of blue light marked the side boundaries. The pilot maintained a standard three degree glide slope as he carried a 110 KIAS all the way to touchdown. *Sun Tzu* had turned into the ten knot wind from the east and carried almost 30 knots of speed as the transport cleared the fantail. The seasoned pilot flared slightly to break most of his rate of descent before touching down firmly on the starboard most of two 1,500 foot parallel flight decks of the new warship. Gray smoke belched from the black tires as they contacted the serrated steel deck, then rapidly blew aft with the forty knot relative wind. The pilot reversed the pitch on her four Zhuzhou WoJiang-6 six-bladed turboprop engines and simultaneously applied maximum braking. The olive drab craft with a large red star on the side of the fuselage shuddered to a stop less than a eight hundred feet down the deck. Even before the props had stopped turning, the wide rear ramp was lowered and Admiral Huang, with his ten man staff, quickly walked down to stand on the expansive deck of his creation and surveyed his dimly lit surroundings.

Admiral Huang Meng was a traditionalist Chinese with a deep and abiding hatred of anything western. He felt the American value system was destroying his beloved China and he fully intended on eliminating that decadent system, with or without the sanction of the Central Committee. He was a quadruple Scorpio: the Sun, Mars, Jupiter and the Moon all in Scorpio at the time of his birth made him highly intelligent, emotionally passionate and with a godlike sense of invincibility. He shared this type of astrological charting with other multiple-planet military strategists like Alexander, Bonapart, Norman Swartzkoff and his idol, Sun Tzu. The blood planet and god of war, Mars, ruled his chart and his I Ching showed repeated *Great Exceeding* and *Abounding* or ambition achieved—all following in line with his approaching birthday of November 18. His confidence, accordingly, showed no bounds.

"You may rejoin the fleet, Captain, as soon as the Y-8G has taken off."

"Yes, Honorable Admiral," Captain Gwok Wei said even as the big transport was being towed to the stern for take off. "I'll show you to the bridge, Admiral…"

"I am aware where *my* bridge is, Captain. I designed it."

"Yes, of course, Admiral, my sincere apologies."

"As soon as we resume our position in the center of the fleet, I want forty knots. I will supply the course. We must get out of this cursed glowing water before the cloud cover clears."

"Yes, sir. But what about the transports? They won't be able to keep up."

"I am aware of that, too, Captain. They'll be in trail at thirty-five knots and I called in four additional destroyers and two additional subs for their screen. We will assume a V formation when we reach the Pacific and you may launch our sub-hunters. You have been apprised that we are under total radio blackout?"

"Yes, sir. Line-of-sight communication only."

AIRSPACE OVER EAST CHINA SEA
Monday, 11 November

With all four *Eagles* aboard, Gears began a right turn toward Hawaii and started a climb. He was about to clear Tom Tallman to bring *Manta* in to dock on the port wing hard point when the sight of the normally black waters of the Pacific and East China Sea stunned him. "And just what the bloody hell is that?"

Kit was busy with the FMS laying out a route to rejoin the KC-10 tanker between their present location and Guam when Gears' question caught him off guard. "Jesus…" he said as he looked down.

Beneath the nose of *Mama Bird*, the normally black nighttime waters had taken on an eerie blue-greenish glow. Lines of what appeared to be wakes from large rapidly moving vessels extended from horizon to horizon with a larger blob of glowing luminescence that covered many square miles to their north.

"Tom, are you picking this up on Manta?"

"Affirmative. It's also visible in IR mode."

"Any ideas?"

"Not a clue. Hang on, let me ask Blaze."

"Ask me what?" she said as she stowed her oxygen mask. She took a good look at the display in front of Tom. The gorgeous redhead pointed at one of the southernmost points of light. "Oh, my goodness! Can you give me a close zoom there in visual spectrum?"

"You bet, Sunshine."

The crystal clear digital image grew as Tom rolled a arrow over with his mouse then tapped out a couple commands on his key board. Suddenly, a Chinese Navy destroyer appeared to fill the screen. Even the bow wake could be seen as it lit up, but astern of the 560 foot vessel, the sea boiled with blue-greenish light. As they watched, the light grew in width and did not fade.

"It's almost like a contrail in the ocean. I've heard about it but never seen it except in pictures on-line!" exclaimed Blaze.

"Yeah, that's a good analogy. What is it?" Gears asked.

"Bioluminescence. Luminescent bacteria, cyanobacter or plankton are stimulated by the agitation caused by the passing of the ships. It can only occur when the organisms are present at very high densities. It's thought to be an associative symbiotic relationship among long chain prokaryotes like Nostoc muscorum and Anabaena spiriodes with bacterium and chlorella. The unique ability of the hetrocystous cyanobacter to fix nitrogen in the presence of oxygen presumably can be attributed to the isolation of the enzyme nitrogenase by the thick walled heterocyst." Gears and Tom glanced at each other like deer in headlights as Blaze continued, "An alternating nitrogen fixation with oxygen creation pattern process has evolved that protects the nitrogenase from the deactivating oxygen. It is believed by some that the bioluminescence is a possible result of the high density production of the nitrogenase."

"Say what?" asked Lanie.

"I read a paper written back in '77 by Ken Farmer, an algologist, for a conference on genetic engineering for nitrogen fixation at the Brookhaven National Laboratories in New York.

"Blaze has a photographic memory," Gears said to Lanie.

"Who'd a thunk it," Lanie muttered.

Gears turned back to Blaze. "What causes it to congregate?"

"Nobody really knows. It can't be much of a defense mechanism, because it gives up their presence. Only on rare occasions do they stay lit up for any length of time. It has been reported in the Indian Ocean by our naval forces fighting pirates off Somalia and as far back as Columbus's logs. Now wait a sec…How big is that blob at our eleven o'clock?"

"Well over ninety miles long. It goes as far north as I can see," replied Gears.

"Do you think that could be the Chinese carrier task force that SecDef Baker is worried about?"

"Think you nailed it, Blaze. Tom, can you get me as much data as you can? We still have a cirrus layer above us, and our visual satellites are useless in these conditions."

"I'll do what I can. Want to get a good look at those ultra-super carriers myself."

"I'll run a spectrometry and full ELINT scan on the fleet and determine what radar frequencies they use and also check out their communications. The DoD will need all the help it can get if we get into a shooting war with all our top fighters disabled," Blaze added.

"When we get back to the airways, I'd like a couple of radar sweeps from altitude to determine the total size of the battle group. They have to bring the ships in close to pass through the Japanese held islands north of Taiwan. Once they get outside the archipelago, they would disperse and make it much more difficult to track," Kit said.

"I'll get it for you, MC. But, I thought you were Army. How do you know about so much naval operations?" Blaze asked.

"I study all aspects of military intelligence and planning, girl. If you aren't growing, you're letting your brain rot." Kit laughed.

"Couldn't have said it better myself," she mused.

DAVIS-MONTHAN AFB, ARIZONA
Saturday, 9 November

It was almost 2200 hours by the time Jack and James Stewart shut the door to Jack's office and headed over to the Officer's Club for a quick nightcap. At least that was the plan. Jack cruised through the parking lot twice without a single spot available.

"What's going on? I don't remember a dining-in being scheduled for this weekend."

"Beat's me, Pop. There's someone leaving, guess we could take his spot."

"He looks familiar. I think I recognize him."

The slightly balding man was almost to his car when he looked inside the General's silver Mercedes 560 SL convertible. The top was up, but he could see the driver's face fairly clearly in the glow of the mercury vapor lights.

"Burner? That you, old dog?"

Jack hit the power window button. As the window silently descended, a smile crossed Burner's face.

"Tom Fox! You low life! How's everything up in Detroit?"

"Great! We're doing well. Four grand kids keep us busy. How's your wife?"

The question hit Burner again for the fourth time that day. But his smile diminished only slightly. *Not his fault. Not everybody got the word.* “I lost her three years ago, Tom. Sorry I didn’t let you know.”

“My turn to say I’m sorry. She was a beautiful woman with a lot of class, Burner.”

“That she was Sly, and thanks…Remember my son, James?”

Tom leaned down to look at the strapping blond pilot in the passenger seat. “Jimmy? Oh, my God! Last time I saw you, you were in Little League.”

“It’s been a couple years, then. Your son Ronnie was my catcher.”

“Small world, guys. Hey it’s great to see you two, but I’m worn smooth out. My day started at 5AM Eastern with meditation and a run. It’s a little past my bedtime. See you at the briefing tomorrow, if that’s okay?”

“Sounds like a plan, Sly. Great to see you and thanks…thanks for coming.”

“Heater told me you guys needed Phantom drivers. That was good enough for me.”

Jack placed his hand on top of Tom’s resting on his window sill. The two old friends simply nodded, and then Tom turned, entered his rental car and backed out of the spot. Jack pulled into the vacated slot and he and James got out. They walked across the parking lot looking at out of state license plates from Colorado, Utah, Texas, Nevada and California.

"Dad, did you guys fly together any place other than at Holloman?"

"Oh, yeah. He was a couple years behind me at the Academy and came to George AFB right after we transitioned out of the 104. Tom was one of my flight commanders at Holloman and went to Fighter Weapon's School a year after I did."

James pulled open the door to the casual bar. The boisterous crowd looked like a scheduled fighter pilot homecoming event. Jack took one look inside and grinned back at his son. "This may have been a mistake."

From across the bar, three guys spotted Jack enter and simultaneously yelled at the top of their lungs to be heard over the boisterous crowd. "Burner!"

Dozens of heads looked and turned around to see Burner waving at his old friends. He was surprised when many got to their feet. Some of them started applauding, and then the whole room appeared to rise and face him. A feeling of gratitude flowed over him followed by a momentary tinge of something upon which he could not place a finger. He shook his head, smiled and held up his hands to try to stop the spontaneous outflow of appreciation. After what seemed like entirely too much time, the crowd finally stopped clapping. Several calls of *Speech!* rang out.

Jack conceded the fact that he had to say something. "Ladies and gentlemen! And both of you know who you are," he continued as the chuckles rumbled through the crowd. "It does an old fighter pilot's heart good to see some very familiar faces as well as some new faces tonight. You and I are here for the very same reason. You are the elite. You are the best of the best aviators America has to offer. Each of you has been asked once again to serve your country and, to the man, have responded exactly as I hoped you would. I can not go into the exact nature of the mission or the threat facing us at this time. Both will be covered in briefings tomorrow for the late arrivals." He paused to look over the crowd for a second. The fleeting feeling he had experienced when he entered the room crossed his mind again and the second time he caught it. *Some of these men will not come back from this mission.* The salute attributed to Roman gladiators came to mind. *Morituri te salutant* or those of us about to die salute you. But this was not Rome, and these were free men, not slaves. "As your commander, I want each of you to know how proud I am of you and how much you mean to me. Drinks are on me! Carry on!"

A raucous cheer went out from the mostly well oiled crowd. James placed his hand on his father's shoulder. "Pop, that's gonna set you back 2K!"

"Closer to three, but who's countin'?"

The two plowed into the throng and tried to find a waitress to take a drink order.

A few minutes after midnight, Jack and James exited the club with their voices almost gone. Trying to talk over hundreds of competing conversations had taken a toll.

"Pop, I didn't know that many combat pilots and WSOs were still were kicking around. Your guys did a hellova job getting that many on short notice."

"Son, that's nothing yet. Most are coming in commercial or military hops starting after daylight. We'll have the Personal Equipment shops busy with checking out helmet O2 and comm gear as well as G-suits, boots and flight suits. Not to mention crew training."

"How are the birds coming?"

"Got fifteen Eagles, ten Phantoms and five F-111s on line today. Have three Starfighters coming up from Florida tomorrow and teams putting together a couple 105s and 106s per day."

"Have to say, I'm proud of the team you picked. If we can keep this cranking for a full week, the Chinese Navy better turn tail and head for home."

"Thanks, I sure couldn't have done it without them. It's amazing how much can get done if you don't care who gets the credit."

AIRSPACE OVER WESTERN PACIFIC
Monday, 11 November

"Hold her steady, Gears. I have Manta five hundred feet in trail for the rejoin," Tom called over the interphone.

"Roger, holding steady as she goes. Maintaining Flight Level 270," Gears responded.

Tom inched forward on the throttle on the console. Without taking his eyes off the video feed, he spoke to Lanie at his side, "Give me red docking LEDs *On*."

She tapped a two keystroke input on her board. "LEDs are on."

"Ah, there you are," Tom said as a single row of lights with a crossing set at each end appeared in the blackness in front of the ray shaped recon fighter.

What looked like a squat capital "I" was actually seven feet long and indicated the location of the electromechanical uplocks for the stealthy craft. Tom sped up until he was positioned some fifty feet below and matched speed with the *Super Galaxy*. The task of docking was not much more difficult than accomplishing a night aerial refueling. In other words, hard, but certainly not impossible. What made it somewhat more difficult was looking through a sensor package. He made tiny control corrections until the crafts were ten feet apart with a closure rate of one foot per second.

"Split screen, mating icon, give me feed from Mama Bird."

"You got it," Lanie replied as a view from the port wing flush mounted camera showed a small Maltese Cross appear on the photochromatic upper surface of *Manta*.

An outline of the cross appeared on the left split screen. It was segmented and seemed larger than the one on *Manta*. In actuality, they were identical in size. As the two ships converged, the one on the recon fighter grew until the two ships were inches apart. A powerful electromagnet would capture the smaller craft.

"Keep it coming up. You're almost there. Closure rate dead on," Lanie encouraged. "One foot…six inches."

A small green *Contact* light illuminated on the video flat screen.

"Lock it up," Tom said matter-of-factly.

Lanie hit the *Enter* button on her keyboard. A light on the video monitor flashed *EM LOCK-ON,* followed shortly by a *MECH LOCK-ON* light.

"Manta shut down checklist, called Gears without hint of emotion or stress.

"Mechanical Lock-On. Confirm."

"Lock is On."

"Throttle-Idle, Fuel Shutoff-Close."

As the two completed the checklist, Dare Phillips stood from the seat often used by Mission Commander Kit Kitaen.

"Nice work, you guys. Compile a full sensor download for transfer to Pearl when we overfly Hawaii. I'm sure Washington will want to know everything about the fleet composition and ELINT we picked up. Anybody need coffee?"

Blaze, Lanie and Tom shook their heads. All planned to get some rest once the refueling with the KC-10 was initiated. Dare stepped forward to the cockpit.

"Gears, you're cleared for cruise climb. Manta is secured."

"Thanks, Boss. I think we got some good stuff for the DoD to look at."

"My thoughts, too. It'll give the Navy plans shop a heads up. Too bad about our targeted Admiral."

"Yeah. Something in my gut tells me he's a key player in all this crap," Kit replied.

"Time will tell, my friend…time will tell."

***

CHAPTER TEN

AIRSPACE OVER WESTERN PACIFIC
Monday, 11 November

"Texaco 59, Galaxy 1, cleared to disconnect."

"Galaxy 1, Texaco 59, roger. Texaco is clear. Have a safe trip."

"Appreciate your help, Texaco. Have a nice flight to Yakota."

"Any time, my friends."

The silver and gray tanker began a turn back to the west over the vast emptiness of the Pacific. Japan lay some four hours flight time away. Hawaii was another seven hours ahead of the C-5M. It would be dawn before the secret aerial battle carrier was in range to deliver their Top Secret data to the receiving station at the west end of Oahu.

DAVIS-MONTHAN AFB, ARIZONA
Sunday, 10 November

The morning wake-up call Jack had set for himself came on time. He forced himself out of bed and splashed water on his face before he looked in the mirror. He was tired and it showed. The pair of dark circles he was staring at did not normally appear after two hours in the club. *Must be the stress.* Jack stepped into the shower and felt somewhat reinvigorated. *This week is gonna require a maximum effort and you can't afford to do that every night. You're not 30 years old any more.* Thirty minutes later, Jack was finished with breakfast and on the way to headquarters.

Mindy, his administrative assistant, was already at her desk with a review of Saturday's status, "Here you are, General. The colonels are still not quite sure why you don't want a stand-up briefing like most staff officers."

"Okay, Mindy, take a message," he replied. "To all 22nd Composite Wing Staff: In my experience, it takes approximately one full hour to prepare and another 30 minutes to hold a morning stand-up briefing. In seven days, that time spent would cost up to one whole work day which we certainly cannot afford. I much prefer to have my people work than to talk about working, whenever possible. Sincerely, blah blah. Okay?"

"That it, sir?"

"In a nutshell. I'm going to call Lockheed. Be on for about 10 minutes. Hold any calls that are not emergencies."

"Yes, sir."

He took the folder into his office and closed the door. Checking his watch, he noted it was only 8:30AM on this Sunday morning back in Fort Worth. Jack pulled out his cellular, checked the number, and then picked up the secure telephone and called—it was answered on the second ring.

"Good morning, Lockheed-Martin, Mr. Perry's office."

"Morning, Kristi. Jack Stewart calling Roland."

"I'll put you right through, General."

"Burner, you're up early."

"Hey, Roland. Yeah, don't have time let the grass grow. How's the company coming with the stealth coating?"

"Doing great, workin' round the clock. You know, it's not really all that different from a vinyl dashboard coating. We have a GM subcontractor over in Arlington cranking it out by the ton. I've got a C-130 scheduled out with the first 100,000 square feet just after noon today."

Jack did the time of flight calculations from Fort Worth to Tucson in his head. "Okay, we can expect it by mid-afternoon. How about sending a couple technicians to train my guys? I want to get started on this ASAP. We really need it on the old iron to help their survivability."

"Gotcha covered. Four of my best are included and your Mindy already took care of their accommodations. Anything else?"

"I owe you. Really appreciate you staying on top of this, buddy."

"We should have the rest of it by Wednesday at the latest. Call me if Lockheed can be of any assistance. The whole company is behind you on this."

"You guys are great. See ya," Jack said as he ended the call.

He glanced at the maintenance reports from the overnight shift. The number of fighters had risen dramatically. The report showed twenty-nine F-15s, twenty-one F-4s, nine F-111s, three F-8s, five F-14s and two each of the older F-104, F-105 and F-106s had been completed as of 0600 local time. *Good work, people.* Some were progressing at a slower rate than others—that was expected. Wide variances in the systems complexities and avionics packages made it difficult to compare airframe to airframe restoration time. One thing he learned as a leader in both his Air Force and Lockheed careers was to trust in his teammates and delegate responsibility. Jack laid the summary on his desk and headed out the door. Passing Mindy's desk, he paused for a second. "Thanks for your help on the Lockheed-Martin hotel accommodations. I'm going to chat with Logistics and Maintenance down the hall. Be on my cell if you need me."

"Yes sir," she replied as she made inputs to her lists of crew members being brought in. "I'll have an updated alpha roster of crews broken down by aircraft type and position when you return."

"You're a wonder, young lady."

"I know," she replied with a wink.

Jack entered the office of the Deputy Commander for Maintenance. As he did, one of the senior NCOs spotted him and stood to attention. Jack motioned him to sit.

"Make some progress overnight, Chief?"

"Yes sir, they're bustin' their tails on both shifts."

"What can I do to help you? Have enough mechanics? How about support equipment, jack stands and the like?"

"We've got plenty of bodies, General. Some of the guys said it would be nice if we had more power tools to tear down the wheel and brake assemblies. Almost all of them have to be rebuilt to insure the wheel bearings and brakes work as advertised."

"Stopping is nice. Always liked to keep it on the concrete. Air or electric impact?"

"We're scattered all over hell and gone out there, sir. Either will work, but we're gonna need some remote generators and or compressors. Plus extension cords or air hoses."

"I'll get someone on it," Jack said. He pulled a card out of his wallet and handed it to the Chief Master Sergeant. "Here's my cell number. Call me direct if you guys come up with anything else."

"Will do, General," the chief said as he placed the card on his desk.

Jack turned and pulled his iPhone out. He tapped the screen to open and slid to his contacts icon on the second page. Thumbing down, he found the one he needed.

"Lars, how's it coming over on the Starfighter line?"

"Mornin', Burner. Wondered how long you could stand it before you checked on my progress."

"Can't say I'm not interested, but I need your opinion on another matter."

"Sure, boss, what's the situation?"

"The boys need power tools to help tear down the wheel and brake assemblies. What would you recommend to get the job done remotely? Air or electric? We probably are gonna need some gas or diesel compressors or generators to support whichever we get."

"For a single job, the Lithium powered electric would do fine, but I'm not sure I'd attempt a whole fleet overhaul with 'em. The job takes a lot of torque, and absolutely kills battery jobs in a New York minute."

"So you're saying go with air tools?"

"Yeah, yeah, but I tell you what might be more of a limiting factor...make sure you had a source of air compressors first."

"Got it. I'll turn this job over to the logistic folks and let them get after it. How many do you think we can fully utilize?"

Lars took a look around the boneyard. It was a mass of moving men and equipment unlike anything he had ever witnessed on the tarmac at Luke AFB. *Looks like somebody stirred up an ant hill.* "Burner, shoot for twenty compressors and eighty impact guns. Plus plenty of hose and quick disconnects. That's my best guess."

"Thanks, pal. Glad to have your experience."

"Any time. And the answer is eleven."

"Eleven? Eleven what?"

"Manned missiles. I think we have enough good parts here to get eleven Starfighters in the air, not counting the Silver Knight."

"Damn! With the three coming in from the Starfighter Demonstration team, that'll give us a whole squadron."

"Just thought you would want to know."

"Ya think?"

A flight of two F-4 target aircraft pitched out and entered the overhead pattern for landing at D-M. They were highly modified for target use in the ranges south of Eglin AFB, Florida. Both aircraft would have required extensive modification to return to the line as fighters, but Jack Stewart had other plans for them and three others that had been destined for similar work out of Tyndall. The two touched down on opposite sides of the wide runway and rolled out to the end. Major Eddie Nash looked around the field. It was difficult to recognize D-M—so much had changed in the ten days since he last departed the field with the *Phantom* he was returning today. *Jesus! What's goin' on?* His wingman, Captain Joe Kreimborg was thinking the same thing.

Both men had been launched out of the Florida panhandle early Sunday morning with a scheduled stop at Holloman AFB, New Mexico for fuel. They were scheduled to attend a briefing at 1000 hours at the base theater. Neither knew what it was about. But suddenly, the two pilots knew that whatever had caused the rash of aircraft crashes the previous week probably had something to do with it. The pair of *Phantoms* was directed to a ramp normally filled with C-130 *Hercules* transport aircraft. Only two *Hercs* were still parked there and both were missing an engine and one also had a second propeller off for overhaul. In their places stood two lines of mismatched F-4s, some with Air Force, some with Navy and one sporting Marine paint.

Nash was marshaled into the next available parking slot and pulled to a stop. He opened the canopy and pulled the two throttles past the idle gate to the shutoff position. As the noise of his own J-79s spooled down, he looked to his left and saw Kreimborg pulling in. A crew chief maneuvered a ladder to the side of his bird and hung it onto the canopy rail. The fresh faced female airman clambered up to assist him unstrap from the Martin-Baker seat. "How's the bird, Major?"

"Good. No writeups. Only six flight hours since I picked it up last week."

"I heard that. There will be a line truck by in a few minutes to run you gentlemen over to the briefing at the base theater."

"We planned to check in to the VOQ first."

"Sorry, sir, base quarters are full. They'll tell you where you're staying at the briefing. They asked me to give you this orientation cover letter. There's a lot going on, as you can see."

"Thanks," he said as he took the letter, folded it up and slipped it into his thigh pocket. He handed her his helmet and followed her down the ladder. *I'm starting to think this mission is a little more involved than the Ops officer thought it would be.*

As the two fighter pilots arrived at the base theater, they noted a long line of olive drab B-4 personal equipment bags as well as bulky parachute and helmet bags stacked along the sidewalk from the parking lot to the theater. The line truck driver pointed to the staff sergeant with a clipboard who stood near the midsection of the sea of green bags.

"Major, check with Sergeant Timms there. He'll get your gear with the right group."

"Thanks…I think," he replied as he and his wingman grabbed their gear.

"Eddie, what the hell is all this? Looks like a major mobility deployment, but we don't have any fighters operational. And who are all the geezers standing in line? Some of 'em gotta be 60 or 70, if they're a day."

"How the hell should I know? Colonel Travis just told us to get our gear and plan for a week deployment to Tucson. I was planning to play some golf. See a lot of out-of-state cars. Must be some sort of reunion, I guess. Those guys are way too old to be on active duty."

Eddie and Joe approached the enlisted man with the clipboard. He looked up and snapped a salute.

"Good morning, Major. Last names and aircraft type, please."

"Nash and Kreimborg. F-4 Phantom."

The sergeant flipped a couple pages and ran his finger down the list. He looked closely at the captain's embossed name on his flight jacket.

"K not a C. Here you are sir…and there's Nash. Gentlemen, you'll be staying at the Marriott Residence Inn off I-10. Just set your bags in that line over on the right. We'll have transport for you after the brief."

"Thanks, Sergeant," replied Nash.

They dropped off their bags and passed a gray haired Lt. Colonel wearing a flight suit, a slightly worn flight jacket and a carrying faded green parachute bag. The two exchanged salutes with the senior officer and heard him address the Sergeant. "Bamhauer, fabulous Phantom driver."

"Hello, Colonel. Glad to have to with us. Marriott Residence Inn. Please drop your bag over there."

The two young jocks glanced back at the older pilot then each other. Major Nash shrugged and then took his place at the end of the line of people waiting to get into the theater. Only then did he notice that a contingent of Air Police had been deployed at the building. All entrances were covered as well as exits. Small signs attached to the glass beside the ticket counter announced the briefing was TOP SECRET POSITIVE IDENTIFICATION REQUIRED. A feeling of uneasiness began to creep into Nash's consciousness. *This is getting weirder by the minute*. Some of the patches on the flight jackets worn by the old dudes in line in front of him were positively ancient, at least to him. The metal rank insignia were under plastic covers, sewn onto the shoulders. *Was that two stars on that old guy's jacket? OMG.* A major general was talking to another older man, a captain, with an F-105 on his sleeve. *Thud drivers*? *And over there is a jock with an F-14 Tomcat and Grim Reaper VF-101 squadron insignia.* Nash didn't have a clue what was getting ready to be briefed, but his curiosity was certainly peaked.

As the 1000 briefing time approached, Colonel McElhenny stepped into the theater lobby and made an announcement. "Gentlemen! Please take your seats inside the auditorium. General Stewart is enroute and the building will be secured before the briefing begins."

Most of the attendees had already moved to their seats. The thirty or so holdouts had been engaged in a spirited renewal of old ties, forged through decades spent defending America's interests across the globe. They moved into the partially empty rows and sat down. Only 167 of the four hundred seats in the auditorium were filled. A second briefing would be held at 1500 hours later that day and a third and final orientation would take place Monday at 1400 hours. The doors at the rear opened. Colonel McElhenny made the order ring out. "Room! Ten-hut!"

Jack, flanked by his son, James, entered and made their way to the front. James stood by an empty seat in the front row where he was joined by Heater McElhenny. General Stewart approached the walnut podium emblazoned with a US Air Force Strike Command logo. He positioned the microphone carefully before he began to speak. "Take your seats, please."

The single spotlight illuminating the General danced off the eight stars on the epaulets of his dress uniform and reflected crazily off his command pilot wings as well the six rows of ribbons. The assembled group sat back down, with their eyes fixed on the silver haired warrior.

"I suppose an introduction is in order. For those of you I have not met personally, I'm General Jack Stewart, Commander of the newly formed 22nd Composite Wing here at Davis-Monthan. The briefing I am about to give you is TOP SECRET/NOFORN. It is not to be discussed in unsecured areas at any time or transmitted over unsecured means. For you young guys and gals, that means no Twitter or Facebook, either."

A chorus of chuckles rolled over the group.

"You were asked to come here because you are the best at what you do, or in many cases, the best at what you did. Each of you was personally selected by my staff or through your commanding officer because we need you." Jack let the words sink in for a second. "Last week, the armed forces of the United States were attacked, without notice or provocation, by forces believed to working at the behest of the People's Republic of China through an insidious high tech computer virus. Our Air Force, Navy and Marine aviation all suffered extreme damage to their ability to defend our national interests as well as substantial loss of life. That damage was aimed at our fourth and fifth generation fighters, stealth bombers and missile systems. As we speak, all are still disabled."

A buzz could be heard growing from the crowd as attendees murmured between each other. Jack held up his right hand to get the silence he needed before he continued. "Discussions with DoD contractors indicate it will take a minimum of six weeks to generate all the replacement hard drives needed for our high tech fighters and missile systems and over two months to get the B-2s back on line."

Most of the crew members found themselves shocked at the news that there were not adequate backup avionics available—thanks to the deep military budget cuts. Suddenly they began to feel the same vulnerability Burner Stewart had felt when he first recognized the extent of the damage that our fleets and air wings had suffered. Once again he held up his hand for silence. "Lights please," he said as he picked up the remote control for the slide projector.

The curtains behind him opened exposing a silver screen usually reserved for Hollywood films. He started the slide presentation with the obligatory security warning statement. He quickly advanced to the next slide, a color satellite shot of the massive twin hulled *Sun Tzu.*

"The Chinese government has demanded six trillion dollars in gold in repayment for their investments in US treasury bonds that are now worth approximately only two trillion. Our government does not have that amount of gold and would not pay their demands if they could. This, ladies and gentlemen, is Sun Tzu, one of two brand new Mao-Class ultra-super carriers the Chinese have made ready for departure. As you can see by the size of the Ju-20s on the deck, she is huge, approximately 1,500 feet in length. She has been tracked at an unbelievable sixty knots via sonar monitors. With three air wings aboard, she is well more than a match for any US CSG in terms of displacement, speed and aircraft. She is part of a huge two carrier task force with over forty thousand ground troops known to be aboard. According to the latest US Navy sonar intelligence, Sun Tzu and her sister ship, Yang Jian, departed the port city of Dalian last night with a massive, but as yet unknown number of capital ships. Presumed destination is the west coast of the United States." Jack left that last statement hang in the air. One could have heard a pin drop, as most people in the crowd could scarcely breathe. The slide of *Sun Tzu* disappeared, replaced by an aerial shot taken of lines of F-4s wrapped in white plastic. "Which brings us back to Tucson, Arizona, home of the 309th AMARG. Most of you know it as the boneyard. We have discovered some information about the old iron that many of you should find interesting. What you are about to see is the last few seconds of an engagement last month between a Lockheed F-104 and a pair of Raptors. Roll the video please."

Jack clicked off the slide projector. A video began with Burner providing the commentary. He pointed out the small dots he had determined to be Bravo 31 and 32. He let the split screen of the overtake and gun camera film speak for itself.

"Bravo 31 kill. Bravo 32 kill. Delta 22, Blackjack, I see you are approaching the southern end of the exercise area. Say intentions."

"Lights, please," Jack said as he clicked the remote of the video controller.

A single pair of hands clapped followed immediately by a growing thunder of applause. Jack held up both hands to help stem the show of amazement and appreciation. The information that a century series fighter had scored not one, but two simulated kills on the previously un-vanquished F-22 had been a well kept secret. Jack had made his point in a big way. The impact on his fighter crews was electric. He didn't have to connect the dots. These men and women were not stupid. In fact, they represented the top five percent of the population in brains and the top one percent in guts and training.

"What we have discovered is a means to detect, track, and target stealth fighters. Working with the fine folks at Raytheon, Lockheed-Martin and other contractors, we now have the ability to engage and defeat the enemy now posing the most serious threat to our country since WWII...and we will do it with specially modified aircraft with which you ladies and gentlemen have proven to be the deadliest operators on the planet. In just a few hours, a C-130 will arrive with the first shipment of radar absorptive material that will be applied to the entire surface of each of the fighters being brought back on line.

"Engineers at Lockheed have the technical data available and will cover that in your individual aircraft briefings. We are under a severe time constraint here, people. Our best intel estimates gives us seven to ten days until the Chinese are in position off our west coast. We are going to be asking a lot of each and every one of you." He looked around at the faces in the auditorium. "We have put together a team to support you in every way we can. Members of the logistics branch will assist you with flight gear and uniform items. The key here is cooperation. I know some of you will be outranking your squadron commanders by several pay grades. We need your inputs and will ask you for your assistance in tactics and planning. Until the aircraft are ready to rejoin the fleets, Navy and Marine crews will train side by side with Air Force crews. We cannot and will not abide any inter-service rivalries or bickering. I mean that. If you become a problem to us, you'll be gone by sunset. I'm serious…gone."

Nash and Kreimborg exchanged glances. *Who ever heard of a four-star wing commander? What did we get ourselves into?*

"There are another 170 crew members being contacted or traveling today. I can only compare our present situation to that of the Royal Air Force in the Battle of Britain. The fate of our country hangs in the balance." Jack paused for a second to allow the group to process what he just said. "I'm going to introduce you to your flight commanders. After the brief, you'll break up into squadrons and they will assign your systems review classes and simulator schedules as needed. We'll be using upgraded AIM-120 AMRAAM on all the birds. Those of you who have been out of the game for a while…are gonna be impressed."

AIRSPACE OVER CENTRAL PACIFIC
Sunday, 10 November

Gears noted the sun creeping over the horizon. *At least going eastbound, the sun will rise quickly and get out of our eyes.* "Max, let Blaze know we're back across the International Date Line and will be in range of Honolulu in ten minutes. It's also about time for a shift change. See that Julio and Bobby get started on breakfast. One more thing…"

"What?"

"Let Tze know we are five hours out. He wanted Doc Long to sedate Mrs. Chen one last time to keep her down until we arrive. She doesn't need to see those Black Eagles in the cargo bay."

"You got it, AC."

Max unstrapped and headed aft to wake Blaze. She was nestled in a gray leather recliner next to Dare—both had crew blankets draped across them. He hated to disrupt her slumber, but she was primary on the Offensive and Defensive System station where the reconnaissance system of *Manta* stored the voluminous files of the mission. He touched her on her shoulder. Her eyelids fluttered a couple times before she tried to bring his image into focus.

"Coming up on Hawaii, Blaze."

Three hours of sleep did not leave her well rested, but she slipped out of the recliner without waking Dare and got herself a bottle of water from one of the many coolers strapped to the floor around the crew compartment. The cool water helped kill the dryness in her mouth. Max woke the two relief pilots and his own backup flight engineer, Gunnz Garner.

Sosa and Mendez pulled their prepared meal trays out of the refrigerator and slid them into the galley oven. Mendez turned the timer knob to fifteen minutes and then headed to the forward lavatory. Sosa twisted at the waist and tried to stretch out some of the kinks from sleeping in the recliners. Gunnz decided to forego the meal and just partake of the very strong Kona coffee. There were still five hours flying time remaining until the *Galaxy* reached Travis AFB near San Francisco. He could eat at any time he wished, since the workload for loadmasters and flight engineers was really light once the

Eagles were back aboard and secured. The *Galaxy* automated most of the flight engineer functions and the Air Force actually had done away with the position.

The Black Eagle Force had highly qualified cross-trained personnel in almost all positions, and loadmaster/flight engineer was no exception. Both Max and Gunnz were Airline Transport Pilot rated flyers in addition to handling the systems and load problems. Max worked his way aft behind the rows of sleeping Raptors and other back-up crew members. He found Tze asleep with Kim watching the rescued Chinese American woman.

In a security conference between Dare, Tze and Kim, it was decided that she be left sedated until arrival on US soil. The CIA wanted a chance to debrief her in depth. Her daughter had committed one of the most serious acts of sabotage ever recorded in US history. If Stacie was anything other than what she claimed to be, her mother could also be a threat to US security interests. Dare wanted no unwarranted breaches of BEF secrets, if at all possible.

"How is she doing?" Max asked.

"Still out," Kim said as she checked her watch. "Where are we?"

"Waikiki will be off the starboard side in 15 minutes."

"Guess it's time Doc gave her the last shot before landing."

"Right. Tze wanted me to wake him when it was time."

"I could use a nap myself. I've never been on such a long plane ride."

"I would say you get used to it, but that wouldn't be true. Still kicks my butt…Morning, Doc. Your friendly wake-up call."

Former SEAL medic, Andy "Doc" Long responded to the nudge and rubbed his eyes.

"Morning this soon? Whoa. Feel like hammered duck poop."

"Look like it, too. Five hours out of Travis, time for mama Chen's last shot."

PENTAGON, WASHINGTON, DC
Sunday Afternoon, 10 November

"Mr. Baker, Admiral Valenti is on line one."

"Thanks, Bill…Charger! I hope you have some good news."

"Mixed, Mr. Secretary. We missed the Admiral by two hours."

"Damn! I really thought we had a shot at heading this conflict off before it gets to be a shooting war."

"It gets worse, sir. The BEF positively confirmed the carrier battle groups are moving out of Chinese waters. They picked up tons of info. My people in intel are beginning to break it down as we speak."

"They used radar to map the disposition?"

"Baker, they used everything they had. I've got low light color real time of nearly the whole damned fleet, plus infrared and the whole ELINT spectrum. We're even able to pinpoint what radar search freqs they are using and counted over 130 ships of the line escorting those two ultra-super carriers. They had the misfortune to stir up some luminescent plankton. Really lit 'em up for us."

"We can probably thank God for that. We're gonna need every edge we can get to try to even the playing field. What about the woman? Did we get her back?"

"Yeah, she's safe. The CIA will debrief her for a couple days in San Francisco."

"Right. Oh, you got the twix about the President wanting a full NSC briefing tonight?"

"Sure. We'll be ready with some detailed DOF analysis. By the way, looks like your boys at D-M are coming through for us. They're actually ahead of Burner's original estimates."

"Yeah, saw that. He's doing something right out there. It was a gamble to turn him loose, but I don't see we had any other choice, do you?"

"If he can get me four or five squadrons of Tomcats and Phantoms by week's end, I'd put him up for the MoH!"

"And I'll sign the recommendation. Keep me in the loop. Gonna be a long week."

"Aye-aye, sir. Charger out."

Baker flicked his intercom button. "Bill, get me the President."

"She's already on two, sir."

Baker just smiled, shook his head and punched the button.

HONOLULU, HAWAII
Sunday Morning, 10 November

Kelli jogged up the hilly street leading to her condo. She slowed to a walk as she turned into the parking lot and pulled the headphone buds out of her ears. He long red hair was pulled in a pony tail and draped over her shoulder as she rolled and tucked the tiny white unit into her lightweight lavender windbreaker. The sun was just coming up over the placid Pacific waters, and her part of Oahu was still in the deep shadows from the central mountain ridges that covered much of the islands interior.

It was only 62 degrees Fahrenheit on the typical Hawaiian fall day, but the effort from her solo run still left her glistening in a light sheen of perspiration. She heard the whine of a large military transport high overhead. Looking up, she saw absolutely nothing in the clear blue sky. Try as she might, she couldn't pick out the actual source of the distinctive hum of four high-bypass turbofans. *That's odd.*

Touching her iPhone to open the contacts icon, Kelli slid her slender finger down to the desired name and opened it up. She tapped a number and waited for them to answer. A slight northwest breeze filled her surroundings with the scent of hibiscus from a huge landscape planting of the gigantic flowers across the street from her building.

DAVIS-MONTHAN AFB, ARIZONA
Sunday Midday, 10 November

"Hold on guys, I've got to take this call, uh, it's my doctor." James said as he checked out the caller ID and got up from the table. "Doctor Johnson, Colonel Stewart. How nice of you to call."

"Colonel Stewart? What the hell is that? Already find another lady friend?"

"No, no…uh, no, I'm having lunch with some of the new guys in the squadron and I…"

"Didn't want to look like the whipped dog you are?"

"No, I mean…well, yeah."

"I miss you, too, you weasel. How's the face? Is the bruising starting to disappear?"

"I miss you, Kel, and it's only been one day."

"That's more like it. You didn't answer the question. How's the face?"

"Great, the topical vitamin E and arnica gel are doing the trick. You're so smart."

"And you only like me for my mind."

"You know better than that. How's Deacon's wife doin'?"

"Devastated, just like I'd be in her shoes. I'm dropping by after church. I'll tell her you were thinking about them."

"Thanks. Listen, sweetheart, don't want to stop talking, but we're on kind of a short schedule here. Call you this evening?"

"You better. It's different without you here on the island."

"I'll be back…Promise."

"And I'm gonna hold you to it."

"Now you're talkin'. Love ya. Catch you later."

James ended the call and slipped the phone back into his flight jacket. He returned to the table with a just little more spring in his step.

CENTRAL MILITARY COMMISSION
MINISTRY OF NATIONAL DEFENSE COMPOUND
BEIJING, PEOPLE'S REPUBLIC OF CHINA
Monday, 11 November

"He did what?" Paramount Leader Hu Jintao screamed.

Vice President Xi Jinping, his head bowed in shame, replied, "Admiral Huang did, in fact, set sail toward the United States last night before 2400 hours with two entire Carrier Battle Groups, most Honorable Leader."

"He did this without the permission of the Committee?" shouted Guo Boxiong, Vice Chairman of the Central Military Commission.

"So it would seem, Comrade Vice Chairman," replied Xi.

"This action is treasonous! Give him orders to return to port immediately!" said President Hu.

"I beg your forgiveness, Honorable Leader, but the fleet is apparently under total communications black out."

"If the United States is not already aware of the fleet's embarkation, they will be in very short order and will be moving up to four of their carrier groups to intercept Huang. They will not tolerate any foreign incursion into their waters regardless of the reason. I fear that our new and very expensive ultra-super carriers will wind up on the bottom of the Pacific

Ocean," said another Vice Chairmen of the Central Military Commission Xu Caihou.

"I think not, Comrade. You will recall Admiral Huang's statement that he had devised a plan that would negate the vaunted American air power, the missile capability of their submarines and Aegis guided missile cruisers. It seems to exceed providence or coincidence that almost fifty of their fifth generation fighters and a B-2 stealth bomber crashed in one day. They have since grounded all of their combat military aircraft except transports. We have heard no chatter on their MILSATCOM, coded or otherwise. There have also been no test missile launches since that day. In my humble opinion, the tiger is now toothless," proffered High General Chen Bingde, Chief of the General Staff of the PLAN.

"I must speak directly with the President of the United States. I do not for one moment consider the Americans to be as toothless as you might think, Comrade General," Hu said.

"Most Honorable Leader, I suggest we wait and let the US initiate contact about the movement of our fleet. For us to precipitate the contact will show guilt or complicity on our part. We can always deny any hostile intent and use the American's standard ploy of 'It's just an exercise'. It will give us time to contact Admiral Huang and determine his intentions."

DAVIS-MONTHAN AFB, ARIZONA
Sunday Afternoon, 10 November

Air Force Colonels Heater McElhenny and Marty "Duke" Ellington along with Marine Colonel "Wardog" Reynolds and

Navy Admiral Snake Sievers finally hung up the phones after many hours spent recruiting pilots to fly the gaggle of birds coming out of deep storage.

"I think I cauliflowered both my ears," said Heater as he stood up from his desk in the Personnel Section.

"Got myself a permanent crick," Wardog complained as he stretched out his arm and massaged his right biceps, and then the back of his neck.

"Tell you what, Wardog. If we ever have to do this again, I'll make sure we get some of those headsets like those telemarketers use."

"Bitch, bitch, bitch! You guys sound like a couple of old women. You don't hear me complaining."

"Duke, you little shit! You didn't get here until 1100. We've be at it since yesterday afternoon. Wipe that grin off your face," Heater spat back.

"Just pulling your chain, big guy. Did we get everybody you wanted?"

"Mostly. Some of 'em couldn't volunteer as result of physical challenges. Found out a few others had passed away. Others were just out of pocket, I guess…never did hear back from them," he replied as he looked at his cell phone for any missed calls.

TRAVIS AFB, CALIFORNIA
Sunday Afternoon, 10 November

The last vestiges of a November bay area fog dissipated under a relentless clear sky. A yellow afternoon sun shone brightly on the 12,000 foot runway as the unmarked dark gray C-5M *Super Galaxy* touched down. A light breeze from the west did little to dissipate the cloud of smoke created from the mass of tires under the monster transport.

"Galaxy 1, turn left at the next high-speed. Contact Travis Ground on 121.8"

"Galaxy 1, roger. Ground on point eight."

"Ground, Galaxy 1 with you for the transient ramp, negative customs, negative maintenance, require refuel."

"Galaxy 1, roger, make a left turn on the inner, right on taxiway six. Follow Transient Alert to parking."

Eight minutes later, the unmarked C-5M shut down all engines. A black Chevrolet Suburban followed two Air Force crew vans to the left side of the *Galaxy* as ground crew members hooked up the grounding wires and fueling hoses. A flight engineer with a powder blue flight suit bearing an embroidered Warbird Restorations, Inc. over the left breast walked down the forward crew stairs and presented a DoD credit card to the fuel technician on the starboard side of the aircraft.

"Top us off, my friend. Beautiful day we have, isn't it?" Gunnz Garner said.

"Yes it is. Don't think I ever saw another private C-5M. Where are you guys based?" the young airman asked.

"We're out of north Texas. We do restorations on old classics from WWII and Korea."

"Must be interesting."

"Yep. Sometimes."

A line of crew members in black flight suits and Raptors in their MCCDU camo uniforms filed out and boarded the crew vans and departed for the short ride to Base Operations. Kim and Tze, both dressed in civilian clothes led a somewhat woozy Lan Chen down the stairs and to the Suburban. When Mrs. Chen was safely seated in the back seat next to a young man wearing a dark suit, Kim turned to Tze and extended her hand.

"Thanks for everything. I won't forget your help."

"Pleasure meeting you, Kim. Let me know if you ever need somebody to make a night watchman pee his pants."

They both laughed and shook hands. Kim initiated a parting hug that was returned by Tze with enthusiasm.

"Call me if you ever get back to Cali," she said with a sly smile.

"That's a promise," he said as she climbed in the back bench seat beside the partially drugged Mrs. Chen.

He watched until the Suburban disappeared behind one of the massive hangars lining the ramp, and then made his way back to the C-5 and nestled into his recliner for a nap.

"Do you want me to order something from the grill? Their salad bar looks okay, but nothing to write home about," Mike Hermann said as he stood in line back of the team members in the operations snack bar.

"I'll stick with the salad bar. I'm not really all that hungry," Jill said as she fished the cell phone out of her flight suit.

She had retrieved it from her locker aboard *Mama Bird* after landing in California. She turned the phone on and checked to find seven missed calls and two messages from her father. She didn't bother to listen to the messages, but did choose to immediately return the call.

DAVIS-MONTHAN AFB, ARIZONA
Sunday Afternoon, 10 November

The four seasoned warriors were almost out of the headquarters building foyer when Colonel McElheney's cell phone vibrated. He pulled it out of his flight suit and checked the caller ID.

"Guys, I have to take this, it's my baby girl. Go ahead, I'll meet you at the club for lunch…Hey, Honey, I've been trying to get you for two days."

"Is Mom okay? You had me worried."

"No, no. She's fine. Just needed to talk to you about something important…I've been called back to active duty and we are really in need of fighter pilots. Good ones."

"But, Dad, the F-22s are all grounded, aren't they?"

"They are, but, we also need top Eagle drivers."

"I thought they were all grounded, too. Besides, I only flew the Eagle for less than two years before I transitioned to the Raptor."

"I know that, but you're one of the best. We need you."

Jill was confused. She was torn between her dedication to her father, her former career as one of the top Air Force fighter pilots and her present one as a Black Eagle Force pilot. Her new job was so cutting edge and secret she couldn't even tell her father what she did.

"Dad, what would I be flying?"

"I can't tell you over an unsecured line."

"Does it have anything to do with the Chinese Fleet deployment?"

Now it was Heater's turn to be surprised. News of the Chinese fleet being on the move was only released hours earlier from the DoD and the information was still highly classified. He tried to remain as noncommittal as possible. He also had to determine the source of her information. A news leak could be disastrous for the operation at this stage.

"Hon, I can't discuss the information regarding this assignment over an unsecured line. Where are you now?"

"I'm in Base Ops at Travis. Why?"

"Call me on Autovon at the number I text you. Give me a minute to get back upstairs, okay?"

"Sure, Dad. I'll find a phone in ops."

Jill sought help from a tech sergeant behind the operations desk and was shown to a room with phones capable of the *Automated Secure Voice Network* commonly called the Autovon System. She entered the number and waited for the line to connect.

"Colonel McElheney," the man on the other end answered.

"Dad, what's going on?"

"We're recruiting top pilots for a special mission, but I have to ask you, Jill. How did you hear about the Chinese Fleet movements? That is highly sensitive information, and I have to find out where you got access to it."

"Uh, I saw it last night."

"You what? Are you talking about a satellite feed?"

"Nope. Up close and personal, but I can't tell you how or why. Have to get clearance from my boss, first."

"Who's your boss?"

"Dare Phillips."

"Iron Horse?"

"You know him?"

"Met him at the War College. Thought he retired."

"He did, just like you."

"Yeah, know how that works."

"Let me talk to him. Call you back."

Jill approached Dare and Blaze at a small table in the snack bar.

"Boss, need your help."

"Sure, Jill, what is it?"

"My dad has been called back to active duty. You two met at the War College."

"Right, his call sign was Heater if I remember correctly. What is it?"

"He wants me to come back to the Air Force and fly the F-15s...but that's not what I need your help about."

"Hold on there, girl. He wants you back? What's your decision and what can I do?"

"The help is about the Chinese Fleet. I asked him if his request concerned the fleet and he weirded out on me. Said he couldn't talk about it. I need your guidance."

Dare paused for a moment, glanced at Blaze then back to Jill.

“Something else is going on.” Dare pulled out his secure Iridium sat phone and selected a number from his speed dial. “Bill, Iron Horse, I need to speak with Secretary Baker.”

***

CHAPTER ELEVEN

PENTAGON
WASHINGTON, DC
Sunday Afternoon, 10 November

"Sir, I'll be happy to connect you. We're glad you made it back safe and sound."

"Appreciate the kind thoughts, Bill."

"Glad to hear your voice, Iron Horse. Sorry the mission timing wasn't a day earlier."

"Yes, Mr. Secretary. We were close, but our high value target slipped out of our fingers."

"I have to hand it to you, though, the intel your team picked up vis-à-vis the fleet was critical. Admiral Valenti was impressed."

"Just doing our duty, Mr. Secretary. The fleet is the reason I called, sir. One of my top fliers was called by her formerly retired father to recruit her back into the Air Force to fly the F-15. She asked if it had to do with the Chinese fleet and he went into classified mode on her. I wonder if you could shed a bit of light on the situation. We were under the impression that the F-15s were grounded. Is there any kind of connection between the fleet and the fighter pilot recall?"

Harold Baker took a deep breath. A determination had to be made on whether to release the information on the status of the efforts underway at Davis-Monthan. *The Black Eagle Force has no real need to be apprised of the situation at this time. Or do they?*

"Dare, what do you know about Davis-Monthan Air Force Base?"

"Just what I studied at the War College, sir. Major Strike Command and Air Guard fighter base, plus the boneyard. Why?"

"Because they are currently the only source of operational fighters in the country. All the newer birds have been compromised by a very virulent Chinese virus that knocked out all our B-2s, fourth and fifth gen fighters and almost all of our nuclear capability except for bombs. Got the picture?"

"Jesus, I had no idea."

"Well it's not what you want to see printed in three inch headlines by the New York Times. I've got a four-star down at D-M running the regeneration effort. We don't have enough trained active duty pilots for all the older birds and we want some of our Top Gun and Fighter Weapons Center grads as well as combat vets to come back and serve. You saw the Chinese fleet and those two monster carriers with your own eyes. We have a week or so before they are in position for a preemptive strike. Basically, we couldn't defend our west coast against the fleet today."

"Almost sorry I asked…Mr. Secretary, you know the capabilities of the BEF as well as anyone in the administration."

"Yes, I do. What are you thinking?"

"With your permission, I'd like to talk to your four-star…"

"He's Jack "Burner" Stewart, by the way."

"Heard of him…MiG ace…Hell of a stick…Anyway, I'd like to talk to him about combining forces with the group out of D-M. We could possibly be instrumental in knocking out those carriers defensive perimeter."

Baker processed the request and tried to imagine what Phillips and his team could do to a carrier task force. *Holy Mother of God. That could work.*

"I'll tell Burner to expect your call. Maybe you're on to something! Damn, what with Bill and now you knowing what I need even before I do…"

"It's called teamwork, sir."

"I guess it is, Dare, I guess it is and thank God for it."

DAVIS-MONTHAN AFB, ARIZONA
Sunday Afternoon, 10 November

"Everybody buckled in?" Jill asked as she slipped her right hand around the throttle and began to ease it forward.

After a short phone conversation a couple of hours earlier, Jack had invited Dare and his BEF to make the short hop from Travis to D-M. A quick demonstration flight in *Eagle 1* was proffered. Burner sat in the right seat normally manned by the WSO. Jill's father, Colonel C.J. McElheney sat directly behind her, flanked by Lt. Colonel James Stewart. Jill glanced back over her shoulder and saw a pair of thumbs pointed upward. The low hum of eight Rotopower rotary engines became an angry roar like a million hornets as she advanced the central located throttle—the small dark craft lifted off the remote ramp. Jill pointed to the small molded plastic handle resembling a wheel and tire and spoke to General Stewart.

"Gear up, please."

"Gear coming up," he replied as he pulled the small handle out, then up to its locked position.

Burner glanced over as Jill touched a *Lizard* icon on her CDU screen; the nose of the craft seemed to shimmer slightly.

"Tower, November X-ray India Tango departing east ramp westbound VFR. Will remain clear of all runways."

"November X-ray India Tango, D-M Tower does not have you in sight. Cleared to cross the active runway. Call when clear."

"India Tango, wilco," Jill said as she pushed forward on the stick and throttle simultaneously. The flight computers on the *Eagle* modified the pitch angle of the vanes at the back of the four nacelles sending the craft forward. All three of her passengers marveled at the acceleration as the Skycar quickly streaked westward across the air base.

“Tower, India Tango clear of all runways. Good day.”

“D-M tower, roger. Maintain VFR.”

Inside the control tower, the sergeant responsible for flight operations lowered his binoculars and shook his head.

“I’m glad they called to coordinate that first. I never saw a thing, did you?”

The airman first class ground controller simply shook his head.

In minutes, the *Eagle* was at 100 feet AGL streaking across the Arizona desert west of Tucson at almost 400 KIAS.

“General, take us up to 2,000 feet. You have the aircraft.”

“Roger, I have the aircraft,” he said as he slipped his right hand over the side stick on the side of the cockpit and shook it ever so slightly. “That Lizard system you activated. Tell me how it works. I can see the nose is changing colors as we fly over different terrain.”

“It requires an electronically activated complex system of sensors to detect optical conditions on opposing sides of the aircraft. The chromatophores in the skin are energized to reflect what is on the other side of the aircraft, essentially making it invisible. It’s similar to what a chameleon does, hence the nickname, Lizard.

“Sounds a little more complicated than the RAM I want to add to the old iron. That’s too bad.”

“One disadvantage is that it makes formation flying a bitch. And it requires a lot of training flights to learn to support each other in a dogfight…We’re south of Phoenix now. I’ll set up the visual display from our URF that we call Manta, and pick out a tank on one of the Luke ranges. I remember some they had southeast of Gila Bend."

She busied herself with the downloaded feed from the high flying unmanned reconnaissance fighter. A view of a line of partially demolished T-60 tanks came into view. The setting sun cast long shadows across the sparely covered desert terrain. She called to Tom back aboard *Mama Bird* parked on the remote spot at D-M.

"Mama Bird, Eagle 1, give me laser lock on the T-60 at the south end of the line."

"At your service, Eagle 1," he said as he slid the crosshairs over the image of the tank and right clicked it. A powerful laser from *Manta* bathed the turret with an invisible beam three feet across.

"Confirm the range is hot for Eagle 1."

"Eagle 1, range is hot from surface to 25,000 feet," Tom replied.

"Eagle 1 copies. We're eight miles out and closing."

Jill tapped in two commands and set up a split screen with FLIR display on the right and weapons status on her left side.

"Burner, I have the aircraft."

"Roger, Lucky, you have the aircraft," he replied as he reluctantly relinquished command.

"Now I want you to roll the tracker ball onto the designated tank," she said as she pointed at the blue ball mounted aft of the weapons CDU. Just move the orange arrow over the tank and left click it."

He followed her instructions—a *LOCKED* icon appeared on the right screen.

"Select one of the Hellfires from the panel on my side. Use the ball like a mouse and click it."

"Got it."

"When we're in range, the LOCKED icon will turn green, and I want you to pull the red trigger on your stick."

"That's it?"

"You want it more complicated, sir?"

"No, I just…oh, there's the in-range signal."

"Fire."

Burner squeezed the trigger. A bright white flame erupted off the top of the left rear strut. A short deafening roar was heard inside the cockpit, followed by a whoosh as the Hellfire lit off and cleared the rail. The pilots could see a plume of white as the rocket streaked upward for several seconds, then turned over and descended almost straight down onto the turret. From a distance the red and yellow flash did not look impressive.

"Tom can you give us a close-up?"

"Can do."

The 1.8 Gigapixel ARGUS-IS cameras aboard *Manta* pulled into a tight, ultra high definition shot. It clearly showed the smoking turret lying twenty yards from the flaming hulk.

"Nice shooting, Burner. How many tanks have you killed?"

"This and one more will make two. Can't believe it's that easy."

"It's all due to the in-depth ground school," Jill joked. "Hang on guys."

The words barely left her mouth when she initiated a Cobra maneuver, and brought the *Eagle* to an abrupt stop from their 400 KIAS a mile from the burning tank. All four pilots found themselves grunting from the four G deceleration. Jill leveled the craft and toggled the switch to arm the G2 coil gun. She activated the new Helmet Mounted Display, called HMD for short that replaced the old HUD system and talked Burner through the process she used to target the next tank in line. Once she had made a laser bore lock with the G2 on the tank, she squeezed her red trigger for three-quarters of a second. A stream of hypervelocity 7mm projectiles filled the air. A faint blue glow of superheated plasma flashed as eighteen of the deadly tungsten steel rods streaked across the darkening sky. On the close-up of the second tank, the impact of the projectiles could be seen in a rapid series of flashes.

"Good hit, Lucky, but I don't see much damage."

"Let's go down and check it out while there's still light."

"You mean land?"

"That's the idea…I forget you guys can't do this with your birds."

Jill made a routine approach and landing. As the dust settled, she opened the crew door on the left side and issued a brief warning.

"Watch your step, might be some really pissed off rattlesnakes left around."

The four approached the tank, the newest hits were obvious—no rust was visible around the new craters. Burner looked at one of the lower holes and could see completely through the turret, the chassis, the offside tracks and deep into the ground.

"My God! That's as much damage as the A-10 inflicts. What do you call that gun again?"

"Sir, it's called the Blaze G2. Blaze Hermann and Gears Formby, our AC on Mama Bird cooked it up."

"Unbelievable. How much armor did you say it can penetrate?"

"I think Blaze says seventy-two inches…but, she tends to be a bit conservative. Anyway, I'd like my Dad to sit up front for the return flight, with your permission, sir. We haven't had a chance to fly together for a long time."

"By all means. Heater, you have the right seat. I think you're gonna like this little bird. I'm certainly impressed."

"You took the words right out of my mouth, Dad. Dare said she took on a MiG 29 with it," Hollywood added.

"It was our two seater…five nacelle version. Guns only. Didn't work out as well as I liked…I lost the bird…and my WSO," Jill replied solemnly.

"You'll have to tell us the story on the way back to base…Didn't know about that either," Heater said as he looked at his daughter curiously. *What else have you not told me ?*

Fifteen minutes later, *Eagle 1* and *Manta* flew a straight-in approach to Davis-Monthan. Tom used the infrared camera to fly on the *Eagle's* wing.

"November X-ray India Tango flight, cleared to land on runway 22."

"India Tango flight, roger, cleared to land on runway 22."

Jill switched on the landing lights as she reviewed the before landing checklist in her head. "Gear down, three green. Cleared to land," she said over the comm. "Keep it over the left side and maintain 120 indicated for Manta. Small movements of the stick, Dad. You're doing great."

"You sure you want me to land?"

"If I didn't have confidence in you, wouldn't have put you in the seat. Besides, you guys are all going to need as much stick time you can get to be back anywhere close to combat ready in a week."

"Got a point, there. How did you get so smart?"

"Good genes…Probably from Mom," she said as she grinned and glanced at her dad.

"No doubt."

Several minutes later, *Eagle 1* and *Manta* pulled to a stop on the remote pad near the gargantuan *Mama Bird.* Dare, Blaze and Mike Hermann accompanied by Kit Kitaen met the pilots as they disembarked from the M600/A.

"See anything you like General?" Dare asked.

"Colonel, you have just what this country needs to help us on this upcoming mission. An invisible stealth fighter with a big nasty gun. I had no idea."

"General Stewart, in addition, our Galaxy has offensive and defensive capabilities it would take over an hour to brief," Blaze added.

"I don't doubt it, young lady...Oh, I remember you now. Tried to hire you at Lockheed when you got your doctorate from Rice. Turned us down flat. Where did you go to work?"

"For myself," Blaze replied with a wink.

"Uh, huh. Well, we received the intel report and images you collected last night. I'm sold. Just where did you get all those wonderful toys?"

"Well, actually, the BEF serves as a test bed for DARPA through the DoD, plus we have our own R & D division."

"Amazing stuff," Hollywood commented.

"General, is there any hangar space where we can keep our birds out of sight. Kinda like to keep them under wraps, if you know what I mean."

"Dare, as you can see, we're pretty committed here. Tell you what...I have my personal hangar that I lease over at Tucson International. There should be more than enough space for ten of your 600s and two Mantas. I can have Lars help you guys put what you have here to bed tonight. In any event, I need to get the Silver Knight over here for a RAM coating."

"By the way, we actually have a total of fourteen 600s and one 200, our two-seater—the wings fold on the 600s and Manta. We can pack them pretty tight. Any asset or personnel we can lend your group, sir, let me know. Oh, and if you wish, we also have one of the new Sea Fighter FSF-1s we can bring in. She's docked at San Diego."

"You have a Sea Fighter?"

"Just got it, we've named her Sea Eagle. She's stealthy, has a flank speed over fifty-five knots and can carry four of our M600s," Dare added.

"Jesus, Mary and Joseph." Burner extended his hand and Dare shook it firmly. "Pleasure to have your team aboard, Dare."

"I'll call my folks in from Denison and Eagle Nest. We'll get the whole team here on our C-130…she's equipped as a Spooky gun-ship. May take a couple of trips. Your teams have their hands full trying to put together that gaggle of mixed birds. I'll get you a spread sheet of our men and equipment."

"Don't you mean our people?" Blaze asked.

"Right. Old habits and all that…"

"You're turning into a regular dinosaur, dear."

"I know, just part of my irresistible charm."

"Glad you think so," she said as she turned to walk back to Mama Bird.

WASHINGTON, DC
SITUATION ROOM
WHITE HOUSE
Sunday Evening, 10 November

It was one minute after 9:00p.m. EST when President Thompson turned the meeting of the NSC over to Secretary of Defense Baker.

"Thank you Madame President. Ladies and gentlemen, inside the folders in front of you, you will find a detailed briefing of all the current information relating to the known disposition of the Chinese fleet. Their current position is approximately 400 nautical miles east of Okinawa. Appendix Two contains the latest updates on the 22nd Composite Wing as of fifteen minutes ago. Preparations are ongoing around the clock. No major unanticipated challenges have been encountered. General Stewart has advised the first fifteen of the modified fighters with the stealth RAM coating have been completed. Lastly, the General has also advised that the Black Eagle Force has volunteered to join the defensive effort and he has enthusiastically accepted their offer."

"What do they think they can do that a squadron of active duty fighters can't do better?" asked NSC Director Austin Roberts.

"A valid question. For those of you who are not familiar with the nuts and bolts of the BEF, they are equipped with very small, but highly effective, stealth fighters and a huge platform for delivering them world wide. Their airborne battle carrier, a C-5M called Mama Bird, also has self contained command and control equipment equivalent to an AWACS, and electronic jamming suite comparable to a B-52 with offensive and defensive capabilities unlike anything else in use in any of our services."

"Now, Harold, is that going to create a problem, using civilians in an active combat support role?" wondered Attorney General Alan Ames.

"Not that I can see, Alan. Most of them are ex-military. As some of you know, we regularly task the BEF under standard protocol contract with the DoD. We could, however, bring them back on active duty if necessary. But, in any case, it's not much different than using civilian contractors as we did in Iraq. Wouldn't you agree, Madame President?"

"Of course. We have a deep trust of the people of the Black Eagle Force. I would certainly not turn down their participation in the face of this current challenge."

Secretary of State Conrad Harper did not approve of the talk he was hearing. He felt he could negotiate a settlement and come out a hero, if not a prime candidate for his party's nominee in the next presidential election. President Thompson noticed a frown on his face and a narrow furrow forming between his eyes.

"Conrad, I see you are dying to offer a different viewpoint. Let's hear it."

He shot a disapproving look at her. *Damn. Is she psychic?*

"Madame President, I find the premise that we are headed for out and out warfare somewhat repugnant. I expect such from Admiral Valenti or Secretary Baker, but I had hoped cooler heads would prevail, helping fend this crisis off before men died."

Valenti shot him a look that let Conrad know the Admiral could cut him up for bait and never think twice. Conrad swallowed hard, and then turned to face the President. "President Thompson, I propose that I should contact Premier Hu directly. I feel if he and I could speak freely, I could persuade him to listen to reason. Have any of you considered the possibility that this Admiral Huang Meng could be acting without knowledge and approval of the Central Committee?"

"Highly doubtful, Mr. Secretary. No nation spends a trillion dollars on such a capability and leaves the keys to a loose cannon," Admiral Valenti offered.

"Conrad, I don't want you to engage them in discussions at this time. We are not certain of their destination. It is a little too early to act as if we are actually threatened when they have six thousand miles of open water to cross before they are in range. We'll meet again at 7AM. The meeting is adjourned…you all have work to do."

President Thompson entered the family's private quarters upstairs, Gunter was pouring himself a cup of coffee from a carafe brought up by the White House kitchen staff. "All done?" he asked, looking up.

"Until seven in the morning…Harold said the entire BEF is joining up with General Stewart at D-M."

"Thought that might come down…Gotta pack, Hon…You know I have to go. Gunnz will need my help. I can get a hop out of Andrews," Gunter said, putting down his cup and walking over to Annie.

As they embraced, she said, "I know…All the way upstairs I kept going over ways to keep you here…I came up blank."

"Sometimes we have choices and sometimes we don't."

"You watch out for our children…and yourself, hardhead. I love you."

"I love you too…Madame President."

WESTERN PACIFIC OCEAN
Wednesday Morning, 13 November

The rays of the early morning sun were just becoming visible through the large brass portal when Admiral Huang Meng sat bolt upright in the lavishly appointed bed in his equally ostentatious cabin decorated with Chinese antiquities aboard *Sun Tzu.* He looked around in confusion for a moment then realized the giant ship was not moving—the impellers of the six powerful, nuclear-driven jet thrusters were at idle. Meng sprang to his feet, rushed to the comm system at his desk and keyed the bridge. "Captain Gwok Wei, why is the ship stopped?"

"Many pardons, Admiral Huang. We ran into the debris field from the Japanese tsunami just before dawn. We sailed into an area similar to the Sargasso Sea of the Atlantic…the currents of the Pacific Trash Vortex have kept the debris concentrated in an enlarged convergence zone. Our thruster screens are clogged with trash and we have a team over side clearing them as we speak."

"My God, man, that tsunami was last year. Why was the field not detected?"

"There is nothing in the field that will show on radar. It was invisible to us during the night. The screens should be cleared in short order, Admiral."

"Make it fast Captain. I want to be back underway by 0900."

"Sir, the field extends as far as the eye can see to the east and south. There are whole houses, appliances, trees, lumber, capsized ships, shipping containers and boats of all types. We have already lost one destroyer and two frigates to propeller or shaft damage. We cannot go forward…Sir."

"Then, bring the fleet about to port as soon as able and take a heading of 035. We'll skirt to the north away from the Japanese current then turn toward Midway."

"Aye, sir. That may take us an additional two days…"

"I know that, Captain. In the end, it won't change anything."

"Aye, sir."

DAVIS-MONTHAN AFB, ARIZONA
Wednesday Morning, 13 November

Major Eddie Nash and Captain Joe Kreimborg finished their briefings for the two colonels who had just completed their ground schools and simulator refreshers. At the next table, four other officers, two pilots and two WSOs who were already on their second flight after their initial requal.

"Boomer, anything else you wanted to add?" Nash asked Lt. Col. Baumhauer at the next table.

"Only that the hard deck is firm at 10,000 feet MSL. Don't want anybody busting his ass trying to make a bad decision into a good one. Knock it off and call for another set up. Okay?"

A round of nodding heads indicated the other eight pilots. With Nash and Kreimborg being some of the very few active duty Air Force pilots with instructor backgrounds and F-4 currency, both were being tasked heavily in the first half of the hectic regeneration effort. They were each flying four missions a day, and logging more time than they ever thought possible in a week. Twenty minutes later, they were gear up and turning west bound to the MOA outside of Yuma MCAS. From their entry altitude of FL 280, the flight of four *Phantoms* could expect the opposing forces to be coming in at any altitude.

To make the training as realistic as possible, Burner had mixed the opposing forces and scheduled two F-8s, two F-105s, two F-106s, two F-111 and a single F-104 in the Red Air Force strike package. The F-106s had not yet been coated with the RAM stealth coating and would be relatively easy for the Blue Force *Phantoms* to pick up, particularly in a turn. A seasoned F-111 veteran with flying time in Vietnam and Desert Storm, Brigadier General Bruce Crimin, was picked as the flight lead in the day's second flight. He had deployed the F-111s and F-105s low, taking advantage of their high speed dash capability, the F-8s and F-106s at FL350 and the F-104 at FL450.

"Cactus, Azure 1 flight entering the block," Major Nash radioed from the back seat of the lead F-4.

"Azure 1, Cactus Control, radar contact. MOA is hot at this time surface to FL600. Hard deck at ten thousand. Multiple bogeys inbound, cleared to maneuver as required."

"Azure 1, copy all," replied Nash as he flipped the red safety cover up on his master weapons arming switch. With his gloved hand, he toggled the silver switch to the *ARM* position. "Weapons are hot, Wardog. Show me what the Marines taught you."

"Here we go," Wardog said over interphone. He waggled the wings on the dull black F-4. Azure 2 slid out to fighting wing three hundred feet on the port side. Azure 3 and Azure 4 moved even farther, out to five hundred and seven hundred feet starboard and descended some two hundred feet as briefed.

"Contacts bearing 265 for 30," Nash commented as he got a return from the pair of *Delta Darts*. "Looks like they're low. Under three-zero-zero."

"Gotcha, Little Eddie. Lock em up," Wardog said on the intercom as he slid the throttles around the stop into burner. "Lead has contacts low at eleven-thirty. Three, take em' high."

Azure 2 followed his leader and entered a shallow dive. He and his WSO/Instructor felt the steady push of the J-79s as the afterburners kicked in to accelerate the vintage craft closer to Mach 2.

"Contacts, confirmed. Call your tally. Keep you eyes open, Colonel. There may be more of 'em than we can track with radar," Joe Kreimborg advised.

"Nothin' yet," replied the sixty-two year old aircraft aommander. His eyes scanned all quadrants as he cross-checked the APG-65GY radar sweeps. A steady beep-beep-beep high-pitched tone from the *Phantom's* radar warning system let him know that the Red Air fighters were in a search mode. Colonel John "Mils" Milbourn glanced inside at his RHAW gear. Four spokes indicated multiple sources of incoming radiation. Suddenly, a fifth spoke appeared.

"Five bandits, eleven to one o'clock. No joy."

"Got a lock on the northern most return!"

“Got it. Azure 2, Fox Two!” Mils called over the Blue Force frequency as he triggered off a simulated AMRAAM at the F-106.

“Azure 1, Fox Two!” Wardog called as his WSO locked up the other F-106. Out of the bottom of his clear visor, he caught a flash of movement well below the *Phantom.* He snapped his head to see the shapes of a pair of F-111s with wings swept back streaking across the desert at 11,000 feet. “Talley ho! Two *Aardvarks* 10 o’clock low!” Wardog tugged the throttles to idle and slammed left rudder and aileron causing the supersonic bird to snap left and shudder under the strain of eight Gs and he tried to pull the nose down and around to follow the fleeing fighter bombers.

“Keep it on the road, Wardog!” joked Little Eddie as the *Phantom* beat the air into submission.

There are many elegant nimble fighters in the sky. The F-4 is not one of them. The *Phantom* shook like a pickup driving on a washboard dirt road as Wardog kept his eyes on the black silhouettes of the F-111s.

“Watch your AOA!” Nash warned as the F-4 bled airspeed back below Mach 1.

Pulling his nose through vertical while inverted—Wardog cross-checked his AOA and altitude on his HUD. Noting the high angle-of-attack, he eased off the stick as he came back with some throttle. He strained at the steady seven Gs and grunted as he tried to form words. “Heaters.”

Back in his beloved F-8 *Crudsader* for the first time in twenty years, Lt. Commander Evan "Ev" Bradshaw let the computing gunsight do all the work. The lead F-4 had rolled belly up and was going for a shot on the two F-111s. He smoothly rolled inverted to match the F-4's descent and slid his finger over the red trigger on his stick. The black *Phantom* filled the gunsight in his HUD. "Red 3, guns."

Beneath him a pair of F-105 *Thunderchiefs* fifteen miles in trail of the F-111s picked up the motion of a second F-4 *Phantom* breaking down toward the *Aardvarks*. Blasting across the Arizona desert at Mach 2, the lead called a visual on the black F-4. "Red 7 tally ho the *Phantom*," he said as he pulled back hard on the stick.

Boundary layer air separated across the huge *Thunderchief* wing. A ragged white cloud formed and then rapidly disappeared as Colonel Richter brought his nose up aggressively to meet the threat to his predecessors. He thumbed the selector atop his stick and selected the AIM-9 infrared missile. As the F-4 appeared in the upper center of his HUD, a steady tone told him the *Phantom* was in range. Richter squeezed the trigger and grunted out the radio call. "Red 7, Fox Two!" He broke hard left and cleared up and to his left where, to his dismay, a pair of black *Phantoms* was starting to break in inverted pulls from their high vantage point at FL280. He instinctively unloaded the back pressure and slammed his throttle to the stops in full burner. "Red 7, bandits eleven o'clock high. A little help here…"

With a 2,400 knot closure rate, the F-4s passing through 22,000 feet slid behind him and were still nose down pointed the other direction. Red 8 was in no position to offer support, as the F-4s were behind him at the same time. But high above the developing furball, a seasoned pilot in his newly blackened *Starfighter* announced his intentions. "Red 1, Fox Two…Fox Two."

The pair of *Phantoms* appeared to hang in the air before Burner Stewart. Of course they were descending rapidly as they tried to chase the high supersonic F-105s who had pulled out a good eight miles ahead of them. Jack was inverted over very familiar terrain as he closed the distance between the re-christened *Black Knight* and the barely supersonic F-4s. The wingman, Azure 4, floated in front of his pipper as the hazy heat from its twin exhausts caused the image to become almost a mirage. At a point sixty degrees nose low, the canopy of the descending F-4 became visible once again to the pilot of the attacking F-104. Jack bumped the stick slightly forward as he thumbed the guns hot. He placed the pipper on the canopy and took a one second burst. "Red 1, guns."

Jack snapped the *Starfighter* through a right 300 degree roll and pulled over to the lead *Phantom*. He barely had time to set up for a gun shot before he overtook the second *Phantom* and squeezed the trigger.

"Azure 3, Fox Three!"

"Red 1, guns!"

The two radio calls overlapped each other on different frequencies. Azure 3 had achieved a valid setup for his AMRAAM shot at the trailing *Thunderchief*. Burner pulled back on the stick and switched to guard frequency. "Red 1 overtaking pair of *Phantoms* at one-six thousand. All elements knock it off. Red Flight, rejoin at one-five thousand for recovery."

Inside Azures 3 and 4, the sight of the sleek black *Starfighter* streaking by at a six hundred knot speed advantage was not a welcome one.

"Holy shit! Where the hell did he come from?" a disappointed Heater McElheney asked.

"Don't know, boss. Hey, four! I thought you were supposed to cover our six!"

"Major, you want to answer that? I never saw zip," the AC said glumly.

"Sorry, Colonel. Guess I should have paid more attention to the RHAW gear. It's been a while."

"Yeah, for both of us."

At the debriefing, Jack was pleased with the information gained from the exercise. Given the relatively small radar system of the F-4E, he was encouraged that the system had allowed a missile shot at a fleeing F-105. The low PRF mod was proving its worth on the AIM-120. Jack was even ready to concede that Wardog got the missile shot off before the *Starfighter's* gun ripped him to shreds. Wardog did not even bother to contest the gun kills.

"General, just like in the NFL, instant replays are a bitch… Why was it that we didn't detect you, again?"

"I didn't initiate my search radar until I had a visual on you two. We still don't have all the tactics down pat for this operation. I do know that if we can offer some form of AWACS coverage, I'm going to recommend that we minimize the fighter's radar usage until needed."

"Is that why you haven't modified the two target birds we brought up from Eglin?" asked Eddie Nash.

"It's one of the reasons, Major. We're working with some R&D folks to give the Chinese a couple headaches they haven't even thought of. It should be ready later in the week. People, great show out there this morning. Even given the handicap of simulated missiles, I'm happy with your instincts and aircraft handling. Don't put too much validation on the numbers from today's little show. The range simulation results show all Blue Force birds destroyed with three of the eight Red Force downed. With our ECM pod mods, we think we can raise our survivability rates substantially. That wraps it up for this brief. I'd like to see the squadron commanders here for a short meeting. Thank, you."

The WSO and instructors got up to leave. General Stewart intercepted Major Nash before he got to the door. Jack motioned for his attention.

"Sir, you wanted to see me?"

"How are you and Joe hanging in there? I don't want to wear you to a nub."

"If we get to the point where we can't go, sir, I'll raise my hand. I know we don't have much time."

"I appreciate your effort, son. Is there anything you would change?"

Eddie thought for a moment. “Sir, I think it would be a good idea if you would have three or four crews sit in on the briefings. It’s kinda like Yogi Berra said, ‘This game is ninety percent mental. The other half is physical.’ I think it would do the guys a favor to try to get their heads into the mission planning and briefing scenario as much as possible.”

“Great idea. I’ll see that it happens. Any thing else?”

Eddie hesitated for a second. “Sir, I don’t want you to take this wrong. Joe and I are not trying to hog time or anything…”

“Go on, say what you feel.”

“Sir the thing is, Joe and I don’t get that much stick time ourselves. We deliver the drones and make our basic minimum time and get a couple BFM rides a year.”

“Your point is…”

“Sir, what I’m trying to say is Joe and I both need a ride in the front seat before we go into combat next week. We’re watching other guys fly and react and being an instructor is just not the same a being a mission ready combat pilot.”

Jack studied the young Major. He thought about his later career and all the time he spent on Wing Staff when his primary duty was not being a line jock. He knew what Nash was feeling.

“Glad you brought it up, Major. I want all my guys to feel confident in their abilities. I’ll make sure you both get a ride before Saturday.”

“Thanks, General. Thanks for caring.”

NELLIS AFB, NEVADA
Wednesday Afternoon, 13 November

The afternoon quiet was broken as a flight of four black F-15 *Eagles* roared overhead. The young airman participating in a FOD walk across the ramp full of disabled aircraft looked up at the unusual fourship.

"I thought they were all grounded," he said to another, more senior airman first class.

"I heard the first shirt talking to the DCM. He said to expect a gaggle of them up from the boneyard."

"Aw, man, there goes our weekend. All those old A and B models are ancient. Some of 'em are older than I am."

"Maybe so, but they're flying and ours are all still tits up."

"Why didn't they just pull the black boxes out of the old ones and stick them in the newer birds?"

"Jonsey, you would be dangerous if you had a brain. Why do you think they have all those avionics black boxes numbered and coded? They don't just swap out from airframe to airframe. There are a lot of differences between models. My dad worked on the first Eagles way back when he was on active duty. Plus he was an avionics specialist. That's how come I know all that stuff."

"So far, all they let me do is brakes and wheels."

"There you go. Another three years plus a couple schools and we might let you touch one..."

"Bite me, Darnell."

Colonel Peterman, flying lead in the first F-15, followed the hand signals of the marshallers into parking. Four rows of the disabled *Eagles* had been removed to a remote ramp and stored until replacement avionics and hard drives were obtained from the suppliers. Peterman's wingmen taxied into the adjoining slots. As the canopies opened on the four fighters, another fourship entered initial for the active runway. Fifteen minutes later, sixty of the familiar, but now somewhat different, F-15s filled the ramp. None of the aircraft bore tail numbers or any external identification for that matter. The lead line mechanic on the shift approached Colonel Peterman. "How was your flight in, sir?"

"Good overall. I got a warning flag in my standby attitude indicator. Can you check it out?"

"Absolutely…Uh, sir? How do you tell bird from bird? They covered over the tail numbers."

"Inside the nose wheel well, there are some numbers painted on the inside of the gear doors."

"That's different."

"Yeah, a little trick we learned from the Russians back in the '70s. All their Bears had the same number painted on the tail. Kept us guessing how many they really had."

"Don't satellites make all that information pretty much common knowledge today?"

"Not if we use hangars and mockups, Sergeant. It's a new day, and a new way."

Peterman grabbed his helmet bag and headed for the crew van. The lead mechanic stood scratching his head.

"Afternoon, Flash, got the briefing room all set up for you."

"Thanks, Rocket, we have a lot to cover for the current pilots. Were you able to get the differences training completed?"

"Oh, yeah. Should have heard the pissin' and moanin'. You'd think we were gonna make them fly Tweets."

"They'll get over it. Wait till they hear about the stealth characteristics and the enhancements we have in the Slammers. The biggest factors we're going to talk about are tactics. We have an experienced Raptor pilot to talk turkey about how to defeat the J-20."

"That I'd like to hear."

Just then, Lt. Colonel James Stewart entered the room. He looked around, noted several familiar faces and smiled. "Rocket Crockett! How've you been, sir?"

"Wonderous…good to see you, Hollywood. You're looking good…Almost."

The two shook hands, then gave each other bear hugs.

"A little worse for wear, maybe. How are Tracy and the kids?"

"Doin' fine. Sorry about your friend Deacon."

"Yeah…Real shame. Fine man," Hollywood said as he tried to steel himself from the memory of his loss. He almost succeeded.

"Bob, you have that flash drive with your briefing slides?"

"Here you go," he said as he removed it from his upper left sleeve pocket.

Colonel Crockett took the drive and walked it over to the audio visual non-com.

An air policeman escorted a pair of Navy officers into the room and approached Colonel Peterman.

“Sir, Captain Heller and Commander Winsett. They were on the attendees list.”

“Thank you, Airman,” he said as he extended his hand. “Bob Peterman, Commander of the 311th Fighter Squadron.”

“The CNO tells me you gentlemen are in need of an overview of our assessment of Chinese Naval Tactics. I’m Mark Heller, F-18 pilot by trade,” the Captain said.

“Colonel, I’m Hugh Carter, from the war plans section under the CNO.”

After the introductions were completed, Bob lead the two Navy fliers to the front row of the already crowded room and showed them their reserved seats.

The door to the briefing room was closed, with a detail assigned outside to insure it remained secured during the highly classified brief.

An hour and twenty minutes later, a group of stern faced pilots filed out of the room. Peterman looked at Crockett.

“What do you think, Rocket? Like getting a drink of water from a fire hose?”

“You could say that. A lot of information in one fell swoop. Looks as if we have our work cut out for us.”

“I’d like to get together with the flight commanders and tactics and training guys before dinner. I want their inputs to evaluate their comprehension level post briefing.”

"You got it."

Bob turned to the Navy briefers. "What's your schedule, guys? I imagine Burner wanted your talents down at D-M."

"Right. He has us set up for a ten hundred talk tomorrow."

"I've got a C-130 going back with crews to pick up more Eagles at 0800 if that works. Otherwise I can have admin set up a commercial to Tucson International."

"Let's go with the Herc. I got to the point where I hate Homeland Security and TSA."

"Not my first choice on where and when to get really personal, either." Peterman laughed.

"So General Stewart really ate your lunch with a 104? Kinda hard to believe," Heller said curiously.

"Mine, plus a couple Raptors, *Phantoms*, and your Super Hornets. Oh. Forgot about the B-2."

"Sumbitch…Kinda lookin' forward to meeting him."

"Shoot straight with him, girls. Don't sugar coat anything. He's also responsible for the regeneration of the Marine and Navy F-4s, F-8s and the Tomcats."

"We have to develop a cohesive plan to counter these Chinese bastards. I just hope that relying on all these old birds is not a strategic mistake," Commander Carter added solemnly.

"You and me, both. But, apparently we don't have a choice," Flash Peterman responded.

DAVIS-MONTHAN AFB, ARIZONA
Wednesday Afternoon, 13 November

Blaze Hermann, Gears Formby and Kit Kitaen sat across a table from Burner Stewart and his number two, Heater McElheney in the spartan conference room as Blaze finished up the briefing on *Mama Bird's* offensive and defensive capabilities.

"Jesus H., Blaze, you were wrong. It actually took an hour and a half to brief us," said Jack incredulously.

"She probably could have done it in her projected hour if I hadn't asked so many questions," C.J. said apologetically.

"Better to ask and know than to not ask and wonder," countered Kit.

"That's an amazing aircraft you've got there. It's almost a flying battleship...and carrying those deadly little VTOLs..." said Burner.

"We actually refer to her as a stealthy flying battle carrier because we can not only launch and recover our Eagles, but have JDAM, JSOW and air-to-air capability along with the umbrella radar and full ELINT package Blaze talked about. Our new sonic cannon hasn't been battle tested as yet, but we have a great deal of confidence in it," offered Gears.

"Brings up a point," said Jack. "Does that quantum entanglement system you use in the S-1 sonic cannon work with any thing else besides sound?"

"Theoretically, it should work with any form of energy. Why?" asked Gears.

"We need to figure out a way to take out a Chinese spy/comm satellite in a frozen polar orbit that runs generally along our west coast every 102 minutes at roughly 1000 km. We don't want to use a ASM-135 ASAT satellite killer missile. Too obvious and detectable," stated Burner.

"EMP," muttered Blaze as she thought out loud.

"Say again?" said Heater.

"EMP. Electromagnetic Pulse," repeated Blaze. "I'm sure we can come up with an electromagnetic pulse generator in short order. Then it's a simple matter to combine a laser with the EMP using a clocking multiplexer to merge the two in real time. Gears and I can design the requisite integrated circuit for the entanglement microprocessor and I already have an idea for multiple fuselage turret mounted projectors for Mama Bird. Burning out circuit boards at a thousand kilometers from thirty-five thousand feet should be a piece of cake."

"Did anyone understand a word she said?" asked C.J.

Gears and Kit both held up their hands and nodded.

"Just the thirty-five thousand feet and the cake part," responded Jack. "We don't need to know how, just so long as it works. Sounds like the perfect solution. A covert satellite killer...What size do you think you can make the beam?"

"Probably down to the size of a basketball or as large as a school bus," Blaze said.

"And I'm sure we can find a few more applications for long range circuit frying," added Kit.

"We can put a turret on the top and one on the bottom of Mama Bird," said Blaze.

"What do ya know? The first directional EMP weapon," offered Heater.

“Necessity is always the mother of invention,” stated Blaze.

“Gunnz and Gunter can install the projectors in less than half a day, once we complete the test firing,” said Gears.

“Gunter? As in the president’s husband, Gunter Hermann?” asked C.J.

“The same. Gunter has been a fixture with the BEF since before they married…along with Blaze here and her brother Mike. Their half-brother, Mickey Williams, son of the president and Gunter, was invited to join after the Sacred Mountain mission. Gunter flew in from Andrews on Monday to help out,” responded Kit.

“Wow. Didn’t make the connection, ‘till now.”

“You know, might be a good idea to install a couple more…one on the Herc and another one on the Sea Eagle, could give us some close-in applications that I mentioned earlier,” added Kit.

“Works for me,” said Jack.

An aide entered the conference room with a folder and whispered into General Stewart’s ear. The aide handed Jack the folder with a teletype that he quickly read—he flipped over to the next page. An aerial satellite picture of the Pacific with circles and arrows drawn across the center caught his attention. A smile crossed his face. “Thanks, Cody,” he said and the aide departed.

“Good news, General?” Kit asked.

“It would appear so. The Chinese fleet appears to have encountered a massive debris field. They are being forced to come about and change course far north of their original track.”

"Japanese tsunami debris…flotsam, and jetsam?" Blaze asked.

"That was the Navy's guess, based on what we could see. There were three ships dead in the water."

"None of the carriers, I take it?" said Kit.

"No such luck. One destroyer and two frigates."

"How much more time will that give us, sir?" Gears inquired.

"Best estimated guess, one full day…two tops."

"We're gonna need all the time we can get. We'll have to set up a ground test of the EMP. Don't want to knock ourselves out of the sky."

"I'll handle it. We can use the emergency divert airstrip at Gila Bend. Remote enough to keep prying eyes away and not interfere with other operations," Col. McElheney added.

"Good thinking, Heater. You're now point man for the EMP satellite mission. Make it happen, people."

Burner Stewart stood up, his back aching a bit from his flight earlier in the week, and made his way out the room without another word…

***

CHAPTER TWELVE

AIRSPACE OVER NEVADA
Thursday Morning, 14 November

"IP in coming up in fifteen," Colonel Karl Richter announced to Lt. Colonel Will Williams in the front seat of the EF-105F—called a *Wild Weasel* back in 1967 when they first flew together out of Korat AFB, Thailand. The two were now paired together in a high-speed run across the vast open deserts on Nevada. They had descended to 100 feet above the sparsely populated terrain and were flying the nap of the earth in high subsonic mode. Red bluffs and green pinion trees streaked into view and disappeared beneath the nose in almost unimaginable succession.

Richter instructed from the seat normally occupied by a specially trained navigator called a EWO, short for Electronics

Warfare Officer. The aircraft had been updated with the ability to carry JADM 2,000 pound bombs internally. A GPS receiver was located just forward of the aft ventral fin leading up to the vertical stabilizer. A small digital readout and input pad was added on the left side of the cockpit where the controls for a Shrike anti-radiation missile had once been located.

Will glanced down at his Garmin GDU 375 GPS map display on his thigh mounted kneeboard. Only the weapons delivery systems in the 1964 model *Thunderchief* had been updated. It lacked any of the newer sophisticated integrated navigation and targeting displays. However, the addition of a moving map with terrain and weather XM satellite feed offered capabilities the pilots could only dream of back in the 60's. The radar absorbing material had made the aging warhorse almost invisible to land or ship based radar beyond a range of eight miles.

"Initial point," called Richter over the intercom.

"Got it," replied Williams as he pulled back hard on the stick and eased the throttle forward to full afterburner.

The *Thud* responded with a dull boom as the Pratt and Whitney J-25 burner lit off. Williams stopped the pitch at forty-degrees nose up as briefed, crosschecked the altimeter as it spun wildly in response to the climb—calling out as the altitude as the pair approached the drop altitude. "Twenty-five for twenty-eight."

"Coordinates verified, confirm weapon is hot."

"Arming switches, *ARM*. Internal store selected."

"Commence your roll," said Richter.

William rolled right until the blackened *Thunderchief* was inverted, still flying upward at a forty-degree angle.

"Release altitude. Bay doors open," called Richter.

Willams flipped the bomb bay position lever to the open position. A slight increase in the already substantial noise level aboard the sixty-five foot fighter bomber could be heard.

"Release and pull," advised Richter.

"Weapon away," replied Will as he pressed the black button on his stick and pulled back gently. The lethal black GBU-31 payload—all 12.75 feet of it—separated from the bomb shackles and drifted upward. He counted silently to three and reached for the bomb bay door lever. A second later, the doors were closed—he pulled back harder on the stick and moved the throttle back to idle. "What say we get out of dodge, Karl?"

"Works for me."

Will continued the Split-S maneuver and brought the big bird back down to 8,000 feet MSL, well below the tops of the Sierra Nevadas to the west of the range. He leveled off southbound at five hundred KIAS.

"Blackjack Control, Whiskey 01, weapons away. Advise strike assessment, over."

"Whiskey 01, Blackjack, roger. Negative radar contact. Stand by for BDA."

Inside the air conditioned range control facility, several non-coms and a couple junior officers monitored video feeds from numerous concrete block target structures scattered around the huge range complex.

"It would have helped if they let us know in advance which building they were going to attack," a tech sergeant said.

"The colonel says that four-star down at D-M don't work that way. He always approaches training just like combat," a first lieutenant replied.

"Nobody even get a nibble on the radars?"

"Not that I see, Sergeant. Whoa! There it is…16 Delta is now history. Friggin' shack with a big boy!" he exclaimed as the two thousand pound smart bomb pierced the ceiling of the structure designated as 16 D. The resulting massive explosion blasted the target into bits of flying gray debris and obscured the target area with concrete dust for several seconds.

"That it is, sir. I'll call the attacker…Whiskey 01, Blackjack."

"Go, Blackjack," Richter replied.

"Whiskey 01, Blackjack, target destroyed. Say your intentions."

"Whiskey 01 will recover at Creech. We're exiting your airspace at this time."

"Copy that, 01, squawk 3200, contact Longshot on 238.8 for handoff to Creech approach. Good day."

"Same to you, Blackjack. Whiskey 01 going to Longshot."

Several seconds passed before either pilot said anything. The dull roar of the air passing over the largest single engine fighter ever to serve in the US Air Force was partially muted by the foam padding inside their helmets.

"Karl do you ever think about the boys we flew with back in the day? All those that never came back?"

“Sure. I named my first son after one of ‘em. Lance Sijan and I roomed together at UPT. He was flying F-4s out of Da Nang…Died in the Hanoi Hilton.”

“Medal of Honor recipient…Tough SOB.”

“Yeah, he was…Why do you ask?”

“Here we are, back driving this old fugitive from an air museum, we hit a target we never even saw, and nobody ever saw us. Doesn’t seem possible.”

“I get your drift. Modern friggin’ warfare for you. Back in Route Pack Six, we’d have scheduled thirty-six sorties to knock out a single damned bridge…Jesus, we lost a lot of folks up there,” Karl said as a wave of sadness suddenly overcame him.

“Just wanted to know if I was the only one who still thought about them. I can still see their faces…Hear their voices.”

“I know, Will. I know.”

WASHINGTON, DC
PENTAGON
Thursday Afternoon, 14 November

“Bill, get me Charger, please,” the Secretary of Defense said.

“Right away, Mr. Baker,” Willamena “Bill” Parker acknowledged on the intercom. In less than ten seconds, she buzzed Baker back. “Admiral Valenti on one, sir.”

“Thanks, Bill,” the Secretary said as he punched line one. “Charger, what’s the current disposition of our Pacific CSGs and our Ohio and Los Angeles class subs?”

“Harold, we have two CSGs in the Pacific theater, but only Nimitz is in range to our coast. She was half a day out of Perth from that good-will tour to Australia when she got the word. Admiral Nelson informed me the Old Salt would arrive in San Diego by tomorrow."

"What's the projection on unloading her wing? Burner tells me he'll have sixteen Tomcats, twelve Crusaders and up to fifty-six F-4s ready by the end of the week."

"Holy crap! That's unbelievable...She's carrying eighty-four fixed wing." He thought quickly before concluding. "We'll have them all removed within twelve hours of docking, sir."

"That'll work. I'll tell General Stewart to apprise Admiral Sievers and Colonel Reynolds to start ferrying the Navy birds out Saturday morning. The drivers will need some live deck practice...Now what about our attack subs?"

"Well, our current Pacific deployment is twenty-five Los Angeles class, eight Ohio class, three Virginia and two Sea Wolf. All are in route to our west coast. Wouldn't make much sense to shadow the Chinese, since we can't keep up, but a picket fence two hundred miles off our shore should give us an effective wolf pack line of defense. They don't have the capability to detect our subs unless they're right on top of one and even then it's questionable."

"Of course the only weapons the subs have available, at least for now, will be the Mark 48 torpedoes...either active or passive programmed search and destroy or wire guided. As you well know, Charger, our wire guided mode would be virtually limited to line of sight."

"Right. But those fast mothers will play hell out-running a Mark 48."

"With what Burner is cooking up, our subs and the Black Eagle Force, I think the Chinese are in for a big surprise."

"So it would seem, Mr. Secretary, so it would seem. I do hope you're right."

CREECH AFB, NEVADA
Thursday Afternoon, 14 November

A pair of F-106's touched down on the active runway followed by two others. A flight of four F-104 *Starfighters* roared into the overhead pattern at almost 320 knots before they peeled off in a left break, one by one, for their landings. Additional air traffic controllers had been brought in to handle the increased work load. The base had never seen the level of activity along the flight line, with additional revetments being set up around the clock. Two fourships of *Thuds* arrived from D-M and entered the overhead pattern as Karl Richter contacted the tower. "Creech tower, Whiskey 01, initial for two seven."

"Whiskey 01, tower, you are number eight for runway two seven, continue."

"Whiskey 01, roger."

Whoa, this thing is really getting cranked up. Karl completed the dogleg to initial then rolled out on the active runway heading. He could see the first fourship initiate their break, their silhouettes clearly visible against the clear Nevada skies.

"Check out the pattern, Willy. I bet there haven't been that many *Thuds* airborne at one time since Nam."

"I wouldn't take that bet, Bossman. Looking good, even if they're painted black."

"Hells bells, they could paint us pink if the radar can't find us."

"Don't know I'd go that far."

Richter hit the break point and pulled the throttle to idle as he extended the speed brake. He rolled into a crisp forty-five degree left bank and deployed partial flaps as the big bird slowed below 200 KIAS. Wings level on the downwind leg, he extended the gear and retracted the speed break. Karl waited until he saw he was lined up with the extension of the inverted chevrons painted on the runway 09 overrun. That meant he was forty-five degrees past the runway 27 threshold. He set full flaps and began his descending base to final turn at 165 KIAS. The last of the previous *Thuds* was rolling out on the right side of the runway and slowing to take the last highspeed taxiway.

"Whiskey 01, cleared to land on 27," called the master sergeant in the tower.

"Whiskey 01, roger, gear down, cleared to land on 27," Karl replied as he passed through the halfway point in his base to final turn. He picked up the VASI and adjusted his descent to maintain the three-degree glide slope with the red lights over white ones. The F-105 touched down smoothly 750 feet down the runway with the two landing gear straddling the centerline stripe.

"Nicely done, Karl," quipped Will.

"Thanks, buddy. Like ridin' a bicycle."

Moments later, the menacing black bird pulled into line with a dozen other parked *Thuds* and Karl cut the power as directed by the ground crewman.

The ride to the operations squadron was somewhat surreal. Inside the packed crew truck, the boisterous gaggle of warriors chattered like a bunch of teenagers on their first field trip.

Karl smiled as he took in the activity. Morale was high. The improvements of the old iron were working better than any of them dared hope for. But inside squadron operations was something none of them had thought of.

Colonel Jim Lake, operations officer of the newly reformed 412st Tactical Fighter Squadron, met the incoming men as they walked in from the personal equipment room. Shed of their helmets, survival vests, and G suits, they looked like all the other pilots who had been milling around the squadron.

"Hey guys, take ten, then we need to see you all in the briefing room."

"What's up, Jimbo?" asked squadron commander Richter.

"McElhenny has some whiz kids contacts who wrote an app for the iPad that displays the disposition of forces from some black ops airborne super carrier. We're gonna put WiFi on all the birds."

"Get outta here!"

"No, really, Karl. I just got back from Nellis and saw the prototype in action on a F-4 Wild Weasel."

"Will it interface with our Slammers and JDAMs?"

"You don't know the half of it. It'll water your eyes."

"Out-friggin'-standing! About time somebody figured out how to get the whole damned Air Force into the 21st century."

"See you inside, Bubba. Got a lot to cover."

Forty-one pilots and EWOs filed out of the briefing room, each carrying their newly issued iPad in a black padded carry case. Karl, Will and Jim remained inside, standing by the podium and contemplating the electronic wizardry just handed to them.

"Guys, when I think about all the time I spent in training to use the bomb drop computers and then these folks come up with a damned Apple gizmo that makes all that crap obsolete. I could just spit!" Will grumbled.

"Burner said he'd pull out all stops to make this mission a go. Guess the SecDef picked the right man for the job. They imply that the Chinese carrier aircraft makes jammers obsolete, too," Richter observed.

"If the enemy can't detect you, it doesn't make sense to transmit search radar or any ECM. Burner did it with his Starfighter without this new fangled iPod," commented Colonel Lake.

"Pad, iPod is for Mp3s. Don't you jocks know anything?" Will chuckled.

"Whatever you say. Don't care…If the damned thing works, we're going to be some deadly SOBs."

Karl smiled broadly at the thought. The world had turned a time or two since he shot down his first MiG at age 23. He had a fondness for the old Republic bird that matched Burner's passion for his re-christened *Black Knight*. Vietnam was a long time past in a land far, far away. This time, the mission that lay before them was over their own home. And more than ever before, he and the *Thud* would be up to the challenge.

"Got that right, Jimmy, my boy. How 'bout we drink to that? I'm buying."

AIR FORCE SPACE COMMAND
VANDENBURG, CALIFORNIA
Friday, 15 November

A disheveled and haggard Stacie Chen sat at her desk staring at her monitor. She leaned back, removed her glasses and vigorously massaged her temples with her finger tips and then replaced them. There were deep dark circles under her eyes as she rechecked one of the lines of code. Two dark suited FBI agents, one male and the other female, sat on opposite sides of the room. A third agent, a male computer program specialist sat beside Stacie, also focused on the screen.

"Don't understand it," the very frustrated Dr. Chen said. "I've been working on this program for a week now and this last sequence is now refusing to recognize my pass code. This can't be…I created it."

"Is neutralization of this last sequence necessary to eradicate the virus?" asked the FBI computer expert, Mark Lowenstein.

Stacie turned and looked askance at him. "I thought you were supposed to be a program expert? Of course it's necessary."

"I'm sorry, Dr. Chen, I do know how to create programs…just don't know how to create a virus. It's not part of our protocol."

"Well it should be. You can't scrub a complex virus if you don't know how it was created." She paused for a moment. "All right, once more from the top. Maybe I just missed one of the digits. I'm so tired."

"Want me to send out for more coffee?"

"No. I'm jumpy enough as it is…There are twenty-seven digits in this pass code alone. Got one more shot at it…"

"Then it locks up, right?"

"Right you are." She handed Mark a note pad. "Here, the code is at the top. Read me the digits…very slowly and confirm my individual keystrokes."

"Can do…Here we go. Capital F…"

"Capital F…"

WASHINGTON, DC
PENTAGON
Friday Afternoon, 15 November

Admiral Valenti rushed into Secretary of Defense Baker's outer office and headed toward the SecDef's door.

"Whoa there, Charger. Have a seat before you blow a gasket. He's on the phone with the President. You don't go in until I tell you. You know the drill."

"Dammit, Bill…"

"Don't you curse at me, Samson Bartholomew Valenti. You know better."

"I apologize. But dang it, you've had my number since I was an ensign."

"Then I shouldn't have to tell you that you can't go in there until I say so."

"Yes, ma'am," replied the Admiral as he started to sit down in one of the antique leather chairs opposite her desk.

"You may go in, Admiral, he's off the phone now."

Charger entered the SecDef's office, walked straight to Baker's desk and laid a folder in front of him.

"Here you are, sir. The latest satellite photos of the Chinese fleet. The bastards started to split the fleet in two about twelve hundred miles out. Sun Tzu's CSG is headed toward San Diego and the other, Yang Jian, toward San Francisco. It's Naval Intelligence's opinion that Sun Tzu is the flag ship. Thought I would hand deliver the information."

"What's the projected time for them to be in launch range?"

"Seventy-two hours, sir."

Baker's intercom buzzed.　　　　"Yes, Bill."

"I have FBI Deputy Director Ben Corbin on one, Mr. Baker."

He punched the button and nodded to Valenti to pick up the extension. "Baker here, Ben. Charger is on the extension. Talk to me."

"Just got word from Vandenberg, sir. Dr. Chen has successfully scrubbed the virus."

"Verified?"

"Yes, sir."

"Charger, there are five channels in the MILSATCOM system, right?"

"Yes, sir."

"Ben, have Dr. Chen lock the top three channels like they're still infected and open the two bottom ones. Far as we know, the Chinese aren't aware that we even have five channels, correct?"

"That's correct," Admiral Valenti confirmed. "We've never used the bottom two, so there's no way they could know. What do you have in mind?"

"A little disinformation. We'll let Admiral Huang Meng think we're still infected. Deaf, dumb and very vulnerable…Thanks, Ben."

"I'll take care of this end, Mr. Secretary."

"Good man." He punched his intercom. "Bill, get me General Stewart."

DAVIS-MONTHAN AFB, ARIZONA
Friday Afternoon, 15 November

Inside the 22nd Composite Wing conference room, Gears and Blaze began to lay out their testing requirements for the laser/electromagnetic pulse weapon.

"The folks up at Kirkland Air Force Base were very cooperative once you got involved, General. They provided the pulse generators that we needed and even offered some advice on shielding our Mama Bird systems from the weapon's destructive power," Gears said.

"Glad I was able to help. Back when I worked for Lockheed, we tested the variants of the F-15s and the Raptors up there as part of the Air Force acceptance process. I understand it's not necessary to put the C-5M on the Albuquerque test pedestal, as you're not the target of the EMP burst. What practical considerations do you see as critical to the actual test?" Burner asked

"We concur. In fact I don't want even to be airborne when we test the laser for the first time. What I'd like is an actual operational air defense radar system and a remote runway within visual range of the radar. We could set down on the strip, target the radar and run our tests. Afterwards, we'd run an intensive self diagnostic on Mama Bird. If everything works as we designed, the air defense radar will be destroyed, without putting us at risk."

"Gears, that laser/EMP is definitely a high risk operation, I grant you. We spend years making our newest systems impervious to high altitude NUDETs back during the cold war. I imagine the concept of bringing an EMP generator aboard your ship is more than a little unsettling." Stewart paused a moment. "Heater, have you set up something over at Gila Bend for the BEF? There are several captured Iraqi SA-2 systems scattered around the Luke range. I think we could put one on an elevated bluff or hillside within sight of the south end of the airstrip."

"Got Luke to designate one of the older mobile units for a test. Should take less than an hour to move into position. How does a fifteen mile shot sound?"

"Works for me. Gila Bend is just a short hop from here. We could get the test completed early this afternoon if you can coordinate the range availability."

"I'll let Heater make those arrangements. We're running hot and heavy on our retraining sorties on most of the ranges in the west, including Cannon, Holloman, Fallon, Yuma, Nellis as well as Luke."

"And the Mountain Home and Hill ranges as well. I'll get you in. How many minutes do you need, Gears?"

Gears looked at Blaze. The actual test would only take seconds. Both had discussed how they would like the airspace clear for the test, so as not to subject non-test aircraft to potential catastrophic damage.

"Clear the airspace within a thirty-mile circumference for ten minutes, Colonel. We also want all civilian traffic clear. Will that be a problem?"

"Shouldn't be. We have the airways closed through the MOAs during training anyway. I'll check with ATC. How are you going to monitor the effectiveness of the pulse?"

"Good question, Heater. I planned to use remote visual sensors from Manta, with a comm link to Luke to monitor the actual radar feed from the SA-2. I assume they have that capability."

"I'll check to confirm. Any thing else you folks at the BEF need?"

"No, sir. Dare asked me to pass on his thanks for your support. If this new weapon works as we hope, it will vastly improve our capabilities," Blaze responded.

“Miss Hermann, it is I who should be thanking you. Oh…have you decided what you’re going to call the weapon?”

Blaze glanced at Gears. “We like TeslaPulse. It’s similar in theory to Tesla’s charged particle beam projector he termed Teleforce.”

“Works for me…Your inputs on the WiFi additions and the iPad can truly revolutionize the fighter world. If we only had more time, I’d like to discuss the transfer of the Lizard technology. That little wrinkle is a real game changer…and one other thing. My squadron commanders are asking for a full scale exercise tomorrow night. They want their crews to see the data link with Mama Bird and Manta in action before we face off with the Chinese.”

“I’ll have to confirm with Dare and Kit, but I’m sure they’d be up for it. Kit has been in talks with the war plans guys for two days. They’re coming up with some coordinated tactics and strategies to maximize our effectiveness,” Gears said.

“I’ll get with them this afternoon and check their status, after I check on the Navy’s. We’re planning on sending the re-qualified Crusaders, Phantoms and Tomcats back to the fleet this evening. Great work, people, keep it up. Latest word from Washington estimates the Chinese will be within range late Monday night. We don’t have much time.” General Stewart’s words hung in a air for a moment. Everyone in the room pondered what the next few days would bring. Each had plenty to keep them busy.

Finally, Heater McElhenny spoke, “I guess we all have our marching orders. Gears, I’ll confirm your range time via cell phone before your departure. Final clearance to fire will come from Gila Bend tower. Will that work?"

"Sounds good. Time to get crackin', little girl."

Blaze's eyes flashed for a moment as she and Gears stood up to leave the conference table. Her friend could get away with calling her a little girl, but only by the barest of margins. She was already planning her payback—and Gears would not know when or where that would come.

USS NIMITZ
PACIFIC OCEAN,
300 MILES SOUTH WEST OF SAN DIEGO
Friday, 15 November

The cold waters of the eastern Pacific were a leaden greenish gray that matched the overcast skies. Admiral Nelson, commander of the CSG, entered the Primary Flight Control, or PFC for short, with a confident air as he awaited the arrival of the first *Tomcat*. The decks of the *Old Salt* had been curiously quiet for weeks, save the occasional launch of a surveillance craft, helo or utility transport. The grounding of all the front line fighters had left the ship's crew feeling somewhat emasculated and defenseless. That feeling was about to change.

"Mornin' Air Boss, what's the latest on our inbound traffic?"

"Morning, Admiral, radar has the transponders of the first flight of four at one hundred-fifty miles, last bearing zero-seven-five."

"Excellent. Captain Witter, what do you say we make the ship ready for the re-qual traps?"

"All hands have received the required differences training, sir. We're as ready as we'll ever be…Helm, bring us into the wind," Witter said into his hand held radio.

"Aye-aye, sir. Coming port to 350 degrees. Aye."

The monster warship groaned slightly as she heeled to port at thirty-five knots.

Captain Witter walked into the CIC and picked up a microphone. He selected *All Stations* on the intercom public address system.

"Attention on board. Attention on board. This is the Captain speaking. First replacement flights will be arriving in fifteen minutes. Deck crews, prepare to stand to."

A feeling of excitement was felt throughout the ship. It had been almost five weeks without normal fighter operations. Older supervisory personnel with experience handling the *Crusader*, *Phantom* and *Tomcats* had been pressed into duty training the younger crew members. Several had been flown in from Honolulu aboard a P-3 Orion anti-submarine craft to supplement the limited numbers of older experienced hands aboard the *Nimitz.* It had been decades since *Crusaders* and *Phantoms* had caught a wire on the *Old Salt.* Most of the current crop of deck handlers had never even seen one of the older birds aboard a carrier. They certainly had never seen a highly modified stealthy F-14. The Admiral glanced at the grease pencil call signs for arriving aircraft that were listed on the glass wall in the PFC. He noted the call sign Romeo 01 flight and the identifying squadron information as VFA-41.

"Who's the new CO of the Black Aces Tomcats?" he asked the air boss.

"Admiral Sievers, sir. Know him?"

"Snake Sievers? Son of a bitch. Somebody up there likes me."

"Sir?"

"Son, if you have to go to war, Snake is the kind of man I would want up front. Can't believe they pulled his ass out of retirement…Do we have him on the frequency yet?"

"Yes, sir. You can use that headset on the console."

Placing the headset on, Admiral Nelson adjusted the boom microphone into position as a smile came to his lips.

"Romeo 01, Nimitz Operations."

"Nimitz, Romeo 01, go."

"CSG Commander has requested a simulated ship attack and high speed waterline check, fuel permitting."

Inside the cockpit of the lead F-14, Snake simply shook his head. *Fuck. Who is that joker on the radio? He probably doesn't know he's talking to an Admiral.*

"Snake, you gonna do it?" asked Captain Bob Harkins, the radar intercept officer, or RIO, seated in the rear of the cockpit.

"Dammit! I just get my wings back and some joker is trying really hard to get them pulled."

Snake thumbed the transmit button on the throttle. “High speed passes are frowned upon, sailor.”

“Who you callin’ sailor, you weasel bastard?”

Snake was taken back. *Weasel Bastard?* Only one person ever called him that. It had been a long time since he heard the voice of his old Naval Academy roommate.

“Hornblower? That you?”

“Snake, do you have fuel or not? Don’t have a hair on your decrepit old ass…”

“Romeo Flight, strangle squawk, five second spacing at fifty feet, keep it under Mach 1.2, okay? The boys down there need a little motivation. Let’s show them what Tomcats can do.”

Sievers eased the two throttles into burner, rolled inverted and pulled. His wingmen each followed suit on short spacing and dove toward the gray waters.

Admiral Nelson grinned as he removed the headset and turned to the air boss.

“I’ll smooth it over with Witter. You might pass the word below and let the folks know what’s coming. They can use a little air show to get their spirits up.”

“Aye-aye, Admiral,” Commander Watson replied. He took a second look back at the Admiral. “Hornblower…sir?”

Nelson laughed as he leaned closer to the seasoned Navy pilot. “My father gave me the middle name Horatio after our famous British Naval ancestor. Sievers always called me Hornblower after the fictional character. I’ll let him tell you why we call him Snake.”

Only minutes later, the four black wraiths streaked across the wave tops and crossed the long grayish white wake trail of *Nimitz* as she slowed to 30 knots for the recoveries. Dozens of mixed flight deck crew in their distinctive colored vests, turtlenecks and wind breakers lined the port deck. Inside the superstructure, every available window had a face pressed against the glass, anxiously awaiting the first sight of the old iron blasting inbound.

"There he is!" shouted a white vested landing signal officer.

"Where?" yelled the aircraft director in yellow.

"Right there!" the LSO shouted back as the wind whipped across the deck. The LSO pointed low to the pointy black dart a mile and a half behind the carrier.

A buzz went through the crowd as the dart grew into the distinctive shape of the F-14 with its wings swept back the full sixty-eight degrees. No one aboard had seen the black RAM coating that made the big bird look even more menacing. As the *Tomcat* approached the stern, it was possible to see the ripples forming across the water as the shock wave contacted the surface. Still silent, the aircraft approached the stern, and then the nose began to rise slightly as the pilot brought it up to barely ten feet above the flight deck level. Almost as a blur, the black bird tore through the sky at 1,400 FPS, easily passing the entire length of the 1,092 foot carrier in less than a second. The blast of the supersonic shock wave of the fighter shook the entire ship and could be heard and felt deep inside, followed by the roar of the two GE F110-GE-400 engines in min-burner.

Passing the bow, the pilot pulled up hard left and extended the speed brake as he maneuvered to join the standard carrier downwind traffic pattern. Excited crew members pumped their fists and exchanged high fives as they anxiously awaited the rest of the formation.

Inside the CAC, a concerned defensive systems operator turned to his supervisor. "Uh, Ensign Waverly, uh, ma'am."

"Yes, what is it?"

"Was that a sonic boom of an arrival?"

"Yes, I believe it was. Why?"

"Ma'am, I didn't pick them up on the target acquisition radar. It's supposed to be on and checked good. I'm still painting the E-2C Hawkeye fine. Somethin's not kosher."

She looked at his display. The AN/SPQ-9B radar appeared to functioning normally, but none of the four *Tomcats* appeared on the screen. Suddenly, a primary target from one of the four F-14s appeared on the downwind. The altitude and speed readout showed 1,500 feet and 240 knots slowing. The ensign picked up a handset and buzzed the PFC. "PFC, Jenkins."

"Jenkins, Waverly in the CAC. Do you have eyes on jet traffic in the downwind pattern?"

"Affirmative. Tomcat just put his gear down. Three more pulling up now. Aren't you guys trackin' 'em, ma'am?"

Checking the radar, Waverly saw a second primary radar return appear on the screen as it entered the downwind.

"Yeah, we got 'em now. Thanks."

She hung up the phone and paused for a second. "I need to speak to the Captain. Be right back. After the fourth F-14 appears, run a complete system diagnostic."

Snake Sievers rolled out three-quarters of a mile in trail of the *Nimitz.* His wings were deployed full forward to the twenty degree postion, with flaps and slats extended. Sievers pulled the tail hook release. RIO Bob Harkins confirmed the *before landing checklist* was complete.

"Romeo 01, call the ball."

Snake smiled even as his heart rate accelerated from the adrenaline rush. Carrier landings were always a challenge, always an element of danger. Night carrier *traps*, as they are called, actually generated a higher physiological stress levels than even combat sorties for most pilots. This was only a day trap, but the first in over seven years for Snake Sievers.

"Romeo 01, roger, ball."

"No pressure, buddy. Just everybody on the boat is watchin'," quipped Harkins.

"Piece o' cake," Snake lied.

"Right, just like back at Yuma, except it's movin'."

"And a whole lot shorter."

The Improved Fresnel Lens Optical Landing System, or *ball* as the pilots call it, was a system of red, yellow and green lights mounted near the stern of the ship. The Landing Signaling Officer operated a manual controller called a pickle to communicate with the pilots if they drifted off the glide slope.

The landing deck differed from the departing deck. It began at the fantail and was angled off the centerline by several degrees. Therefore, it required a pilot to maintain constant glide slope on a drifting, moving target that pitched up and down with the sea conditions. If it was easy, everybody could do it—but it was not.

The green *cut lights* flashed, indicating Romeo 01 could continue the approach. Snake jostled the throttles slightly to maintain the 115 KIAS final approach speed that Bob had computed for their current weight. As the *Tomcat* closed in on the ship, the height of the six foot seas could be better gauged from the cockpit.

"Six to eight feet today," Snake commented. "Not bad."

"Keep it coming, looking good," replied Bob, his heart racing as well.

Snake made rapid but small adjustments to the slight wind gusts as he closed in on the angle deck. He felt the old familiar feelings come back to him as the quick crosscheck between deck aim point and visual glide slope came faster and faster. The gray steel deck rushed up as he maintained the 700 feet-per-second sink rate all the way to touchdown. The massive tail hook, thicker than a man's arm slammed to the deck creating sparks a fraction of a second before the main gear tire made solid contact and spun up to speed. Even before the smoke boiled off the tires and was blown away by the forty knot winds angling across the deck, Snake had punched the two throttles into full burner. Both lit off, but their combined 55,600 pounds of thrust was no match for the second arresting cable. Snake had caught the *two wire* and he and Bob were slammed forward against their locked shoulder harnesses. The *Tomcat* lurched to a complete stop. Snake pulled the throttles back to idle and followed the hand signals of the green shirted arresting gear crew. In moments, Romeo 01 was being marshaled to an alert pad and being set up for refueling.

Behind him the LSO held the pickle high over his head until the first F-14 was clear. He reset the ball for Romeo 02 and the landing sequence began anew. Captain Witter and Admiral Nelson emerged from the superstructure as the fourth was disconnected from the wire. They were waiting on the deck when Snake climbed down the crew ladder. A beaming Admiral Sievers snapped a salute to the flag, then to Captain Witter.

"Permission to come aboard, sir?"

Witter snapped a salute, then extended his hand. "Nice job, Admiral. Glad to have you aboard."

Snake shook Witter's hand, started to salute Nelson, and then lowered his hand back down and extended it. He pulled it back when Nelson reached for it, and stepped forward for a bear hug instead.

"Hornblower, you old sea dog! How's it hanging?"

"Super! I see you haven't lost a step. Still trap with the best of 'em."

"Yeah, maybe. Have to admit my mouth is a little dry…been a while…Dammit, where the hell's my manners? Want you guys to meet Bob Harkins, best RIO in the fleet."

"Easy for you to say, Snake. I'm the only RIO in the fleet," Bob laughed as he saluted the flag. "Permission to come aboard, sir?"

GILA BEND AIR FORCE STATION, ARIZONA
Friday Afternoon, 15 November

The C-5M pulled into position in the run-up area at the south end of the single runway. Overhead, *Manta* orbited at 37,000 feet as the crew of *Mama Bird* ran through their checklist for the first live fire exercise involving the *TeslaPulse* laser/EMP weapon. Blaze Hermann identified the SA-2 mobile launcher atop a 100 foot tall butte almost twenty miles south of the airstrip.

"Target identified, targeting laser…Locked," she said to herself as she ran through the checklist. The gorgeous redhead pressed the intercom switch. "Gears, confirm all personnel are clear from target area. Target locked."

"Roger, Weapons, standby," Gears said as he transmitted to the Gila Bend control tower. "Tower, Eagle 1, target identified and locked. Confirm all range personnel are clear."

"Eagle 1, tower, be advised all ground personnel are at least one statute mile west of target area. Cleared to test at your desecration."

"Eagle 1 copies cleared hot."

Gears reached for the PA system selector. "Attention all stations. We have been cleared to fire the weapon. Monitor ship's systems and report any anomalies as briefed."

Blaze took in a deep breath. All the preparations over the last few days were on the line. If they didn't shield their own ship properly, there was more than a good chance that the weapon could do as much damage to *Mama Bird* as it did the mobile SAM launcher. Dare laid his hand on her shoulder for support as he monitored the shot on the feed from Manta.

"It's your baby, Red. Show us what she'll do."

She lifted the red plastic cover over the firing mechanism. Her finger pressed down and a blue *System Operating* light illuminated on the panel, and then went out as she lifted her finger.

"That's it?" Dare asked.

"And what did you expect, honey? Photon torpedoes?" Blaze responded. "Gears, test complete, SA-2 radar transmissions were terminated within one second."

Gears reviewed his caution and warning messages. None appeared and all systems were operating normally.

"Roger, AC reports no system abnormalities. Anything from Manta?"

"Sensors showed no visible damage, but the truck engine quit at the same time the generator and radar went off line. I'd say it was a solid kill," Tom Tallman added.

"Let's check it out. General Stewart was nice enough to loan us a Huey."

Six minutes later, Gears, Blaze, Tom and Dare were poking around the mobile launcher. Inspection of the control panel indicated massive damage to the circuit board and evidence of arcing from high current leads. The batteries for both the truck engine and the launch generator motor had faulted internally and melted the cases.

"Home run," said an excited Gears.

WASHINGTON, DC
WHITE HOUSE
OVAL OFFICE

The northwest door of the Oval Office opened and White House Chief of Staff Mark Carter escorted the Chairman of the Joint Chiefs, Admiral Valenti inside. President Thompson and Secretary of Defense Baker were seated in the two facing creme colored couches centered in the room in front of the large ornately carved Resolute desk.

The desk was a gift from Queen Victoria to President Rutherford B. Hayes in 1880. Built from the timbers of the British Arctic Exploration ship *HMS Resolute*, the desk had been almost in continuous use in the Oval Office since Kennedy. The only president not to use it was Johnson, primarily because it was on loan to the Smithsonian.

"That will be all."

"Uh…Yes, Madame President," the shocked Chief of Staff stammered as he exited the Oval Office.

"Mark looked like he'd been hit in the face with a dirty diaper," remarked Baker.

"I found it prudent to reduce the powers of the Chief of Staff and play it closer to the vest since that incident with my former CoS, Ralph Anderson."

"Life in Levenworth. He's damn lucky he didn't get the death penalty…I think he should have," offered Valenti.

"Not sure that I don't agree…But on to the matters at hand. I'm activating Continuity of Government. Harold, I want you in the Nightwatch E4 and Admiral, I want you at Cheyenne Mountain."

"I think this is the first time COG has been activated, isn't it?" the Secretary asked.

"I believe you're right Harold. The closest we've ever been before was the Cuban Missile Crises back in '62. Kennedy stood up to the USSR, I can do no less to the Chinese. Maybe they'll back down too."

"We can hope, but the difference is Kennedy was dealing directly with Premier Nikita Khrushchev. I truly believe we are dealing with a rogue."

"DEFCON 2, Madame President?" Valenti asked.

"DEFCON 2, Admiral, but unannounced except to the top military brass. I want to keep the Chinese in the dark and this is the only way."

"Where will you be, Madame President?" asked Baker.

"Right here. I don't want those hens in the NSC to be involved either…not in the mood."

"What do you wish me to tell General Stewart?" the Secretary asked.

"I want his people and the BEF at maximum readiness. We won't attack the Chinese fleet unless they launch their planes… Then he's to hit them with everything he's got. I'll not have a foreign power on American soil or in the air over her…not on my watch. Am I clear, gentlemen?"

***

CHAPTER THIRTEEN

NAVAL BASE SAN DIEGO
Friday Evening, 15 November

USS *Nimitz* was docked alongside the pier without the usual fanfare. No crowds of anxious wives, girlfriends and children had been standing twenty deep awaiting the departure of a disembarking crew. *Nimitz* was actually homeported at Bremerton, Washington, and no leaves were scheduled during the short stay in southern California. In eight to twelve hours, after the compliment of incapacitated F-18 *Super Hornets* were removed by the three cranes servicing the mighty warship, she would put back out to sea. Fresh perishables were brought aboard, as were modified munitions and a portion of the replacement fighters. Technicians from Raytheon and Boeing installed modifications to the ship's target acquisition radar systems and stored similar upgrades for the remainder of the carrier support group. Helicopters would later deliver the upgraded parts and technicians to the cruisers, destroyers and frigates assigned to the defensive perimeter of the *Nimitz.* Just before 0200, *Nimitz* put out to sea, ready once again to do battle.

NELLIS AIR FORCE BASE, NEVADA
Saturday night, 16 November

Hollywood Stewart pulled the olive drab G-suit out of his locker and began to strap it on. The events of the past week had become a blur of training flights, briefings and conferences. He hadn't flown as many sorties in one week since he checked out on the F-22. The other F-15 *Eagle* squadron commander, Bob Peterman had the locker beside him as the two geared up for the night sortie.

"Hard to believe we're flying as simulated Chinese J-20s tonight. How do you think the old birds will fare against us?" Bob asked as he pulled down his helmet from the top shelf.

"That's anybody's guess. They're going to use the feed from that C-5 to keep up with their deployment and any radar skin paint they can pick up from us. Don't know how it will shake out. I imagine Dad will throw in some wrinkles we don't expect."

"The General is a sneaky son-of-a-gun at that. He had them work up some telemetry to trigger our warning systems if they take either radar or IR missile shots at us."

"Should make it interesting," Hollywood said as he slipped his helmet into his green nylon bag. "Some of the older guys are bitching about the new coating on their old brain buckets. Technicians at Lockheed said the radar returns off the smooth round poly carbonate shells were as much as the whole planes after we added the RAM."

"Kinda miss the old Easy Rider motif I had. It's been my signature since I got out of UPT. Guess it falls into the category better to live and fight another day than die stylin'," Bob said wistfully.

"Got that right. We Raptor guys got used to it. Dang sure ain't pretty, but most modern warfare isn't."

"Twenty years from now, folks will ask us why we just didn't use drones. Bet there won't even be fighter pilots in the future."

"Won't take that bet, Flash. We might even see some Chinese drones in this action."

"Damn, Hollywood. You sure know how to pep up a fella. Any word from the NSA on those? Or, are you just yanking my chain?"

Hollywood just grinned and shrugged as he turned to walk out the door. Bob stared at his back for a second and followed him outside. The Nevada dawn would be breaking in just over an hour. The skies above would be full of fighters and a very capable C-5M battle carrier working the kinks out of America's last line of defense.

One thousand kilometers above the earth, the Chinese *Jìjìng dí límíng* or Silent Dawn satellite crossed over the north pole as made its way round the globe. Its path on this trip would cross over eastern Alberta, parts of Montana, Idaho, Nevada and Southern California before overflying Mexico and the Pacific ocean. Aboard the reconnaissance platform, a series of very sophisticated cameras and radar sensors responded to the needs of the Chinese military, or in practical terms, whatever Admiral Huang Meng desired.

Eighty miles north of Phoenix, the crew on *Mama Bird* was set up for their most ambitious test of the *TeslaPulse* weapon. President Thompson had authorized the use of weapons against Chinese space assets. She had not bothered to ask for a ruling from her Attorney General Alan Aimes. Once she had made the decision on COG, niceties like international space protocols were just so many pieces of paper. The Chinese certainly hadn't been deterred by them—American assets had been lost and American blood had been spilled. The Black Eagle Force was the pointy end of the spear to carry out the first definitive action in the defense plans coordinated with the Department of Defense.

"Four minutes until she crosses the horizon," Dare relayed to Blaze as she initiated the checklist.

"Copy, four minutes," she replied calmly.

Tom Tallman sat at the *Manta* station beside her with the feed from his laptop laid out on the right side of his seventy-two inch flat screen display. Real time tracking from NORAD headquarters inside Cheyenne Mountain, south of Colorado Springs, monitored the exact position of every satellite and thousands of pieces of space debris encircling the earth. *Manta* was ten thousand feet above and six miles in trail of the massive airborne battle carrier. Her high powered ARGUS-IS 1.8 Gigapixel camera system with four arrays—each contained ninety-two five-megapixel imagers with a refresh rate of fifteen frames-per-second. Lanie Hayes was monitoring the ARGUS and would be able to define up to sixty-five independent video windows within the image and zoom in or out on command. The cameras were locked on the exact location where *Jìjìng dí límíng* would become visible to the *Manta*. Thin cirrus clouds moved underneath the C-5M as she crossed over the south rim of the Grand Canyon. A dusting of snow could be seen on the north rim, causing Aircraft Commander Gears Formby to speak, "Gonna be a beautiful day, once the sun comes up."

"Yep, it is. Nice day for flying, if you like dawn patrol," retorted Bobby Mendez. "Want another cup of coffee?"

"Sounds like a plan. We're 'bout ready to take our shot. Hustle back or just wait 'till it's done, okay?"

Bobby slid his seat back and made his way aft to the galley. He quickly poured two cups of the hot black liquid and eased back up to the cockpit.

"Tom just said two minutes to go," he said as he handed a mug to Gears.

Tension became almost unbearable as the time crawled by. Dare sensed the stress in Blaze as he placed his hands on her shoulders. He began a gentle massage at the base of her neck after moving her mass of flaming red hair aside.

"Ooh," she purred. "Don't start something you can't finish, Colonel," she teased.

"Colonel? Getting formal, are we?"

"You *are* back on active duty, aren't you?"

Dare laughed. "Well, not exactly…Baker let us choose to remain on contract status. Jill's dad and his wing are on active duty. Not a whole lot of difference, I guess, once the shooting starts."

"Clearing horizon now," Tom announced as *Manta 1* picked up the shiny dot. Flying much higher than *Mama Bird*, the satellite was bathed in the bright morning sun, while the *Lizard* cloaked C-5M cruised in starlight. Tom increased magnification digitally to three thousand times. As the dot grew in size, two huge black wings of solar cells became visible, splayed out either side of the twenty-foot polished titanium cylinder. Blaze tapped a keyboard command to lock the *TeslaPulse* targeting laser to the image relayed by *Manta 1*.

"Target confirmed visually and locked," Blaze announced. "Autotrack, enable," she continued to herself.

A green light on her display confirmed the top turret laser tracking module was functioning as designed. She mentally reviewed all systems were in the *go* mode and lifted the cover on the firing button. The blue *System Operating* light confirmed the pulse generator engaged. Blaze held the button down for a full six seconds. Two seconds were all the system needed to accomplish its mission.

Six hundred miles above Fort Smith, Canada in the Northwest Territories, the electromagnetic pulse struck the extended solar array, frying the delicate circuitry and sending a damaging surge of current through the stabilizing gyros as well as the hard drives used to record and store the image data files. As on the SA-2 launcher, the batteries suffered permanent internal faults, causing one to explode.

"AC, firing sequence is complete. You are cleared to resume the training mission as briefed," Blaze called over the intercom.

"Copy that," he said as he rolled into a turn back to the northwest.

"When will we know if the shot was successful?" Dare asked.

"SETA should be able to tell us that PDQ. They will be looking to pick up any downloaded transmissions from the Silent Dawn. My guess is that she just lived up to her name. Just a high dollar piece of space junk."

"That's gonna make the boys flying tonight over Nevada happy, knowing the Chinese aren't watching every move," Dare replied. "I'll notify the SecDef when he wakes up."

The lights of Sin City shone bright to the south and west of *Mama Bird* as she picked up a heading of 335 degrees. In the skies over the Nellis range, eighty mixed fighters flew toward their designated entry points and altitudes, all anxious for the complex training mission to get under way. *Manta 2* orbited over the northern end of the range as Lanie aboard *Mama Bird* checked in, "Blackjack, Eagle 1 with you at entry point Charlie Two."

"Eagle 1, Blackjack roger. Negative radar contact."

The master sergeant turned to the four-star seated behind him watching the radar screen in the control room.

"General, did you want the airborne control craft to squawk?"

"No, son, I did not. Let's keep it as close to combat as we can. Initiate and see what happens."

SANTA MONICA , CALIFORNIA
Monday Morning, 17 November

The fifth US Army Patriot Missile detachment pulled off the Pacific Coast Highway and turned onto the beach road. The lead HUMVEE rolled down the deserted beach and set up between the paved bike and rollerblading path and the beach. A couple hard core joggers passed by and glared disapprovingly at the uniformed soldiers. *How dare they camp out on a public beach. This isn't Iraq.*

One of the soldiers hopped out of the HUMVEE that had braked to a halt on the four hundred yard wide strip of sand. He took a look at the waves crashing against the sand. Unmanned red lifeguard stations stood as mute sentinels to the mid-November beaches, yet PFC Jones immediately recognized the setting as a typical Baywatch location.

"Man, I can't believe we're really here. I've never been to the ocean before."

"Move your ass, Jonesie. After we're up and operational, you can go freeze your nuts off in the water," snapped his sergeant.

"You got it, Sarge. It's just that, two days ago we were chillin' at Ft. Bliss and now I'm on the beach…Sweet."

"Whatever, dude, but we've got a job to do, so just get it done," he growled as he pulled out a handheld radio. "Lancer control, Bravo Troop."

"Bravo Troop, Lancer, report."

"Lancer, Bravo Troop in position, estimate operational on the hour."

"Copy, Bravo, battalion advises commander call at eleven hundred hours at Charlie Papa."

"Bravo Troop copies all, clear at three-five," the sergeant said into the handheld as he watched a formation of five *Blackhawk* helos thunder overhead enroute to Malibu.

Similar scenarios were taking place all along the west coast at exposed beaches near urban areas. War planners had identified likely targets for the Chinese to hit to cause maximum disruption without destroying the economic base they coveted. Highway checkpoints, fuel storage depots and of course, the myriad of military installations within reach of a carrier based fighter force were being protected with the Patriot Batteries, HUMVEE based Stinger antiaircraft units, and *Blackhawks*.

Any fighters or helicopters that made it past the old iron and the Black Eagle Force were in for a very rude reception.

DAVIS-MONTHAN AIR FORCE BASE, ARIZONA
22nd Composite Wing HQ
Monday Morning, 17 November

After the early Sunday morning exercise, General Stewart had mixed emotions. Overall, the planning, training and briefing sessions had paid off. The crews performed beautifully for the most part, as did the aircraft. One F-4 lost an engine to a possible bird strike, neither crew member saw a bird, but the sound of a solid thump was heard before the number one engine exploded. Fragments of the compressor section sheared fuel lines and the resulting fire could not be brought under control. The pilot initiated the ejection sequence at just under 500 knots. Both men were hospitalized, but expected to recover. Burner briefed the SecDef about the overall results of the mission and then confirmed the complicated refueling logistics plan for the fighter wing offensive plan. Once the Chinese carriers turned into the wind and began to launch their fighters, the American forces would commence their attack.

The last of the F-4s departed Arizona for their temporary homes at March Joint Air Reserve Base near Riverside, a short forty miles east of Los Angeles. All the modified *Phantoms* were quickly hustled into a pair of the large maintenance hangars to keep them out of sight as much as practical. C-17 transports departed behind them with ground support men and equipment.

Burner reviewed the dispersal of his aged fleet. He closed his eyes and re-imagined the tactical disposition of the disparate assets and wondered if they would be enough to stop the onslaught of China's best.

EASTERN PACIFIC OCEAN
CHINESE CARRIER SUN TZU
Monday Morning, 17 November

Admiral Huang Meng flew into a rage at the intelligence briefer. Captain Gwok Wei held back for a moment then tried to come to the aid of the junior officer. "Admiral, may I point out that Shao Xiao Wan is merely the messenger. He is not responsible for the interruption of service from Silent Dawn."

"Silence! I was not speaking to you, Shang Xiao. Why is the satellite not functioning properly? How long will it take to get it back on line? I need that intelligence now. We launch in only fourteen hours and we are blind!"

The captain knew when to stand up to the narcissistic fleet commander and when to stay mute. He stared impassively at a map on the glass top of the backlit forces display table.

"Sir! My operators are very skilled in the retrieval of information from the *Jìjìng dí límíng*. It is not responding to any commands at all. Data from the tracking computers indicates it is still in orbit. Request permission to contact our Space Command Committee in Beijing…" the young lt. commander protested.

"Permission denied! Have your technicians initiate a complete system power down and reboot. Report when you have reestablished contact. Dismissed!"

AIRSPACE OVER PACIFIC OCEAN
Tuesday Morning, 18 November
0400 Hours

Light from a billion stars twinkled through the thin air at 34,000 feet over the dark waters of the Pacific. Behind *Mama Bird*, the coast of California was lit by the lights of the plethora of cities that dotted the prime coastal real estate. Tom Tallman controlled *Manta 1* orbiting three hundred miles west of the Channel Islands. Lanie sat beside him on an adjoining station at the joystick tied to *Manta 2,* which was in an unseen orbit west northwest of San Franciso. Beneath the two ray-shaped URFs, the Chinese super carriers began to slow to launch speed of 30 knots. Lanie took a sip of coffee from her personalized mug and noticed the digital speed readout change from the crystal clear image provided from *Manta 2's* sensors.

"Heads up everybody. *Yang Jian* just dropped speed. She's slowing through 56 knots."

Tom checked his display—*Sun Tzu* was powering back also.

"Same here. Keep your eyes on the elevators. They turned into the wind to launch, but all their planes are still below deck."

EASTERN PACIFIC OCEAN
CHINESE CARRIER SUN TZU
Tuesday Morning, 18 November
0400 Hours

The mess steward cleared the empty gold trimmed china plates off the Admiral's private dining table. Huang Meng dabbed his thin lips with a linen napkin, rose and stepped to his dressing area. His shipboard valet held the elaborate white uniform coat as the Admiral slipped into it and studied himself in the mirror. Meng liked what he saw. The valet placed the round wheel hat with a heavy gold wire embroidered dragon across the bill on his head. An almost imperceptible smile came to the old man's face—he waved his fingers as if shooing away a pesky fly. The steward bowed and backed away with his head lowered.

A knock came to the door.

"Come," announced the admiral in a deep voice.

The ship's executive officer entered, flanked by a pair of the Admiral's personal guard, dressed in white and gold naval uniforms that appeared to be toned down versions of the Admiral's uniform.

"Most worthy Admiral, Captain Gwok Wei wishes to inform you Sun Tzu and Yang Jian are ready to launch the attack fighters. We have just turned into the wind. A glorious victory awaits."

"What of the Jìjìng dí límíng? Were efforts to reactivate the satellite successful?"

"Regrettably no, Admiral. A catastrophic failure has occurred. All attempts have been for naught. I did take the liberty to monitor satellite television transmissions from several American stations in our target areas."

The admiral raised one eyebrow. Fleet regulations prohibit contact with Western unfiltered news outlets without express permission and supervision by a representative of the Select Committee. *Surely the XO knows about such regulation, but he is readily admitting his indiscretion to me.*

"I was able to deduce that normal operations of their local stations were continuing in the face of our imminent arrival. Their imperialistic news outlets also made no reference whatsoever of our presence. I checked CNN, FOX, ABC and CBS. Many of the transmissions were concerned with the sale of national consumer goods. Their decadence knows no boundaries, Admiral. It is my professional opinion that we have achieved the element of surprise your brilliant plan envisioned."

"Is the American's MILSATCOM system still inoperative?"

"Yes, Admiral. Only static is being broadcast."

The XO bowed slightly in deference to the admiral, who raised his upturned palm, indicating the younger officer could stand erect. *Perhaps this officer deserves a higher post. I shall see to it in the coming days.* The admiral turned to the door, followed by the XO and the ceremonial guard detail. The four made their way to the bridge elevator.

DAVIS-MONTHAN AIR FORCE BASE, ARIZONA
22nd Composite Wing HQ
Tuesday Morning, 18 November
0404 Hours

"Execute Operation Vulcan, authorization India Mike Whiskey," General Stewart said into his handheld sat phone.

Inside the *Nightwatch E4* orbiting at 36,000 feet over western Montana, Secretary of Defense Baker received the word needed to initiate force against force threatening the United States. Unlike the use of nuclear weapons, this defensive action did not require the *Football* with its leather bound strike authorization book.

"Baker acknowledges Operation Vulcan is a go at 1204 Zulu, counter sign Delta Delta Alpha," the SecDef replied as he nodded to the chief master sergeant at the computer console. He, in turn, right clicked a command authorization bar on the keyboard in front of him and hit the enter button. A red bar across the bottom of the screen followed the notification message transmittal and turned green in less than a second as the secure satellite link forwarded the launch messages across one of the two newly activated secret MILSATCOM channels at the speed of light. A second bar began to appear as each message recipient confirmed their receipt. Eight seconds later, the bar turned green and showed a 100% contact rate.

"General, all parties are confirmed with Vulcan *go* message," Baker somberly intoned into the handset.

"Thank you, Mr. Secretary," replied Stewart as he looked at his reflection in the headquarters office building window.

Outside the building, a staff car waited for the aging General. The headlights of the blue sedan shone across the smoothly polished river rocks used in the desert landscaping outside the headquarters. Stewart had no intention of commanding this war from a desk, and Baker knew it.

"I personally want thank you and your team for all their hard work, General. God speed and good hunting, Burner."

"We'll do our best, sir."

As Baker closed his end of the call, Burner took his sat phone and secured it in his survival vest. He took down the embroidered flight jacket with the silver *Starfighter* emblazoned across the back off a brass hook on a coat rack near the door. He smiled as he slid the somewhat garish gift on and zipped it up. Next followed the G suit and survival vest. When he was ready, Jack picked up his helmet bag and specially modified iPad from the carpeted floor next to the coat rack.

He opened the door to the outer office and was surprised to see the hallway lined with support officers and non-coms. All wore battle dress camouflage with Kevlar helmets. The 22nd Composite Wing Deputy Commander for Logistics called the assembly to attention, "Wing, ten-hut! Present…arms!"

The lines of men and women snapped crisp salutes and held them. Jack transferred the computer carrying case to his left hand and assumed the position of attention. A lump involuntarily formed in his throat. He had gone into combat plenty of times before, but never with a personal sendoff other than a crew chief or flight commander in attendance. He returned the salute, then gave an order of his own, "Stand at ease, people."

Colonel Robinson stepped forward and extended his hand. "Give 'em hell, General."

"That's the idea, Robbie. Thanks for all the hard work. Couldn't have done it without your team's fine efforts...that goes for all of you. I mean that from the bottom of my heart."

The assembled group began to applaud enthusiastically. After a few seconds, he held up his hand. "All of the fliers appreciate your contributions, but you'll have to excuse me...I have a plane to catch."

A ripple of chuckles passed throughout the crowd. Burner began to make his way down the hall, shaking hands and nodding as each person wished him well. By the time he got to the stairway down to the foyer, the lump in his throat had grown. As he exited the building and approached the staff car—a tear slowly ran down the left side of his face.

"Are you okay, General?" the staff sergeant asked as he gazed at the silver haired flyer in the rearview mirror.

"Never felt better in my whole life, Sergeant. Never felt better," he said as he stared out into the darkness.

AIRSPACE OVER PACIFIC OCEAN
Tuesday Morning, 18 November
0410 Hours

Inside *Mama Bird*, Tom observed the first two launches of the J-20 stealth fighters as they blasted off *Sun Tzu's* parallel decks on the large screen linked to *Manta 1's* cameras.

"Here they come," he said somewhat impassively.

"Same from Yang Jian," reported Lanie from Manta 2's monitor.

"That's all I need to see. Select the closest picket ship and let Blaze get to work opening a corridor," Dare said.

"You got it, Boss," the six-foot-eight former Army officer replied as he rolled the stick left and banked *Manta 1* into a turn back east toward the California coast.

Gears glanced at his Mach meter. He had the big, four engine transport at max maneuvering speed to close the gap to the far flung defensive perimeter surrounding the southernmost Chinese carrier group.

Dare picked up the mic from the comm station and adjusted the frequency. "Attention all units. Sun Tzu and Yang Jian launching fighters. Repeat, launching fighters. Operation Vulcan now active." The *Global Information Grid* or GIG notified all linked units in real time.

The fight was on.

VANDENBERG AIR FORCE BASE, CALIFORNIA
Tuesday Morning, 18 November
0412 Hours

"Forge Flight check in," Colonel Richter called on Vandenberg ground frequency. His seven wingmen responded in seconds. The extensively modified F-105 *Thunderchiefs* were carrying two deadly 2,000 pound GBU-31s internally and eight 750 pound GBU-38s under the wings. The sinister black craft sat inside portable temporary field shelters lined up along the outer edges of the crowded ramp. All had been hooked up to external power cart with their pre-flight checklist complete up to engine start. The crews had been assembled in a central briefing tent reviewing the real time disposition of forces displays down loaded from *Mama Bird*. Two crews were assigned to each Chinese cruiser with secondary targets of destroyers and frigates. Once the signal was received by alert fighter crews, they clambered up the crew ladders and were strapped in by a seasoned crew chief.

"Light 'em up!" Karl called over the radio a moment before he transmitted the call for taxi clearance.

"Vandenberg Ground, Forge Flight taxi for takeoff."

"Forge Flight taxi runway 30 via Alpha. Hold short at arming area. Altimeter 29.89. Winds are 270 at 12. Contact tower on 326.2 when ready for departure."

"Ground, Forge Flight, roger taxi to 30, hold short at arming area. Altimeter 29.89"

The sound of eight power carts roaring to life echoed around the ramp as the all the *Thud* pilots selected the start valves open. The Pratt and Whitney engines answered at first with a low whine, then a steady, throaty growl as the pilots brought the throttles out of the cutoff position. Hot exhaust gasses blew out of the back of the eight canvas covered aircraft shelters. Once the pilots gave the signal, ground crews disconnected the APUs from the engine start ports and followed up with the bulky black power cords. They snapped the access covers closed and rechecked that the cover fasteners were flush. Nothing was left to chance.

Karl Richter signaled to pull the chocks. Sergeant Markham stood in front of the nose and marshaled *Forge 1* out of the ersatz hangar and toward the active taxiway. He moved to the side of the taxi route and snapped a salute with his flashlight equipped with a long orange luminescent cone. Karl returned the salute as did Colonel Kurt Hiller, his veteran EWO. The first of eight *Thuds* passed by Markam. He remained at the position of attention until the last had taxied past, then began the short walk over to the F-111 parking area, where he offered assistance to his fellow airmen readying the two flights of *Aardvarks*.

Minutes later, the first four *Thuds* pulled into position on the 15,000 foot runway. The two pairs of two were separated by 250 feet as Richter signaled to power up. White cones of fire lit the night as the J-79s roared to 24,000 pounds of thrust. At 230 KIAS, he pulled back on the stick and the heavily laden fighters lifted off into the night sky. Once the gear came up, Richter rolled left to a heading of 265 for the Chinese cruiser *Yangtze*.

EASTERN PACIFIC OCEAN
Tuesday Morning, 18 November
0415 Hours

Aboard *Sea Eagle*, all four of the BEF M600/A Eagle detachment were powered up and ready to launch. Captain "Shoehorn" Stienke, in the gray leather futuristic chair on the small bridge of the oddly shaped fighting vessel spoke to the helmsman. "Helm, bring her about to 275 degrees and slow to thirty knots."

"Aye-aye, sir. 275 and three-zero. Aye."

The nimble craft rolled out on the new heading as the jet thrusters beneath the twin-hulled ship slowed slightly. Dark waves passed between and around the hulls as the digital readout slowed to the desired speed. Stienke moved the boom microphone down into position on his headset as he monitored the red forces moving into range on the disposition map. *Manta* had identified all the naval forces assigned to the southern carrier battle group.

The closest Chinese ship, a frigate named *Sholin*, lay forty miles off the starboard bow—escorting a three-wide line of transports moving at full speed toward the California coast. Still beyond the horizon, the frigate had no way of painting *Sea Eagle*. The stealthy design of the new ship would not reflect any energy back to the radar receivers.

The six-foot-three Captain placed his index finger on a red rectangular switch light on the outside of the armrest. He pressed it, causing flashing red lights to activate in every portion of the 264 foot ship. External navigation lights extinguished.

"Attention all hands. Battle Stations. Eagles cleared to launch."

On the deck above the bridge, the single crewman in the flight operations area station released the first BEF *Eagle*.

"Eagle 1, cleared for take off."

Jill McElhenny pushed the single centrally mounted throttle up as she concentrated on a single spot in front of her. The glow of the night vision goggles was a familiar sight as she called back, "Eagle 1, off port side."

She lifted off to an altitude of twenty feet before she rolled slightly to the left and called for her WSO, Bug Haug, to retract the gear. The pair flew around the forward superstructure of *Sea Eagle* and picked up a heading to intercept the *Sholin.* Seconds later, *Eagle 2* followed off the starboard side and trailed her into the black night. *Eagles 3* and *4* departed off the port side for a rendezvous with the frigate *Foshan*, named after a city south west of Guangzhou.

Captain Stienke turned *Sea Eagle* back to a heading of 325 degrees to intercept the line of transports. Far to the west, a squadron of Chinese J-20 air superiority stealth fighters had assembled, flanked by three squadrons of J-10 fighters, each considered to be comparable to the USAF F-16 or US Navy F-18 fighters. Shoehorn could not miss the fact that as every minute passed, another four red dots departed each of the carriers on his large monitor. The US Navy had designed the *Sea Fighter* as a littoral warship designed for close-in coast skirmishes. With the BEF, the addition of the G2 electromagnetic, multi-barrel coil gun and the *TeslaPulse* weapons were intended to transform the stealthy little vessel into an unseen deadly heavyweight. That was the plan. Stienke had never gone into battle during his twenty-year career without possessing the advantage of air superiority overhead. He looked at the thin lines of blue dots approaching from the east and counted the blue numbers across the vast expanse of the western US coastline—he was not reassured. Not by a long shot. *First time for everything.*

AIR SPACE OVER MONTANA
NIGHTWATCH E4
Tuesday Morning, 18 November
0415 Hours

"...Yes, Madame President, Operation Vulcan was activated four minutes ago. The Black Eagle Force is moving into position to open penetration corridors in both the north and south Chinese fleets. The first wave of General Stewart's forces will be airborne in the next twenty minutes," Secretary of Defense Baker informed the president.

"Fine, Harold. However, I want you to have Charger arm thirty B-52Hs and get them airborne in the event we have to go to DEFCON 1."

"Yes, ma'am, already thought of that and Valenti's standing by at Fast Pace ready to go to Cocked Pistol. We discussed having half come out of Minot AFB's 5th Bomb Wing and the other half from Barksdale's 2nd Bomb Wing. We'll have the 917th Reserve Wing at Barksdale on standby with another fifteen...if needed."

"Harold, now listen to me. The last thing I want is to be the first president in history of the United States to go to DEFCON 1...but you know I will if I have to."

"No, ma'am…my gut tells me that it won't be necessary. I think that General Stewart and Dare's Black Eagle Force are up to the challenge."

"I pray to God you're right, Mr. Secretary. I pray to God you're right."

***

CHAPTER FOURTEEN

AIRSPACE OVER PACIFIC OCEAN
Tuesday Morning, 18 November
0420 Hours

Kit Kitaen deliberated over the initial targeting display as blue icons merged closer to the outer ring of the southern Chinese carrier group. His computer-like grasp of all the varied assets allowed him to make rapid decisions in the hot seat next to Blaze. He directed a small red laser pointer at the icon for the heavy cruiser *Yangtze*. Two icons identified as F-105s bore down on the 580 foot ship at just under Mach 2. *Yangtze,* like three other Chinese cruisers, began its life as a Russian warship. But Kit cared nothing about its past. He was only concerned with the present.

"Take 'em out, folks," Kit said as he sought the next player in the deadly game of 21st century warfare.

Tom Tallman locked *Manta's* IR target laser on the superstructure. Blaze ran through her targeting sequence and fired once the *TeslaPulse* weapon matched the target location. She sent a five-second stream of the searing EMP down on the unsuspecting cruiser. Without a moment's hesitation Kit pointed at the icon for the frigate *Sholin.*

"Next."

EASTERN PACIFIC OCEAN
CHINESE CRUISER YANGTZE
Tuesday Morning, 18 November
0420 Hours

Captain Han Lee reacted to the massive electrical destruction across the various bridge flat screens with an involuntary shout. Smoke poured out from behind three of the screens—all the bridge lighting went dark and the backup battery systems failed to kick in. Acrid smoke began to fill the room; the light from the stars was the only thing providing any illumination in the pre-dawn darkness. Lee tried to compose himself as best he could—he reached for the handset on the wall. "Engineering, bridge...Engineering, come in," he spoke loudly into the useless device. Lee slammed the handset back onto to the wall, missing the cradle.

Two of the sailors began to cough in response to the smoke. The helmsman began to shout excitedly, "Get an extinguisher on that electrical fire. Open the door. Do something!"

The Central Committee's political officer stumbled out of the bridge and into the darkened deck passageway. His burning, watery eyes never saw the stairwell to the lower deck—he missed the first step and took a header down to the base of the steep metal stairs where his lifeless body laid still.

AIRSPACE OVER PACIFIC OCEAN
Tuesday Morning, 18 November
0422 Hours

Colonel Richter initiated the pull-up from twenty feet above the wave tops as he reached his IP thirty miles from the first warship inside the corridor. The Mach wave signature across the cold black waters dissipated as the *Thud* rocketed upwards at 40,000 feet per minute. His wingman followed suit, 800 feet abeam. Thirty seconds later, Richter called for a laser ID from *Manta One*. "Mama Bird, Forge 1."

"Forge 1, Mama Bird, go ahead," Tallman replied.

"Light up contact at twelve o'clock and twenty."

"Can do, easy," said Tom as he slid the cursor atop *Yangtze* and activated *Manta's* targeting laser. The laser bathed the crippled cruiser with the invisible beam.

Richter and his wingman simultaneously rolled inverted and pickled their deadly cargo. They continued their split-S maneuvers back down toward the water and sought another ship as the GBU-31s arced gracefully directly toward *Yangtze*.

EASTERN PACIFIC OCEAN
CHINESE CRUISER YANGTZE
Tuesday Morning, 18 November
0424Hours

Seamen ran up the stairwell to the bridge carrying flashlights and electric work lanterns. They excitedly tried to explain the unknown calamity that had befallen them to the beleaguered captain. They never saw the muted shape of the pair of JDAMS falling at supersonic speeds. The first hit the center of the helipad, passed though two decks of steel and exploded in the engine room. The blast tore through the warship, sending the remains of the inch-thick steel plates flying over the bridge and onto the missile launch platforms. The gas turbine engines were wrenched off their mounts and seized in seconds as the twisted propeller shafts thrashed uncontrolled—wreaking havoc on the bodies of the dead sailors.

The second JDAM entered the gaping hole created by the first; punched through the pile of debris on the engine room floor, and then hit the ship's keel before it exploded. The blast lifted the ill-fated 11,450 ton vessel amidships, breaking her back in half and detonating the weapons storage magazine. In a brief, but tremendous ball of fire, she was gone.

EASTERN PACIFIC OCEAN
CHINESE CARRIER SUN TZU
Tuesday Morning, 18 November
0425 Hours

Admiral Meng stood on the bridge, his hands clasped behind his back, confidently watching his J-20 fighters simultaneously launch from the deck of his ultimate creation. Abruptly, a flash of light from his four o'clock caused him to turn in time to see a ball of fire lighting up the night sky no more than ten miles away.

"What…" he started to say as he brought the binoculars hung around his neck to his eyes and watched as munitions and missiles on board *Yangtze* cooked off.

"Sir, Yangtze just exploded," shouted the petty officer who had been scanning the horizon.

"I can see that, Hai Jun San Ji Shi Guan! I want to know why." He strode quickly to the comm link and picked up the mic. "Radar control, this is the Admiral. What are you tracking on radar or sonar?"

"The only radar returns we have are our own ships and our aircraft that have been launched, sir. We do have distant returns from civilian commercial airways at appropriate altitudes," came the reply. "Sonar reports two rapid explosions and then the sounds of Yangtze breaking up. We did not pick up any torpedo sounds prior to the explosions."

"CIC, were there any distress signals from Yangtze?"

"Sir, no sir…only that we lost contact," was the report from the Communications Center. "We are now losing data contact with other ships in the fleet, as well."

Meng hesitated for a moment as he tried to comprehend what was happening, then said, "Sound General Quarters."

AIRSPACE OVER PACIFIC OCEAN
Tuesday Morning, 18 November
0425 Hours

Tallman monitored the impacts on *Yangtze* with *Manta's* ARGUS-IS imaging system. "Whoa…sucks to be them."

"Get me the destroyer in this location," Kit said as he pointed to the next major target in the southern corridor.

"You got it."

"Looks like Eagle 1 and 2 are engaging the first frigate," Blaze commented.

"Lanie, have Spooky engage the cruiser here. Follow up with these two destroyers," Kit said as fingered the intended targets. He turned his attention to *Manta 2* and the northern CBG.

Lanie nodded and keyed her mic, "Spooky, Mama Bird."

"Go, Lanie," Harlen "Big Dog" Hambly replied as he climbed through FL280.

"Target identified and tagged, engage when ready."

"Spooky copies all. Will call you back when pulsed," Big Dog replied. He quickly switched to interphone. "Ronnie, lock up the ship with the yellow ring around it and fire. Let big bird know when it's done."

Ronnie Carpenter saw the target Kit had designated on his flat screen display and gave the distant ship a four second burst. "Mama Bird, Spooky. Target 1 engaged." Mere seconds after the word left his mouth, a second yellow target circle appeared on the screen. In six minutes, the lanky former Air Force master sergeant had effectively blinded a third of *Yang Jian*'s battle group.

Bobby Mendez in *Eagle 5*, rolled into a strafing pass on the frigate *Jade Prince.* Coming in from the stern, he lined up his targeting laser on the area that Naval Intelligence had briefed was the bridge. The ship's power was out, but her momentum was still carrying the totally dark vessel forward. Spooky's *TeslaPulse* had done its job once again. He squeezed the red trigger on his side stick. Hypersonic ferromagnetic projectiles poured out of the six-barreled electromagnetic coil gun in the nose at 13,000 feet per second. Faint blue trails of ionized particles appeared, then faded as Bobby released the trigger.

"Eagle 5 off left," the smooth talking native of Puerto Rico transmitted as he broke off the attack.

"Eagle 6 in hot," Trace Askins called from a mile in trail.

EASTERN PACIFIC OCEAN
CHINESE FRIGATE JADE PRINCE
Tuesday Morning, 18 November
0425 Hours

The sound of metal tearing and men screaming filled the air as sixty-six hardened tungsten steel projectiles ripped through the superstructure like it was butter. Trapped in the darkness, the officers and men of the Chinese ship were terrorized by their unseen attacker. White hot spalling from the bridge's aft steel wall tore limbs from bodies and splattered the forward wall with gore. The sailor at the helm slumped to the floor, trying to hold on to the wheel as his life's blood flowed from the stub of his mangled leg.

Jade Prince's rudder responded to the unintended input, coming starboard fifteen degrees. A deck below, a survivor in the unscathed, but inoperative Combat Control Center fumbled with a latched storage closet in pitch blackness. He grabbed a yellow rubber coated flashlight and thumbed it on. The ceiling dripped blood through inch diameter holes in the deck of the bridge above. Blood ran down the glass of the fused weapons status display boards. The sight turned the young man's stomach as the awful thought that his first sea voyage would be his last ran across his consciousness.

The staccato sound reminiscent of a dozen massive gongs being struck, rung though out the warship. In the engine room and fuel bunkers, a series of holes appeared in the side of the ship two feet below the water line. Water sprayed into the first compartment with the force of a dozen fire hoses. The forward-most fuel bunker was over half empty, and a half dozen white hot G2 ferromagnetic projectiles ignited the diesel fuel vapors in a blast that would be heard twenty miles away. The ship's ragged prow dug into the cold unforgiving water at over twenty-five knots, tossing crew members forward like so many rag dolls into unyielding bulkheads. Fire quickly spread to the adjoining fuel storage area damaged by the first blast. There was no one to fight the blaze, and in mere minutes, both missile batteries on the foredeck exploded. *Jade Prince* listed hard to port as she slowed to a halt. Burning diesel fuel lit up the darkness while her funeral pyre raged on unabated.

AIRSPACE OVER PACIFIC OCEAN
Tuesday Morning, 18 November
0430 Hours

Two squadrons of the new J-20 stealth fighters were formed up and released to surge inland as planned. Six squadrons of the J-10 ground attack fighters were already airborne, but two of those had been assigned to carrier defense before the launch of the major attack. Once the damage reports became a torrent of bad news, the planes of the carrier defense air fleet were tasked to protect *Sun Tzu* and *Lang Jian*. Without an enemy on the radar, the J-20 fighters were helpless to actually do anything in the pre-dawn skies. Sixty miles east of *Sun Tzu*, the first waves of J-20s began to pick up a radar return from an enemy fighter.

"Tiger Flight, Tiger Lead has a enemy bearing 100 degrees at sixty kilometers," the senior flight leader reported. "Speed eight hundred, two thousand meters above us."

The QF-4 drone was cruising at FL360 and was being driven directly at the massed Chinese fighters at thirty thousand feet. As range closed to thirty-five miles, the electronic signal to fire the F-16 simulator missiles was given. In groups of four, the seven foot long missiles were launched as the QF-4 parent climbed higher. Each emitted a signal identical to an F-16 radar cross-section, tailored to the Chinese fighter search radar.

Using cutting edge technology "borrowed" from the Russians, Italians, Israelis and United States, the designers of the Chengdu J-10 and its newer stable mate, the Jian-20, or as the Chinese referred to it, the Annihilator-20, created formidable platforms. The pair were designed to compete head-to head with the F-18/A *Super Hornet* and F-22 *Raptor*. The J-10 possessed an *Infra-Red Search and Track* system, as used on the Russian SU-27 holographic heads-up display and *Forward Looking Infra Red (FLIR)* thought to have been reverse engineered from shot down US systems recovered in the gulf war with Iraq. It was known to have a established a 13:1 kill ratio on the J-11A in simulated dogfights.

Some models incorporated a helmet-mounted display system, eliminating the HUD. All the J-10s carried a sophisticated ECM suite and external BM/KG300G jamming pods. The PLAN pilots felt supremely confident in their aircraft and their personal abilities. What the Chinese were not prepared for was the genius of General Jack Stewart.

Sixteen F-16 decoys were joined by eighty others in the southern battle space as F-106 *Delta Darts* flying high above the QF-4 drone added their decoy missiles to the barrage screaming toward the J-20s. Aboard the Chinese stealth fighters, the unexpected arrival of dozens of presumed F-16 aircraft into the fray was completely unexpected. Each man had been briefed that the *Vipers* had been disabled by superior Chinese computer science. Yet, there on the HUDs was proof the *Vipers* were in striking distance of the fleet. J-20 automated targeting systems locked on the approaching decoys and the Chinese pilots engaged them as trained. Once their bomb bay doors opened, each J-20 fired two ShanDian-10 air-to-air missiles. The large fire-and-forget weapons lit off with a brilliant white flash and streaked across the inky skies as they accelerated to Mach 4. In less than thirty seconds, the missiles closed with the incoming fighter simulators. Proximity fuses detonated the 438 pound SD-10s, blasting some, but not all, of the drones out of the sky. Frantically, the Chinese pilots fired more missiles to intercept the rest. Chinese cockpit warning systems identified multiple enemy radar systems had been turned on. Additional inbound threats were identified as AIM-120s that had just seconds earlier had roared off the rails from undetected F-15 *Eagles*.

EASTERN PACIFIC OCEAN
CHINESE CARRIER SUN TZU
Tuesday Morning, 18 November
0434 Hours

The young sailors at their posts monitoring US secured satellite frequencies on channels one through three, excitedly began to call their intercepts up to the Combat Control Center. Dozens of calls could be heard from ship-to-aircraft and between fighters, as they called targets bearing and range. What was particularly frightening to the sailors was the Navy fighter jocks were talking about *Sun Tzu*, *Yang Jian* and dozens of other ships in the two carrier strike groups by name.

One of them turned to his section commander and exclaimed, “Shao Xiao Tian. The American Navy is attacking us from the west! We have confirmed two squadrons are gathering at 10,000 meters.”

“Calm yourself. It is obvious that this is the first sea battle you have even seen,” he curtly replied before reaching for the interphone hand piece. He glared back at the seaman, “Did I tell you to stop listening?” He picked up his handset and keyed the bridge. “CCC, Intelligence Officer Tian.”

“Make it quick, Tian,” came the short reply.

“Commander, we have intercepted the American pilots talking on their supposedly secure satcom. They are massed for an attack from the west. The call signs match those of Nimitz and Stennis.”

“Thank you, Tian. I’ll advise the Captain.”

“But the American system was disabled by our spy, according to Admiral Meng!” growled the agitated senior officer. Shang Xiao Gwok Wei glanced around the control center. Information from numerous Chinese sources had the Americans attacking from all sides, except the west. The Admiral’s plan was falling apart from the onset. Unseen forces had attacked and sunk much of his defensive screen and supposed disabled fighters were reported to the west. A decision had to be made, or *Sun Tzu* would be at risk.

"Air Commander, launch the reserve fighters, configured for air-to-air. Deploy west until further notice."

AIRSPACE OVER PACIFIC OCEAN
Tuesday Morning, 18 November
0436 Hours

Blaze checked the status of her computer hard drive to confirm the taped naval chatter transmissions were operating as planned. Six hours of canned electronic misdirection had been recorded at General Stewart's request—all part of a master plan to confuse, delay and undermine the enemy fleet's numerical and technological advantage. The BEF had transmitted the information up to the MILSATCOM system on the only channels known to the Chinese. Channels four and five, newly encrypted channels previously unused, and unknown to the enemy, provided the real situational awareness to the US forces defending the west coast.

Further south, Lt. Colonel Hollywood Stewart lead sixteen F-15 *Eagles* in attack spread formation on the J-20s. F-106s had successfully confused the J-20s with the F-16 decoys and a fusillade of AMRAAMs before they disengaged and broke away toward the water. Six Slammers with the modified low PRF seekers had tagged their quarry, sending a half-dozen of the vaunted *Annihilators* down in flaming arcs. Hollywood selected the *ACTIVE* mode on his radar for six seconds, just enough to locate the J-20 attempting to get a heat-seeker lock on one of the F-106s. He triggered a Slammer off the inboard port pylon and quickly turned his search radar off. With a blinding flash, the AIM-120 missile was away streaking down at almost 3,000 miles per hour.

"Steel 1, Fox Three," the squadron commander transmitted as he jinked left, rolled and pulled the stick back to his lap. He groaned as he strained against the rapidly building G forces.

The Chinese pilot in the J-20 took a PL-9 infrared missile shot at the supersonic F-106 descending through 4,000 feet. His supply of SD-10s had been expended on F-16 decoy missiles, but he was still game to defeat the impertinent American fighter pilot in the unknown black craft. For the eighth time, his bomb bay doors opened and a missile lit up the darkness. The PL-9 trailed a white smoke trail across vast Pacific as the F-106 pilot tried in vain to gain separation from his attacker. The Chinese major reacted instantly when his HMD flashed a warning of a rear quarter radar missile attack. He activated his ECM pod to jam the American AIM-120, then wondered what went wrong with the PL-9 as it detonated on an unseen object three thousand feet behind the delta winged fighter.

Inside the F-106, Colonel Pete Simmons clicked the flare button a third time as he strained to glance back over his left shoulder. Another pair of the foot long enclosed cylinders blasted free of the fuselage and activated a 1,200 degree Celcius exothermic chemical reaction. Another BEF contribution to the fray, the flares did not burn like magnesium with its telltale white flame. Rather, they rapidly heated the stainless steel container that emitted a heat signature within the normal operating temperature range for an afterburning turbofan engine. Pete gritted his teeth as he focused on the missile coming down fast from his six o'clock high. *Six seconds to figure somethin' out.*

But the missile was not aimed at him. It impacted the J-20 just aft of the cockpit, severing the two wings and turning night into day for a fraction of a second. Simmons checked his blue force disposition on the iPad strapped to his left thigh. He checked his fuel totalizer and made a slow turn slightly north to intercept the closest KC-10. *Thank you, Jesus, and thank whoever is in Steel 1.*

Ninety miles south west, Wardog noted the buildup of Chinese fighters west of *Sun Tzu. All right you dumb chink bastards. You took the bait.* He had previously dropped a total of eight JDAMs on the ships damaged by the BEF *Eagles*. His sector began to look a bit target poor, with burning oil slicks and only one badly listing destroyer left beneath his squadron. His heart was pumping a mile-a-minute, just like the old days. And it felt good. Damned good. The Marine colonel studied the iPad and checked his fuel status. Airborne just over a hour, the *Phantom* would be bingo fuel in less than forty minutes, as would his wingmen.

"Little Eddie, what say we skedaddle back and get some more push-water?"

"Works for me, Wardog."

"When we come back, gonna be in the mood for some Chinese takeout."

"Getting a little hungry myself…I am."

EASTERN PACIFIC OCEAN
USS NIMITZ
Tuesday Morning, 18 November
0450 Hours

Inside the Combat Control Center, the air boss acknowledged the impending return of the first fourteen *Phantoms*.

"Launch the reserve F-4s, I want the Tomcats rigged up air-to-air only and standing by. The Reds have taken the bait."

Up on the flight deck, Admiral Snake Sievers was itching for action. His fighters had been held cocked and locked beside the primary catapult as last ditch defense for the carrier. Now that the bulk of the Chinese sea defenses were neutralized, the time to hit the J-10s massed west of *SunTzu* had come.

A wave of nausea swept over the aging warrior. It was not a sudden bout of sea sickness and Snake had never admitted to feeling fear. But the pancreatic cancer in his abdomen didn't care how brave or battle tested the man was. It just kept dividing, multiplying and spreading as if tomorrow would never come. He grabbed hold of the canopy rails for support, then dropped his left hand down to the mic switch on the throttle. "Volcano Basin, Anvil 1."

"Anvil 1, Volcano Basin, What's on your mind," the air boss answered.

"Any chance me and my boys are gonna get off this tub tonight?"

The air boss looked out as the first of the returning *Phantoms* trapped on the angle deck two wire. In ten minutes, the first would have an air-to-ship Harpoon missile strapped to the centerline hardpoint. Hot refueling would take five minutes to top off. He could use the room on the deck as the elevators brought up another blackened F-8 *Crusader*. They may have been called *The Last of the Gunfighters*, but those single seaters had four AMRAAMs added to them. The plan called for the F-8's to lead the final assault on the Chinese air arm.

"Anvil 1, Volcano Basin."

"Go."

"You have eight Gunfighters ahead of you, Snake. Get ready."

"Born that way," Snake quipped and a smile came to his face as he ended the call and clicked the intercom. "What'cha think about a little cruise in the moonlight, Robbie?"

"Anything…as long as we can get inverted for a while. My ass is startin' to feel welded to this seat."

The fifth Type 071 LPD troop carrier out of the line of twenty fell victim to the G2 coil gun mounted at the stern of *Sea Eagle*. Stienke had neutralized her first with the *TeslaPulse* to suppress return fire and eliminate radio chatter that could expose *Sea Eagle's* position.

Damaged boats appeared to fall out of position in the darkness and did not respond to radio transmissions. Shoehorn raked the LPD fore and aft with hypersonic rounds ripping into men and equipment with impunity. Fires broke out on the heavylift helos assigned to bring the tanks ashore once the hovercrafts had landed and secured the beach. Stienke checked the bearing to the next troop carrier and lay in a course to intercept.

AIRSPACE OVER PACIFIC OCEAN
Tuesday Morning, 18 November
0510 Hours

In the area northwest of San Francisco, Colonel Bob Peterman led two flights of F-15s as they engaged the last of the J-20s in an aerial dual to the death. Earlier, waves of F-4s and F-106s had followed the BEF *Eagles* into the northern Chinese fleet—refurbished Air Force *Thuds* and *Aardvarks* were used to duplicate the operational success against the southern carrier battle group. One of the first J-20's launched somehow slipped past six layers of fighters and approached the US coast line only forty miles west of the target area assigned to Peterman's flight, Travis Air Force Base. A Patriot Missile Battery picked up the distant faint radar return off the stealthy craft by using low PRF radar modifications updated into the system. Peterman made a snap decision and transferred command to a flight commander from his regular home squadron.

"Steel 23, you have the lead…22 you're with me," he called out as he performed a slicing reversal and smashed both throttles to their stops.

"Steel 22, roger that," Major Teddy Carter, his wingman grunted as he fought against the eight G turn to follow Peterman. Teddy could see the twin cones of fire from the commander's *Eagle* as it accelerated ahead of him. Carter smacked his own throttles against the stops.

The lights of San Mateo and San Francisco were glowing bright, low against the eastern horizon as Peterman attempted to visually locate the Jian-20. The waxing moon was fast approaching a point where it would crest the distant Sierra Nevada range. He could see two closely spaced dots moving right to left above the barely perceptible horizon. "Tally ho the J-20, three degrees above the mountains." Peterman called out.

Got ya, you son of a bitch. Flash selected the AIM-9 and tried to bore site the J-20 exhaust nozzles. He centered the two in his HUD, but got no tone. *Shit. Outta range.* He swapped over to the AIM-120 and locked up the stealthy bird at 7 miles—pulled the trigger, sending a Slammer off the starboard outside pylon. He winced as the white hot flame seared his eyes, momentarily taking his night vision from him. "Steel 21, Fox Three!"

"Steel 22, Fox Three!"

"Come on, baby," Peterman urged his *Eagle* to go faster, but she was already at the limit. The Mach 2 tail chase pitted two fighters at their max speeds, but the AMRAAM could do much more.

Just fifty yards from the cliff above the crashing Pacific surf, a first lieutenant barely over two years out of West Point commanded the three missile batteries assigned to that particular sector of California. He monitored the radar screen as the upgraded phased array refreshed the display. "No IFF on that one?" he asked the operator seated at the screen.

"Negative, Lieutenant. I pinged him twice."

"Lock him up. Stand by to fire."

"Yes, sir!" replied the specialist fourth class. "In range now."

"Fire one."

One second, the forty foot Patriot missile was lying there on the launcher—the next, it was supersonic, already hundreds of feet away. A huge cloud of dense white smoke billowed out and almost covered the entire launcher. The team had fired the missiles dozens of times in the simulator, and got to shoot a real one once at Fort Bliss in initial training, but never had made one single real launch at night. The blindingly fast disappearing anti-aircraft/anti-missile missile was more than impressive. Lt. Wagaman stood there with his mouth agape for a second. Finally he found words to express his feeling, "Holy shit!"

Inside the Jian-20 cockpit, the three incoming missiles triggered multiple warning in his HMD. The eight-year pilot reacted by pulling back hard on the stick. The nose of the J-20 responded rapidly and his craft climbed almost three thousand feet before the Patriot proximity fuse detonated. Steel rods impacted the belly of the J-20 as the first AMRAAM followed suit fifty feet above the aircraft's canopy, followed shortly thereafter by the second. The fighter disappeared in a thunderous blast heard all the way to Santa Cruz.

"That's what I'm talking about!" Peterman radioed to his wingman. "Nice shootin', 22."

"Back at 'ya," his wing man replied as he turned west once again to follow Peterman's *Eagle* back into the melee.

EASTERN PACIFIC OCEAN
Sun Tzu
Tuesday Morning, 18 November
0525 Hours

The bright yellow gibbous moon cleared the mountain tops east of Santa Monica, starting to bathe the coast with a mellow glow. Fires from the burning cruiser *Sholin* cast a pall over the western horizon. Inside the Combat Control Center, Captain Gwok Wei approached a stunned and transfixed Admiral Huang Meng staring at the electronic holographic table. The remains of his once vaunted fleet assigned to *Sun Tzu's* support, only a single destroyer, more than forty miles west, was left afloat. *This was not supposed to happen on my birthday—my chart is never wrong*. "Shang Xiao, you have something to say?" he said lifelessly.

"Admiral, the XO of *Snow Tiger* advises us they have taken a torpedo and are dead in the water. The captain gave the order to abandon ship just before he was killed."

The Admiral tried to digest the news. He noticed the three dimensional electronic image of *Snow Tiger* as it flickered and disappeared. His head jerked ever so slightly to the side and took on an even stranger countenance.

"Perhaps it is time for you to take a transport to *Yang Jian*. She still has a cruiser and two frigates… "

"Silence!" Meng thundered, interrupting the captain. "Never would I retreat. Your flyers and sailors have disgraced us both. They have comported themselves in an abysmal manner that showcased their gross incompet...."

The lights inside the center snapped off without warning. Throughout the ship, anything electronic had simply ceased to function. The controls to the elevators were locked. No radios worked and the automated ship defenses failed in their last position. The normally taciturn and reserved Captain exploded—he knew what was coming. He didn't know how the resourceful Americans did it, but he now knew exactly what had transpired aboard the ships that had met their fates. Wei turned back to his once exalted Admiral. "Meng, you arrogant bastard. You have killed us all!"

***

CHAPTER FIFTEEN

AIRSPACE OVER PACIFIC OCEAN
Tuesday Morning, 18 November
0525 Hours

"Dammit!" Blaze shouted to no one in particular, but Dare Phillips reacted with a start.

"What? What's wrong?"

"The EMP generator. I got an Off flag and System Electrical Fault."

Gears called back on interphone, "We have an electrical master caution. The number two A/C bus automatically dropped off line. What's your situation?"

"We lost the TeslaPulse. I ran it for twenty seconds as we walked the beam the length of the carrier."

“May have overloaded its design parameters. Any thing else?” Gears asked.

“No, I think…”

Her response was cut off by Gunter Hermann who was glancing aft at the large metal box enclosing the guts of the EMP generator. “Hey! We’ve got smoke back there.”

“Crap! Gunnz, get an extinguisher on that,” Kit called up to the cockpit.

Gunnz unstrapped, but Gunter beat him to the nearest one. Both men raced back and unsnapped the cover latches on the front of the box. Gunter shoved the nozzle of the CO2 extinguisher inside and fired the bottle for ten seconds.

“That should get it, Gunter.”

The elder Hermann checked the gauge. “Got more if we need it.”

The carbon dioxide dissipated in seconds; Gunnz pulled out a small LED flashlight and looked inside the box. Puddles of melted plastic insulation told him all he needed to see. “Make a great trot line weight now. This bad boy is toast.”

“‘Fraid so. Worked like a champ for while, I’d say.”

“It did, it did,” agreed Gunnz as he snapped the cover closed.

AIRSPACE OVER SOUTHERN CALIFORNIA
Tuesday Morning, 18 November
0528 Hours

The auto shutoff on Jack Stewart’s *Starfighter* triggered a light in the KC-10. The boomer sat in a large leather chair looking out a three foot wide by eight inch high window at the black *Starfighter* beneath him—called to terminate the operation. "Vulcan 1, Dino 15, I see you are topped off. Cleared to disconnect."

"Vulcan 1, roger. Vulcan Flight is clear at this time."

He retarded the throttle slightly and backed away from the drogue and basket, pulling his refueling probe free. Jack eased forward on the stick, entering a shallow dive and slow left turn. His wingmen followed suit, staying in tight formation by reference to the other aircraft's position lights. The KC-10 continued northbound on the airway to San Francisco.

A flight of F-4s pulled in to take the place of the F-104s as two dozen of the mobile gas stations coursed up and down the west coast.

Jack called the flight to change to tactical frequency preset, "Vulcan flight, button six."

As they checked in, Burner led the two flights of four into a climb at military power—the bright lights of Century City were almost directly beneath. It was easy to see the Santa Monica mountains surrounding Century City and Burbank. Jack had visited the LA area dozens of times with his wife. He glanced down to see the lighted sign proudly proclaiming the movie capital of the world. *Hollywood.* The sight could not help jar him for a second. Jack wondered silently where his son James was at that instant. Hopefully he was in one of those little blue dots between the *Starfighters* and the Chinese fighters struggling to survive west of *Sun Tzu*.

"Vulcan 9, Vulcan 1."

“Vulcan 9 has his ears on.”

“Stop your climb at angels three-three. We’ll continue up to four-five-zero. Maintain spacing as briefed.”

“Roger, angels three-three for Vulcan 9 flight.”

Burner’s mind evaluated all the battle space as he glanced at the iPad on his knee board. Less than twenty red icons were left marking the location of Chinese J-10s or J-20s in the area west of *Sun Tzu.* He compressed the display and slid the northern carrier battle group down, then spread it out to enlarge. Between the fingers of his Nomex gloves he could see perhaps thirty planes airborne. Some were attempting to land for refueling, as best he could make out with his cursory examination. Highway 101 passed under the nose of the *Zipper*, with Interstate 405 almost directly under his feet. It was filling up with morning traffic in both directions—completely oblivious to the carnage occurring offshore.

“Vulcan Flight, spread ‘em out, kill your lights.”

One by one, the outboard aircraft in the formation peeled off to assume a tactical spread and extinguished their position lights. Even in the moonlight, they no longer could see one another and relied solely on the disposition displays to keep abreast. Missiles, flares, and tracers twinkled in the distance. An explosion far off shore indicated an air-to-air missile had detonated, and a flaming pile of debris tumbled toward the ocean surface. The question on Burner’s mind was clear—*Whose aircraft was it?*

Eight hundred feet over the recently dusted Santa Monica mountains, a Rockwell B-1B *Lancer* from the 7th Bomb Wing at Dyess AFB, roared low over the picturesque mountain tops casting a shadow in the moonlight on the pristine new-fallen snow. With its wings laid back the full 67.5 degrees, she resembled a shark, and this predator already had its morning meal picked out.

Captain Roger Morton and his copilot Captain Phil Klein prepped *Hammer 1* for their bombing run on the stricken *Sun Tzu*. Neither knew the electronics were already savaged on the big ultra-super carrier. She was under way, but in a slight right turn. Her nuclear reactors had shut down electronically, but the residual heat from the two reactors had plenty of energy to continue to power her steam turbines—at least for the next few minutes.

"Feet wet, taking it down to three hundred feet," Morton remarked as he crossed over the Pacific Coast Highway. The sonic boom rattled the windows along the coast as the black bird, called *Bone* by the men who flew her, passed overhead at six thousand feet at Mach 1.2, just under its redline top speed.

Klein set up the weapons fusing and entered the initial target coordinates into the bomb computer. Updates once the B-1B came into radar contact with *Sun Tzu* would allow them to place their JDAMS and JSOWS precisely where they wanted.

"Damn! These boys have been busy," Morton remarked as he picked his way around the first line of burning transports. Smoke spread across the ocean for miles from the wrecks.

"Gotta admire their handiwork, Mort...Jesus! Was that a *Sea Fighter* off our right wing?"

"What?"

At a flying speed of 1,380 feet per second, things went by the B-1B in a flash. Mort never saw the almost invisible boat. He checked his blue forces display. The map showed a blue icon two miles behind them. Every passing 3.82 seconds put the *Sea Eagle* another mile back.

"Guess so. The IP is coming up in 10 seconds. Ready?"

"Go for it, cat daddy."

Morton keyed the mic and transmitted on the battlefield operation frequency for the first time.

"Attention all stations, be advised, Hammer 1 inbound on X-ray Charlie One."

Phil noted the arrival over the initial point designated on the magenta line laid out on the crew's flat screen nav system display. "IP," he said with a little more excitement in his voice.

"Roger that," replied Morton as he pulled back hard on the stick. The black shark nose rose quickly to forty degrees above the horizon, leaving the dark waves far below like a homesick angel.

"Sniper XR is hot. Weapons - Arm, Automated bomb drop - On. All systems - Go. Keep her coming, Mort."

Morton concentrated on keeping the two flight directors centered over the aircraft symbol in the ADI, or attitude directional indicator. He knew the Lockheed-Martin Sniper Advanced Targeting Pod, designated AN/AAQ-33 for the US Air Force, was taking high res pics of *Sun Tzu* with its third generation *FLIR* and CCAD camera. All he had to do was get the aircraft to the right spot in the sky to allow a clean release and the ATP would guide the smart bombs, both JDAMS and JSOWS to say hello in a dramatic fashion. Forty-five seconds later, *Hammer 1* reached that point and the bay doors opened automatically. Two of the one thousand pound Joint Stand Off Weapons, or JSOWS, and five of the two thousand pound GBU 38 smart bombs cleared the bay of the still climbing *Bone*. The doors closed, triggering a light in the forward panel.

Captain Morton rolled inverted lazily and started pulling the nose down smoothly. He took his hands off the stick.

"I say, old Chap!" he said with the most affected English accent he could muster. "Might you want to have a go at the other bloke?"

"Capital idea, Guv'na," his flying buddy of four years responded. "Bloody good show."

The twenty-six year old took control of the 300 million dollar jet and continued the slicing, descending turn to the north while the deadly warbird screamed toward the wave tops. Four hundred miles away lay *Yang Jian*—and *Bone* was still hungry.

"Gears take us back up north. We have the heavy metal off target on *Sun Tzu*. Anything else we would do is in the category of overkill," Kit said over the C-5M intercom.

"You got it," came the reply.

Kit studied both the screens. Eight blue icons raced across the southern battle space in a wide, but shallow, *W* shaped formation, followed by an identical one approximately ten miles in trail. He clicked on the center of the first one; an ID tag showed the call sign *Vulcan 1, General Stewart*. They were sixty miles away from a multiple aircraft engagement with eight blue dots and twelve red ones. *Here comes the cavalry.*

Jack Stewart looked at the same layout, albeit on a much smaller screen. His plan to knife through the Jian-10s was derived from an old time US Army Air Force patriot fighting a faster and more maneuverable foe. General Claire Chennault, in command of the US Volunteer Group, UVG for short, or *Flying Tigers* as they were more famously called, determined the best way to fight the Japanese *Zeros* and *Kates* was to blast through the enemy formations at high speed, taking advantage of the Curtis P-40 *Tomahawk's* superior speed in a dive. It couldn't turn with the *Zeros* and Chennault had no intention of trying to fight the enemy's fight. Stewart learned the lesson well and drilled it into his *Starfighter* pilots.

"Vulcan flights, Vulcan 1. Time to let the big dogs eat... Burners, now!"

Sixteen pilots responded as one, lighting the sky with sixteen foot cones of blue-white flame and thrusting the pilots deep into the back of their ejection seats. One of them called out a rebel yell, "Yee-Hah!"

Jack couldn't help but smile. His adrenaline was really pumping and he never felt more alive than when he was entering battle. The mach meter passed 1.6 when he issued his command. "First Vulcan flight, take it down. Clear to engage at will."

AIRSPACE OVER EASTERN PACIFIC
Tuesday Morning, 18 November
0535 Hours

Twenty-three miles to the west, a desperate air battle pitted a single blue dot against five new Jian-20 Chinese fighters. Snake Sievers and his RIO had competed a full ace in daily air kills in only eighteen minutes. But by 0535 local, *Anvil 1* was completely out of missiles and down to 232 of his 20 mm HE rounds for his M-61 multi-barreled gun. He had made a move to disengage, but was cut off by three J-10s and not amused at all when two additional fifth generation fighters closed in behind him. They must have been out of missiles, too, because neither took a shot at him when they were five miles in trail. The lopsided melee, called a furball by old time and newly christened fighter pilots alike, swooped, cut back, reversed and zoomed in a no-holds-barred fight to the death. Snake felt the sweat run down into his eyes. He blinked twice to try to clear them as he broke left again at the direction of his RIO. Robbie tried to keep the mental image of the three dimensional chess game in focus as the smallish iPad provided the only full display of the battle space. Snake strained to check his seven o'clock where a stream of green tracers that passed between his twin vertical stabilizers had originated.

Night battles were the pits under optimum conditions, and the Chinese were close enough to pick up both radar and heat signature of the swing-wing *Tomcat*. Bleeding off airspeed in a hard reversal break into the shooter, the F-14 wings swept forward automatically and the leading edge slats deployed, grabbing the air like a drowning man grabs at a rope. Snake heard himself groan at the onset of the Gs, not certain if it was the rapid acceleration or the anaconda crush of the G-suit over his cancerous pancreas. The metallic sound of a single 23 mm round tearing through his right vertical stab didn't offer any encouragement. Snake knew he was in a world of hurt. Suddenly, another sound, one more beautiful than any he could ever remember, came to his ears.

"Vulcan 1, Fox Two, Fox Two!"

A pair of recently modified AIM-9X heaters streaked down at Mach 2.5. The newest software upgrade, compliments of Blaze and Gears at the BEF, completely disregarded the twinkling magnesium flares that burned brightly as they arced silently through the early morning darkness. The J-10's Saturn AL-31FM turbofans were cranking out almost 31,000 pounds of thrust, and just the right heat signature for the nine foot long Sidewinders. One flew literally up the tailpipe of the targeted fighter. The resulting explosion blasted the empennage completely off and ignited what little fuel was left in the agile craft. Flames lasted only two seconds, and then any visual evidence of the fighter's existence disappeared. The second bird faired little better. The heater's proximity fuse detonated 100 feet above the J-10 and sent lethal metal rods ripping through the cockpit as well as the left wing root. The wing separated, sending the wreckage tumbling end-over-end in a flaming spiral to the cold waters of the Pacific.

Jack pulled aft and rolled hard left to engage the enemy fighter on the far side of the former furball. He squeezed the trigger enough to get the gun targeting radar and camera to engage. Placing the pipper where the green splash on the radar detected the J-10, the seasoned warrior fired a short burst. His near miss was close enough to convince the rookie Chinese pilot to unload and break down and away from the red tracers. The *Vigorous Dragon*, as western military planners called the Jian-10, sped away only to be picked up by an AMRAAM from *Vulcan 10.* Sometime you get the bear, sometimes the bear gets you. The rookie pilot who had scored a kill on an F-4 early in the battle died without a second victory.

Jack began a three G pullout at 26,000 feet and sped toward a pair of J-10s twenty-five miles west.

Admiral Sievers took the opportunity to disengage the fight for good. With the last local J-10s tied up with the newly arrived *Starfighters*, he broke away and separated himself and his WSO from the remaining enemy fighters in only seconds.

"Snake, we're bingo minus two," Robbie reported from the back seat. He placed a gloved finger over the gas pump icon on the iPad. "Looks like the closest fueler is that C-5M, but she's a hundred miles north and going away."

"Crap. Looks like our only shot....Eagle House, Anvil 1."

"Anvil 1, Eagle House."

"Eagle House, Anvil 1 is emergency fuel and unable to make it back to Nimitz. Any chance you can help?"

"Stand by, Anvil," Gears said. "Mile Charlie, AC."

Kit clicked the intercom. "Go, Gears."

"We have an emergency request for fuel from an Anvil 1. Can we handle?"

Kit assessed the situation. *The Herc could work over Yang Jian as required. Besides, the C-5M had lost its most powerful weapon when the TeslaPulse went tits up. The battle is going our way, a few minutes saving the Admiral's butt won't change the output.*

"Tell him the store is open all day."

Gears chuckled. "You betcha....Anvil 1, Eagle House turning south at this time."

"Eagle House, you're a lifesaver," Snake replied. "Any chance you can drop down to angels two-eight? I'm not sure we have the gas to make it up to three-five."

"Make it easy on yourself, Anvil. The boss man said to tell you we're open all day."

It was Snake's chance to smile. "Do you clean the windshield, too?...Jesus! Look at that!"

EASTERN PACIFIC OCEAN
CHINESE CARRIER SUN TZU
Tuesday Morning, 18 November
0540 Hours

Off to the east, the five JDAMs from the B-1B finally had reached their intended target, *Sun Tzu*. A pair of the one-ton GBU 38s penetrated the steel runway decks on each catamaran before exploding deep below. The fifth carved its way into the superstructure, burrowing through the ceiling and decks until the delayed fuse set it off one deck below the Combat Control Center. The resultant five blasts sent the two nuclear reactors to the sea floor as the twin keels broke in multiple places. Aviation fuel as well as ordnance stores exploded, adding to the carnage as steel and flesh was rendered alike. Two seconds later, the JSOWs, winged glide bombs with incredible range and accuracy smashed into the stern of each wrecked catamaran hull. Hangar bays of attack helicopters were engulfed in uncontrolled fires. The worst damage occurred when the solid fuel missile motors of the sixteen intermediate range ICBMs detonated in unison.

The once proud flagship of the People's Liberation Army Navy became a sinking graveyard of one man's narcissistic ambitions, taking the seven thousand officers and men aboard with her. A mushroom shaped fireball rose three thousand feet in the air. Early risers along the southern California coast marveled at the sight as they sipped their morning cups of coffee.

AIRSPACE OVER EASTERN PACIFIC
Tuesday Morning, 18 November
0540 Hours

"Man, would you look at that!" Tom Tallman blurted as the feed from *Manta 1* relayed the full affects of the B-1B attack.

Blaze glanced over at the screen and gasped inaudibly.

"Isn't that overkill?" she asked to no one in particular.

"I don't think Strike Command has that word in their lexicon," Dare offered.

He studied the northern display. Six scattered fighters, one missile frigate and the ultra-super carrier, *Yang Jian*, were all that remained of the CBG. The southern group was reduced to four Chinese fighters versus thirty-nine American birds with dozens more coming back off the tankers. The harried J-10s tangled up with the fleet aircraft were low on fuel and several had already flamed out, trying in vain to break away. Abruptly, Dare had a idea. A crazy one. *What if we captured Yang Jian? Was it possible?*

"Kit, if we wanted to capture the remaining carrier. How would you go about it?"

Kit spun around and faced his boss. He had been a major planner in the overall attack strategy. But the idea of capturing a defeated carrier never even came up. The plan had been to try to prevent a Chinese invasion.

"You serious?" Kit asked. When Dare nodded, Kit's mind raced. "First, we'd have to a call off the *Bone.* In two minutes they'll be in range. Maybe call them and ask for a surrender? Have the Herc or an Eagle knock out their helm, maybe their rudders."

"If we can slow them down, we could put the Herc on the boat. Let our Raptor teams take over," Dare replied.

"Hell, worth a shot. That ship's an engineering masterpiece. Major wow factor and serious loss of face for the Reds to lose it. Your call, Boss."

"No, it's the General's call…Vulcan 1, Eagle House."

The silver haired general had fired his last two AIM-120s at the sole remaining J-10, splashing the nimble craft with the first one, the second impacting the wreckage on the way down. He was ready to issue a recall order to the fighters in the south when he got the transmission from Dare. "Eagle House, Vulcan 1 go ahead."

"Eagle House request permission to attempt capture of the remaining carrier, over."

Jack was thunderstruck. *Capture Yang Jian?* With any other man making the recommendation, Stewart would have been laughing. But this was the head of the Black Eagle Force. *If Dare Phillips thinks such a mission was feasible, hell, by all means.*

"Go for it, Eagle House. What do you need from me?"

"Have Hammer stand down, sir. Give us thirty minutes. If no luck, we can always send her to the bottom."

"Vulcan 1 copies. Break…Hammer 1, Vulcan 1."

"Vulcan 1, be advised Hammer 1 is ninety seconds from IP," Captain Morton replied.

"Understand Hammer. Stand down. Repeat, stand down. We're gonna try to take *Yang Jian* in one piece. Remain in the area until advised, over."

Morton looked over at his obviously disappointed copilot and shrugged. "Hammer 1, standing by as requested."

Back aboard the BEF's C-5M, Dare considered all the facets of the daunting tasks ahead. *Where the hell is Tze Yen when you need him?* He remembered the counter intelligence operation Blaze was running over the MILSATCOM.

“Blaze, I need you to discontinue that program on the satcom channels one through three.”

She looked at him for a second, then considered he must have a good reason. He would tell her why when he had time, she thought. She right-clicked the program icon and selected *Discontinue Program* on the drop down menu.

“Eagle 9, Eagle House.”

“Eagle House, 9 is with you,” Tze Yen replied.

“Eagle 9, I need your language skills. Opportunity of a lifetime.”

“What?” the confused *Eagle* pilot asked.

Twenty miles west and 10,000 feet below the C-5M a scared and dispirited Chinese first lieutenant wondered how long he had to live. All but two of his squadron mates were dead and he barely survived a slew of missiles that had impacted other aircraft in the crazy shoot out south of *Yang Jian* main carrier battle group. He had escaped by diving to the deck and heading south, then climbed to conserve fuel.

Looking up, he saw a strange sight glistening in the moonlight—four short, but very distinct, contrails appeared heading south. They were close together, like four aircraft in tight formation, but he could see no aircraft. It wasn’t a civilian craft, he reasoned, because it had no position lights. On a hunch, he decided to check it out. He turned off his search radar. It hadn’t worked well against the American fighters, anyway. If those contrails belonged to a stealth bomber, the lieutenant planned to exact a modicum of revenge for the massive losses his country had suffered on that historic night.

"Anvil 1, Eagle House is level angels two-eight, slowing to 300. Rejoin on starboard side for a basket snag."

"Anvil 1 copies, we have a visual on you and are turning in trail at this time. Nose is cold," Sievers advised after having Robbie place the *Tomcat* search radar in *Standb*y position.

Julio Sosa looked at Gears. "Did he say visual?"

Gears glanced back at Bobby, then clicked the intercom. "Weapons, AC, say Lizard status."

Blaze clicked on a drop down menu as she replied, "Standby, I'll check."

A second right-click on the *Lizard* icon and a third on the *System Status* told her the answer. "AC, Weapons, Lizard functioning normal. Why?"

"Not sure, I'll call you back."

Bobby extended the refueling drogue from the starboard wing pylon between the two massive General Electric TF39 engines. It rolled out almost 100 feet of flexible hose that hung slightly lower than the bottom of the gigantic engine nacelles.

Admiral Snake Sievers stained his eyes to find the massive airframe that was generating the contrails. Try as he might, he could only see slightly opaque ragged blasts of ice crystals forming and rapidly dissipating in the dark skies. Suddenly the familiar faint circle of white lights appeared. He focused on the tiny LED lights embedded inside the refueling drogue. On the second attempt, his probe looked in solid.

"Eagle House, Anvil 1 is hooked up."

"Roger, Anvil 1, pumps coming on," Sosa said as he reached overhead to energize the transfer pumps. "Positive pressure," he relayed once the pump lights illuminated.

"Totalizer's rising." Robbie noted from the rear cockpit of the F-14. "Nothing like cutting it close there, Snake. We we're down to 1,100 pounds."

"Told you to have faith, buddy."

"Anvil 1, Eagle House, for clarification, what did you mean when you said you had a visual on us?"

"We could see short cons in the moonlight. Assumed that was you, over."

"Eagle House copies. How's the transfer coming?"

"Doin' fine. We're a little over 5,500 pounds now. It's a little cold for a night swim, I'm told," Robbie answered.

Blaze noted a change in the direction and speed of one of the red icons on her screen. She clicked it and saw the Chinese bird was climbing and accelerating rapidly. Its search radar was not transmitting.

"All stations, enemy fighter incoming!" she shouted over the *Super Galaxy* intercom.

"Anvil, emergency break! Fighter inbound, five o'clock," Gears radioed as he checked his display.

Snake thumbed the speed brakes open, immediately tugging the *Tomcat* away from the refueling apparatus. He pushed over slightly to increase separation from the C-5M, then snapped inverted and pulled hard to split-S into the incoming threat. He pushed his head back as far as the ejection seat headrest would allow and saw a missile coming up from the blackness below. He instinctively started to break back to the right, but the trajectory told him instantly that the move was not needed. The Mach 3 missile was not targeted at Anvil 1. Even before Snake had the *Tomcat* three-fourths of the way through the maneuver, the PL-9 streaked overhead. He followed it for a half second before he snapped his head around to the HUD. Robbie had the AN/APG-71 radar back up and running. Snake acquired the J-10 just as it closed to gun range. He centered the incoming fighter and fired a burst. Red tracers crossed paths with inbound green tracers. Snake saw the looming 23mm rounds growing larger, but they stayed in the same relative spot in his canopy. That meant one thing and one thing only. If he didn't do something quick, he and Robbie were both dead men.

"Missile Incoming!" Blaze yelled over the intercom. She knew it was not a radar guided one, as *Mama Bird's* suite of jamming and detection gear did not pick up search radar before the shot. She keyed the command to activate a series of flares that would protect the gargantuan craft. A message on the screen appeared. *Number 2 AC Bus Fault. Flares not available.* The stunned beauty sat motionless. *Of course. The TeslaPulse and flare systems were on the same circuitry. Dammit.* There had not time to add additional wiring to *Mama Bird* when the new system was added. No one had imagined a complete bus failure after the successful test at Gila Bend.

"Oh, God, no." She reached out and grabbed Dare's hand. He looked at her and tried to read the unspoken anguish in her face just before the infrared missile struck the number two engine.

EASTERN PACIFIC OCEAN
CHINESE CARRIER YANG JIAN
Tuesday Morning, 18 November
0540 Hours

The carrier intel officer could not believe what he heard over the American satellite frequency he had been monitoring since the battle began. The aircraft chatter was gone and a single voice claiming to be a representative of the President of the United States was requesting to talk to Shang Xiao Bohan Tao. His Chinese was impeccable. What bothered the intel officer most was that he asked to talk to the captain by name. The lieutenant responded with a lie, "There is no one by that name aboard."

"Do not disgrace yourself with a lie! I know the Captain's name. I saw his picture in your headquarters in Hangzhou. Not a flattering likeness I might add. You know the dire straights the remains of your pitiful fleet is in. If you want to live, sailor, notify Captain Tao immediately!"

That command, coming across the radio with the venom in Tze's voice spurred the young man to action. His throat was dry and the reports that three of the fleet's submarines had just been torpedoed by American attack subs clinched the deal. The situation looked hopeless indeed.

"Sir, I will contact the Captain as you desire."

In less than a minute, Tze found himself on the radio with Captain Bohan Tao.

"Captain, the President of the United States has authorized me to extend surrender terms to you. Our forces have, as you no doubt have seen, the ability to obliterate your vessel at will. It is the desire of our government to stop further needless loss of life. Your men have fought bravely in a losing battle, Captain. It would be honorable to think of your crew and their loved ones back home. What say you?"

AIRSPACE OVER EASTERN PACIFIC
Tuesday Morning, 18 November
0540 Hours

The blast sent parts of *Mama Bird's* giant turbofan engine flying in all directions. A huge section of the compressor tore into the port side of the fuselage and wrought havoc before it exited the starboard side. Master caution lights lit up the flight deck as electrical, hydraulic and pressurization systems normally powered by the left inboard engine ceased to function. All the fight deck crew members quickly donned on their oxygen masks as cabin pressure rapidly dropped to 18,000 feet MSL.

"Oxygen Masks - On, 100%," Gears commanded as he began to run through the *Loss of Pressurization* and *Engine*

Failure bold face memory items on the emergency action checklists. “Gunnz, grab a walkaround bottle and let me know what the situation is back there!”

“Mayday! Mayday! Eagle House under attack, any available aircraft please respond.”

Colonel Bob Peterman checked his iPad and tapped the blue icon to confirm he was actually looking at the C-5M display. Orbiting at FL550 and only sixty miles north of the stricken aircraft, he quickly computed fuel requirements. Thankful his F-15C model had the conformal *Fast Pack* fuel tanks, he turned his fighter to intercept the rapidly descending transport. He bumped the stick forward, lit the burners and rechecked his weapons status. Bob still had a single AIM-9 and a AMRAAM as well as four hundred rounds of 20mm. He knew his bird would top out at Mach 2.6 in the dive and cover almost 27 miles per minute.

“Eagle House, Steel 22 coming from the north. ETA two minutes.”

Gunnz was stunned by what he saw. Blood was spattered everywhere near the station assigned to Kit Kitaen. Dare was holding pressure to a wound in Blaze’s thigh. Tom Tallman held an oxygen mask to Lanie’s face and tried to calm the badly injured girl as best he could.

Gunter had reached the first aid kit and was moving back to the prone Kit carrying two emergency oxygen bottles with him. Gunnz noted damage to the fuselage on both sides, but electrical smoke from the damaged mission command screen was not a problem. Wisps of smoke were quickly sucked out the nearest holes along with the pressurizing air from the remaining three engines. He bounded down the stairs to the almost empty cargo bay, and quickly made his way to a viewing port on the crew entrance door. The sight of the bare number two engine pylon was not unexpected, but the seasoned veteran felt the loss personally. *Mama Bird* was *his* aircraft, a part of him and his heart was touched. As he reached the top of the crew stair, he saw Gunter spreading a crew blanket over Kit's body. The two Marines shared a knowing glance for a couple of seconds, then Gunnz walked slowly back to the cockpit and hooked back into the comm system. "Coulda been worse, AC...We lost Mike Charley. Lanie is in real bad shape. Doc's working on her now, but says there's not much hope. Blaze has a leg wound. The bird is okay, but number two engine is history."

"Weapons, AC, say status."

"AC, Weapons, defensive flares are off. Jammers still functioning, over," Blaze yelled as she tried to ignore the wind noise in the damaged fuselage.

"Blaze, I thought you were injured."

"Dad is applying first aid. Thanks, but I'm hanging in there."

Snake smashed the stick to the left trying to avoid the incoming 23mm tracers from the J-10 cannon—he almost did. But a couple rounds hit the rear canopy and three impacted the starboard engine compressor, shaking the whole airframe like a rag doll as the turbine blades shelled out the GE F110 in a second. Flames came out of the intake and exhaust then blew out as the *Tomcat* rolled almost uncontrollably.

Reacting to the line of red cannon tracers coming out of empty black skies, the Chinese junior officer yanked full aft on the stick, going completely vertical, but not before three of Snake's 20mm rounds found their target. One blew a fist sized hole in the starboard canard. A second tore though the wing root and clipped a hydraulic line. The final hit disabled the right inboard flap actuator.

Inside the damaged F-14, Snake secured the starboard engine after regaining control. The *Tomcat* had *wrapped up,* as pilots say, when a roll rate gets out of the pilot's ability to track the horizon. The rapid 720 degrees per second roll rate in pitch black conditions had rendered Snake temporarily disoriented. He centered the stick and added right rudder to compensate for the loss of thrust—leveled off at 20,000 feet and checked on his situation. "Robbie…you okay? Robbie?"

His heart sunk as the sound of his own rapid breathing was the only thing he heard. Snake turned back as far an he could in the seat. The sight of Robbie's shattered helmet confirmed the worst. He turned back, snapped the Hughes AWG-9 X-band radar out of *Standby* and back to *On.* No time to play cat and mouse. That son-of-a-bitch in the J-10 killed his back seater and was still a threat to the *Super Galaxy*. Snake planned to find him and kill him.

Dare slid into the bloody crew chair previously occupied by Lanie. He tried to ignore the torn leather and focus on the job at hand. Tom had reconfigured the screens to spilt the two *Manta* feeds to a single feed to his split screen. Dare now had overall BEF Mission Commander responsibility after the death of his best friend, Kit Kitaen. The veteran Marine *Super Cobra* pilot was no stranger to losses in combat, but Lanie was the first woman he had ever lost under his command. Doc had tried valiantly, but the massive internal injuries were even beyond his capable hands. Now, he had taken over for Gunter and had removed the small piece of compressor blade from Blaze's right thigh. He injected the leg with Novocain, cleaned the wound and stapled it shut. Doc monitored her for shock while she tracked the movement of the last J-10 in the sky.

"Dammit! He's turning back our direction!"

Gears was torn between concerns for the Galaxy airframe damage and the threat of another missile attack from the stern. Diving at 300 KIAS through FL190, he turned to Gunnz. "Any chance of main spar damage?"

The aging Marine shook his head. "Too far forward for the wing spar. No fuel imbalance or major hydraulic leaks, at least none that I can detect. I'll go back and watch for tears in the side walls. We're not that heavy, roll it on up to Vmo, AC."

Gears trusted his crew chief. There was nothing he didn't know about the C-5M. That is, nothing except the fact that the *Lizard* system was compromised aft of the fuselage turbine damage.

Blaze took a sip of the water Doc handed her. She looked at her options, wishing she had not used all the AIM-120s mounted on the lower pylons. *Mama Bird* still had plenty of JDAMs tucked away in their vertical storage compartments, but they were of no use for defending from an attack from above.

The J-10 pilot finally recovered from his near death dual with the American fighter. He was convinced he destroyed the unseen craft, whatever it was, because he did see a flash or explosion just before he entered the breakaway climb. Pulling inverted as the J-10 topped out at over 55,000 feet, he looked down at the ocean and saw the distinct shape of a massive pair of wings and a tail in the moonlight. *Must be some super secret American bomber*. The shape was unfamiliar, but it didn't matter. The J-10 was almost out of fuel and felt he had to restore honor to his squadron. He pulled the nose down through the moon-lit horizon and dove for a last chance gun pass at the unknown craft. This time he would finish the job.

Peterman roared across the airspace at his limiting Mach. The range to target was barely within an AIM-120's maximum, but he chose not to take the low percentage shot. Another blue dot was closer, much closer. He tapped the iPad for an ID. *Who is flying Anvil 1?*

The fuel ran out in the Shenyang Liming WS-10 as the J-10 screamed through 20,000 feet in a Mach 2.2 dive. The lieutenant paid it no heed as the RAT deployed to provide hydraulic power for the flight controls. Wind-milling engine RPMs kept the generators humming as he lined up the giant transport in his Helmet Mounted Display. Range was six miles and closing fast.

Snake Sievers had lost eight thousand feet altitude in the encounter with the J-10. When he recovered, he put the badly damaged bird on a heading to rejoin *Eagle House*. There was no way to follow the J-10 up stairs with one engine shot out. But once the J-10 made a move to re-attack, he made his decision. He lit the burner on number one and took the swing-wing fighter up to all she was worth, Mach 1.2. His G-suit hissed full and he groaned as the tumor in his side sent a lightening bolt of searing pain to his brain. The shape of the underside of the Jian-10 zoomed larger and larger in his canopy until the bottom centerline tank was as wide as the entire night sky. That was the last thing Admiral Snake Sievers would ever see.

"Oh my God," Colonel Bob Peterman said as he watch the two dots, one red and one blue, merge on his iPad. An explosion at his twelve o'clock confirmed the act of sacrifice. Flash Peterman was speechless for a second. He keyed the mic and swallowed. "Eagle House, Steel 22. Be advised Anvil 1 cleared your six. I've got you now."

***

EPILOGUE

SANTA YNEZ, CA.

On the side of a mountain in the picturesque Santa Ynez Mountains south of Lompoc on the California coast, sat a modest well-kept log cabin nestled in an isolated copse of conifers. White smoke curled from the chimney. Inside, Lan Chen sat with her legs curled up to the side on a comfortable chocolate leather couch in front of a rock fireplace with a roaring fire. She had a multicolored hand-crocheted throw over her legs and looked up as her daughter, Stacie, came through the door from the kitchen with a porcelain tea set on a carry tray.

"Tea, mama?"

"Oh, wonderful, Stacie, thank you. Even with the fire, there seems to be a chill in the air."

Stacie set the tray on a hand-crafted coffee table in front of the couch and began to pour the tea. There was also a small plate of pastries topped with blueberry jam on the tray.

"I just love your cream scones, honey."

"Thank you, mama." There was a pause then Stacie spoke again, "I just don't really understand why President Thompson pardoned me…not that I'm complaining. But…but I was responsible for so many American pilot's deaths…That's something I'll never get over…" She paused again and stared at the flames in the fireplace. A tear began to roll down her face as she thought about Boom Boom.

"Sweetheart, Meng lied to you when he kidnapped me. There was no way you could have known about that hidden part of the worm that incapacitated all those planes…That's what I told the President."

"You talked with President Thompson? How? When?…" Stacie stammered.

"Let's just say Annette and I had a long mother-to-mother chat. She's really quite nice…I like her," Lan said as she sipped her tea then added, "I think everything has worked out better than we planned…considering."

HONOLULU INTERNATIONAL AIRPORT
HAWAII

Hollywood exited the secured concourse and went through the revolving door into baggage claim. Most of his fellow passengers were dressed in brightly colored vacation and resort wear that contrasted with his olive drab flight suit. He looked around for a familiar face and was somewhat disappointed to see no one. Suddenly, from behind a unpainted concrete pillar, a lithe figure of an Air Force doctor in uniform stepped out with a smile that lit up the room. Hollywood caught sight of her and his mood changed instantly.

"Afternoon, Colonel, did you have a nice flight?" she asked as he approached with a quickness in his step.

"You're gonna have to do a lot better than that, Lady," he said as he swept her up in his arms and kissed her passionately.

EAGLE NEST RANCH

Blaze hobbled into the spacious den of the two hundred year old Hermann home using Gunter's old cane. Dare, Jill, Maria and her brothers, Mike and Mickey were seated, already nursing Shiner Bock beers.

"Well, come on in, Hopalong…your beer's gettin' warm," Mike said teasingly.

"Bite me, Mike…How's the work comin' on Mama Bird?" she asked Dare.

"The wiring and damaged skin has been replaced. Gunnz and Partsman should have the new engine installed by this afternoon. Your dad's supervising. We'll do a little test fly tomorrow."

"Good, can't wait," Blaze said.

"You aren't going anywhere near an aircraft, young lady, 'till the Doc says you're past clotting danger. End of discussion," Dare said sternly.

WASHINGTON, DC
WHITE HOUSE
OVAL OFFICE

Secretary of Defense Baker, Chairman of the Joint Chiefs Admiral Samson Valenti, Secretary of State Conrad Harper and General Jack Stewart sat in the high-backed wing chairs in front of President Thompson's desk.

"General Stewart, I don't know how this country will ever be able to repay you. What you, your people and the Black Eagle Force accomplished is nothing short of a miracle," the president said.

"Repayment not necessary Madame President. I took an oath many years ago swearing to defend the Constitution of the United States against all enemies, foreign and domestic…an oath is forever. Dare has asked if I would join the Black Eagle Force as Operations Officer. I told him I would, but not to expect me to fill Kit Kitaen's shoes…He wanted me to join them at Eagle Nest this weekend, but I'd made a previous engagement with a friend in Vegas." Burner paused and glanced at the flag behind the president's desk and then continued, "My only regret is the loss of some irreplaceable people."

"General, as long as our flag waves, there will be patriots willing to go into harm's way for this nation."

"Yes, ma'am. It's just that some of those we lost were personal friends."

"We all share your loss, Jack," offered Valenti. "I lost some good friends too."

"As did I…But, on the upside, we won't be hearing from the Chinese for some time. They not only lost virtually their entire navy…we have their surviving carrier…but probably more important to them is…they lost face. Major face. President Hu Jintao is not even admitting they ever had ultra-super carriers," stated Baker.

"What I find most interesting, however, is the coup the ROC staged on Taiwan the same day we were wiping out Meng's fleet. The government of the Republic of China is now firmly reestablished in Taipei after driving the PLAN's occupying troops back to the mainland and taking the Central Committee's representatives prisoner," said Harper.

"The PLAN had no back-up forces available and were in such a state of disarray because of Meng's actions that the ROC had almost no casualties in overthrowing the Communists and retaking Taiwan…I think it stretches coincidence a bit far that the coup was staged at exactly the same time we were engaged defending our shores against the might of the People's Republic of China," offered Admiral Valenti.

"You think?" replied President Thompson with a knowing look in her eye.

****

PREVIEW OF THE NEXT EXCITING NOVEL

BY

KEN FARMER & BUCK STIENKE

THE NATIONS

CHAPTER ONE

THE INDIAN NATIONS- 1885
WEWOKA
SEMINOLE NATION

Wewoka, a Seminole word that meant *barking waters,* earned its name for the small rapids found in the creek that ran on the north side of the town. It was a farming and ranching community as were most of the towns in the Nations.

A lone rider walked his tired red roan gelding down the main street of the capital of the Seminole Nation. He was a handsome young man of twenty wearing a spiffy black morning coat with a tall starched collar and a burgundy cravat. A dark gray uncreased low-crown Stetson with a stiff, flat three inch pencil-rolled brim, sat atop his head, cocked at a jaunty angle—neatly trimmed dark hair showed out from underneath the back. Unlike many of the men of his time, the young man wore no facial hair.

The main street had begun to fill up from the towns' people and farmers coming in for supplies or to market their wares. One wagon with several wooden crates of chickens and two pigs tied in the back had pulled up to the front of Haney's Butcher Shop, next door to Franklin's General Store and Mercantile.

The young man drew rein and eased his roan up to a water trough between two hitching rails in front of Franklin's and allowed the grateful horse to dip his nose to the water. After a few moments, he lifted the reins and side-passed the gelding to the hitching rail on the right side of the trough, dismounted and tied up. He dusted his clothes down, straightened his vest, grabbed his saddlebags and stepped up on the eight-foot wide boardwalk. He was all of five feet-seven, a tight one hundred-fifty pounds and moved with a somewhat confident, if not arrogant air.

He turned the knob and pushed the door open to Franklin's, ringing a three inch brass bell attached to the doorjamb overhead. There was only one other customer in the store—a man on the far right side looking at garden tools. A balding middle-aged store-keep in a white shirt with black garter half-sleeves and a white apron stood behind the counter. He looked up when he heard the bell. "Come in, Pilgrim. If we ain't got it, you don't need it. That's our motto. Whatcha lookin' for?"

"Oh, just need some supplies," the young man said as he walked over and flipped his saddlebags on the counter. "You can start by fillin' up those saddlebags with some Bull Durham smokin' tobacca, canned peaches 'n some stick candy."

The clerk took the bags, turned around and grabbed a couple cans of peaches and the Bull Durham and put them in one side of the leather bags. He turned back around, laid the bags on the counter and reached for the large round glass jar packed full of cinnamon, butterscotch and root beer stick-candy.

"Oh…yeah, and all the money in yer cash register there."

"Wh…what?" said the stunned store-keep as he looked up.

The young man pulled a pearl-handled Colt, cocked it and shot the store clerk between the eyes. "Damn. I hate it when people act like they did not hear what I said."

He reached over, opened the cash register, cleaned out all the paper money, grabbed most of the hard stick-candy from the jar then stuffed the booty in his saddlebags. Just as he turned around, he met the business end of a swipe from a hickory ax handle across the forehead. The Stetson went flying backward as his eyes rolled up and he dropped straight down to the floor.

The store owner, Millard Franklin, rushed out from the back store room with a ten gauge long barreled shot gun to his shoulder when he heard the pistol shot. "What the Sam Hill…"

"I'm sorry Millard…He shot Barkley 'fore I could get to him. Most cold-blooded thang I ever saw. Just shot him dead, right there…on account of him askin' what the man said," said resident Deputy United States Marshal Stan Oakley.

"Who is he, Marshal?"

"Damn if I know," Oakley said as he slipped the toe of his boot under the unconscious man's shoulder and rolled him over on his back. "My God in Heaven...This here is Ben Larson, the youngest of the Larson gang. Got a new dodger jest yesterday on 'em. They's a two thousand dollar re-ward on Ben here and his older brother, Wes. The most bloodthirsty bunch since Quantrill's Raiders...Jesus Christ o'mighty!" Oakley stood there for a moment just shaking his head. Then he looked at the ax handle, quickly dropped it and drew his Colt Peacemaker. "Git some rope, Millard...A lot of it, and let's git him tied up good 'n proper. Gotta send a telegram to Fort Smith. Hope they's a Tumbleweed Wagon in the area."

It was Indian Territory, 1885—comprised of most of the eastern half of what is now the state of Oklahoma, given primarily to the five Native American civilized tribes or nations—the Cherokee, Choctaw, Chickasaw, Seminole and Creek by the Indian Removal Act of 1830. The forced removal of the five tribes from their ancestral homeland in the southeastern part of the United States, beginning in 1831, became known as *The Trail of Tears*. The Cherokees called it *Nunna daul Tsuny* or *The Trail Where They Cried*. Over four thousand of the fifteen thousand relocated Cherokees alone, died en route.

The land of the Red Man became the stamping ground for outlaws from all over North America. The Territory, also called Robber's Roost or simply the Nations, was under the jurisdiction of the Federal Court for Western Arkansas at Fort Smith, presided over by Judge Isaac C. Parker...known far and wide as the *Hanging Judge*. This area of nearly 74,000 square miles was policed by a small, but courageous force of 200 white, black and Indian Deputy United States Marshals along with local Indian Police known as *Lighthorse*.

Deputy Marshals often traveled in wagons in which they served warrants and collected their prisoners, many of them hardened criminals, and transported them back to Fort Smith to await trial. They received 10 cents per mile for expenses and board plus $2.00 for each fugitive arrested. These marshals served nearly 9,000 writs or warrants during Parker's twenty-one years on the bench from 1875 to 1896. A prison wagon like this would drift back and forth across the territory like an uprooted, windblown weed and it is from that analogy it got its name…the *Tumbleweed Wagon*, the Great Wagon of the law.

ADA
CHICKASAW NATION

The green covered wagon creaked slowly toward town, as the team of four black-nose Tennessee mules plodded on, indifferent to the cold north wind at their backs. The wooden axle-grease pail swung to and fro from its hook just in front of the rear tailgate. Deputy Marshal Hank McGann held on to the four reins and kept a sharp eye out for any sign of trouble. Beside him sat Deputy Marshal Joshua Nelson, a stocky black man. Both men wore dark sackcloth suits and had their collars turned up to ward off the chill of the late winter cold front that was passing through. Hank had wrapped a charcoal colored woolen scarf around his neck and ears. Nelson was singing softly to himself an old Negro song, *Swing Low, Sweet Chariot*, he had learned from his grandfather who had been a slave in Mississippi before the war. The song had a direct reference to the Underground Railroad used for runaway slaves.

"Coming for to carry me home…Swing low, sweet chariot…"

"Hope that there chariot rides easier than this old prairie barge, Josh. My butt is about wore to a nub."

"Yessir, Hank, this seat is as hard as a widow-maker's heart. Could stand another cup 'o Arbuckle, too."

"Think I see the steeple of the First Baptist Church yonder. See there? Just to the left of the road where it crosses the rise."

"Cain't make it out. Yer eyes be better 'n mine. Never was as sharp as yern's."

"Should be rollin' in just before noontime. How's eating somebody else's cooking sound to you fer a change?"

"Is that a complaint? Thought you liked my cookin'."

"No complaint. Jest thought you might like to sit down inside and get out of the wind, not to mention have some vittles without the work."

"Never was afraid of work, but some fried chicken, mashed taters'n sweet-milk saw-mill gravy would stick to my ribs jest fine, I'm thinkin'," Nelson said as he grinned.

"Whoa there, boys. Hold on up, now," Hank coaxed the team to a halt outside the town livery. He set the foot brake and looped the reins around it. Joshua stood up, stretched his back out before he picked up his rifle and climbed down off the wagon. Hank followed suit and both men eased up beside the lead mules and began the process of unhitching the team from their traces. A young man in faded blue bib overalls and brogans exited the livery office door and approached McGann.

"Good day, Marshal. Y'all stayin' over?"

"Nope, just stoppin' fer a bite. Water 'em, check their hooves, give 'em a bait of grain and some hay," McGann replied. "Any place you speak highly of?"

The stable boy pointed down the street. "Lots of folks 'er partial to The Fried Pie."

"We were kinda thinking more about lunch than dessert."

"No, Marshall. That's the name of the cafe, The Fried Pie."

Joshua looked quizzically over at the boy. "Ain't never heard of frying a pie."

"It's somethin' Gussie May, just come up with, I guess. They sure are good, 'specially when you pour some fresh cream on top er some melted butter."

"Well, I'm game to try somethin' new. How 'bout you, Hank?" asked Joshua.

"Same here. If we didn't try new things, we'd all still be nursing…way I figure."

The boy blushed. Joshua let loose a deep laugh. He glanced at Hank and grinned. "That would be a sight to see."

Joshua licked the crumbs off the four-tined fork and set it reluctantly on the plate. "That fried apple pie makes me want to slap my momma, it was so good."

"Well, that just gives me an idea of a new trail dessert, if you have the fixin's," said Hank.

"Got everything, but ground cinnamon and vanilla. Think I'm gonna make me a stop by the mercantile a'fore we get outta town."

"Pick up some canned peaches while you're at it. That's what they used in this peach pie. It's worth a trip to Ada, all by its lonesome. Stable boy was right 'bout the fresh cream."

"We just might have to tip him a nickel for his suggestion."

"Uh huh, jest…"

"Howdy there, gentlemen. Willy over to the livery told me I could find y'all here."

The two looked up to see a gaunt man of fifty wearing a badge. They started to get up.

"Keep yer seats, boys, finish yer coffee," town marshal Burton Raines said as he pulled out a chair. "My lunch break, too."

Gussie May Davis, a portly woman in her fifties with her gray hair up neatly in a bun, approached the table. "The usual, Burt?"

"You know me too well, Gussie May, but I'm kinda extra hungry today, double up on the dumplins 'n bring me a glass of buttermilk."

"Comin' right up. You marshals need anythin' else?"

"No, ma'am, fuller'n a tick. That was mighty good," answered Joshua.

"I'll bring your ticket when I bring Burt's lunch," she said as she walked away.

"How's everything in Ada, Marshal?"

"Fine as frog's hair, Hank. Good to see you and Joshua. Guess you boys are working warrants out this way. Don't have any customers for ya, myself."

"Didn't figure you would. You keep most of the riff-raff on the scout away from Ada. We been strikin' out so far on this trip."

"That's what the folks pay me for. Oh, hell! So busy flappin' my gums, I almost forgot to give you this here telegram from Fort Smith," he said as he pulled back his lapel and drug out a folded piece of yellow paper. "You're gonna love this one!"

Hank and Joshua exchanged glances. Hank took the paper and read it aloud to Joshua, who could cook like nobody's business, but reading was not his long suit. "To US Deputy Marshals McGann and Nelson. Stop. Proceed to Wewoka, Seminole Nation. Stop. Pick up prisoner Benjamin Larson. Stop. Additional personnel will meet you for transport assistance. Stop. Confirm this message upon receipt. End. Signed United States Marshal Fagan."

"Benjamin Larson? Ben Larson? They caught Ben Larson in Wewoka?" Joshua asked incredulously.

Burton Raines leaned back in his chair and smiled broadly. "Even a blind hog finds an acorn sometimes."

***

THE AUTHORS

Buck Stienke – Captain – Fighter Pilot - United States Air Force, has an extensive background in military aviation and weaponry. A graduate of the Air Force Academy, Buck (call sign 'Shoehorn') was a member of the undefeated Rugby team and was on the Dean's List. After leaving the Air Force, Buck was a pilot for Delta Airlines for over twenty-five years. He has vast knowledge of weapons, tactics and survival techniques. Buck is the owner of Lone Star Shooting Supply, Gainesville, TX. As a successful actor, writer and businessman, Buck lives in Gainesville with his wife, Carolyn. Buck was Executive Producer for the award winning film, *Rockabilly Baby*.

Ken Farmer – After proudly serving his country as a US Marine (call sign 'Tarzan'), Ken attended Stephen F. Austin State University on a full football scholarship, receiving his Bachelors Degree in Business and Speech & Drama. Ken quickly discovered his love for acting when he starred as a cowboy in a Dairy Queen commercial. Ken has over 39 years as a professional actor, with memorable roles *Silverado, Friday Night Lights, The Newton Boys* and *Uncommon Valor*. He was the OC and VO spokesman for Wolf Brand Chili for eight years. Ken now lives near Gainesville, TX, where he continues to write and direct award winning films like *Rockabilly Baby* and write novels.

Buck and Ken have completed four novels to date. The first was *BLACK EAGLE FORCE: Eye of the Storm,* published by Tate Publishing. *BLACK EAGLE FORCE: Sacred Mountain*, second *Return of the Starfighter*, third. A historical fiction western, *The Nations*, the fourth and we are almost complete with our fifth novel, this time back to the Black Eagle Force series: *Black Eagle Force: Blood Ivory,* all published by Timber Creek Press.
Contact: blackeagleforce1@yahoo.com

TIMBER CREEK PRESS

www.ingramcontent.com/pod-product-compliance
Lightning Source LLC
Chambersburg PA
CBHW051532250626
47157CB00001B/14

* 9 7 8 0 9 8 4 8 8 2 0 3 8 *